RIPENESS IS ALL

Joyce Muriel

Cromwell Publishers

Cover Illustration by Frances Bickerdike

First published in 1999 by
Cromwell Publishers
Eagle Court Concord Business Park
Threapwood Road
Manchester M22 0RR

Paperback ISBN 1 901679 51 9

Chapter One

Looking back, Cleo could never truthfully say why but the exact moment of her decision was perfectly clear. It was in the middle of an after theatre supper party in their flat - a small, intimate gathering of friends who knew and accepted her as Marcus's lover and who presented no danger to his unsullied reputation. Elizabeth was a little intoxicated as usual and was getting somewhat amorous with Paul, Brenda's husband. Paul absent-mindedly removed her straying hand and continued his earnest discussion with Steve about market forces. Brenda was, as always, absorbed with the food. It was, one might think, a routine evening. Marcus, sitting opposite her, was playing the perfect host but she could tell that he was bored and longing for them to go. He gave her a little smile which meant, "Thank God, we shall soon be alone!" After all, their time together was necessarily limited, not only by his work in Parliament but also by the legitimate demands of his wife, which Cleo had never denied.

She waited for Steve to say something about 'dependency culture' and the need for individuality and the need for enterprise and, as he did so, she had a brief vision of the people she had recently seen lying on the pavements and in the doorways, as she had daintily made her way from the theatre to where Marcus had parked his car. Why didn't Marcus say something, she thought. But then did he care? He tolerated her Christian 'eccentricities', as he called them, but what did he really think? He was after all a good party man, as he had to be.

She felt again that terrible surge of anger which sometimes threatened to overwhelm her. It wasn't just anger but a kind of disgust. Why did she feel like this? Her fingers tightened on the stem of her glass. She longed for a moment to throw it across the table so that it would smash and its red liquid stain the pale surfaces. What would Marcus do? As she looked across at him, he smiled once more, a smile just for her.

Cleo studied him dispassionately for a moment. He was handsome, tall, dark and lean with a beguiling and tender smile, with blue eyes under level brows which always remained watchful. Once that smile had delighted her but now she was more aware of the eyes. Passionate he could be, but self interest was never forgotten. Suddenly the smile made her feel sick, or was it perhaps the pressure of Stephen's hand on her thigh, constant in spite of his apparently serious conversation? He too smiled at her from time to time.

She removed Stephen's hand and stood up. "I won't be long," she said, as she walked out of the room.

She walked down the corridor and into the bedroom which she and Marcus had shared spasmodically for nearly two years. It was comfortable and elegant, like the rest of the flat. They had planned its furnishing and decoration together. It was not just a place where they had made love but a place where they had talked and had, at times, seemed to be very close. Now, however, it no longer pleased her. She felt imprisoned there.

She stood in front of the dressing table and looked at herself in the mirror. She knew she was beautiful and desirable; many men had told her so from her earliest years. Now she wondered what it was that made her so. Was it her black, shining cap of hair? Her large, long lashed green eyes? Her red lips, with their tempting curves? Or her naturally perfect figure? She removed the jewels in her ears and from her fingers. As dressed by Marcus, she murmured cynically as she surveyed herself in her so elegant, so perfect black dress. She found the sight revolting. People who talk about the 'dependency culture' should look at me, she thought with sudden self disgust.

She walked to the bedroom door, shut it and turned the key. The time had come, she told herself. Why, she asked? She could only shrug her shoulders. There seemed to be no clear answer. She knew that she had perhaps, almost subconsciously, been thinking about it for a long time. But at this moment none of that seemed to be important. All that mattered was her desire to get away and quickly, without a scene, without an argument, for, if there were one, she felt she would be betrayed by her need for Marcus.

Taking off her dress, she hung it up and took out a suitcase from the cupboard. It was only necessary to take a few things for she had money and Jane, her elder sister, would always take her in for the night.

"Cleo, is there anything wrong? You've been ages!" Marcus was at the door.

"No, of course not. I won't be long." She closed the suitcase and checked her handbag.

He turned the door handle impatiently. "What on earth are you doing? Why have you locked the door?" Although concerned, he was also irritated for, as she knew, he liked to have everything well regulated and under control.

"Just a moment," she called out, and pulled on a pair of trousers and a jersey.

"For heaven's sake, hurry up," he said, still trying to keep his voice low. "Everyone will be wondering what has happened to you."

"Then they need wonder no more." She picked up the suitcase and a jacket, turned the key and opened the door.

Marcus stared at her in amazement. "Where the hell do you think you're going?"

"I'm leaving," she replied calmly.

"Don't be ridiculous," he advanced towards her and she retreated back into the bedroom. "You can't. It doesn't make sense."

For a moment she stared at him and felt nothing. Even her fierce anger had evaporated. "Perhaps not," she said finally, "but I'm going all the same."

"But why? What can possibly have upset you? Was it Stephen? You know he's a bit of an idiot."

So he had noticed. "No, it wasn't Stephen, particularly. It was nothing really." She paused. "I suppose you might say that I came for no good reason and I'm going for no good reason." She moved away from him. It was important to remember that even Marcus was her enemy at the moment.

"This is nonsense," he said, but very patiently. "We came together because we both wanted it. And that's not changed."

"I don't want it any more, that's all."

He stared at her. "Why are you so hostile?" he asked.

"I'm sorry." She picked up her suitcase and firmly pushed past him. "Don't try to stop me. It'll only make an embarrassing scene and you'd hate that. Tell the others I'm sick. It's probably true in a way. I'll be at Jane's for a few days, if you want to get in touch with me. But I don't think there'll be much point in that." She left him standing there, apparently too paralysed with shock to try to stop her or perhaps too unwilling to make an unpleasant scene. Much more likely the latter, she thought cynically, as she closed the door of the flat behind her. No one apparently noticed her departure.

Once she reached the street, she felt an exhilarating sense of freedom, as she stepped out firmly, looking for a taxi. She would afford that luxury for the last time as it was so late. She stopped suddenly remembering that Jane had no inkling of her impending arrival. She was a very indulgent elder sister but even so an erring younger sister might not be completely welcome, especially so late, even if it was a Friday night.

Fortunately, there was a telephone kiosk quite near, she remembered. It was a relief when Jane answered and not Robert, her husband. "Hello Jane," she said brightly. "It's Cleo." She rushed on before her sister could say anything. "Can I spend the night with you? I've just left Marcus."

"Why?" Jane replied in the uncompromising way she always had. "Have you quarrelled?"

"No, not really. I've just left him, that's all. I would explain but I don't really know what to say."

"Well, don't bother now," Jane said briskly. "Save it until later."

"Then you will put me up?"

"Of course, silly. But how are you going to get here? I don't think Robert would want to get up to fetch you."

"I'll get a taxi and be with you in about half an hour."

"Fine. I'll put the sheets on the spare bed and get some coffee on the go."

"Thank God for a good sister," Cleo thought as she signalled a cruising taxi.

It was about forty five minutes later when she found herself at the gate of Jane's neat semi-detached in one of North London's pleasanter suburbs. There was a welcoming light shining through the window of the front door but, even so, Cleo hesitated for a moment. Once she had knocked at that door, she felt that there would be no turning back and the unknown future suddenly seemed a little frightening. Dismissing such pointless thoughts, however, she walked firmly up the little path and rang the bell.

She was confronted with a cosy looking Jane in dressing gown and slippers with her soft brown hair hanging loose about her shoulders. The sisters smiled at one another. Jane opened the door widely, "The coffee's waiting," she said comfortingly. Cleo put her suitcase down in the hall and followed her sister to the small kitchen.

"Hello there," Robert with dark, tousled hair and wearing striped pyjamas leaned over the banisters. "What's this? The return of the prodigal? Why wasn't I informed? We might have killed the fatted calf or at least the three ancient chops in the freezer."

"I thought you were asleep." Jane turned round and gave him a warning look. "But, if you're not, you might as well join us for coffee."

"No thanks." He grinned amiably. "I'd rather leave you to your girlish chats. I need my beauty sleep. All explanations can wait till morning." He vanished with a wave.

Cleo followed Jane into the kitchen. "He's being very tactful," she remarked.

"Not at all." Jane poured the coffee into the mugs. "He's never interested in anything that happens after 11pm, even on a Friday. But I am. So let's go into the sitting room and have a chat."

Cleo followed her and settled herself comfortably on the rug in front of the gas fire, while Jane curled up in a nearby armchair. "How do you do it?" she asked admiringly.

"Do what?" Cleo raised her eyebrows.

"Always manage to look just perfect and very seductive, no matter what you're wearing. You've always been the same, while I've always been plain and ordinary. It isn't fair that you should have all the good looks."

Cleo sat up. "Don't talk rot," she said firmly. "It's just a matter of application. I made it my business. You just didn't bother. I may have the good looks but you have the good character. You bothered about more important things, like being a nurse and getting married. You've achieved a real job, a devoted husband and a home, while I'm just a….." she hesitated striving to find the right word.

"A what?" Jane prompted her.

"A mistress, and a model. Unemployed in both capacities as from tonight."

"What on earth do you mean? Isn't it about time you told me?" Jane leaned forward to look more closely at her sister. "What's happened?"

"Nothing really," Cleo replied casually. "I simply got up from the supper table, went to our bedroom, packed a few things, changed and walked out, leaving Marcus in shock."

"Just like that?" Jane stared at her.

"Yes, just like that."

"But why? I don't understand. Had you quarrelled or something?"

"No, certainly not. We've never quarrelled. I suddenly felt that I wanted to go. I wanted to change my whole life. I suppose it's rather like having what people call a conversion. Like Saul on the road to Damascus or something."

"Oh, no!" Jane stared at her in horror. "You're not going to tell me that you of all people have turned religious?"

"I don't see why not." Cleo sounded almost piqued. "I'm not such a dreadful sinner, after all. It's an idea, anyway. I rather fancy myself in a habit and a veil. I always thought the nuns at school could have looked very attractive, if they'd only made an effort."

"As you very well know that's not quite the idea. I do wish you'd stop fooling about and tell me what's happened."

"But I have told you," Cleo protested. "I simply did what I said. The trouble is I don't seem to have a reasonable explanation. I simply decided that I didn't want to go on living like that anymore. That's all there is to it really."

"But what are you going to do now?"

"Don't worry," Cleo smiled at her. "I'm not thinking of living with you. I'll be off in a couple of days or so. I've got quite a bit of money from the various modelling jobs I've done from time to time." She paused. "I thought quite a lot coming here and it suddenly occurred to me that it might be nice to use my brains for a bit. After all I have got a good Oxford degree. I also thought that I'd like to get away from men for a time, if not for ever. It was difficult to find an answer, once I'd rejected the idea of a convent but at Wood Green I had an inspiration." She paused.

"Go on. What on earth was it?"

"Well I thought I could become a teacher in a girls' school, preferably a girls' boarding school, miles from anywhere, like ours was. Are there such schools nowadays, do you know? Other than convent schools, I mean? Or have they all become co-educational with sex orgies and drug parties?"

"I think there are still quite a few single-sexed schools," Jane replied cautiously. "In fact I think they're becoming more popular because girls are said to be doing better in them."

"Well, there you are then," Cleo announced triumphantly. "Isn't it a marvellous idea?"

"I can see a few objections," Jane began cautiously,

"Well, I can't see any." Cleo put down her mug emphatically. "I have a good English degree with first rate testimonials from my tutors. I did think of being a teacher once. I thought I would be quite good at it, in fact. I can just see myself now."

"Well, I can't," Jane said brutally. "it's a preposterous idea and anyway you haven't any training qualification."

"You don't need that for a private school," Cleo retorted, showing herself surprisingly knowledgeable "and you can't deny that it would be a complete change and it would get me away from men."

"You'd never stand it. You've never been able to do without them. There's bound to be some men and you'll just cause havoc as usual."

"No," said Cleo firmly. "I renounce my so-called fatal fascination. I'm bored with the whole business. I want to do something. I want to be me, not Marcus' mistress or someone else's."

Jane laughed. "I don't believe a word," she said. "it's just one of your fantasies. In any case, if you really want to do something, why don't you go back to Oxford? You were doing quite well there before you decided to chuck it all suddenly."

"You don't understand, do you?" Cleo replied sadly. "That would just be the same world, and mostly the same people."

"But why does it have to be something so extreme?"

"It has to be. Or there's no hope for me. Anyway, you ought to be pleased. You've often told me I ought to do something useful."

"Oh dear!" Jane picked up the mugs and stood up. "I ought to know better than to argue with you after all these years. I don't doubt you'll do what you want, however mad it seems to be. Just think about it, please."

"Oh, I have," Cleo replied triumphantly. "It came to me just as I got out of the taxi. There's a paper called *The Times Educational Supplement*. I'll go out early tomorrow morning, buy a copy and look for a job. Having found it, I'll write a scintillating letter and start my new career."

"You seem to have overlooked a few things."

"Such as?" Cleo raised her eyebrows.

"Such as (a) there may not be a suitable job. In fact it's highly unlikely and (b), if there is, it's not very probable that they'll want you. I doubt if any headmistress of a select girls' school would consider you suitable, not when she sees you, at least."

"You're very discouraging but fortunately I believe in Divine Providence. I have decided to be a Good Girl and so the opportunity will be given to me. I don't see what objections you can make to that. You ought to be pleased."

"I shan't attempt to make any further objections," Jane replied somewhat wearily, as she rinsed out the mugs.

"Good," Cleo said cheerfully. "Now I suggest we both go to bed and get our beauty sleep and stop worrying till tomorrow. Come along." She walked into the hall and, after picking up her suitcase began to climb the stairs. "As for my appearance," she whispered, "I intend to do something about that. I realise that I don't quite look the part at the moment. And anyway I don't intend to encourage any males."

"There won't be any," retorted Jane.

"Don't be silly, there's bound to be a gardener or a caretaker or somebody."

"Surely they would be a bit beneath you, especially after Marcus?"

"My dear," Cleo said impudently, "as you know, no man is immune when I choose to exert my fatal fascination."

"You're a conceited devil," Jane whispered fiercely. "But I bet you'll be glad to get back to Marcus."

"Didn't you hear me say I'd given up men?"

"All men for ever?" Jane looked unconvinced and she might have been even less convinced had she followed Cleo into her bedroom and seen her without her frivolous mask.

"Why ever have I done it?" Cleo asked herself as she sat down an her uncomfortable single bed and remembered Marcus as she had last seen him. "Don't be idiotic," she told herself. "You've started and you're going to see it through. Courage! You've got to win through or perish!" She began to brush her hair vigorously.

Chapter Two

There was a tempting smell of toast and coffee as Cleo bounded down the stairs early on the Saturday morning. "That smells good," she exclaimed loudly above the noise of the radio. Robert, who was standing by the stove quietly eating his toast and waiting for the coffee to percolate, wheeled round, almost dropping his toast.

"God, you gave me a shock! I'd forgotten you were here! In fact, I'd imagined that you might just have been part of my dreams."

"No such luck for you." Cleo broke a piece off a slice of toast and nibbled it. "Jane still in bed, I suppose?"

"Yes. I'm taking her breakfast up." He indicated a small tray on the side.

"Marvellous!" Cleo looked at him admiringly. "I sometimes wonder why I didn't marry you myself, instead of letting Jane snaffle you."

"I'm simply not in your class," he replied amiably. "You know it and I know it. That's why we're safe."

"Possibly. It's a great relief anyway." She took another nibble, watching Robert while he poured out two cups of coffee, one for himself and one for Jane. He never was very hospitable in the morning. which was strange. since he always got up early.

Noticing her glance, he grinned. "Help yourself. 'There should be enough left."

"No thanks," she said vigorously, "I haven't time to stop for breakfast now. I must dash out to the newsagent's."

"Whatever for?" He paused at the door with his tray.

"To buy a copy of *The Times Educational Supplement.*"

"I would hardly consider that light reading."

"It isn't. It's very serious. I want to get a job. Don't stand there, looking so unbelieving. It's not very flattering. Ask Jane.

She knows all about it and will be only too ready to tell you, I'm sure. Now I must dash. I believe it's very important not to hesitate once one has made a decision." She had already passed him and was on her way to the front dear, where she paused. "I'll have some toast and coffee when I get back. That'll fortify me for my serious study." With a wave she was gone, leaving Robert to mount the stairs with a somewhat dazed air.

"Cleo seems to be madder than usual," he announced as he pushed open the bedroom door. "Or perhaps it's just that she's mad in a different way. Anyway, she said you'd explain to me, so perhaps you'd better try, while you eat your breakfast. It might be better to be forewarned." He gave her a quick kiss and putting the tray on her lap sat on the side of the bed. "Fire away. It should be entertaining at least."

"It's no joke," Jane replied miserably. "I wish it were. I'm really worried about her."

Robert groaned. "Don't you think it's time." he asked, "that you stopped worrying about this sister of yours? You're only four years older after all and she is twenty four. You may not like her way of life but it seems to suit her, so why should you worry about it?"

"I'm not worried about that." Jane replied. "I'm worried that she's giving it all up. She's left Marcus."

"Oh, that'll soon sort itself out," Robert replied easily. That sort of thing's just a ploy. She's only bullying him a bit. Forget it and don't get involved."

"And that's your considered advice, is it?" Jane looked at him pityingly. "I feel sorry for your clients. Don't you ever ask them for the story before giving them your counsel? It isn't at all what you think. Let me explain."

Ten minutes later she was still explaining to an incredulous Robert. "It simply doesn't make sense!" he exclaimed. "She must be joking. But I still think my idea's basically right. It's just an elaborate game with Marcus. He'll be ringing up before long, you can bet, and she'll be making better terms."

"Why do you always take such a low view of human nature?"

"I'm a solicitor, my darling, and I've seen human nature at work."

"But that doesn't mean you know everything," she protested. "Cleo's my sister and I know her better than you do. I always thought she might do something unexpected one day."

"Rot!" he said. "You never expected anything of the sort." He picked up the tray and moved towards the door. then stopped as the front door bell and the telephone began to ring simultaneously. "What did I say?" he declared triumphantly. "Cleo and Marcus. That will be him on the phone and she's arrived back just in time. Very typical! Which shall I answer first?"

"Be really clever and do both," Jane suggested.

Depositing the tray on the dressing table. Robert ran downstairs, With one hand he picked up the phone and with the other he opened the front door. Cleo came in triumphantly carrying her copy of the *Educational Supplement,* Recognising the familiar voice at the other end of the line, Robert offered her the phone but she shook her head firmly. "Not now. Tell him I'll be in later," she mouthed, then retreated to the kitchen, shutting the door firmly behind her.

Somewhat nonplussed, Robert returned to the phone, It seemed better to play it safe. "Sorry Marcus, old man," he said in his most courteous tones, "I was interrupted, What were you saying?"

Marcus repeated his wish to speak to Cleo. "Cleo? Oh yes, she turned up late last night. I was three quarters asleep actually. We haven't really communicated as yet. I think it would be a good idea if you tried again in about an hour." To his relief

Marcus accepted his message without question and rang off, merely asking Robert to tell Cleo he had rung.

Putting down the receiver. he made his way to the kitchen, shouting a reply to Jane's anxious enquiry. "Yes, it was Marcus and, if you want to know more, you'll have to stop slummocking about in bed and crawl down to the kitchen. I'm going to have a word with your darling sister." Without waiting for Jane's reply, he went into the kitchen to confront Cleo. He felt righteously angry with her. She had disturbed the well earned peace of his weekend and, worse still, she had caused him to lie to Marcus, who had probably not believed a word.

He discovered her sitting comfortably ensconced on a kitchen stool with a mug of coffee and a thick slice of bread and marmalade in front of her. She appeared to be so utterly absorbed in the pages of the TES that she did not even bother to look up when he came in.

"Well!" he said bitterly.

"Well what?" she asked, looking up briefly.

"That was Marcus. Don't you want to know what he said?"

"Marcus." She seemed to be trying to remember who that was. "Marcus, of course. I suppose he wanted to speak to me." She seemed to be restraining herself with difficulty from returning to the perusal of her paper.

"Naturally."

"And what did you tell him?" She took another bite of bread and marmalade.

"I lied. I told him you'd probably be around in about an hour, and he said he'd ring again."

"Good. Not that I've really anything more to say to him. But I suppose I'd better say something, although it all seems rather irrelevant now."

"What do you mean?" Robert asked fiercely?"by 'rather irrelevant now'? Was he or was he not your lover until last night? Surely that's a matter of some importance?"

Cleo looked up at him reluctantly. "It depends how you look at things, I suppose," she replied. "It no longer seems at all important to me, that's all." She turned a page.

"You shock me. And that's a shattering admission to have to make because I thought neither you nor anyone could any more."

"What's a shattering admission?" Jane appeared in the doorway

"Your unbelievable sister has actually managed to shock me. I really thought I had got beyond that by now. She appears to have no interest whatsoever in Marcus, who was after all her devoted lover of two years until last night when something apparently happened, although Heaven knows what."

"I told you what happened," Cleo said firmly. "There isn't anything else to tell. I'm sorry I didn't seem very interested in what you had to say. It's just that my mind is full of other matters at the moment." She returned to her study of the TES.

"Don't apologise," Robert retorted. "I mean what does it matter - a small thing like that? You've invaded my home, upset the quiet weekend I'd planned, so why should I bother about having to lie for you to Marcus. who was undoubtedly more than a little upset and just as bewildered as I am."

"Robert." Jane expostulated?"I don't think..."

"Did he sound upset?" Cleo asked with a flicker of interest.

"Ah! I thought so," Robert exclaimed. "I knew that was what it was all about. You just want to twist him round your little finger, or something. Well, I don't doubt, if you play you cards right, as you usually do, you'll manage it. Well, all I say is, please just hurry up about it. Get on the phone. Persuade him to give you whatever you want, then you and he can have a touching reconciliation and Jane and I can return to our humdrum, drama-free life." He turned towards Jane with a triumphant look. "What did I tell you?"

Cleo smiled at him. "I don't blame you, Robert." she said gently. It's natural that you should think like that but, unfortunately, I don't want anything, at least not anything that Marcus can give me. I thought Jane had explained this to you."

"I did," Jane interrupted her, "but being the conceited fool he is, he didn't believe me."

"It's strange how foolish clever people can sometimes be," Cleo said sadly. She picked up the TES again.

"Now look here." With a quick, unexpected move Robert snatched the paper from her. "I want your full attention and I want a bit of sense. You surely don't expect me to believe the rubbish you and Jane have concocted about being tired of men?"

Jane and Cleo looked at one another. "The trouble with men is," remarked Jane, "that they can never believe that women can do without them."

"Or their money or their other temptations," added Cleo.

"Spare me that feminist propaganda," Robert groaned, "and tell me what you really mean."

"I have." Cleo replied simply, "but you won't believe me."

"Do you really mean that you don't intend to go back to Marcus? That you're not just holding out on him?"

"Yes. I have not quarrelled with Marcus. I am not holding out to gain some advantage. I have left Marcus because I want to start a fresh life."

"But why? Why this sudden access of virtue? Isn't it a bit late?"

"Surely it's never too late to repent?" Cleo said virtuously.

"Perhaps not. But why? Why now?"

She shrugged. "How I can I tell? The mood seized me. I suppose."

"Don't tell me you heard a voice from heaven?"

"Well, no, I can't really claim that. I rather wish I could. I just had a strong feeling that this wasn't for me any longer. I wanted... Oh dear, it's all rather impossible to explain. But it needn't worry you, Robert, I've no intention of staying here for long, although it's going to be a bit difficult, if you won't even let me look for a job." She buttered another piece of bread philosophically.

"Very well." Robert handed over the TES somewhat grudgingly. "Although I can't imagine there will be anything suitable for you in there. What sort of an advertisement are you expecting to find?"

Cleo ignored him and returned to her study of the advertisements. There was a long silence. "I've got it," she yelled suddenly. "Just the very thing. It must be right. Listen. 'Wanted immediately a Teacher for English. Some GCSE and 'A' level work. Graduate preferred. Accommodation available. Write or phone: The Headmistress, St Elizabeth's School, Barton Leas. Telephone Barton Leas 208'" They both stared at her silently, "What do you think?"

They looked at one another. "I sincerely hope." said Robert finally, "that you are not seriously suggesting that this job is the answer to your prayers?"

Cleo raised her eyebrows. "You're being very obtuse, Robert, even for you. It's obvious. I have an English degree, I'm a female and they'd naturally prefer that in a girls' boarding school, although they can't say so. The headmistress has an urgent need of a teacher, I have an urgent need of a job. It's clearly what I'm looking for."

"Do be sensible, Cleo," Jane urged, "I mean do you actually know how to teach a GCSE?"

"Not exactly," Cleo admitted, "But I'm sure I can find out."

"Perhaps more to the point." Robert said, "do you know what sort of a place Barton Leas is? I'll go and get the motoring guide." He left the kitchen.

"He's right, you know you don't want to bury yourself in some horrid little place, doing a job you've no aptitude for and will probably hate. You can always stay here for a time, if you and Marcus have really split up."

Cleo looked up from the advertisement she had apparently been studying. "Thanks Jane," she said. "Don't worry about me. I may sound frivolous but then you know I've always been like that. I don't care where it is or what it's like. I want this job, if they'll have me. I need it. Please don't try to stop me. I'm afraid I might listen to you." Her face was strangely grief stricken as she looked at her sister.

"I won't," Jane said impulsively. "Dear Cleo."

"Well. it's just as I thought," Robert said triumphantly coming into the kitchen with his guide. "It's a small village almost in the middle of England, miles from anywhere. No hotel, just a garage. It'll be a dead and alive hole."

"Splendid," declared Cleo. "I couldn't ask for anything better. It's just what I want. All I need now is the telephone code."

"I'll get that for you, too," replied Robert, "since you're determined to be mad." He departed once again for the hall."

Cleo picked up the newspaper, her pen and a notebook. "I'll make the call straightaway, if that's all right." As she stood up the kitchen door opened suddenly.

"Sorry to have to be the bearer of bad news," Robert announced with a certain glee. "Marcus has just pulled up outside and he's making for the door looking very determined."

"Thank you," Cleo replied with dignity, "Is it all right if I see him in the dining room. I think it would be better if we were alone."

"Of course," Jane said quickly. She felt quite unable to cope with Marcus.

The front door bell rang. "Get into the dining room," Robert said, "and I'll let him in. He deserves to be treated with proper respect. It's not every day we have such a distinguished visitor."

Cleo went quickly. The bell rang again. "Good morning, Marcus," Robert said politely, as he opened the door. "Cleo's through there in the dining room." He pointed to the door.

"Thank you." Marcus did not waste any time but with a quick polite smile made straight for the dining room and shut the door firmly behind him.

Robert retreated thankfully to the kitchen. "He looks very determined," he remarked. "Cleo's not going to find it easy. Let's hope he makes her see sense."

"What is sense?" Jane asked.

Robert groaned. "Don't get metaphysical. I've had enough. My brain needs a rest on Saturday." he looked out of the window. There was a patch of blue in the sky and a sniff of spring in the air. Their small garden suddenly looked inviting. "I think I'll go and indulge in some rural pursuits. I might even plant some lettuces. Tell me when the battle's over."

"Coward," remarked Jane lightly. "Marcus won't stand a chance with Cleo in her present mood. I remember she was just like that when she was six."

"Oh God." Robert looked exasperated. "More childhood memories. What happened then?"

"She decided that Mother must send her to another school, because she was bored and she didn't see why she should be."

"So?"

"She went to another school eventually."

"History might have been different, if she'd been soundly spanked."

“I doubt it.” Jane stood up. “Some people don’t respond to spanking. They need loving. Anyway I’ll get lunch for three.”

“You’re just like your mother used to be. You spoil her.”

Robert departed for the garden with the uncomfortable feeling that matters would not easily return to normal.

Chapter Three

In the dining room Marcus stood against the closed door and looked at Cleo as she sat at the dining room table, facing him. He seemed to be waiting, so Cleo finally spoke. "I thought you were going to ring up later."

"I didn't intend to be put off again by Robert." He moved towards the table but did not sit down.

"You didn't believe him then?" Cleo smiled faintly. "He was afraid you hadn't."

"Of course not. He did his best to be convincing, but he sounded uncomfortable. He doesn't like lying." He paused for a moment and their eyes met. She did not turn away but faced him squarely. "But I didn't come here to talk about Robert. I came to ask you some questions." She was surprised how calm and reasonable he sounded, even though she was accustomed to his habitual self control. "I suppose it's, quite simply, why? What has gone wrong? What do you want from me?" He sat down, apparently prepared to wait.

"I'll start with the last question first," she said slowly. "I don't want anything, at least not anything that you can give me. You may think I want to gain some advantage. Robert certainly does but I don't. We have never had that kind of relationship. Surely, you believe that?"

"Of course. I was really asking whether there is something I should have done and failed to do? I just can't understand why you left and I would like you to come back."

"Aren't you angry? You ought to be. I behaved very badly."

"I'm not sure if I should be angry until you answer the 'Why'."

"Why are you so reasonable?" she demanded. "You ought to be angry or something."

He smiled slightly. "You'd prefer it, if I made a scene?"

"Why not?" she said belligerently. "If you'd left me like that, I'd probably have made a terrible scene." She stood up. "Oh, this is ridiculous. I told you why I was leaving I didn't want to stay. I was bored with the situation, not really with you but just with everything. I'd slipped into it because it was easy and pleasant and now I just wanted to slip out of it."

He stood up too and put his hands on her shoulders. "Cleo, my dear," he said quietly, "I love you. You know I do. We've had some wonderful times together. Surely that isn't all you've got to say?"

She moved away a little impatiently. "Yes, we've had some wonderful times but something is lacking now. Do you remember when you took me to the flat just after you'd decided to buy it?"

"Of course, I remember. I do have normal feelings, you know."

"You asked me to come and live with you there. And when I wasn't sure what you meant, you smiled and said, 'I'm making a dishonourable proposal, and then you said, 'Come live with me and be my love."

"And you said," he interrupted, "that you would and quoted the next line 'and we will all the pleasures prove.'"

"And we did," she continued, "and you're right, it has often been wonderful but it isn't any longer and I must leave."

"I don't understand you. Why?" He too moved away.

"It's no longer enough for me. You have your career, your life with Sarah, as well as your time with me. Apart from you I have nothing that really matters to me. It has been fun but it no longer is. I have to move on. I have no security."

"You have the security of my love for you. Do you want more? Is it that you really mean that you want me to persuade Sarah to divorce me? She knows nothing about you but I told you about her from the beginning. I made no secret that, although I no longer loved her, I had a definite loyalty to her and a dependence on her help to some degree. I thought you accepted that. But do you now really want us to divorce? Is that the real truth?"

"No", she said decisively. "I don't want that. I have always understood your situation. It would be very wrong for me to insist that you sacrificed your career and all your hard work. It would be a futile gesture anyway for someone as fickle as I am. I didn't suggest that at the beginning and I'm not suggesting it now."

"What are you suggesting then?"

"I'm trying to tell you that it doesn't work any more. It did but now it doesn't. I have to live my own life and this is the only way I can do it."

"Don't you think this is a very brutal way?" he asked. He was very pale but still apparently quite calm.

"I'm sorry," she said. "I suppose it is. I'm a wayward, heartless person. I've stayed with you, far longer than I've ever stayed with anyone, probably because we never tried to make any ties. I accepted Sarah's importance to you and you accepted that I didn't want marriage or a permanent arrangement. We came together freely. Now you must let me go freely."

"Where are you going?"

"I don't know but I want to get a job out of London, doing something that is worth doing or at least something that will enable me to be independent. I never really intended to spend much time being photographed for glossy magazines. I went on longer than I meant because of you."

He moved closer to her again. "Why are you treating me as an enemy? I wanted you to be happy. I mistakenly thought you were."

"I was but I no longer am. It's the sort of person I seem to be. It always happens to me. I need to get away by myself. But thank you for everything." She kissed him lightly on the cheek. She did not trust herself to say more or to do more.

He tried to hold her but it was as he had feared. She was cold and unyielding. For some reason she had put an impenetrable barrier between them. He dropped his arms and moved away. "Are you saying that you never want to see me again? I don't believe it." Looking at her averted face, he felt that she was desperately unhappy but there seemed to be no way he could reach her. "Well is that what you are saying?" he repeated. "that you never want to see me again."

"I don't know," she said slowly. "I really don't know, Marcus."

"How shall I get in touch with you," he asked coldly. "when I need to?"

"Jane will have my address when I have one."

He felt deserted and betrayed by her return to Jane who had never approved of him. "I see you have returned to Jane again. I suppose it was inevitable."

"I'm not staying here very long," she replied quickly. "I must live my own life."

"And that's all you have to say, Cleo?" It was impossible to tell whether he was hurt or angry.

"Yes, I'm afraid so. And please don't say you love me, Marcus. Love means commitment and we never had that. Perhaps it would have been better if we had."

"Do you think so?" he paused for a moment. There was so much he wanted to say but he needed first to try to understand and even more to come to terms with his own feelings. He moved towards the door. "Very well, then, if that's what you want, I'll say goodbye."

"I thought you would. You're a realistic politician, not a romantic."

He smiled back. "Perhaps." He paused at the door, and, as he opened it, turned one last time. "I'll be around, if you change your mind." He was gone without waiting for a reply.

Cleo, hearing the front door close behind him, walked to the window and watched him get into his car and drive away without a further look. She was still standing there when Jane came in a few moments later. "Are you all right, love?" Jane asked anxiously walking over towards her sister. "Was there an unpleasant scene?"

Cleo turned round to face her. "Not a bit. It was rather unflattering really. He took it so calmly. I thought I might have been worth more of a fuss. But he's always got Sarah to console him, I suppose."

"I thought you said that they weren't at all close."

"They're not. That was unfair of me. I don't think for one moment that he'll go to her. It's just the way he is: pragmatic, I suppose you'd call it. He'll probably find someone much nicer. He's not one to waste his time on the unattainable."

"You sound quite sorry. You could go back, you know. He wouldn't object to that, would he?"

"No. He said he'd be around if I changed my mind. But I'm not going to, so stop being sentimental." It was time to resume her cheerful mask before Jane started getting worried. She walked towards the door, determined to hide the shock she felt at Marcus's abrupt departure.

"That's over now. I haven't any more time to waste. I must go and make my phone call. I don't want to miss that opportunity. I regard that as a definite sign from heaven."

Jane sat down and waited. There seemed to be nothing else she could usefully do. She could hear Cleo's voice but could not distinguish the words. It seemed very unlikely that the headmistress of such a prestigious school would be interested. Poor Cleo! Jane felt a sudden rush of love for her wayward, unpredictable younger sister. Three years ago it might have been possible but hardly now.

Suddenly the door was thrown open and Cleo burst in. "Well, that was short!" Jane exclaimed. Obviously the headmistress had quickly realised that Cleo was not the sort of person she was looking for.

"Yes. She was absolutely charming. As soon as I mentioned my Oxford First and my reference from Professor Harding, (she'd heard of him, of course), she was interested."

"Really." Jane looked at her sister, feeling slightly dazed.

"Yes, but I'm afraid," Cleo said thoughtfully, "that it was really father's cousin, Edward, that clinched it."

"What on earth do you mean?"

"Well, he was a Canon at Markhampton Cathedral, don't you remember? They stayed with us once and mother said they were always cadging off their relatives."

"I do remember now you mention it. But what has that got to do with your telephone call?"

"Oh? everything, " Cleo said firmly. " The headmistress, her name's Miss Stephens, asked me if I was a relative of the late Canon Lafay. It's such an unusual name, she thought I must be. Well, naturally, I said yes and I was in. I'm to go for an interview on Monday."

"I'm afraid I don't quite see the relevance."

"Well, it's a Church of England school you see. They go to the Cathedral for special services, so when I told her I was related to the late Canon - well that was it. Oxford helped as well, of course. At least I think it did but the Canon was my badge of respectability."

"You devil!" Even Jane was astounded. "Your badge of respectability! I don't know how you dare to sit opposite me and say it! What about the last few years?"

"Well, I sort of said I'd drifted around a bit."

"One would have to be very charitable to call it that."

Cleo ignored that remark. "I said I'd tried one or two things but had recently decided that I was wasting my time and that teaching was what I really wanted to do and that a girls' boarding school would really suit me. That went down well."

"Just as you calculated it would. You really are a most frightful hypocrite." Jane looked severely at her sister. I suppose you didn't bother to mention that you're supposed to be a Roman Catholic?"

"No, but I'll slip it in at the interview, if you insist, although I don't honestly think it's very important as far as I'm concerned. I could hardly call myself a pillar of the church." She paused and looked at her sister. I'm not quite happy about that word 'hypocrite'. It's not very pleasant."

"It wasn't meant to be. But don't you think that perhaps you are being one? I happen to think that teaching is a serious job and that you shouldn't just take it up to solve the problems of your love life."

"I'm not just doing that, Jane, honestly. I really want to live a different life and teaching appeals to me as something worth doing that I might even be able to do. I don't think my last two years have anything to do with anyone else. I'm a reformed character now."

Jane laughed. "You've always been the same and so I'll try and believe you. But do you have to go to such extremes burying yourself in the country in a girls' school?"

"It's the only way I can do it, unless you'd prefer me to go to a convent? But you do see that, don't you? It has to be a drastic change."

"Perhaps I do." Jane stood up and gave Cleo a quick hug. "Anyway I wish you well."

"And you'll take back 'hypocrite'?"

"I'll take back 'hypocrite'."

"Good, that's a relief. Now let's go and tell Robert. It'll amuse him, anyway. Then, we'll go and buy some suitable clothes for me. Hurry up and get dressed." She gave Jane a little push."

"Not so fast! You forget I've got a husband to think about and he'll want some lunch after slaving in the garden all morning."

"Resting on his spade you mean."

"All right, he may have rested on his spade but he'll still want some lunch as a reward."

"Well, I help you get the lunch, then we'll buy my clothes."

"I don't see why you need to buy clothes. You brought a case full with you."

"Ah, but then they're not suitable for my new life. I want some 'school teacher clothes' - a neat little suit or something. I want to look quite different and I need your advice."

"All right, if you insist. But tell me," Jane asked as they went to the kitchen, "when would you start this job, if they are crazy enough to offer it to you?"

"As soon as possible, so I won't need to upset your life too long."

"That's fine. But why, may I ask, have they got this sudden vacancy in the middle of a term? Isn't that a bit suspicious?"

"Oh, I don't think so. Miss Stephens explained that to me. They had a new person last September but she's had a breakdown and had to go into hospital or something, so they're a bit desperate."

"That doesn't sound too good. I hope that won't happen to you."

"Don't be ridiculous. I'm too tough for that."

"Yes, probably the school will break down this time!"

"Possibly but I hope not," replied Cleo blithely as she went after her into the kitchen.

Chapter Four

"Well, here you are then, love." The taxi driver jumped out and opened the door for Cleo. "Here's the college. Just go up the drive, through the front door and the secretary's office is on your left."

Thank you very much," Cleo spoke in a soft voice as she got out carefully and primly, giving the driver at the same time a very shy smile, or what she hoped was a very shy smile. She was making a big effort to fit her voice and manner to her newly acquired dull shoes and her plain suit with its loose badly fitting jacket and unfashionable length of skirt. It was difficult but she felt that she had had considerable success so far. Not a single man had given her a second glance since she had left Jane's home that morning. The young business man seated opposite to her in the train had actually found his copy of 'The Times' more interesting and at Markhampton station not one porter had volunteered to help her. It had been an unusual and rather interesting sensation. I shall soon be able to write a book, she thought about life as a dowdy and unattractive female in the last decade of the twentieth century. That should make the feminists sit up. Banishing such foolish thoughts, she hastily paid the waiting and obviously unimpressed taxi driver.

Jane had been right, she thought as she walked up the wide drive lined with impressive old trees, dowdy clothes, absolutely no make-up and a pair of horn-rimmed, tinted glasses which successfully obscured her best feature did make a great difference. But she must also remember Jane's further warning. "Watch it," she had said, "it's not just how you look, it's how you move and how you behave."

She paused as she reached the end of the drive and looked with approval at the imposing red brick building in front of her. The school was obviously large and had an air of success. The garden and lawns in front were immaculate and it had pleasantly peaceful and cloistered air on that sunny January morning. The village too as they had passed along the main street to the school had been quiet and attractive with its many old houses and central village green. She sniffed the air. It was fresh and slightly perfumed by the almond blossom drifting down from several trees. This was, she thought, a different world from London.

As she approached to open the main door, Cleo took a deep breath. This was a testing time. She pushed open the glass door and entered the large, pleasant entrance hall. It was light and airy and smelt faintly of wax polish. There were several bowls of tastefully arranged flowers on oak tables. She turned to the left and found the secretary's room. She knocked with suitable timidity and entered, The secretary, a friendly, middle aged woman took charge of her efficiently, as soon as Cleo introduced herself.

"Good morning, Miss Lafay. Miss Stephens is expecting you. I'll take you to her office." She led Cleo briskly down a broad corridor, then suddenly turned left through a door into a slightly narrower corridor. This had a hushed and somewhat luxurious air, having thick carpeting and elegantly papered walls. Cleo was motioned to sit down on an oak settle opposite an oak chest, dark with age and gleaming with polish, on which was a magnificent bowl of flowers. This was obviously the approach to the holy of holies, she decided.

The Secretary approached a white painted door, listened briefly, then tapped lightly. She then opened the door and announced Cleo, who took a few tentative steps into the room and then paused as Miss Stephens rose to meet her. Her first impression was one of light and space, then of an impressive personality, as Miss Stephens moved around her large oak desk to greet her. She was tall and well built, dressed comfortably in tweeds and moved firmly but easily with a relaxed but slightly regal manner.

"Good morning, Miss Lafay. How good of you to come at such short notice. I hope you had a pleasant. journey. You did say you were coming from London, didn't you? I trust you found your way quite easily?" As Cleo assured her that she had, she seated herself again on the opposite side of the desk. Cleo straightened her jacket nervously then looked up to find Miss Stephens's amazingly clear blue eyes fixed on her. There was a humorous twinkle in them, however, and she was smiling encouragingly. For a brief instant they scrutinised one another. Miss Stephens was in her late fifties, Cleo decided and with her white hair and relaxed manner there was something very reassuring and almost motherly about her. She was probably a very good headmistress and not a person to be easily deceived but there was no time for reflecting on that now.

"You did say you were at Oxford, I think?" Miss Stephens asked briskly, looking down briefly at the paper in front of her. "First class Honours in English, that's very satisfactory?" she murmured. Then, looking up, "You have a testimonial, I believe?"

"Yes, from Professor Harding." Cleo fumbled in her handbag and produced a long envelope which she handed to Miss Stephens.

"Ah, yes." Miss Stephens took it from her, opened it, took out the testimonial and read it carefully. "Well, that also seems very satisfactory," she began.

Cleo braced herself. The difficult part was about to begin. This headmistress, as she had thought, was not going to be an easy woman to deceive. Miss Stephens glanced down once more at the paper in front of her. "I see that you said that you had no previous teaching experience and that you obtained your degree three years ago."

There was an obvious question in her voice. Cleo took a deep breath. "Yes," she began, "as I mentioned I spent a year in further study….." She hesitated, now for the difficult bit. "Then I….." A loud plaintive miaow followed by a soft scratching interrupted her.

"I'm afraid that's Candida," exclaimed Miss Stephens. "She has just come back from her morning stroll." She walked across the room and opened the door. A large, superbly white cat glided majestically in, paused for a moment, surveyed Cleo with an insolent green-eyed stare, then leapt gracefully on to the arm chair next to Miss Stephens and fixed her unwavering stare on Cleo. Cleo involuntarily looked back. It was ridiculous but she felt that Candida was a kindred spirit and might see through her. Cats often had an odd effect on her. She shivered slightly and looked away.

Miss Stephens sat down. "Have you had a nice walk, Candida, poppet?" she asked caressingly. Candida stood up and casually leapt on to her mistress's knee, where she settled, purring, as Miss Stephens tickled her under her chin. Her green eyes, however, remained unblinkingly fixed on Cleo. "This is Candida," Miss Stephens announced.

"She is very beautiful," Cleo answered her with a genuine admiration which obviously pleased Miss Stephens. She looked down at the paper in front of her again. "You have no previous teaching experience, I think you said?" Cleo waited for the obvious question. She had been saved once by Candida but she could not expect such a lucky intervention again and she did not feel that she could easily lie to Miss Stephens who, at the moment, appeared to be absorbed in stroking her cat. There was a brief silence. Miss Stephens looked up. "But that need not necessarily be a serious objection, if you do, as you say, feel that after your past experiences that you would now like to teach.

Sometimes, a decision like that is better made when one is more mature."

"Yes," Cleo agreed swiftly, seizing the opening offered her. "I had really no idea what I wanted to do when I left Oxford but now I feel I would really like to try teaching specially in a girls' school." It was easier to look straight at someone when your eyes were masked with spectacles but she didn't feel that she sounded very convincing. She waited apprehensively, for the first time realising how much she wanted this job.

Suddenly Candida gave a little shake, leapt down from Miss Stephens' lap and approached Cleo. They regarded one another for a moment and then with a soft purr Candida began to rub herself against Cleo's legs.

Miss Stephens smiled broadly. "Well, Candida clearly thinks you belong here. She doesn't usually show her approval so obviously. Do you, poppet?" Having expressed her opinion, Candida returned to her mistress's knee. Cleo waited. "We have several young staff here," Miss Stephens said unexpectedly" so you won't find it too lonely. We have a staff house, where you can have a room. You did say you would want accommodation, didn't you?"

"Oh, yes, that would be very helpful." Cleo felt a little bewildered.

"You wouldn't object to examination work, I imagine?"

"Oh, no, of course not," Cleo said fervently with vague and distant ideas of GCSE and 'A' levels. There would surely be time to find out about them.

"I'm afraid Mrs Lang left GCSE and 'A' level groups but I always think it's probably better to plunge straight in," Miss Stephens continued smoothly. You'll find that both the girls and the staff are very helpful. We always make a great point at St. Elizabeth's at making newcomers feel at home."

Cleo smiled; she could think of nothing particularly appropriate to say. She was, in fact, wondering, if she could possibly ask whether or not she was being offered the job. Before she could speak, however, Miss Stephens continued. "I suggest you go on a brief tour of the school now and then we can have another little chat. Miss Wilson, the Head of the English Department, will be here in a moment to take you round." As if on cue, there was a light tap at the door. "Ah, that will be her now. Come in." As the door opened, Candida jumped from her mistress's lap and advanced with a disdainful air. She did not rub herself against the newcomer's legs but walked straight past her stretching herself arrogantly and disappeared into the corridor.

Miss Wilson was just as Cleo had expected. She was small and angular with short grey hair framing a sallow face with many unhappy, anxious lines. Her skirt and jumper, although originally expensive, had seen better days. She seemed nervous and scarcely smiled when Miss Stephens introduced them. Cleo's confidence in her new appearance rose considerably at this point.

Whatever further remarks Miss Stephens might have been intending to make were cut short by the ringing of the telephone. As she picked it up to answer it, she gave a bright smile and a little wave of her hand which was obviously intended to be one of dismissal. Cleo found herself ushered into the corridor by Miss Wilson who appeared to be regarding her with some irritation and disfavour.

"I suppose I might as well take you to the library first as it's quite near. We have a good selection of books. I see to that. The only trouble is that the majority of the girls never trouble to use them. Not that the staff are much better." She sounded disillusioned and weary and Cleo thought it wiser to make no reply.

They proceeded back to the main corridor and went along it to the library. There was a buzz of noise which subsided abruptly as Miss Wilson entered. Everyone of the many girls seated at the long oak tables suddenly seemed to be absorbed in her work. "The Sixth Form use the Library for private study," Miss Wilson explained as she began the tour. "There is supposed to be a rule of silence." There was silence now but nevertheless Cleo was aware of many eyes following as she was conducted round by Miss Wilson and shown the various sections of the Library, especially the English section of which Miss Wilson was obviously very proud, and justifiably so, it seemed to Cleo as she remembered her own school days.

"Well, I think you've seen enough of this," Miss Wilson suddenly said unexpectedly ushering Cleo out of the door at the other end of the long room. "Now I'd better show you as much as I can of the rest." With almost breathless haste Cleo was shown in quick succession the dining room, the laboratories and several classrooms. They seemed to go up and down innumerable short staircases and traversed endless long corridors. Miss Wilson spoke as little as possible and then apparently reluctantly, scarcely, it seemed, expecting or desiring any reply.

Cleo, quite bewildered, suddenly found herself once again in the main entrance hall. Miss Wilson paused and consulted her watch. "Miss Stephens won't be free to see you for another ten minutes. so I'll take you to the staff room and show you my syllabus." She hurried off once more down the corridor and Cleo followed her.

The staff room was not very prepossessing. It was a large room filled with cupboards, desks and tables and very untidy. There seemed to be papers, exercise books and folders strewn everywhere. The only chairs were straight and hard. It certainly needed redecorating and refurbishing but Cleo decided that probably dedicated teachers did not worry about things like that. It was empty except for one or two women at the other end who appeared to be deep in their marking. "We do have a staff sitting room," Miss Wilson explained, "but this is where we work. She stopped suddenly at a fairly large table in the middle of the room, opened a drawer in it and began to sort irritably through a pile of papers. "Here it is," she exclaimed triumphantly, producing two rather crumpled duplicated sheets stapled together. She looked at them vaguely. "I think this should be quite clear." She handed them to Cleo who hoped it might become clear when she had time to read it. "And this," she added producing another sheet of paper, "is a copy of Mrs Lang's timetable. You will see that she taught mainly in the Upper School and had quite a bit of Sixth form work which should suit you. You can see from the syllabus the books she has been using. I will see that you have copies. It is difficult, of course, to take over in mid-term." For a moment her voice expressed something almost like human sympathy but she repressed it briskly and continued, "But you should be all right after a week or two."

Cleo clutched the papers, feeling overwhelmed. "Nothing has been settled yet.. Miss Stephens may not want me. I've never done any teaching before, you see. She may not think I'll be up to standard."

Miss Wilson unexpectedly laughed. "I don't think you need to worry too much about that. I might as well tell you that we desperately need someone and there aren't many, even if they are free, who would want to bury themselves in a girls' boarding school in the middle of nowhere. Most people who come here these days, if they don't live in the area, are divorced or separated and looking for a refuge or want one for some other reason." She gave Cleo a sharp, enquiring look. "But it doesn't seem to me that you fit into that category?"

"No, I don't," Cleo replied firmly. "I have decided that I want to be a teacher and I thought that this might be a good place to make a start. But perhaps you don't think so?"

"Don't take any notice of me," Miss Wilson said with unexpected affability. "I'm leaving at the end of this school year and going back to academic life. I don't fit in here. It's not exactly challenging, you know. The daughters of the rich aren't always bright and many of them who come here seem not to be. With your qualifications you might find it a bit dull. I thought I ought to warn you." She gave Cleo an almost kindly look as from one academic to another.

Cleo was not sure how to respond. She had not expected this. "I'm not sure that Miss Stephens will want me anyway," she murmured.

"Oh, you don't need to worry about that. You're just what the parents like - young with a good Oxford degree and the right connections. The job's yours, if you want it."

"What do you mean?"

"You are related to Canon Lafay aren't you?"

"Yes," Cleo admittedly almost shamefacedly, "but I don't see what that has to do with it."

"No?" Miss Wilson actually smiled. "Well, perhaps not. But take my advice you'd better think quickly and decide whether this is really the job you want. Now we'd better be going. Miss Stephens will be ready for you. If you do decide to take it," she added unexpectedly, "I shan't be sorry."

Miss Stephens was ready and waiting for them, together with her Deputy, Mrs Maitland. Cleo's confused impression of her was that she was plump, middle aged and pleasant with a rather motherly air and a constant smile. Miss Wilson departed but not before Miss Stephens had had a quiet word with her in the corridor. In the meantime Cleo found herself being urged to sit down by Mrs Maitland and being offered a cup of coffee and a biscuit. The coffee was excellent, the cup was fine china, the biscuit was delicious, and Mrs Maitland was most charming and friendly, as was Miss Stephens when she came back into the room. None of the questions Cleo had expected were being asked and she was adroitly prevented from asking any awkward ones herself

"Well now," said Miss Stephens finally, putting down her cup, "can we take it then that you would be ready to start next week, Miss Lafay?"

"Yes, if you want me." Cleo felt suddenly like panicking but that was ridiculous.

"Of course we don't know exactly when Mrs Lang will be back but it's very unlikely to be before the end of the summer term, so I think that we can safely say that there is employment for you until then. And we might review the position at that time. The bursar will settle the salary details with you. Is that agreeable to you?"

"Oh, yes, if you think I will be suitable." There seemed to be nothing else that she could say.

"Mrs Maitland and I were only saying how well we thought you would fit into St Elizabeth's with your background and qualifications and I'm glad to say that Miss Wilson agrees with us." She stood up, obviously terminating the interview.

Mrs Maitland coughed and then said diffidently, "Don't you think, Miss Stephens, that Miss Lafay might like to see her room?" She smiled in a kindly manner at Cleo.

"Yes, of course, but perhaps I can leave that to you, Mrs Maitland." She glanced at her watch. "There is time for Miss Lafay to see the bursar and her room before she needs to leave for the station." She turned to Cleo with a gracious smile. "Goodbye Miss Lafay, we look forward to seeing you on Sunday. Mrs Maitland will look after you."

Mrs Maitland certainly wasted no time and everything was arranged with an ease and speed which left Cleo marvelling. The bursar was businesslike but friendly, the room was small but more pleasant than she had expected and the Secretary booked a taxi for her in time for the midday train, after she had refused an invitation to lunch with Mrs Maitland in her House.

In an amazingly short time, she found herself once again in the entrance hall waiting for the taxi, with a bag full of books and papers which Miss Wilson had given her and a school prospectus which Mrs Maitland had procured for her from the Secretary. She felt overwhelmed and hoped that she might be able to sort herself out before Sunday. As she had a few minutes to spare she rang up Jane from the telephone there.

"I have been offered the job," she said, "but I don't quite know why, unless it's because of dear, old Canon Lafay which doesn't seem exactly flattering. I'll tell you all about it later." But what would she tell Jane she wondered. Somehow it was not as she had expected.

At the same moment, Mrs Maitland was looking a little anxiously at Miss Stephens. "Do you think she'll be all right? We know very little about her."

"I'm quite sure there's a lot more to learn about her," Miss Stephens replied cheerfully, "but she has a good degree, she's related to Canon Lafay, she'll go down well with the parents and she fills a gap in the timetable." She sat down at her desk, ready to pass on now to the next problem, while Mrs Maitland retired with a smile and a murmur of apparent agreement.

Chapter Five

The telephone call from Marcus on the Friday evening at the end of her second weary week at Barton Leas was completely unexpected. Three weeks had passed since she had parted from him and his lack of further protest had caused her to think, on the rare occasions when she found time to think, that he had relinquished her without too much pain and that all she might expect would be a polite request through Jane to remove her belongings as soon as she conveniently could. She had even found a wry amusement in this - a confirmation of her new view of life and of their relationship.

Now, however, it seemed that she had once more misjudged the situation. He was in Markhampton he told her, to her amazement, and wished to meet her the next day. "Why?" she asked, for she had become convinced of the permanency of their parting.

He had brushed this aside, however, as irrelevant at the moment. "We can discuss that," he replied firmly, "when we meet. Let's just say I'm curious. Will you have lunch with me tomorrow? I don't know what the food's like but it's supposed to be the best hotel in this place, so I think we might risk it."

The offer was tempting, all the more for being unanticipated. She had been dreading another lonely weekend in an almost empty school for, although she was beginning to know some of the staff with whom she shared the staff house, most of them went away for the weekend or part of it. Furthermore, she was seen as a passing visitor from another world and there seemed to be a gulf of suspicion and almost of hostility between them and her. It was a feeling familiar to her from her schooldays when she had felt separated from everyone else by her lack of family. Now, Marcus, at least, wanted to maintain the link between them.

"I teach until midday," she replied cautiously,, "but I could get a taxi and be with you at about a quarter to one."

"Good." He sounded pleased but unwilling to say more at this moment. "Now that's settled, I'll go and look for some food, before everything closes down."

Before he could put down the receiver, she asked abruptly, "And then what?"

"That's entirely up to you," he replied coolly, "I'm here until Sunday morning. We could spend the night together. I hope we will. But, if you decide otherwise, I'll return you to your cloistered refuge."

As she walked slowly back to her room, she wondered whether she should have accepted so easily. Of course, there were matters which needed to be discussed because of her precipitate departure. But was that the true reason for her easy agreement? She looked with distaste around the room which she had first thought of as fairly pleasant but which now seemed small, shabby and decidedly dreary.

The narrow sash window opposite the door looked on to the main High Street but had to be kept closed most of the time because of the unexpected amount of traffic. By day there was a constant stream of cars and after midnight when the village had been quiet for a couple of hours, the lorries began to grind their way along the narrow, winding street, apparently finding it a convenient by-pass. It was rare indeed to find the village as peaceful as it had been when she had first seen it.

The long, heavy curtains had once been a rich brocade but they were now faded and did not match the more recent covers of the divan and its cushions. The carpet had obviously been good once but it too was now worn and faded. There was an old fashioned and far too large oak wardrobe and next to it an equally solid but somewhat dilapidated chest of drawers. Walking over to this, she took off her unnecessary glasses revealing her large and expressive green eyes then released her hair so that it fell into its normal, shining black waves and gazed at herself in the mirror above. "What sort of a person are you, Cleo," she asked. Feeling unable to answer herself, she moved across to her table covered with books and papers and switched on the room's one good feature, the angle-poise lamp. At least, the invitation had given her a much needed incentive for tackling her marking and preparation.

Now, seated opposite to Marcus in the spacious, oak-panelled dining room of what had obviously been an old coaching inn, she admitted to herself that the meeting had so far been easier and pleasanter that she had expected but this was probably due to Marcus and his ability to stage manage most events smoothly so as to avoid any unnecessary difficulties. He must have disliked her dramatic exit intensely.

Studying him, as he examined the menu critically, she decided not for the first time that he projected an excellent image of the successful young, Conservative politician with a future. Then, why not. Since this was the truth? Casually but expensively dressed, he was decidedly handsome. His dark brown hair had a natural wave, his features were clear and good, his smile was attractive but his apparently candid blue eyes concealed more than they revealed, as always. She could not tell what his feelings about her now were.

Suddenly, she realised that he had put down the menu and was smiling at her. "I was dreading something more nunlike, he said with obvious approval of her appearance, "but, thank God you haven't changed. What would you like to eat? I would suggest you kept to the simpler dishes. They sound tolerable."

"I will but don't you want to talk to me?"

"Naturally but I'd prefer to eat first, if you've no objection. Then we can talk freely in my room. What do you think?"

Realising that she was in fact hungry, Cleo agreed readily. It would be delightful, she admitted to herself, to eat any meal after the tasteless and limited offerings of St. Elizabeth's. She turned her attention willingly to the menu.

It was nearly two hours later when she faced him in his hotel bedroom. It was a strangely discouraging place for their discussion, particularly as it was somewhat dominated by the large double bed with its heavy, ornate cover. Doing her best to ignore this, she sank into one of the supposedly comfortable but very stiff armchairs giving, she hoped, an impression of being at ease. Marcus sat down in the other armchair opposite her. "Now perhaps I can have a convincing explanation, at last," he said with unusual severity.

"You're angry," she replied, looking at him, surprised. She could not recall ever having seen him really angry.

"Angry? Of course not! Why should I be angry?" he asked with obvious irony, "when my..." he paused obviously looking for a suitable word.

"Try 'mistress'," Cleo suggested lightly, "it's a bit old-fashioned but accurate."

He accepted that but he didn't smile. "When my mistress walks off in the middle of a supper party without any explanation and even refuses one the next day and then decides to disappear so that I have to beg her disapproving sister for her address, why should I be angry?"

"I suppose that's why it took you so long to do it," she suggested. "It wasn't very thoughtful of me, I agree and I think it's very magnanimous of you to came all this way to see me."

"It certainly is," he agreed, somewhat grimly. But I'm glad to hear that you do agree that your conduct wasn't what I might have expected. Even Jane, although she naturally disapproves of me, seemed quite shocked at the way you had treated me."

"She was, I think, and I imagine she still is. But I haven't had time to find out, just as I haven't had the energy to get in touch with you. I'm sorry."

"So you're finding your new life difficult, are you? Good. You deserve to. But I still want to know why the hell you did it and in that outrageous way. Couldn't you have told me at some more convenient time that I no longer attracted you or that you'd found someone else?"

"I couldn't tell you either of those things because they weren't true," she replied swiftly, "as I think you suspect."

"Then why?" He was frowning but he seemed less angry.

Cleo considered this as she had done on many previous occasions. "I'm not entirely sure," she admitted. "I suppose it had really been coming on for some time but I suddenly seemed to see everything differently and very clearly." She paused. He waited. "It was a sort of conversion, like St. Paul on the road to Damascus."

"Oh, I see. Are you trying to convince me that after two years you suddenly remembered the teaching of your Church and repented of your sin of adultery with me?" He sounded ironical and disbelieving. "Do you actually mean that, in spite of all we've agreed in the past, you want me to confess all to Sarah and ask her to divorce me? You disappoint me, Cleo. I would have thought that, if you wanted to change our mutual agreement, you would have told me openly." He looked at her with genuine surprise. " Surely you weren't trying to force me into divorce and remarriage because of you new found conscience?"

"Of course not," she replied coldly. "in any case there's a flaw in your argument. I'd still be living in sin, as far as the Church is concerned, so why should I bother?"

"True," he admitted, "I'd foolishly overlooked that. So what is the reason? You seem to have eliminated most of them."

"I think it's a matter of love, really," she said slowly.

"And what is that supposed to mean?" he asked aggressively. "You haven't denied that we were living happily together. You have to agree that our sex life has always been successful and enjoyable. Are you now trying to tell me that our life together lacked some subtle romantic flavour called 'love'? If so, you amaze me. You've never spoken like that before. In fact, you always said you liked our arrangement and never wanted to talk about love which you seemed to consider as a kind of 'illusion'."

"And I meant that." She stood up restlessly and walked over to the window. Looking out she saw the pale grey river, with its grey stone bridge and fringe of bare trees and in the distance the dark thrusting spire of the cathedral. It was depressingly remote and cold and the white winter sun did little to alleviate it. Turning round again she realised that the room too with its minimum of conventional modern furniture, and its pale striped walls scattered with several pallid prints had no comfort to offer her.

She became aware that Marcus was watching her intently but he made no move towards her. He was obviously not going to risk another repulse such as she had given him on the Saturday three weeks before. She almost wished he would. It would be comfortable at this moment to have his arms around her. How could she make him understand? Why should she bother? What difference would it make?

"Aren't you going to explain yourself more?" He asked impatiently.

She came back to the table and sat down opposite to him again. "I didn't mean romantic love at all. It wouldn't have been suitable for us. You're quite right." She smiled at him and put out her hand across the coffee table which separated them. "We had good sensible reasons for coming together and we have always known that. I had recklessly left Oxford, broken my engagement to a very suitable young man and then taken that ridiculous modelling job and then found myself lonely, frightened and badly needing some security and affection. You offered me that and I didn't want more."

"And I, for my part, wanted companionship and a warm sexual relationship which Sarah, in spite of her excellent support to me in my career, has denied me for years. I never pretended to be a great lover. I admitted that I was pretty selfish and very ambitious and didn't want to risk losing her support or that of her very influential father. You accepted this, I thought, and didn't want more."

"You're right, I didn't," Cleo responded quickly. "I didn't want a binding commitment. I still don't, I suppose. I don't want to put all my trust in one person and be let down. I suppose that all began when my mother deserted us and my father didn't want me any more."

"And I'm not free to take on a binding commitment, as you know. But surely that doesn't mean that we can't continue to comfort one another as we have been doing for two years? What has changed? I still don't understand?"

"The truth is that it didn't seem to comfort me much any more," she replied sadly. She was aware that he was looking at her closely and trying to understand. He could have made an emotional appeal or exercised the considerable physical attraction he had for her but he was too intelligent to do either. He released her hand and leaned back.

"You said earlier," he reminded her, "that it was a matter of love and I think that I rather crudely misunderstood you."

"Yes," she agreed, "I meant love as I think you have now guessed in a very wide sense."

"Is that why you brought in St. Paul?"

"Yes, I had a sort of religious experience, at least that's the only way I can describe it, though I'm not sure it's the correct description." She shut her eyes and the scene was vividly before her as it had been several times in the last three weeks. But why? It was so trivial. But then what happened on the road to Damascus might have seemed trivial to the people standing around. She opened her eyes.

"It sounds crazy," she said uncertainly, " and it probably is."

"It may be," he replied firmly, "but I still want to hear what it was. After all, it can hardly seem crazier than what happened next."

"I suppose not." His calm acceptance steadied her. This is so like Marcus, she thought, he rarely, if ever, allows himself to get over emotional. But then she thought there are times when I wish he could care deeply. She decided to tell him, nevertheless. She owed him that, at least. "Do you remember," she asked him "that when we were coming out of the theatre that night there was a man sitting huddled on the steps?"

"A beggar, you mean?" he replied with a certain contempt.

"Yes, a beggar but also a human being."

"I remember you stopped and gave him something and seemed to take a long time about it, which irritated me."

"It was terribly cold and nobody even noticed him. His coat was thin and inadequate. He didn't ask for anything but I put a note into his hand and he thanked me very pleasantly."

"I'm not surprised," Marcus commented sarcastically. "I don't suppose he expected such luck."

"I stood and looked at him," Cleo continued, disregarding Marcus' comment. "He had a pale, patient face and remarkable eyes. I said I was sorry he had to be there. Then you called me rather crossly and he smiled at me and said, 'You'd better go. Your friend doesn't want you to get cold.' I felt he was sorry for me, because he understood how I felt at that moment."

"And how was that?" Marcus asked ironically.

"I said you'd think it was crazy but I'm going to risk telling you any way. It seemed to me at that moment that all the sorrows of the world were reflected in his eyes and all the patience of the rejected in his smile. He reminded me suddenly of all the things I've tried to disregard and to forget." She paused and then said defiantly, "I saw the face of Christ in him." She waited but when Marcus made no comment, she continued.

"As we walked away, if you remember, Steve made mocking remarks about my weakness for beggars and said I was old enough now to have realised they were all frauds. And later at supper he brought it up again and everyone joined in, making cynical remarks about the dependency culture and benefit frauds, etc. You didn't say anything but you didn't support me. They were all complacent and horribly smug. I was very angry with myself and everyone. I felt like throwing my glass across the table but I walked out instead. I just wanted to get away. I felt stifled. I knew there was something I ought to be doing and this wasn't it."

"And so you came to Barton Leas?"

"Yes," she smiled ruefully. "Don't tell me it's stupid. I think I'm probably the world's worst school teacher. It's been a humbling experience. What was meant to be a great experiment seems to have become a mundane, rather dreary failure.

'Whither is fled the visionary gleam?

Where is it now the glory and the dream?'

I was attempting to study Wordsworth with the Sixth Form and it occurred to me that he had just about expressed my feelings. And that's about the end of my pathetic confession. I'm not even sure now that what I did was right at all."

Marcus said slowly. "I'm sorry, Cleo but I'm afraid I can't help you. I'm not much of a dreamer and I've never given much thought to religion." He paused. He was obviously making an effort to find the right words. "I suppose you're trying to tell me," he said finally, "that you suddenly found the meaning of life or something like that?" He could not keep the scepticism out of his voice.

"And you think it was not only silly but futile?"

"To be honest, Cleo, yes. I think all this sort of thing is a waste of time and rather morbid. In my opinion, life is for living as fully as possible. I rather thought you had the same belief. I didn't realise that you went in for philosophic speculation."

"You haven't understood me properly," she stated as firmly as she could. "I wasn't talking about philosophy or even theology but about a sudden glimpse of truth - something almost beyond words and only half grasped."

"Ah, now, you're being mystical, I think, and that's quite beyond me. I'm firmly attached to this world and its pleasures. Of course, there are bound to be disappointments and failures but my aim is to overcome them."

"And, if they can't be overcome?"

"Then I accept them as cheerfully as possible and carry on."

"You can only say that so confidently because your life on the whole has been comfortable and pretty successful." Perhaps I'm being unfair, she thought, remembering the partial failure of his marriage.

It did not seem to occur to him, however, as he quickly answered her main point. "I'm willing to concede that," he replied, "but then so has yours. You're intelligent, beautiful and have the advantage of an excellent education. You can be very successful, if you're prepared to work at it. It's time you settled down to a career with a future. Give a few pounds to a beggar, if you must but don't imagine yourself called to be another Mother Teresa."

"I don't. I'm not such a hypocrite."

"I don't think you are either," he replied. "Perhaps just a little too impulsive at times. After all, Cleo, most beggars are beggars because they've chosen to be at some point and they're only too eager to batten down on generous people like you."

"I think you're being unjust," she retorted.

"Perhaps. But what are you doing about it? Have you improved your life or anyone else's by running away?"

"I don't know." she replied uncertainly. Perhaps it was a necessary step."

"I doubt that," he said firmly. "of course you can say that I have a vested interest in getting you back, since you contribute considerably to my enjoyment of life but that's not my only reason. I'm actually very fond of you and I don't want to see you throwing away all your chances which is what you seem about to do."

"Then what do you suggest I should do? Go back with you as if nothing had changed?"

"Of course not. That would be ridiculous. The work you were doing could never have satisfied you for long. You need a career which uses your ability to the full. In a few years you could be successful and rich. You could also be my partner. What's wrong with that?"

"You really are trying to tempt me, Marcus!" She smiled at him uncertainly.

"Then follow Oscar Wilde's advice and give in to it! We could have even more fun together. I am not so foolish as to think that you'll always be satisfied with our present relationship. One day I expect you'll find you want something more permanent but, until that day arrives, why shouldn't we continue? I'll accept that you thought you had some sort of a vision, although I can't understand it but you can't make something as ephemeral as that a reason for changing your whole life. Can you?"

"Perhaps not. I just don't know any more." For a brief instant everything had seemed clear but now she felt deeply confused.

She was touched by Marcus' unexpected attempts to help her. Perhaps he was right. There was no one else to ask.

He stood up. "Let's have a truce," he suggested "and forget our problems while we explore Markhampton. The cathedral is supposed to be fine and there are some other interesting buildings. What do you say?"

As she too stood up, ready to agree, he put his arm round her and kissed her. "I still enjoy being with you and I don't want to lose you." He kissed her again. She did not answer but returned his kiss. His closeness was as warm and comforting as she had earlier imagined it would be. Perhaps this was the best she could hope for.

As they walked towards the lift, he asked suddenly, "Why did you leave Oxford just over two years ago. I've often wondered but you've never really told me. Was it for the same sort of reason?"

"Not really, except that you'd probably think it was just as foolish."

"Why not try me," he suggested, as they moved into the empty lift.

She shrugged. "Very well, since you insist on knowing. My first love came back into my life and somewhat disrupted it. I was angry with him and decided that I didn't want to remain, where I wouldn't be able to avoid him. He couldn't be expected to leave, so I did. There were other reasons but that was the immediate cause. I told you that you'd think it was silly. It's unimportant now." She hurried on before he could say anything. "Do you think we could visit the shops as well as the cathedral? I'd like to buy a new dress to wear tonight. I left most of mine behind."

"How can I resist such a plea?" he replied, as they entered the foyer.

It was cold and already dark when they finally re-entered the brightly lit foyer, after an enjoyable afternoon. Contrary to her usual custom, she accepted a whisky and relaxed in a quiet corner of the lounge close to the fire. Marcus sat opposite to her sipping his own drink. He smiled approvingly at her. "I'm surprised you accepted that," he declared. "But it's probably wasted on you. You're a Philistine as far as whisky's concerned."

She laughed. "It's warm and comforting."

"Like me or like I could be," he suggested. He looked challengingly at her. "I think the decisive moment has come, Cleo. Will you spend the night with me or must I take you back after dinner and solace myself with more whisky?"

For a moment she hesitated and then wondered why she should. He was right. He was warm and comforting and she dreaded returning to the loneliness of the last three weeks. It might be a denial of her vision but hadn't she already denied that by meeting him? It would be enjoyable and she wanted to enjoy it. She admitted to herself, almost with disappointment, that she lacked the strength to deny herself this pleasure. She looked across at him. "Why not?" she asked.

"Why not what?"

"Why not stay with you?"

"It's not exactly an enthusiastic acceptance but I suppose it will have to do." He sounded disappointed.

Immediately ashamed that she had been so grudging, she smiled warmly at him. "We'll have fun," she suggested. I'll have a shower and put on my new dress."

"Good. Then don't let's waste too much time down here." He put down his glass and waited impatiently for her to finish her drink.

It was amazingly easy to return to their former intimacy, she realised, as they entered the bedroom. He kissed and embraced her with growing eagerness as she made for the shower. "Don't be too long," he said, "and don't bother to put the dress on yet. I'll be waiting. I'll order a bottle of champagne. What do you think?"

"Fine," she called out as she pulled herself away and went to the shower. "But don't give me too much. You know it makes me sleepy."

"And I certainly don't want that," he agreed.

It had been a most successful evening she reflected hours later, as she lay in the darkness. Marcus had always been a thoughtful lover and she found it easy to respond to him and this evening they seemed to have regained their earlier delight. It was pleasant now to lie in this comfortable bed with a warm, friendly body next to hers. She reached out a hand and touched him gently. "You've been wonderful, darling," he murmured sleepily. "But then you always are. I hope I haven't disappointed you." She didn't answer but moved closer to him in reassurance but at the same time she thought how strange it was that her body could be so content while her mind or was it her soul could remain so detached and uninvolved?

Chapter Six

It was only on the Monday morning during school assembly that Cleo admitted to herself how easily and completely she had capitulated to Marcus. This was a good time for thinking for, providing that she sat quietly in her place at the back of the balcony, no one would think of interrupting her. She looked down indifferently at the stage framed with crimson velvet curtains and observed the choir mistress giving her last instructions to her well drilled choir as Miss Stephens swept in resplendent in her gown and well cut suit.

It was a cold, grey morning again and, as she stood up for the opening hymn, and looked through the long windows that lined each side of the hall the gaunt trees could be seen shuddering under the impact of the gales from the upper moorlands. She, however, saw only herself once more having a final lunch with Marcus in Markhampton. Pleased with their reunion he had delayed his departure until after lunch and was cheerful and relaxed. As the waiter left them with their coffee, he said confidently, "I can expect to see you then in London in a fortnight's time at half term. I can't be there until Sunday afternoon but we can have several days together. You haven't changed your mind, have you?" he asked, as she didn't immediately reply.

"Of course not," she responded quickly. Where else was there for her to go, she wondered? She might descend on Jane but hardly for a week, so soon after her last visit. She hadn't taken holidays into account but the real truth was that she wanted to go back, she wanted the comfort of Marcus.

"You really must look for another job while you're in London," he continued, I'll speak to a friend of mine in the City and arrange a couple of interviews for you. You don't belong to this provincial backwater. You're wasting your talents. They won't appreciate you, on the contrary, you'll just make them feel uncomfortable."

There's some truth in that, she thought. No one accepts me at St Elizabeth's and I'm no good at the job. Whatever talents I may have, teaching doesn't seem to be one of them. It was the feeling of rejection, however, that she minded most, she knew that. The dread of being different. It was that which had always hurt and frightened her, ever since that day twelve years ago when her mother whom she so closely resembled and so much loved had left with her lover without warning and had vanished somewhere. She had turned to her austere father for comfort but he too had rejected her in favour of the older and much less emotional Jane. Finally he had sent her to join Jane at the convent boarding school where she had just entered the Sixth Form. Jane had always been kind but it had never been easy to bridge the gap of age and temperament between them. And now with Jane happily married and planning a family the gap was greater than ever, especially as Robert unwillingly found his beautiful, young sister-in-law attractive.

It was at this point that she became aware that the assembly had ended and the girls were beginning to file out. Standing up, she moved quickly after them but, as she hurried down the stairs from the balcony to get to her first class, she was surprised to be greeted by Cynthia Drew, the Art Mistress, who also had a room in the Staff House.

Cynthia was a tall, slim woman of about thirty, who always drifted around with a vague, dreamy air accentuated by loose dresses usually in soft grey or beige. Her rather long face, framed by soft brown hair drawn into a loose bun, was pale, her eyes were grey, large and surprisingly expressive. Her voice was soft and languid and she had a wistful charm that seemed to have gained her several friends during the four years she had been at St Elizabeth's.

"Hello, Cleo," she said with a friendly smile, "did you have a good weekend?" On seeing Cleo's startled look, she explained quickly, "I saw you dashing off in a taxi on Saturday. I thought you must be catching the London train. I wished I was too."

"Nothing as exciting as that," Cleo replied with some relief. "I was just meeting a friend in Markhampton."

"It's good to get away at the weekends," Cynthia remarked. "I do it whenever I can. Fortunately my family only live about twenty five miles away." They had reached the foyer and paused before separating to go to their different classes. "I was wondering," Cynthia asked diffidently, "if you would like to join me for a coffee in my room after supper? Several other people are coming so it'll give you a chance to get better acquainted. What do you think?"

Cleo accepted readily, pleased at this unexpected friendliness. "Good," Cynthia concluded, as she moved off, "I'll expect you about seven thirty. My room's no. 4 at the back. I must go now, I've a Third Form waiting. See you later." With a gentle smile she drifted away casually.

Was it because of that encouragement, Cleo wondered later, that her first lesson seemed to he happier and more successful? Feeling suddenly more confident she dared to try out an adventurous idea for creative writing and was delighted with her class's positive response. Emboldened by this, she felt able to experiment more with her other classes and ended the day feeling pleased for the first time. She felt that she might at last have begun her career as a teacher. Although she had a lot to learn, she was beginning to believe that she might have something to give and that was an unusual and exciting feeling.

Cynthia's room was larger and much better furnished but this was because, as Cynthia explained, she had provided the soft furnishings and ornaments herself. The delicate water colours which Cleo admired were hers, the set of jugs in deep blue had been made by her as had the divan cover with its delicate blues and pinks and greens, colours which were repeated again in the handmade rug which hid the shabbiness of the carpet.

No one else was there and on seeing Cleo's surprise at this, Cynthia explained that she had deliberately invited them for a little later so that she could have time to get to know Cleo before they arrived. "But there's no reason why we shouldn't have a cup of coffee by ourselves," she said. "I can always make some more."

As she poured the coffee into attractive china mugs, Cynthia talked with a certain gentle humour about the school. and its staff, several of the more dedicated of whom had spent almost their entire working lives there. "But apart from those and the married women who come in daily, it's a kind of refuge for people who can't cope with the world outside for one reason or another. I imagine you," she smiled at Cleo with slightly raised eyebrows, "are one of the transients we occasionally have?"

She paused there and Cleo felt obliged to reply to the implied question. "I left London because I wanted to sort my life out. I felt I needed space, so I suppose I am a kind of refugee too." She did not feel obliged to explain any more.

"But not for long, I think," Cynthia remarked as she passed her coffee to Cleo. Then perhaps sensing a barrier, she abruptly changed the subject. "You have an Oxford degree, I believe, so you ought to have a lot in common with Bridget Russell, our Head of Modern Languages. She was at Oxford but about fifteen years before your time, I imagine. She trained there too, then went into the State system for several years. Is that similar to your experience?"

"No," Cleo replied hastily, "the only teaching I've done is a bit of part time lecturing which I was given to do while I was supposed to be working towards an eventual doctorate. But I decided then I'd had enough of Oxford and took a job in London.

Someone I met offered me a chance to be a photographer's model. I thought it'd be fun, so I took it, especially as it was only for the more refined monthlies."

"And was it fun?"

"For a while yes but then I got bored with it, so I decided to get away and sort myself out properly." She wondered anxiously if this brief explanation would be accepted but, fortunately, Cynthia seemed to be more interested in explaining herself.

"I've been a teacher for eight years," she responded, "it was necessary for me to have a steady income. There's never been much money at home, since my father became ill and there's also a younger brother and sister. "It was lucky I was trained and could take a job almost straightaway."

She spoke quietly but Cleo detected a note of weary resignation in her voice. Once she would probably have ignored it but now she was aware of Cynthia's need to confide. "But you're not happy are you?" she asked.

Cynthia looked surprised and seemed about to make a denial but suddenly changed her mind. "I don't know how you know but you've guessed right. It's hard to accept failure when you're only thirty."

"Surely it's too soon to do that?" Cleo replied energetically.

Cynthia shrugged slightly. "Perhaps but it might be more sensible. I'm not a particularly good teacher- and I don't like the job very much. When I was twenty I wanted to be an artist." She paused.

"Then why didn't you?"

"I wasn't sure I had enough talent and what was worse I didn't even have the courage to put it to the test, so I became a teacher."

"But surely that's a worthwhile job," Cleo responded swiftly. "At least you can help others to develop their talents." That was the argument she was using to convince herself, she realised.

"Perhaps, if you have a vocation although it doesn't always seem like that, I'm sure. The trouble is that I'm a teacher without a vocation. Now you see what a hopeless person I am." She smiled wistfully.

For a moment Cleo felt exasperated but the consciousness of her own failures and indecision held her back. "I know a bit about courage," she said instead, "I'm having trouble with that myself I want to change my life but it's not easy."

"Don't be tempted to stay here too long," Cynthia warned her. "It can seem a very comfortable refuge."

"Hardly that," Cleo laughed, thinking of her ugly, little room and the uninspired meals.

"It's the routine that's so comfortable," Cynthia replied seriously. "Don't be misled, it's very insidious. As long as you conform, everything comes easily - food, meals and the comfort of belonging to a community. But it can be a very narrow life. We tend to become obsessed with our own little world." She paused for a moment and then, as if thinking she had perhaps said too much, she abruptly changed the subject. "How are you finding teaching then?" she asked.

Cleo told her, glad to have a chance to talk to discuss something less personal. It was also a relief to have a chance to talk about her difficulties and newly acquired hope with someone who understood.

"You're doing fine," Cynthia generously reassured her. "Don't forget the girls are always ready to welcome someone different with interesting ideas. But you should concentrate on the Sixth Form. With your fresh academic background, you're just what they need. They often feel isolated too."

A knock at the door, followed by the entry of two other guests, prevented Cynthia from giving any further advice. As they came in, Cleo recognised them as Pam Richards, the young PE teacher and Stella Harvey, a junior member of the

Mathematics Department who also played the violin in the school orchestra. She had been introduced to them at the beginning of term but had not since spoken more than a few brief words to them. After cheerful greetings, they helped themselves to coffee and settled on the divan together. They appeared to be friends, although they were obviously very different.

Pam, still wearing the navy blue track suit she seemed to wear most of the time, was short, stocky and fair. Her hair was brushed back and tied in two bunches. Her face with its slightly plump rosy cheeks and bright blue eyes had a scrubbed, little girl look which was not, however, unattractive. As soon as she sat down, she produced a bottle of ready mixed cocktails from her duffel bag, announcing in her bright, clear voice that she thought they ought to celebrate Cleo's arrival with something a little stronger than coffee. Agreeing that this was a good idea, Cynthia went to her cupboard and produced the necessary glasses. It seemed to Cleo that perhaps such celebrations were not unusual, Stella also brought some appropriate snacks from her bag. "Thanks," Cynthia responded "but we won't start our feast until Bridget comes."

"I didn't know Bridget was coming," Stella said, as she settled herself gracefully on the divan. Taller and slimmer than Pam, she was wearing a dark green dress in some clinging material which emphasised her figure and the simplicity of which was only relieved by a many coloured chiffon scarf, tossed elegantly around her throat. Her straight, dark hair was cut fairly short, framing her face on either side and hiding most of her forehead with a fringe which came close to her heavy dark eyebrows. Her wide set hazel eyes were heavily lidded, her face was square rather than oval and her generous mouth was brilliantly outlined. Except when she smiled, her expression was brooding, almost sombre, as if she was secretly meditating on the sorrows and injustices of the world.

She smiled now as she looked speculatively at Cleo but Cleo was not convinced that it was a truly friendly smile. "Where did you get that magnificent tunic?" she inquired. "The colours are lovely, just right for you and the design's fantastic. It must be hand-knitted. You didn't knit it yourself, did you?"

"I'm afraid not," Cleo confessed. "I bought it at a little boutique in South London."

"You wore a similar one the other day," Pam remarked, "I liked that even better. Did it come from the same shop?" Without waiting for an answer, she continued, "I love quality clothes like those but I can't afford them on my salary."

Her childish curiosity was obvious and it seemed reasonable to satisfy it. But how far? "I wasn't teaching," Cleo paused, wondering how much to say.

"Cleo was a model before she came here," Cynthia interposed. "So she naturally has some suitable clothes."

"You exchanged that for this!" Stella sounded incredulous.. "I can't imagine why?" Her tone was suspicious almost hostile.

Cleo wondered how she should reply. How could she possibly say, 'I had a vision' or 'I'm looking for the meaning of life.' It would sound absurdly pretentious and invite Stella's hostility. Seeing her embarrassment, perhaps, Cynthia intervened. "We all have our reasons," she said, "which may not sound very convincing to others. I came because I found it easier to teach in this environment and because I wanted to be nearer my family."

"And I came because I wanted to be near my boyfriend, so we could see each other every weekend," Pam cheerfully announced. "It'll be convenient when we get married too."

"And when is that going to be," Stella asked, managing to imply doubt.

Pam was unmoved. "Next year, if we can get enough money saved." She turned to Stella. "You're the only one who belongs here. You haven't been away from Markhampton, except for college and the year you taught in the South. Haven't you ever wanted to get away?"

Was her question quite as innocent as it sounded, Cleo wondered as she noticed the quick flush on Stella's normally pale face? Whatever her feelings, however, Stella replied calmly, "Why should I? I like it and my mother needs me now she's on her own. I'm just unadventurous, I suppose."

It was becoming obvious to Cleo that, in spite of their outward appearance of friendship, there was a certain hostility between Pam and Stella. She was intrigued but decided that it would be wiser for her to say as little as possible since she had sensed a certain hostility towards herself in Stella. In view of that decision, Stella's next apparently artless question was more than a little annoying.

"Was that your boyfriend I saw you with in Markhampton on Saturday?" she asked.

Cleo's obvious surprise caused Cynthia to intervene once more. "That's one thing you'll have to learn about this place, Cleo. Everybody likes to know what everybody else is doing and, if the staff don't gossip, the girls will. It adds spice to life."

"It's pretty awful!" Pam exclaimed. It's a bit like 'Cranford', only worse because people are so malicious."

"I don't know why you should say that," Stella retorted. "Be honest. You don't object to a bit of gossip."

Pam shrugged, "I don't mind when it's good natured but not otherwise."

"But it never is good natured, is it? at least not in my experience," Stella replied bitterly.

"Don't let's be so depressing?" Cynthia said quickly, "or Cleo will think we're much worse than we really are." She turned to Pam. "We're not really as bad as that, are we?"

"Of course not," Pam replied cheerfully. "All we need is a few more men about the place to distract us." From her irritated expression it was clear that Stella did not agree but, before she could speak, Pam continued, "Which reminds me, Cynthia, is Nicholas coming tonight?"

"I'm afraid not. He thought he ought to go home." Cleo was surprised to see that Cynthia too had flushed, although her tone was as calm as ever.

"What a pity?" Pam retorted. "He's missed an opportunity of trying out his charms on Cleo! Or perhaps you didn't tell him that?"

"Who is Nicholas?" Cleo asked, feeling that some curiosity was expected of her.

"Do you really mean to say you haven't noticed our middle aged Romeo?"

"I don't think so."

"Oh, you'd know if you had. He's fat, fortyish, married unhappily, of course but he still thinks he's every woman's dream lover. And believe it or not, he's had some success, so beware!"

"You're being ridiculous," Stella snapped. "He's just pleasant and friendly."

"Well, you should know," Pam replied imperturbably, "especially since you joined the orchestra and became his confidante."

Cleo was becoming uncomfortably aware of the growing tension in the room. Pam was like a naughty girl bent on mischief; Stella was very much on the defensive and even the languid Cynthia was undoubtedly ruffled. The evening was not turning out as she had expected. It seemed that Pam secure in her own relationship was amusing herself taunting both Stella and Cynthia in some way. Could it be that they were rivals for Nicholas's attention? The atmosphere was quite different from what she in her ignorance had imagined it would be. She realised at this moment that Pam was addressing her and warning her that she would probably be the next object of Nicholas's attention. "None of us will have a chance when he sees you," she declared.

Bridget's arrival, fortunately, made it unnecessary for Cleo to reply to this remark which seemed to her unnecessarily provocative. She was pleased to meet this cool, self possessed woman whose calm control over the pupils had impressed her on several occasions and whom, she thought, might initiate a more intellectual level of conversation.

Bridget appeared to be older than the others, probably in her late thirties. She was tall and slim with short, pale fair hair, cleverly styled and brushed back from her smooth, broad forehead. She was wearing well tailored green trousers and a crisp and elegantly simple white blouse. She looked directly at Cleo when they were introduced, seemed to consider her for a moment and then smiled pleasantly. Feeling strangely reassured, Cleo smiled back. On her arrival, the tension eased visibly and even Stella seemed to relax. It was also a signal for Pam to open her bottle and for Cynthia to pour the drinks into glasses.

As she sat down in a vacant chair next to Cleo, Bridget apologised for her late arrival. "I'm afraid I forgot the time while I was listening to the news," she said, accepting her glass.

"Was there anything particularly interesting?" Cynthia asked. "I haven't heard anything since this morning early."

"I don't suppose you've missed much," Stella remarked, "It's usually boring and repetitious."

"It was a discussion about euthanasia, which particularly interested me," Bridget continued, ignoring Stella's somewhat ungracious comment.

"Oh, not that again," Pam exclaimed. "There's an awful lot of talk about that these days. It seems pretty morbid to me."

"I suppose it's something we have to consider," Cynthia remarked mildly. We might be faced with the problem ourselves."

"I don't see why," Stella retorted, "Why can't we just let people get on with it quietly, as they have been doing for years, I imagine? But the media always has to have something to talk about."

"The media has a good excuse this time," Bridget replied. "A well known paediatrician in the Midlands has just been charged with allowing a seriously handicapped baby to die quietly by feeding it only on painkillers and water."

"How dreadful for everyone," Pam exclaimed.

"Was the baby very handicapped?" Cynthia enquired.

"Very, I believe," Bridget replied. "It could only have expected a short and painful life. The parents, it seemed had rejected it. Everyone agrees that the doctor is a very caring man and was only doing what he thought right in the circumstances." She spoke calmly and it was difficult to tell what she felt.

Cleo thought with tremendous pity that it was probably best for the baby to have died and thus to be spared the added pain of rejection. She said nothing, however, afraid that the others would not understand her feelings and that, in any case, it might be too self revealing to admit them.

"How was it discovered then?" Stella asked angrily. "I suppose someone let him down. There's always somebody ready to do that."

"I'm not sure exactly how it happened," Bridget replied. "I only know that a Catholic organisation who are against abortion and euthanasia reported him to the police and so of course the police had to act and he will now have to go for trial."

"Poor man," Cynthia exclaimed. "His career could be ruined. But I suppose they thought they were doing what was right," she added a little doubtfully."

"Rubbish." Stella declared emphatically. "They're just interfering pious do-gooders who think they have a right to judge everyone. And they call themselves Christians! A lot of Catholics are like that. They seem to think they have a monopoly of the truth."

Cleo reluctantly felt obliged to intervene at this point. "Not all Catholics," she said. "In any case they're not really judging the people. They simply think that life is sacred." As everyone looked at her she added quickly, "I'm not much of a Catholic now but I was baptised one and educated in a convent boarding school."

"Where the nuns taught you all the usual hell fire and damnation stuff, I suppose?" Stella asked.

Determined not to get angry, Cleo replied quietly, "Not exactly. They taught us that we must hate the sin but love the sinner."

"And that's suppose to include this kind of rotten behaviour, is it?" Stella asked angrily. "Ruining a man's life just because he tries to be merciful."

Cleo would have liked to retreat from an argument she had not really wanted. She was uneasily conscious that her own ideas were not as clear as they should have been. "I understand how you feel," she said quickly, trying to placate Stella, "but it is possible that human beings can go very wrong when they try to act like God. It's not really possible for us to judge."

Stella continued, however, ignoring Cleo's last remark. "It's all very pious to say you don't condemn the sinner but it doesn't actually feel like that to the 'so-called sinner'. I suppose you take the same view of abortion?" Her scorn was as obvious as it was surprising.

"I don't believe Cleo actually gave us her own opinion," Bridget interrupted quietly. "You were just trying to explain how some people might think, weren't you?" she asked. smiling at Cleo.

"Of course she was," Pam burst in before Cleo could reply. "As for abortion, I'm not sure I approve of it, at least not when people do it just for convenience."

"It's all very well to talk," Stella said quickly "but have any of you ever thought just what you'd feel if you found you were going to have an unexpected and unwanted baby, especially if the father didn't want to know? If you haven't, perhaps you should." She looked directly at Pam and then at Cleo.

Pam answered her quickly. "Oh, I know. John and I have talked about it when it happened to some friends of ours. It wouldn't be entirely convenient but we'd just get married sooner, that's all."

Bridget smiled. "I'm afraid it doesn't apply to me any more. I haven't had a love life for several years and I'm quite happy without one. It's simpler that way. A woman has a right to choose but it might be easier if she chose her lover more carefully in the first place."

"That's roughly my opinion," Cynthia agreed. "I wouldn't want to be in that position but, if I were, I think I'd choose to have the baby." There was a longing she could not hide in her voice and it seemed to Cleo that Bridget felt herself to be a failure in this direction also.

"And what about you, Cleo?" Stella asked. "You've explained the Catholic viewpoint but you haven't actually told us what you think or what you would do. You have a boy friend. Surely you must have thought about it?"

It was humbling to Cleo to be forced to realise how little she had thought about it. She had, she supposed, roughly accepted the Church's teaching but had never really considered it how it might apply to herself. Did that mean that she was hopelessly naive or that she had been able to trust the men she had loved?

"You don't seem very sure," Stella remarked. "Perhaps you haven't actually thought of applying the teaching to real life?"

"I suppose you're right," Cleo admitted "I've never really had to think about it in a personal way."

"Lucky for you," Stella said with some irony. "But what if you had trusted someone and he left you as soon as you found you were pregnant? It does happen to people you know. And it's easy to look the other way." Her voice was harsh and bitter.

Oh God, Cleo thought with a sudden flash of insight, it must have happened to her and she's particularly angry with me because she thinks I take 'a holier than thou' attitude simply because I've been lucky, although I'm no better than she is.

While Cleo was trying to think of a reply, Cynthia intervened with the suggestion of another drink. "Can anyone tell me," she asked as she refilled their glasses, "what the arrangements for the Sixth Form parents' meeting are? I gather it's all to be changed."

"I didn't know there was one," Cleo said, feeling that it was not exactly a pleasant surprise but that it would be a safer subject to discuss.

They all laughed. "You'll learn," Pam said gaily. "You have to realise that the parents are our real bosses. You must please them, whatever you do."

"And how do I do that?"

"Wear a dress pretty enough to charm the fathers but not so pretty as to alarm the mothers," Pam suggested.

"Oh, so that's the secret of your success, is it?" Cynthia remarked. "I always wondered what it was."

"But you must always look and sound efficient," Stella added "and be sure to fit the right girl to the right parents. Which isn't always as easy as it seems." She sounded relaxed for the first time. "But seriously, Bridget," she continued, "you must have some idea. After all you are part of the hierarchy."

"It's nothing to worry about," Bridget answered. "It's simply going to be more informal with a buffet."

"And how on earth is that supposed to work?" Stella exclaimed. "How are we to deal with food, coffee and parents at the same time?"

"All with be made clear by HM at the Staff Meeting on Wednesday," Bridget replied, somewhat evasively.

"It's all quite simple," Pam suggested. "We don't eat or drink. We just pretend to."

From then on, to Cleo's relief, the conversation centred on school matters. There was the usual discussion of various pupils and their examination prospects, with light-hearted suggestions as to the best ways of dealing with parents. Cleo felt relieved. This was more as she had expected.

Stella was the first to leave with the excuse of marking to finish.

"Phew!" exclaimed Pam as the door closed behind her. "That was tricky earlier. She's so bitter about everything."

"I suppose it was my fault," Bridget said. "I should be more careful what I talk about."

"Of course it isn't," Cynthia answered her quickly. "It's just that Stella so easily gets worked up about things and takes everything personally."

Cleo listening to them could not decide how much they might know or suspect but thought it wiser to make no comment.

"And now she's determined to get Nicholas," Pam observed. "Some people never learn, apparently."

"You're not fair to Nicholas," Cynthia protested. Pam only shrugged and made no reply. Bridget began to collect the glasses and cups on a tray. "Shall we help you to dispose of these?" she asked tactfully. "It's about time we were all moving off."

It was obvious to Cleo after she had taken a few cups to the kitchen on the landing that the others would now be quite happy to see her go and so with many thanks she departed back to the quiet of her own room which now seemed strangely like a refuge. As she looked through her window into the quiet and empty High Street she tried to sort out the many conflicting impressions she had received during the evening. Suddenly she wished that she had someone she could communicate with, someone who was close to her. That was a futile thought, she decided, for there probably never would be any such person. She closed the curtains and began to prepare for bed. She had learned to accept over the years that life was a lonely business for people like her.

As she brushed her hair she wondered what verdict the others would pass on her but decided it would be more sensible not to speculate.

Chapter Seven

It became increasingly obvious to Cleo, in the days which followed, that the party in Cynthia's room had done nothing to improve her position, in fact it might be said to have worsened it by underlining the differences in both background and attitude between them and her. Furthermore they had revealed much of themselves but she with her habitual reserve had not made any personal confidences, even when invited. Nor had they cared much for the moral views she had stated, apparently considering them in some way to be hypocritical. She was intelligent enough to understand that all this would inevitably be resented but vulnerable enough to wish that it could be otherwise.

Bridget, although always courteous, remained busy and unapproachable, while Cynthia, obviously regretting her burst of confidence, avoided her. Pam cheerfully made it clear that she considered that they had little or nothing in common which was probably true, Cleo admitted. Stella spoke to her when they met but always with a latent hostility, which became open on the Thursday morning when Cleo innocently joined her and Nicholas Barnes for coffee.

She had not suspected that this greying, obviously middle aged man whose stomach bulged over his tight fitting trousers could possibly be the Romeo of whom Pam had spoken, until Stella reluctantly introduced them. He greeted Cleo warmly while giving her a decidedly speculative glance from his deep set grey eyes. He had charm, Cleo had to admit, and he was using it on her. Remembering what Pam had said, Cleo kept herself strictly in check, although it was hard not to respond to some degree. It was soon clear, however, that Stella was resenting her attraction and Nicholas's obvious susceptibility to it and, on seeing Cynthia determinedly approaching their table, she stood up and reminded Nicholas that he had promised to look over a difficult passage of music with her before the end of break.

Apart from giving Cleo an almost conspiratorial smile Nicholas made no protest and he and Stella were departing just as Cynthia reached them. Although they apologised, they still went, leaving Cynthia clearly annoyed and most unwilling to talk to Cleo. Feeling herself unwanted, Cleo hastily swallowed her coffee, made her excuses and left for her classroom ten minutes before the end of break. As she sat at her desk she felt more rejected and isolated than ever before. It seemed that her colleagues were determined to make it quite clear that she did not and could not belong to their world. It was a relief when her class arrived, ready apparently to be stimulated by her and she was able to plunge herself into an activity which she was beginning to find both increasingly rewarding and enjoyable. Here, at least, were people who responded to her and with whom she could establish a friendly relationship.

The attitude of several of the younger staff did not, however escape the vigilance of the pleasant and approachable Mrs Maitland, who as Deputy Headmistress kept a motherly eye on both staff and students. Later that morning she mentioned it to Miss Stephens during one of their regular meetings at which staffing problems were often discussed.

She was facing Miss Stephens across the large walnut desk the leather top of which was, as always, immaculately tidy. The study with its high ceiling and its long windows giving a view of the chapel gardens was light and airy. The book-lined walls gave it a suitably intellectual atmosphere while the carriage clock on the white marble mantelpiece quietly marked the passage of time, so important an aspect of school life.

The meeting was coming to an end. Mrs Maitland consulted her notebook, then almost tentatively, it seemed, asked Miss Stephens for her opinion of Miss Lafay, the new member of staff. "She seems to have settled in well and happily," Miss Stephens replied after a moment's consideration. "At least that is my impression but you think differently, perhaps?"

"I think she has settled in well as a teacher but I doubt very much if she is happy," was Mrs Maitland's somewhat hesitant reply.

Miss Stephens slightly raised her heavy white eyebrows and gave her deputy a curious glance from her unusually brilliant blue eyes. She smiled tolerantly. "Explain yourself, Rosemary."

"Well, I do agree that the girls seem to have taken to her but the younger staff, as we have observed before are very.." she paused trying to find the right word.

"Uncooperative?" Miss Stephens suggested.

"Yes, I'm afraid they tend to close ranks against newcomers, especially one who is so obviously different as Miss Lafay undoubtedly is."

"If by 'different' you mean that she has an unusually good academic background together with a more varied one, shall we say, and is, at the same time, exceptionally good looking and stylish, then I agree with you. She is also, I imagine, reserved. People like that can't expect to be accepted by their more average colleagues. It's hard for her but," she shrugged lightly, "she's probably used to it. She should be an asset, while we have her. The parents like to know that we're willing to take on bright young staff with a fresh outlook on life." She closed her notebook and put down her pen.

As far as Miss Stephens was concerned, the matter was ended, for her primary concern was, as always, the success of the school but the sympathetic Mrs Maitland thought otherwise. "I agree with you," she replied, but I wasn't just wanting to see it from that point of view. I think that as a Christian foundation it is our duty to care for the well being of our staff."

"And what exactly does that mean with regard to Miss Lafay?"

"I think she may be particularly vulnerable because she takes life more seriously than many and is perhaps searching for a vocation. In which case we ought to give her some help. I also think that she is not unhappy simply because of the staff here but there is a deeper cause for it, a cause which sent her from London to the 'wilderness' here. Didn't it occur to you, too?" She spoke quietly but was obviously not prepared to give way.

Miss Stephens considered her deputy's words for a few moments. She was not unaware of the importance of the wider issues which Mrs Maitland had put before her and was too humane a woman not to be concerned. "You mentioned 'vocation'," she said finally, "that's not a word we hear often these days but you may be right. Obviously there was some strong impulse which brought her here so suddenly. I rather thought it might be an unhappy love affair but I must admit that I didn't give it much consideration since her arrival was so very opportune. As always you are more concerned with these problems."

"I regard it as very much my concern," Mrs Maitland replied gently.

"In that case, ought you not to take her under your wing? You have two grown up daughters, after all, and would seem to be well qualified."

"I'm not sure I'm the right person," Mrs Maitland replied after a moment's thought. "I don't think she would respond to being mothered."

"In that case, why don't you have a word with Jean Wilson."

"With Jean Wilson!" Mrs Maitland sounded astonished.

"Yes, why not? She's in Jean's department It's her responsibility."

"But Jean Wilson, as you know, is unapproachable and so very critical. The younger staff, especially, avoid her as much as possible."

Miss Stephens smiled tolerantly. "I accept everything you've said, particularly with regard to the younger staff but, as you yourself also said Miss Lafay is different. Jean Wilson and Cleo Lafay may have more in common than you have realised. They are both products of Oxford, both have outstanding academic records and both, I imagine are perfectionists in their own way. Although there are many differences, they should be able to communicate. Jean definitely needs some help at the moment, especially with dealing with the Sixth Form and who is better qualified to do that than Miss Lafay, whom they will regard as an obvious role model."

After considering this novel idea, Mrs Maitland looked at her Headmistress with considerable approval. During the years they had worked together Isabel Stephens had frequently impressed her with her lucid grasp of essentials and with the swiftness and accuracy of her decisions. She knew that she was needed to point out many of the human problems but once they were pointed out, Isabel could be relied on to solve them at once. St Elizabeth's owed much to her. "I'll try it," she said, "and you're quite right, Jean does need help with Sixth formers, especially those in her House. I'll speak to her after lunch."

"Well there you are," Miss Stephens declared, "two difficulties solved." She stood up and put on her gown as the bell sounded. With a smile, Mrs Maitland too stood up and opened the door.

As a result of this conversation Cleo to her surprise found herself being invited to coffee after supper in Miss Wilson's flat, It was 5.45pm on Thursday evening and she had just finished her last lesson. On Thursdays she taught all day and it was very tiring. The pupils had been listless also. This was not an invitation she had expected since Miss Wilson had scarcely spoken to her since her first day but she supposed it was part of the necessary vetting. Whatever the reason, it was not an offer to be refused.

After making her arrangements with Miss Wilson, she went quickly to her room, only pausing to collect an unexpected note from Marcus. 'Darling,' he wrote, 'tried to ring you without success. Your switchboard appears to be manned by morons. I wanted to tell you I can arrange an interview for Wednesday of half term but must have a quick answer. Ring me on Thursday, if possible. Yours always, but in haste now. Marcus.'

Entering her room she threw the note and her folders on the table and collapsed wearily on the divan. The room seemed even more unwelcoming than usual. She could hear Pam chatting cheerfully to someone on the landing and Stella calling out to Cynthia that she was wanted on the phone but no-one approached her. Even having coffee with the prickly Miss Wilson might be better than spending another evening alone in her room.

Earlier in the day she had bought the requirements of a simple meal, feeling that she could not face another school supper. Fortunately it would not take much preparation and she could read while she ate which would be better than conversation that was no conversation. Why on earth had she been so crazy as to come here, she wondered as she took out a crusty roll and the butter, and the ham and salad to go with it. She poured herself a glass of Chardonnay. It wasn't brilliant but it was much better than she had hoped to find in the village shop.

Leaving Marcus had probably been a quixotic, badly thought out gesture which, she decided, she had tried to glamourise with some romantic nonsense which Marcus was right to mistrust. She would ring him before she went to Miss Wilson and accept the interview and, if she was offered a well paid job, she would leave St Elizabeth's as soon as she decently could. She had been a failure here anyway and Miss Wilson was probably only going to tell her that.

Having made these 'sensible' decisions she turned to her supper and her book. She chose to refresh herself with some of the medieval literature which had been the object of her study before she left Oxford. It seemed particularly delightful to reread 'Sir Gawain and the Grene Knight' which had been written six centuries before by an unknown poet probably in this very part of England. It would be pleasant with a suitable companion to explore the probable background of the poem she thought as she read of the deep forests, the high hills and the frozen streams in a land where wonders could still happen. Might still perhaps?

Rousing herself from these delights she realised that it was time to seek Miss Wilson's flat, high on the top floor of St Elizabeth's newest building. As she reached the landing, Jean Wilson came to the door to welcome her. She was wearing her usual shabby but expensive clothes, chosen it always seemed to make her look as dull and as inconspicuous as possible but unusually she was smiling pleasantly as she welcomed Cleo into her surprisingly spacious living room. The long picture windows were covered with rich velvet curtains. Only a standing lamp and one reading lamp were lit, leaving most of the room in shadow with a pool of light surrounding the coffee table and the two chairs arranged before the comforting electric fire.

It was not quite the room Cleo had expected being austerely tasteful rather than dull and untidy and gave ample evidence of Miss Wilson's interests. There were stacks of classical CDs and several over-filled bookshelves. Left to herself while her hostess hurried off to prepare the coffee, Cleo amused herself by looking idly at the books. A name, once well known to her attracted her attention - 'The Golden Rose' by Merlin Evans. Intrigued, she picked it up as Jean Wilson came back with the coffee. "Ah," she remarked, “I see you’ve picked up ‘The Golden Rose’. I suppose the writer must be known to you? He was long after my time,” she continued as she busied herself with the coffee cups, “but he must have been lecturing when you were up?”

“He was,” Cleo answered slowly “in fact, he helped me quite a lot.”

“You were fortunate,” Jean Wilson replied, offering Cleo a seat by the fire, “he’s a brilliant teacher, I believe. I read his book on the fourteenth century alliterative poetry and thought it excellent. I was rather surprised to see that he’d written a novel, particularly one that sold so well.” She poured the coffee into the elegant Royal Doulton cups and offered one to Cleo.

“Yes, I believe it did,” Cleo agreed. It was strange to hear him talked about.

“Have you read it?”

“No, I’m afraid not, “ How could she say that she had purposefully avoided it? “Is it good?”

“I have to admit it is,” Jean Wilson smiled reluctantly, it seemed. “I thought it might be a pot boiler but it isn’t. The medieval background is impeccable, as you might expect; it’s thoughtful and beautifully written. Quite a triumph, in fact. I think you’d enjoy it, particularly if you’ve met him. Would you like to borrow it?”

Much to her surprise, Cleo found herself accepting the offer, not simply to please Miss Wilson but because she now actually wanted to read it. Perhaps there would be something she could learn from it? She did not, however, wish to talk about its author any more, so she adroitly changed the subject by asking Miss Wilson how long she had been at St Elizabeth’s.

“Nearly six years”, was the sharp and quick reply, “and I’ll be glad to leave at the end of the Summer term.” She spoke with considerable decision.

Surprised by her unequivocal answer, Cleo was emboldened to ask for the reason.

"It's never been the job I expected it to be," Jean Wilson replied without any hesitation. She paused then, as if unwilling to reveal more and offered Cleo a plate of biscuits. "You'll like them," she said, "They're home made."

"Did you make them?" Cleo asked as she took one.

"Yes, cooking's one of my hobbies," was the somewhat unexpected reply. "I like good quality food and a few years' ago, I decided that the best way to make sure of having it, was to cook it myself.

"I'm sure you're right," Cleo agreed. "I cook myself for the same reason. I prepared supper for myself this evening in my own room. It was simple but it was good."

"I do that as often as I can," Jean Wilson declared. She looked keenly at Cleo. "Perhaps you would like to have supper with me here one evening," she suggested.

Amazed at receiving such an invitation, Cleo readily accepted and it was quickly arranged for the Tuesday after half term, after which Jean pouring out more coffee, returned abruptly to Cleo's original question. "St Elizabeth's is a good school in many ways but it has disappointed me because it doesn't have the standards I think are essential. Oh, I know people say I am difficult and impossible to please and I probably am as far as they're concerned but they simply don't understand the importance of excellence. We do have a broad intake here and that makes for difficulties but the real problem is that the majority of the staff are too complacent and too easily satisfied. I find that intolerable, since I want to see the best pupils achieve the highest they can. The girls, naturally are affected by the attitude of many of the staff, so one has to fight all the time." She spoke with considerable passion.

Listening to her, Cleo realised how wrong her first impression had been of this apparently grey, uninteresting woman. How easy it was to allow oneself to be misled by preconceived ideas. She felt a great rush of sympathy, although she was unsure exactly how to express it. While she was searching for the right words, Jean spoke again.

"I hope I haven't offended you by my frankness?" she asked "But I have rather formed the impression that you don't fit in here any more easily than I do, probably for similar reasons. I think perhaps that you are also somewhat of a perfectionist. The Sixth Form have already praised your teaching of them and I gather the Middle School is happy too. But it isn't my intention to speak about such subjects tonight. I rather hoped we might get to know one another better. Don't be afraid to say what you think. I'm not as intolerant as some people suggest. I do think it's important to have a serious purpose in life and to aim high. That doesn't make one popular, of course. But I think one has to be true to oneself, What do you think?"

"I think you're right about that," Cleo agreed slowly, "but my difficulty is that I don't seem to know myself very well and so it's not easy to know what my purpose should be. I thought I had some idea when I came here but it all seems a bit distant now."

"You're still young," Jean said kindly. "You've got time to make mistakes."

"I've already done that. I meant to make a fresh start when I came here but now I'm not so sure I did the right thing."

"You don't have to answer me, but was it perhaps because of an unhappy love affair that you came here? I'm sorry," she added quickly, "I had no right to ask that."

"I'm not sorry you asked," Cleo replied swiftly. It seemed quite a relief to speak to someone at last. "You're right, of course. It was. He didn't want to end it. I did. And now I'm not sure I was right. I may be making another mistake."

"One can often learn a great deal from one's mistakes. Perhaps you are wrong to think you have to make a choice. You don't need to narrow your possibilities too much. I'm inclined to think sometimes that I did that. I concentrated on work so much that I didn't give myself time to consider a husband and a family. Sometimes I have rather regretted it but now, at last I've got the job I want. At last, I'll be dealing with real high fliers in a school that aims at excellence and where my views are respected."

"I'm so glad that you are," Cleo smiled at her. "I can see the fascination of that kind of work but I'm not sure that it's what I want. I think perhaps I really want to help the 'Failures'. The ones who have been rejected and need love and understanding." As she spoke she realised that she had, at last, put into words something of her vague vision, She felt grateful to Jean Wilson for forcing her to do this.

"Yes, that may be right for you. You may not be really sure yet but it's important that you don't stop caring and searching. That's what ultimately matters." Jean looked directly at Cleo and smiled encouragingly at her. "I think you've made a brave start." For a few minutes they didn't speak but continued to drink their coffee companionably, then Jean spoke again, "Since you like helping people perhaps you would be willing to help me? Mrs Maitland suggested that you would be the right person."

Although she was doubtful as to the correctness of Mrs Maitland's opinion, Cleo readily intimated that she would be willing to try and listened patiently to Jean Wilson's account of her problems with the Sixth formers in her House, one of whom at least she suspected of coming in after midnight. It appeared that the only means of entry left was by the gate which led into the Staff House from where it was easy to gain access to the school. Mrs Maitland had apparently decided that this gate was to be locked as from that night, so that the suspected absentee might be caught, if she tried to re-enter. If Cleo was willing Miss

Wilson would give her the key since her room directly overlooked the gate and she could intercept the girl and bring her back to her Housemistress. The staff had been informed and could still enter by the main gates to the car park behind the Staff House.

"I can only hope," Jean Wilson concluded, "that I am mistaken in my suspicions. But, if a foolish girl is doing this, then she must be stopped for her own good and for the good of the others. And I have a suspicion from something I heard that she may be out tonight."

"And what will happen to her?" Cleo asked.

"Naturally, I shall report her to Miss Stephens in the morning."

"And that means?" Cleo pressed her.

"Expulsion probably. A great pity but it's not my decision. I can't worry about things like that. I've told the girls it is foolish but it seems they don't want to listen to me. I can only deal with the matters which are my concern." It was obvious that Jean Wilson did not consider it part of her duty to try to understand and help the girls in her House.

Although Cleo found herself disapproving of this aspect of her character she nevertheless accepted the distasteful task reluctantly in the hope that it might prove unnecessary. Moreover, she thought, it did not seem wise for a seventeen year old girl, however foolish to be locked out. She could spare her that, at least and the rest, she supposed, was rightly left to Miss Stephens.

It was quite late when she finally returned to her room and settled to the marking she had left unfinished. Sternly putting all other thoughts out of her mind, she considered the answers to the question she had set the Sixth Form, 'If Iago had not been such a consummate villain, we would have despised Othello. Discuss.' It occurred to her as she picked up her pen that it was not a question the seventeen year old girls would find easy to answer. It was obvious that they had felt this themselves and had mostly taken refuge in assembling all the well worn clichés and accepted views. There were few, if any individual opinions and little indication of enjoyment or interest. They had worked quite hard and most would probably achieve their 'A' Level but was this the proper education for them? Was this work much of an improvement on what she had been doing? The personal contact in lessons had been good but this was depressing. She forced herself, however, to continue.

It was nearly an hour later that with relief she picked up the last essay. To her surprise it was good! Here was someone with style, who having read all the necessary critics still managed to express an individual point of view with enthusiasm. She read the name - Victoria Evans - she remembered her as a thin, dark girl who spoke little but who occasionally showed lively appreciation. The last time she had spoken to her, however, she had felt that the girl's reserve hid a deep unhappiness. I must make a point of speaking to her again, she thought. Perhaps she needs encouragement just like me.

It was about half past twelve when she completed her task. All the night revellers and their cars had departed from the 'pubs' and the lorries would not start rolling for another two hours. She relaxed enjoying the peace and decided that Jean Wilson's fears had apparently been groundless.

It must have been about ten minutes later that she heard a car draw up and stop. This was followed by the noise of someone trying with increasing agitation to open the gate. She heard a girl exclaim, "Oh God, the gate's locked. It never has been before!" The man with her replied inaudibly and then he too tried the gate.

Cleo quietly opened her window and leaned out. "Wait there," she called softly. "I've got the key." Grabbing a torch, she crept swiftly down the stairs, through the front door and to the gate.

Arriving there, she shone her torch on the two figures - the boyfriend had at least stood his ground prepared to give support. "Stephanie St John!" she exclaimed as she saw the girl. She would never have expected it to be this quiet, rather undistinguished member of the Sixth Form.

As she unlocked the gate, she took a quick glance at the boyfriend. He was older than she had expected, probably in his late twenties. He was tall and dark, wearing jeans and a jacket and definitely good looking. He did not appear to be particularly disturbed by the situation. "I take it she'll be all right now," he said casually. "I'll be off. See you," he said to Stephanie, who appeared to be close to tears.

Cleo was infuriated by his attitude. "Don't you realise," she asked, "that Stephanie could be in serious trouble? Don't you think it's a bit irresponsible of you to bring her back at this hour?"

"Better now than in the morning, I should think," he replied with a shrug.

"I don't understand men like you," Cleo said angrily, "you're old enough to know better."

Before she could say any more Stephanie interrupted her. "Please don't blame Mike," she said. "It's isn't his fault. He's just brought me back. I was at a party and had a quarrel with my boyfriend. He dashed off and I didn't know how to get back. Mike gave me a lift."

Mike grinned amiably. "That's about it," he agreed, "I'll leave you to deal with it." He looked at Cleo. "Be human," he added. "I reckon, she's had a tough time tonight." With a quick wave he was gone.

Cleo turned her attention the woebegone Stephanie. "Why on earth have you taken such risks?" she asked irritably. "It's not as if you don't have quite a bit of freedom, anyway. You could be expelled."

Stephanie burst into tears, "My parents will be furious, if they hear about it. Please Miss Lafay don't tell Miss Wilson."

Cleo stood undecided. "I really ought to," she said.

"It isn't fair," Stephanie suddenly burst out. "We can't even go to a harmless party, while some of the staff can get away with anything. We can't help knowing when we see cars parked outside the Staff House half the night. I think.."

Cleo interrupted her forcefully, "I don't know what you're talking about Stephanie but, in any case you're in no position to criticise anyone, so I think you should be quiet."

"I'm sorry, Miss Lafay," Stephanie apologised unhappily. "I know you're right but I'm so miserable. Everything's gone wrong. Please help me."

Cleo made her a quick decision. She sympathised with Stephanie who was after all nearly eighteen. How much wiser had she been then? "All right," she said in what she hoped was crisp schoolmistress voice. "I'll overlook it this time. Just go quickly back to your room and don't ever be so silly again or you will be in serious trouble and I won't be able to help you."

After fervent thanks and promises of future good behaviour, Stephanie quickly disappeared into the shadows. As soon as she had disappeared, Cleo turned to open the gate. As she did so, she became aware of a car coming into the park behind the Staff House. By the light of the porch lamp she recognised Stella Harvey and Nicholas Barnes, and as the door at the rear of the house closed firmly behind both of them, it was obvious that he had no intention of leaving soon. So that was what Stephanie was referring to, Cleo thought as she went through the gate and locked it behind her. It was apparent that Cynthia's suspicions too were not unfounded. And I imagined that I was coming to a quiet place devoted to hard work and high endeavour, she reflected with some amusement.

Chapter Eight

The usual depressing Saturday evening quiet had settled over St. Elizabeth's as Cleo returned to her room after tea in the staff sitting room where a glowing fire and hot buttered toast had alleviated the February gloom. It was worse than usual since this weekend was the last before half term and very few students had obtained exeats. Most of them, reluctant prisoners together with their housemistresses were now settling down to an evening's television.

As she made her way towards her room, Cleo shivered in the chilly wind which had all day brought a threat of snow with it. The tall buildings of the school with their many pallidly lit bare windows had a threatening air more reminiscent of a Victorian workhouse or prison than that of a comfortable refuge for the offspring of the wealthy, reminding Cleo of her own often unhappy schooldays.

It was pleasanter to remember her recent friendly literary chat with Miss Wilson over tea. Unfortunately that brought less comforting thoughts of her deliberate evasion of the full truth with regard to Stephanie. Once again she told herself it had been the right thing to do. Miss Wilson had been reassured and the now repentant Stephanie was safe and free from further temptation since the gate was now securely locked every night as a precautionary measure.

The staff house had a deserted air as she entered it. Only the lights on the hall and stairs were switched on. There might be some lights at the back but from the front it seemed that everyone was out. Bridget had gone to a Languages conference. Pam had rushed out immediately after the end of morning school, determined to buy a new dress for a celebration with her boyfriend and his family. And Cynthia....

As Cleo locked her door, she clearly recalled Cynthia her wistful pallor heightened by the softly draped grey dress she was wearing. Since they seemed to be the only two survivors they had shared coffee after lunch. Cynthia was obviously in a very unhappy mood. It was not her usual melancholy resignation but something far more wounding and bitter. She gave no explanation but the cause became obvious when a vibrant Stella put her head round the door and enquired if they had seen Nicholas. "I was supposed to meet him here but I have to see Mrs Maitland. If he turns up, will you tell him I won't be long. I don't want him to think I've deserted him." She had an air of triumph and included both of them in her brilliant smile. As Cynthia did not respond, Cleo hastily replied that she would.

There was an unhappy silence after she had gone, as Cynthia stared straight in front of her. Suddenly she looked up at Cleo. "She makes it pretty obvious, doesn't she?" she asked bitterly. "She wants us all to know that she has succeeded at last." Then, as Cleo did not reply, she continued. "I suppose you think we're pretty stupid and immoral battling over a married man?"

Cleo decided that it was preferable to be honest. "I don't think he's much of a catch anyway," she remarked. "I doubt if he's the faithful sort. But I'm in no position to make moral judgements. I'd lived with a married man for over two years before I came here."

"I suppose he promised you marriage and then let you down?" Cynthia was ready to sympathise with a fellow sufferer but, feeling that it would be dishonest to allow that, Cleo replied frankly, "No, we had an understanding from the beginning. I didn't want to marry him and he, for good reasons, didn't want a divorce."

"Then, why did you come here? Frankly that puzzles us all and you've never thrown much light on the subject. Not that you have to, of course," Cynthia added hastily.

"That's probably because, as I told you earlier, I don't really know the answer myself. Life suddenly seemed deeply unsatisfactory and I thought I ought to make a change, though what change wasn't quite clear."

"Was it perhaps because of your convent upbringing?" Cynthia suggested. "I mean you must have been firmly taught that adultery was very wrong and it suddenly affected you."

"You may be right," Cleo responded smiling, "but I don't seem to have had any conscious thoughts about that, although perhaps I should have done."

"It certainly doesn't seem to be worrying Stella," Cynthia said bitterly. "She positively exults in it."

"Did it worry you?" Cleo felt impelled to ask.

Cynthia flushed deeply. "You're right, of course. I'm just being a hypocrite. Who knows what I would have done, if Nicholas had been pressing. But he wasn't and now he's clearly found someone more amenable." She put down her coffee cup firmly and stood up, "It's over and it's about time I started making sensible plans for my own future." She moved towards the door. "It's also about time I began my journey home. The sky's getting very heavy. Have you any plans?"

"Nothing much except I want to read a book Miss Wilson has lent me. I shall be glad of a break, anyway."

"Have a restful time, then. I'll see you tomorrow evening, I expect." She went quickly.

Thinking over that conversation as she entered her room, Cleo was surprised to realise how lightly she had accepted the idea of an adulterous existence and yet how seriously she had been troubled at not telling Miss Wilson the complete truth that afternoon. Honesty was apparently more important to her than sexual purity. That was something she had learned in early life for her mother's betrayal had taught her that. Without honesty there could be no trust and without trust there could be no lasting relationship in life. Unfortunately her mother's action had left her reluctant to trust anyone and so perhaps she had not always been as honest as she should have been. She was determined that this should no longer be the case.

She switched on her fire and tried to settle down in front of it but thoughts of her half lie to Miss Wilson now kept troubling her. Was she not condemned herself by admitting the great importance of honesty? She had always been taught that lying was always wrong but she had also read that St Augustine had conceded that the intention made a difference. If the intention was good, as hers had surely been when talking to Miss Wilson then the sin was negligible. Then why was she worried?

She tried not to face this question for the answer was bound up with so much that she had done. Had her relationship with Marcus really been as honest as she had pretended? Had it not really been a convenience to avoid facing up to wrongs she had committed earlier, to lies she had told? Suddenly being faced with the stark reality of a homeless man's existence had somehow forced her to see her own life for the shallow thing it was.

But was it any better now? She had come to seek another world and instead found herself surrounded by frustrated, disappointed women who seemed to think she was foolish for having left the delights of her life with Marcus. Of course others like Miss Stephens, and Mrs Maitland were different but she could never be like them. Her life had been too tumultuous.

She suddenly admitted as she looked round her dreary, little room that she was very lonely. She desperately wanted someone to talk to, someone who lived in, what she had now come to consider as the real world. She stood up and walked over to her dressing table, gazing resentfully at that beautiful face which so often prevented people from seeing the real person, who was so lonely and insecure.

Impulsively, she decided that she would go out. A brisk walk down the mile long village street would at least invigorate her and she might even find the courage to go into the local pub at the end of the High Street, disregarding the more fashionable ones in the centre. Quickly she pulled on a heavy jade green jacket over her brightly coloured knitted tunic and jade trousers and marched defiantly down the stairs and into the street.

It was a long, cold struggle down the winding, village street for the wind blew in her face all the way, bringing the occasional stinging flakes of snow with it but, at last, she stood outside 'The Royal Oak' with its brightly lit windows and its promise of comfort and warmth. As she hesitated on the threshold belatedly afraid that she might not be welcome there, a man, hurrying to enter from the opposite direction, bumped into her. She turned to apologise realising that she was blocking the doorway but, before she could speak he exclaimed, "Hi! Fancy seeing you here! You're a bit off course aren't you?"

She stared at him, surprised and puzzled. The black curly hair, the friendly grin and the aggressive stance seemed familiar. "You don't remember me, do you?" he continued. "I'm the bloke you accused of treating Stephanie badly. Remember now?" He grinned wickedly at her. She remembered with some embarrassment and apologised once again.

"Forget it," he said easily, drawing her to one side as someone else approached the door. "What are you doing here? Teachers from the college don't come here, especially by themselves."

"Don't tell me it's forbidden," Cleo asked crossly.

"No, it isn't forbidden but, as one of the favourite characters of my youth used to say, 'It's not wrong but we just don't do it'"

"But I want to do it," she protested. "I'm bored, I want a drink and I want to see some real people."

"Instead of those tabby cats up at the college, you mean? Can't say I blame you. I didn't think you fitted in there. `Too good looking, for one thing." He regarded her for a moment. "Tell you what," he said finally, "why don't you risk it and come in with me? You owe me a drink anyway for insulting me. Bloody cheek it was."

She laughed. His directness appealed to her. She had never been cautious, so why start now?"Come in under your protection, you mean?"

"Why not?" he retorted, "You might need it. There are some pretty horny blokes in there and you're tempting."

"But how can I be sure I'll be safe with you?"

"You'll have to risk that, won't you?" he replied. "I can only say that I've never forced a woman yet - never needed to."

"I'll accept the challenge," she said quickly. "I think I'm equal to it."

"I bet you are," he answered as he pushed the door open for her. The lounge was warm and inviting and there were not many people there at this early hour. He led her to a table close to the fire. She undid her jacket, handed him a note from her pocket and warmed herself while he made his way to the bar, where he was cheerfully greeted by the barman and a couple of other men standing there.

He was the best looking man there, she decided as she watched him make his way back to her. Wearing a leather jacket and jeans, he looked taller than average height. He was broad but there was not an ounce of waste flesh on him and he seemed in good trim. As he handed her drink to her, she observed him more closely. His dark curly hair was cut short, the lines of his face were good and clear, his eyes were dark brown and he had a pleasant smile.

Before he sat down, he took off his jacket and put it with hers on the back of another chair. He was wearing an open necked blue check shirt. His neck and face were brown as if he had been much in the open air. His hands brown too looked strong and capable and slightly calloused. He was not a man who worked in an office, she thought.

He sat down and looked directly back at her, placing his hands firmly on the table. "Well, what have you decided, " he challenged. "Will I do?"

"Not bad," she replied, smiling at him.

He studied her for a moment. "Pretty good," he gave his opinion. "Quite classy, in fact." They both laughed, both confident in their attraction and sure of themselves in that respect. " Mike Donovan," he introduced himself. "Twenty five, completely unattached, long distance truck driver, at present."

"Cleo Lafay," she replied. "Twenty four, temporary school teacher, at present."

"Attached?"

"Not very firmly," she replied, "and not wanting to be. In fact, I should warn you I don't want anything except company and conversation."

"Suits me," he said casually, then sipped his beer. Someone greeted him and he waved back, then turned his attention to her again. "How's Stephanie? You didn't rat on her, did you?"

"No, I should have done but I fixed it instead. She was miserable enough, anyway."

"Good I hoped she'd be safe with you." He took another drink. "She's not a bad kid, just stupid. She ought to know that Pete is useless but women are like that, always wanting to hang on to some bloke, no matter what he's like."

"Some women," she corrected him coldly, her brilliant green eyes flashing.

He grinned back at her. "OK. Some women, if you say so but I've never met one who was different."

"That was before you met me."

"How come you're here, anyway?"

"I suddenly needed a job with a home, so it suited me."

"Where do you come from? You don't belong in these parts."

"So every one is determined to make me realise," she said bitterly. "But, if you must know London and before that Oxford."

"The University, I suppose," he said with some irony. "Degrees and all that shit? Only the best."

"Of course." She turned her attention to her drink.

"I thought so. You have the manner. I graduated from the local comprehensive with two 'O' Levels and I've tried several jobs including the Army. Now I'm driving trucks from Scotland to Dover and sometimes to Italy and Spain."

"Do you enjoy it?"

"It suits me. I like driving and I prefer to be my own boss, as far as possible. It's also quite risky and I like that; it keeps the adrenaline running. I can't stand monotony." He stared at her. "How about you? Do you like teaching?"

"I've only done it for three weeks but I quite enjoy it so far."

"How's that? What did you do before then?"

"You'll never guess."

He studied her carefully. "I haven't a clue but with a face and figure like yours you could have been a model or an actress. If you weren't, you were wasting your opportunities."

"Brilliant!"

"You don't mean I guessed right, I was just fooling."

"I was a model for two years then got bored with it and the life that went with it, so I just left and came to St. Elizabeth's because I needed a job and a roof over my head."

"That was bloody drastic, wasn't it?" He looked keenly at her. "Don't tell me," He exclaimed finally. "There has to be a bloke behind this, am I right?"

Annoyed at his perception which she felt confirmed his opinion of women, she was tempted to tell him that it was no business of his and to keep her own counsel which was her usual habit. But his frank, friendly manner made it churlish not to be honest in return. Besides, had she not adopted honesty as her new policy? "You partly right, of course," she admitted. "I'd been living with someone for two years and I just realised that I couldn't stick it any longer."

"You mean you no longer fancied him?"

She frowned. "It wasn't just that. I simply didn't like the kind of life I was living. It wasn't real. He's married. His wife's his business partner and I supply what she lacks."

"So what?" Mike asked casually. "People don't worry about that sort of thing these days, though I don't care much for it myself. I think if you actually marry someone you ought to stick to them."

"I suppose deep down I do," she admitted, somewhat to her own surprise. "I was brought up a Catholic and it sticks, I suppose, even if I don't practise."

"Snap", he replied cheerfully. "That's about my position too," he explained. "I've committed most sins but I draw the line at murder, lying and adultery. I'm not particularly keen on abortion, either." He grinned cheerfully at her and finished off his drink.

"It didn't seem like adultery, at first," she found herself confessing, because he and his wife had stopped sleeping together long before he met me. We were both lonely." She was amazed at herself. It was a relief, however, to talk to a friendly stranger. "But..."

"There's more to marriage than sleeping together," he interrupted her. "My Mum taught me that, and I believe her."

"She's right. So where does that leave me?"

"You tell me."

“I don’t know so I came here to sort things out and to see if I could perhaps be a teacher. I used to think I’d like to be one, once.”

“What does your family think? Can’t they help you? Mine do all the time, though I can’t think why.”

“You’re lucky. I haven’t really got a family. My sister’s married and hasn’t much space for me. When my mother went off years ago, my Father sent me to a boarding school. He couldn’t get rid of me fast enough. So I’ve always had to sort things out for myself.”

“Tough,” he sympathised. “That’s not so good. But don’t let it get you down. Have another drink. It’s my call.” As he stood up, he was accosted by a friend. “Hi, Mike,” he exclaimed, “I didn’t expect to see you here. I thought you were meeting Kay in Markhampton tonight.”

Mike shrugged easily. “I was,” he said, “but not now. Bugger off, Jack, I know what you’re after. You’re out of luck, mate.”

“I don’t think you should bother about another drink, Mike,” Cleo said firmly, “If you’re supposed to be meeting someone else.” She stood up. “I’ve had fun talking to you but it’s time to go.” She picked up her jacket.

“Not so fast,” Mike protested, restraining her. He looked at his watch. “Kay’ll have given me up by now anyway. I was already late when I met you. I needed a pint to strengthen me.”

“But you can’t just let someone down like that,” Cleo protested.

“I can,” Mike replied, “I’ve done it often. I was only going to meet her because she kept ringing up home and pestering my Mum, who thinks she’s a nice girl. She’s so bloody eager, she deserves all she gets. If a girl demands it, I give it to her but I don’t consider myself under any obligation.” He looked at her challengingly. “I don’t pretend to be the sort of gentleman you’re used to.”

"That's obvious," Cleo replied frostily. "Anything but."

"But I'm honest," he said, "and that's more than you can say about many so called gentlemen."

"That's probably true," she admitted.

"So," he continued, "how about you forget Kay, who's probably had a lucky miss. I'm making you an honest, straightforward offer of supper in Markhampton. I bet you haven't eaten."

"You're right." Cleo realised that she was very hungry and had no means of getting into Markhampton herself.

"What would you prefer an Indian or a Chinese?"

"An Indian. But how do I know that I can trust you?"

"Because I promise that you can and I always keep a promise. Supper and chat and then I'll bring you back. After that the night's my own, unless you want to carry on."

"I won't," she said firmly.

"Fine. Then I'll bring you back by eleven. How's that?"

"I agree but only if you let me pay for myself." She wanted no favours.

"OK, we'll split the bill, if that's what you want."

Forty minutes later Cleo agreed with Mike that she was enjoying herself. The Indian restaurant was newly opened and competing to be the best in Markhampton. As it was still fairly early in the evening, there were not many customers, so they received quick and friendly attention. Once the meal was decided with much knowledgeable advice from Mike and the drinks ordered, they sat back and relaxed.

Cleo looked around the long, almost empty dining room. Decorated in rich dark colours with many Indian pictures and rugs, it was dimly and discreetly lit. Soft caressing music was being played and one couple had obviously come as much for amorous dalliance, as for the food, Cleo decided. She became aware that Mike was studying her with a mischievous glint in his brown eyes.

"Tell me," she demanded, "did you choose this place for the food or for the sexy atmosphere?"

"For both, but especially for the food."

"Good, because it's the food I intend to enjoy."

"You will," he promised. "you don't need to be so suspicious."

"It's natural. The nuns always told us not to trust any man. I still believe them." She smiled at him.

"What do they know about it?" he asked. "If they do, they shouldn't, anyway."

"I used to wonder about that sometimes," she admitted.

"How long was it before you tried it out for yourself?"

"Longer than you might think. I was nineteen and at Oxford."

"What happened then?"

"I fell in love, seriously I mean." For a moment she allowed herself to remember the wonder and joy of those brief months.

"Then what? Were the nuns right? Did he let you down?"

"It ended," she said flatly. Even if it had been possible, she had no desire to talk to Mike about this. "How about you?" she asked. "Did you get any useful advice?"

"Not really. By the time my Dad got round to it, I'd already found out. I was an early starter."

"And what had you found out, O wise one?" she asked mockingly.

"That most girls are liars. They pretend they like you but all they want is to get their claws into you and tie you down. So all I do nowadays is love 'em and leave 'em."

"Hence Kay left lamenting?"

"That's right."

She looked at him, amused and somewhat intrigued. "I'm not sure," she remarked, "are you warning me or what?"

"Not really." he smiled cheerfully. "I'm just being honest. It's up to you what you believe. I think you're different. You seem pretty honest, in fact."

"I've tried to be," she replied seriously. I enjoy talking to you but I don't want to get my claws into you or anyone, especially as I still haven't completely broken off my present relationship."

"I believe you," he said, then added cynically, "I'm not the sort of bloke you'd want to be tied to anyway. Stockbrokers and lawyers and blokes like that are more your type. I can't afford you, so we're both safe."

"What a sordid point of view!" she exclaimed. "Don't you believe in love at all?"

"Do you?" He stared straight into her eyes for a moment and then shrugged. "Oh yeah, I believe in it but I also believe that most English people are bloody snobs and that's what matters in the end."

"I don't think it's as simple as that," she retorted "but my family's partly French and partly Irish, so it doesn't apply to me anyway."

"And I'm half Scottish and half Irish, so perhaps that's why we get on. We're both outsiders, in a way. We're not satisfied."

"There's something in what you say," Cleo agreed, "But it doesn't really have much to do with race or class." She sampled the food which had just been placed in front of her. "You're right about one thing, at least! This food is delicious!"

It was a happy meal. Cleo felt more at ease than she had done for weeks and Mike, encouraged by the wine, the food and her appreciation talked freely and amusingly of his life and its adventures. He had tried many jobs, all of them to some degree hazardous and his favourite hobby was riding a motor bike, somewhat recklessly apparently. "Most people," he declared, "like nothing better than to be stuck in a comfortable rut but I hate it. Me, I like risking my neck. I like to feel the adrenalin flowing. The best time was when I chucked up everything and went on a 'piss-up' round Europe for months. It was great. The trouble is it can't last for ever."

"So are you settling down now," she asked, partly sympathetic and partly exasperated. Was she so very different from him, she wondered?

"I suppose so," he said reluctantly. "A couple of months ago I was offered a good steady job with a big, international haulage company. Good, steady pay, prospects of promotion and pension at the end if I stick it."

"You don't sound exactly pleased," she commented. "Isn't it what you wanted?"

"It's what I've been saying I wanted for the last two years."

"And now you're not sure you do?"

"It's crazy, isn't it? When I was working my balls off, driving an old truck for this cowboy company all over Europe, risking my neck almost every day, I was always telling myself that, as soon as I had enough experience I'd get a secure job with good guaranteed pay. And now I've got it, look at me." He stopped and grinned at her.

Cleo smiled back, sympathising with him. "So what's wrong? Isn't it as good as you thought?"

"The job's all right," he replied gloomily. "I'm just not sure I can hack it."

"Why not?" She sensed the deep depression which had suddenly struck him as it sometimes struck her A vague dissatisfaction was something she could understand.

"It's too fucking organised, just like the Army was and I couldn't stick that. Everything has to be done in a certain way and they want to know where you are practically every bloody minute. I hate it. Sometimes I just want to say 'Fuck you' and walk off but I don't suppose you know what I mean."

"In some ways I do, I'm quite good at walking off myself."

"I expect that's why you're here."

"Have you told your family?" she asked quickly, not wanting to discuss herself any more.

"No. They're so pleased I've got a secure job at last. They think I'll soon be settling down, getting married and all that."

"Perhaps you should."

"Not me," he replied quickly. It'd be a disaster, if I did. I Couldn't stick to anyone for long. I'd just walk off one day and I wouldn't care a damn." He looked defiantly at her. "It's the truth," he said.

"I did something like that myself," Cleo replied, "so I do believe you. But it's not a right way to behave, is it?" She suddenly felt depressed.

"I think the right way is to avoid putting yourself in that situation, if you know you're not the faithful sort."

"I suppose you're right but it's lonely, isn't it?"

"Sometimes but you can always have a short term relationship, as long as you don't pretend it's anything else. So why worry?" He helped himself to rice and chutney, then looked up. "How about you?"

"Oh, I'm a hopeless person," she admitted. "I haven't stuck to any job or any person, either. I'd like to change but sometimes I doubt if I will."

"Don't get too depressed about it," Mike said. "Have another drink. That's what I do." He refilled their glasses. "A short life and a merry one, that's my motto. You can always top yourself, if the pain of life gets too much."

"Don't say that," Cleo shuddered. My Mother did that. I can't bear to think about it. It's not a joke."

"Sorry. Don't take me too seriously. There are other things you can do, after all."

"Such as?"

"I've often thought of joining the Foreign Legion. An Army mate of mine did. It'd be tough but it'd keep the adrenalin running."

"I can hardly do that."

"Well, you could become a missionary nun and go to one of those flea bitten places in South America or somewhere, where there's a revolutionary round every corner. It'd suit you. I can just see you as Sister Cleo, all beautiful and holy, caring for the poor and the sick. You wouldn't be lonely then."

"Thanks," she replied dryly. "If I get desperate, I might consider it."

"There you are then! All problems solved. What could be better? Of course, you're supposed to be celibate. That might be tricky."

"The way I feel at the moment, it might be a relief."

"Not for me he said. "I need women like I need drink."

"Don't be disgusting," Cleo retorted, "and don't ever think I'll fit into that plan."

"I won't," he assured her. "You're different. You're the first girl I've ever been able to talk to and I'm enjoying it."

"Good, then let's change the subject, shall we? I'd like to hear more about your family. Families interest me."

Time passed quickly as Mike had definitely inherited the Irish talent for telling a good story, with more regard to entertainment than literal truth, she suspected. It was after half past ten before she noticed the time. "I'm afraid, we'll have to leave, if you're going to get me back by eleven as you promised." To her relief, he made no demur and in five minutes they were driving back to Barton Leas.

It was a little after eleven when they drew up in the staff car park. He did not attempt to kiss her but said "I've got your phone number, I'll be in touch but not until the week after next, as I'm soon off to Spain. I'll ring you when I get back."

"Good," she replied easily. "I hope you will." He leaned out of the window as he drove off. "See you," he called out, as she waved to him.

As she turned to walk towards the door, she noticed that a car was parked near the entrance. Stella and Nicholas got out of it and walked into the house together. If Stella was aware of Cleo, she made no sign. They seemed to be absorbed in one another.

"Is that what Stephanie meant?" Cleo asked herself. "Is he now going to spend the night here or most of it?" It seemed a reckless thing to do when they could so easily be observed from the Sixth Form Wing. It was no concern of hers, she decided. It was pleasanter to remember her unexpectedly diverting evening. It had been a relief to talk freely to a kindred spirit, even if she never saw him again. At least she had stepped outside her dreary limits and found it much easier than she had imagined.

Chapter Nine

The cold winds during Saturday night brought a heavy, although not unexpected fall of snow but by the Sunday morning the wind had dropped leaving a crisp, white stillness everywhere. The school and the village assumed a new, sparkling beauty and the girls were out enjoying it until the orange sun disappeared behind the brooding horizon of heavily massed purple clouds.

Cynthia arrived back before dark, determined to avoid an evening journey. Many of the resident staff were still enjoying tea around the blazing fire in the staff sitting room. The maid had just brought in a plate of hot, buttered toast and a fresh pot of tea. Cold and tired from her journey, Cynthia quickly helped herself and joined Cleo and Bridget in a corner near the fire. Bridget and Cynthia compared the difficulties of their journeys, while Cleo commiserated with them both.

"You may have had a boring weekend here, Cleo," Cynthia remarked "but at least you've been spared icy roads and reckless drivers."

"I don't think Cleo's had a boring time," Stella's voice intervened. "On the contrary." Cleo looked up quickly and met her somewhat sardonic look. Wearing a deep red velour leisure suit with lipstick to match, Stella had a triumphant, self satisfied air. "I saw your boyfriend bringing you back last night," she explained.

"Not my boyfriend," Cleo said coldly, "just a friend who took me for a meal in Markhampton." Her tone expressed clearly the irritation she felt at Stella's interference but Stella was unperturbed.

"Really," she replied in a disbelieving and mocking tone.

Cleo decided it was time to retaliate. "I also saw you, arriving back with Nicholas. I imagined that you were too absorbed to notice me."

"Where did you go for your meal, Cleo?" Cynthia hastily broke in. "Was it good?" Cleo told her in some detail, glad to change the subject.

"That sounds good," Bridget remarked tactfully. "Why don't we try it sometime, Cynthia?"

"We will as soon as the snow's gone. Perhaps you can come and show us the way, Cleo?"

"I'll leave you to your discussion, then," Stella said, obviously now bored. Putting down her empty cup and plate, she drifted away.

"Stella seems to be very pleased with herself," Bridget observed. "She also seems to have her knife into you, Cleo. You should be careful. She can be quite unpleasant."

"I don't see why she should bother," Cleo replied casually.

"She's jealous of your good looks and your boyfriends," Cynthia explained, "particularly now she hopes she's caught Nicholas. She thinks you might be a rival."

Cleo laughed. "What nonsense!" she explained. She had begun to hate this kind of conversation which seemed far too common in the over heated atmosphere of the school.

"Hi!" Pam's cheerful voice interrupted them. She was once again wearing the inevitable track suit with the normal youthful bunches of hair. Her rosy face was devoid of make up but she looked refreshingly wholesome and pleasant. Cleo was very glad to see her. Pam stopped, helped herself to a couple and cream cakes and a cup of tea, then walked over to them.

"I bumped into Stella in the corridor just now. She's looking very pleased with herself. She positively purred over me." She sat down, took a bite of a cream cake and then continued. "Matters must have progressed with Nicholas this weekend. Did you notice anything, Cleo?"

"She did come back with him late last night." Cleo admitted reluctantly.

"And?" Pam queried, then, as Cleo did not reply, she put her question more clearly. "Did he stay?"

"I really can't say."

"There's no reason why you should," Bridget intervened firmly.

"Miss Stephens would be furious if she found out," Pam said with some relish. She bent forward to warm her hands at the fire and, as she did so, a ring on her finger flashed in the light of the flames.

"That's a lovely ring!" Cynthia exclaimed. "It looks like an engagement ring."

"It is," Pam answered happily.

"So that's what the party was all about," Bridget observed. "You kept that a secret. Congratulations!"

"Have you finally fixed the date then?" Cynthia asked.

"Yes. It's to be in the summer after the end of term." She held out her hand for them to admire while they all gave her their congratulations.

"You must meet Tony," Pam remarked to Cleo. "On second thought," she added smiling happily, "I'm not sure I really want you to. You're too much of a 'femme fatale'. He might fall for you. Oh gosh," she continued quickly seeing Cleo's dismayed look. "I'm sounding just like Stella. I'm sorry."

Cleo smiled back but once more she felt excluded.

"I think it's about time we briefed Cleo a little more about the Sixth Form Parents Evening," Bridget intervened tactfully, especially as it's her first."

"I wouldn't mind hearing something about it," Pam remarked. "I didn't think Mrs Maitland was exactly informative about it at the Staff Meeting, especially as the arrangements have been changed."

"It's in the hall, isn't it?" Cleo asked.

"Yes," Bridget replied. "We each have a table with our name on it and the parents queue up to see us."

"You only need to look efficient and competent," Cynthia advised.

"And how do I do that?"

"Attach your mark sheets to a clipboard and have one or two businesslike notebooks to consult, if necessary," Bridget suggested. "We sit in Departments, so Miss Wilson will be nearby, if you need help."

"What worries me," Pam remarked, picking up her second cream cake, "is the food."

"When doesn't it?" Cynthia asked, as they all laughed.

"No, but seriously, I shall have spent the whole day in the Gym or on the playing fields and I shall be ravenous. What's supposed to happen?"

"The idea is that you help yourself to food as soon as you come in," Bridget explained, "before many parents are there and eat quickly before they catch up with you."

"That's not very likely," Pam rejoined. "I can imagine myself chewing a chicken bone and spitting all over some unfortunate parent as I try to talk."

"It's much more likely," Cynthia complained, "that we shall end up eating practically nothing. Some enterprising parents are bound to seek us out as soon as they arrive. Comments will get more and more acid, as we see all that delicious food disappearing. Whatever is the idea, Bridget?"

"Miss Stephens thinks it will be friendlier and less formal," Bridget replied piously." We shall have to see. It may be better than you think."

"Well you don't need to worry, Cleo, we're all novices at this. With all the practice you've had as a model, you'll probably outshine us all," Cynthia said consolingly.

"Thanks," Cleo replied, standing up. "I just hope to get by. Now I must get some marking done before tomorrow. See you later." She went out quickly, glad to escape to her own room. However pleasant they were, she always felt that there was an underlying criticism which prevented her from relaxing in their company.

Four days later on the evening of the Parents' Meeting, Cleo dressed herself carefully. A long black skirt and matching loose jacket together with a crisp, white blouse, relieved only by gold filigree earrings and a matching gold brooch at her throat, seemed to her the most suitable outfit. She would at least look competent even if she wasn't.

As she gathered together her papers, she realised that she was both apprehensive and bored at the thought of the evening ahead. This was not what she wanted to be doing. She had not run away from London to find herself in another narrow, privileged life, especially not one that brought her among so many young women whose sole aim often seemed to be to be to find some sexual partner.

But what right had she to criticise them when in three days' time she would be with Marcus again in their flat? She remembered how outraged and distressed Jane had been when she told her. For once it seemed to her that Jane was right, reluctant though she was to admit it. This was simply weakness, the weakness that had sent her to him in the first place. She should not be going back. What had happened to that brief vision that had driven her to seek a richer and more fulfilling life? The truth was that she was a coward, she decided, as she brushed the black shining waves of her hair and outlined her mouth delicately with lipstick.

She reminded herself as she walked towards the hall that she had decided to be honest and had recently been more successful, particularly during that entertaining evening with Mike. Then, at least, she had moved outside her normal bounds. Mike might be her passport to a different life. This was no time for further thought in that direction tonight. For the next two hours she must conform and fit herself into the expected routine.

The large hall, the scene of many splendid productions and concerts, with its lofty ceiling and cavernous balcony, looked smaller and friendlier that usual as the stage and tall windows were masked with rich, red velvet curtains and the brighter, harsher lights were switched off, leaving everything bathed in a warm golden glow from the side lights and table lamps. At one end there were several trestles covered with snowy, white cloths on which was the evening buffet with wine and coffee served discreetly by the maids.

Feeling overwhelmed, Cleo quickly helped herself to a finger roll and a glass of wine and looked for her table. Once she had assembled her papers there was no time for her to collect any more food as parents were already waiting for her. It seemed that Cynthia's worse prognostications were correct for a steady stream of parents, some unashamedly anxious, others self consciously casual came to consult her. It seemed amazing to Cleo that they should place so much reliance on her amateur opinions. But fortunately perhaps they could not know how inexperienced she was.

At nine o'clock she was feeling weary and ready for at least a coffee, which might now be possible as the crowd was definitely thinning. As she sorted her papers she was startled to hear herself addressed in a friendly tone. "Cleo! I never imagined that I would meet you here!" It was unbelievable! But surely that attractive, musical voice could not belong to any one else? Her heart seemed to race and she found herself struggling to speak. It must be a mistake.

Looking up, she found herself being scrutinised by a pair of deep set dark eyes under straight black brows. A firm but well shaped mouth was curved in a familiar, slightly ironical smile. It was impossible not to recognise that lean, brown face with its long straight nose and clear jawline. His black hair was brushed firmly back and he was immaculate in tailored suit and crisp, white shirt. He was obviously waiting for her to speak.

Somehow she forced herself to do so, in spite of her powerful feelings. "Merlin!" she managed to exclaim lightly. "I wouldn't have expected to meet you here either! Surely you haven't acquired a seventeen year old daughter?"

"Certainly not! But, in case you're suspicious, I hasten to assure you that I am here on legitimate business, as the newly appointed guardian of my niece."

"Then you must have known I would be here," she flashed at him. "Every parent had a list of their daughter's teachers."

"I certainly did not," he protested, "since I only came into this indirectly through my mother who had lost her list. She simply gave me a list of my niece's subjects and trusted to my initiative. The first time I heard your name was from Miss Wilson five minutes ago and even then I didn't believe it could actually be you. But why this mistrust?"

She found it difficult to explain. "It is just that I was so utterly surprised while you seemed to be calm and in control, as always."

"Not always," he replied with an ironical smile. "Certainly not the last time we met."

That was dangerous ground and Cleo hastily moved away from it. "You said you'd come about your niece. Who is she?"

"Victoria Evans."

I should have known, Cleo thought, remembering the thin, dark girl and her challenging essays. Aloud she declared, "She's very good. Even you need not worry about it. She's keenly interested and definitely able. I'll tell you what I have learned about her." She opened her folder.

"Thank you," he responded quickly. "But may I get us some coffee before you start. You must be tired and I know I am."

"I would like that very much," she replied quickly, grateful for his consideration. She watched him as he walked briskly away and tried to gain control of her disordered thoughts and emotions. Before she had had much success, he came quickly back with two cups of black coffee. He had remembered her preference. For a few moments they were silent while they enjoyed the stimulating drinks. Then Cleo determined to come back to the purpose of the interview. "Why are you here, instead of Victoria's parents?" she asked him. "This is an important evening."

"I know." He put down his cup. "The truth is that we have an awkward family situation. Soon after Christmas, my brother announced that he had to go to the Far East on business for several months and shortly afterwards his wife, who has never been particularly faithful, inexplicably decided to abscond with her latest love. Since then, apart from one or two notes to Victoria, nothing has been heard from her. Edward has typically decided that he can't or won't come home and has asked mother to take in Victoria." He paused.

"How dreadful for Victoria!" Cleo exclaimed. "I can understand only too well how she must feel! I thought she seemed unhappy when I spoke to her only a few days ago."

"She is, I imagine. Mother took her in and has been very kind to her but she's unfit to travel much. Hence my appearance on the scene." He sounded weary, Cleo thought but he made no further comment.

"And what are you supposed to do?"

"All the boring things a father should do, I imagine without the satisfaction he may be expected to have." He sounded indifferent but as Cleo remembered that was his usual way of avoiding any praise for being kind. He had always tended to insist that altruism was extremely rare, if not impossible.

"So what is your main object tonight?"

"To try to discover whether Edward's idea that she should read English at Oxford is feasible."

"I can't imagine anyone better qualified than you to do that. She is fortunate in having a well known Oxford scholar as her uncle. But I'm sure Miss Wilson thinks it's a good idea, doesn't she?"

"She does but she recommended me to speak to you. She thinks, as I do, that you are very gifted but, more important than that, Victoria has responded to you she says and trusts you. Miss Wilson thinks that Victoria needs extra tuition because her lack of self confidence recently made worse and that you are the right person to give that extra tuition. What do you say?"

She could not avoid looking directly at him, as he asked her that. She managed this, even though she was aware that her hands were tightly clenched under the table. She forced herself to speak calmly and to appear as unemotional as he apparently was. "You helped me greatly when I was unsure, I'll be pleased to help Victoria."

For a moment they were both silent as they finished their coffee and then, as he put down his cup, he added, "You will undoubtedly understand Victoria's feelings, as her experience is similar to your own, though not as terrible, I think. It is very generous of you to do it, in view of what has happened between us."

"I don't really think so," she replied. It was time to be honest, she thought. "I was cruel and unjust in many of my accusations two years ago. I'm sorry." It was a relief to have said it at last.

"But then I was inconsiderate and selfish," he said quietly, "and I too want to express my regret."

"I think it's time we left," Cleo replied shakily, "practically everyone has gone and the maids are waiting to clear away." She stood up, picked up her papers and led the way to the door.

"I'm afraid I've kept you later than I should have done," he apologised. His tone was formal again. The brief moment of friendliness was gone. It was sad but probably best, she thought. At least they had put matters right that had long been waiting to be put right and that was good. Now they would both be entirely free of the past.

As they reached the foyer at the bottom of the staircase, he suddenly put his hand on her arm. "Will you have supper with me?" he asked.

Cleo was almost too astonished to answer. "It really isn't necessary," she stammered at last.

"But I think it is," he replied, smiling, "for three good reasons. Firstly, I can tell you more about Victoria; secondly we can celebrate our peace making and thirdly and perhaps most important we can satisfy our hunger. I'm ravenous and I have a suspicion that you may be too."

She could not deny that. "You're right," she admitted. My last meal is a distant and somewhat unpleasant memory."

"In that case," he said, in the decisive way she remembered so well, "Don't let us hesitate any longer. There's a good Italian restaurant in Markhampton and I know you like Italian food. Don't worry, Cleo," he continued as she still hesitated, "I'm not seeking anything but good company and good food. I'll bring you back before midnight."

"In that case, I'll come."

"Good. Then you'd better get a coat. It's extremely cold. My car's outside. Can I pick you up somewhere."

"No just wait here and I'll be back in about five minutes." As she dashed off, refusing to allow herself to consider this unexpected development, she was aware of Stella regarding her curiously. "Oh God," she thought, "I've made myself conspicuous again."

Less than half an hour later they were seated in a warm and brightly lit Italian restaurant. They had just finished ordering the food and Merlin was studying the wine list. He looks older, she thought and different somehow but then two and half years had passed since their last disastrous encounter. Sensing her gaze, he looked up and smiled at her. "Do you want to choose?"

"No, I'll happily leave that to your superior judgement, weak minded though that may be," and then, as the waiter deposited the first course before her, she exclaimed, "Oh, I love fresh gnocchi with creamy cheese and real tomato sauce!"

"I see you're still enthusiastic about your food," Merlin remarked, smiling at her again.

"Don't try to be superior," she retorted, "you're just as bad as I am."

"I think we both needed it," he replied between mouthfuls, I've had a long and busy day with little time for food and I imagine yours has been the same."

"I'm very grateful to you," she said, "you're quite right. But now you must tell me more about Victoria, as you promised. Is she very unhappy, do you think?"

"I have no personal knowledge but my mother certainly thinks she is."

"I expect she's lost confidence and personal esteem," Cleo suggested, remembering her own feelings.

"I expect you're right. Now I'm her guardian, I intend to find out more for myself. I shall have an opportunity this half term. I shall take her to my mother's home and will certainly take her out during the week before I bring her back."

"How can you do all this?" Cleo was puzzled. "Shouldn't you be in Oxford?"

"I left Oxford last Summer."

She stared at him, utterly amazed. “But you can’t have done! You belong there and you’ve done so well!”

“Nevertheless,” he smiled. “I have left. I accepted a Professorship at Wheaten, starting a new department, which combines all my interests - quite an exciting experiment in fact.”

“I know Wheaten has a decent reputation but you can’t compare it with Oxford, surely?”

“It’s where I prefer to be at present.” He seemed disinclined to discuss the matter further and Cleo felt herself silenced. After all, she had no right to question his career decisions. Even when they had been lovers he had made that clear.

“And what are you doing here?” he challenged her. “I never expected to find you teaching at St. Elizabeth’s. That’s not exactly Oxford, either.”

“I’m only here temporarily.”

“Which makes it all the more mystifying. So you didn’t marry Simon Woodward?”

“No, I went to London.” She felt his penetrating gaze fixed on her. There was no evasion possible, there never had been with him. She tried, however, to speak lightly. “I accepted a tempting contract as a photographer’s model and decided to live a frivolous and pretty parasitic life. I took a very obliging lover and have been with him for two years.”

“Then why are you at St. Elizabeth’s?”

Suddenly she was angry. “Because I choose to be just as you choose to be at Wheaten.”

“And I have no right to ask impertinent questions. That’s perfectly true and I apologise again.”

“I’m sorry,” she answered quickly. “I didn’t mean to sound rude. The trouble is I’ve decided once more to change my life rather drastically and I’m not completely sure about anything at the moment.”

"I think I may understand." He looked at her sympathetically and refilled her glass. "I did something rather similar last Summer and it can be confusing for a time."

"But I'm sure you were much more sensible and organised. I was as impulsive and crazy as always."

"Just as you were when you left Oxford?" he queried quietly. "You made a thorough job of disappearing then."

"I intended to. The opportunity was there so I took it. You might have found me, if you'd cared to look hard enough." As she said that, she realised for the first time that it was what she had secretly hoped for in the first couple of months after her arrival in London. But that was now past.

"Unfortunately, I was unable to." Again, he seemed disinclined to add anything to his explanation.

Cleo sampled her wine appreciatively and then decided it was better to change the subject. "I was particularly surprised to meet you again just now, as I have only just finished reading your book. Miss Wilson strongly recommended it and lent me her copy. She's a great fan of yours."

"So I gathered," he replied casually. "But what did you think about it? That interests me more."

"I think it's brilliant." He didn't answer but continued to sip his wine thoughtfully. "You don't seem very pleased."

"That could mean all or nothing," he remarked coolly.

"Really Merlin," she protested, "what can I say when the eminent reviewers have already said it all?"

He smiled at her. "It's not vanity," he said. "It's simply that I would still value your opinion. But perhaps you don't believe that?"

"Of course I do and I'm flattered." Then seeing that he was still regarding her, she decided once more on honesty. "I think it's beautifully written and compassionate, Miss Wilson was impressed with your scholarship and style but I was more impressed with your understanding of life and people. I was very moved by it. I hope you're going to write a sequel?"

For a moment, he didn't speak then he said quietly, "Thank you, Cleo. I'm planning a trilogy. I've already started the second. That was another reason for moving to Wheaton. I have less ties and I can live right away from the Campus."

There seemed to be an even greater gulf between them and it was harder than ever to imagine the closeness there had once been until she had angrily rejected him finally. It had been the right thing to do, even though it had been done in the wrong way. He had been right to pursue his ambitions.

"You're very thoughtful," he remarked.

"I was simply considering how successfully you have achieved so many of your ambitions. You must be happy."

"There are even more important things than that in life," he replied seriously. "I was made to realise that some time ago."

Cleo was puzzled. there was something here she could not understand but she was afraid to ask too much. "And that led you from Oxford?"

"Yes, that's right," he agreed but said no more. Instead he looked at his watch and suggested they had better leave without coffee, if she was to get back in good time.

Realising that he had still to get back to his own home after that, she agreed with alacrity, feeling also that the evening was definitely over. There was no need it seemed for any more.

They scarcely spoke on the way back as the winding road was icy and treacherous. He delivered her to the front door but, as he was turning to go, he unexpectedly paused. "I shall be bringing Victoria back next week," he said, "perhaps we may meet?"

Surprised, she replied quickly, "I shall be in the foyer with the other staff. We apparently have a sort of welcoming committee."

"Good. I'll look out for you. Enjoy your half term." With a quick wave he was gone. As she walked into the entrance hall, still disconcerted by his final unexpected words, Cleo was accosted by Pam, who was coming out of the sitting room.

"You're going a bit beyond the bounds of duty aren't you?" Pam queried as they walked up the stairs together.

Cleo stopped outside her door. "Whatever do you mean?"

Pam laughed. "Don't look so innocent! Stella saw you going off in a very friendly manner with a parent. Or so she said. Was she right?

"I did go off for a meal but it wasn't with a parent exactly. He's an uncle and a guardian."

"That still makes you a pretty fast worker!" Pam exclaimed with some admiration. "Stella is certainly envious."

"I can't think why," Cleo expostulated crossly. "In any case you're both completely mistaken. Professor Evans was my tutor and friend years ago in Oxford. We were pleased to meet again and went out for a chat. Whatever's wrong with that?" It wasn't the complete truth but she saw no reason for saying more.

"Don't get cross with me," Pam said quickly. "it's Stella who causes trouble. You need to be careful with her."

"Thanks for the advice but I don't intend to bother about her too much. It's time she sorted herself out."

"We all need a break," Pam replied. "Thank God for half term."

Cleo wasn't sure that she agreed with that, since half term offered her more problems but she contented herself with a friendly good night.

Chapter Ten

It was depressing to come back to St. Elizabeth's and to have to accept the fact that this ugly little room was now her only home and a temporary one at that. While she unpacked Cleo tried not to think but once she settled down to a solitary snack and a cup of coffee, the thoughts would not be denied. The ending of her relationship with Marcus had been so unexpectedly easy.

It had begun with Marcus's telephone call on the Sunday morning during which he told her that he would not be with her for lunch, as he had promised but would arrive in the evening. Sarah had arranged a special luncheon party for several of his chief supporters in the constituency and he was obviously obliged to be there. It had happened before when they were living together and Cleo was accustomed to it but now it seemed to make clear to her the true nature of her position. Sarah was the wife on whose superb organisation and support he depended, while she was the mistress who entertained him and satisfied his sexual needs.

She had always known this and it had not worried her but now as she listened to his excuses and protestations of love, she wondered how she could ever have thought that this would satisfy her for long. For two years she had persuaded herself that it could last and was all that she needed. He had told her that he loved and needed her, while his marriage to Sarah was little more than a business arrangement and she had accepted this. Suddenly, it was no longer possible to believe any of it.

On that solitary Sunday she had forced herself to look at several truths. The comfortable flat to which she had longed to return now seemed like a prison. She had taken a bus and walked along the Embankment. The February sun was shining palely but it was very cold and there were few people to be seen.

As she leaned on the wall and looked down at the grey waters, she felt utterly chilled, empty and very alone. The pitying glance of a homeless man had made her admit the worthlessness of her life and from that moment, it had been impossible to continue with it. The real folly had been to think that she could go back to that materialistic, self indulgent existence. She had enjoyed the comfort and apparent security but she had never loved Marcus, nor had he loved her, in spite of all his protestations. His real commitment was to Sarah and, therefore, it was Sarah he loved and she had no wish to intrude any more.

As she finally moved away and walked back to the bus, it occurred to her that her unexpected meeting with Merlin had made it easier for her to realise how little she had ever loved Marcus, for the six months she and Merlin had been secret lovers in Oxford had been the only really happy months she had known. Circumstances had been against them, particularly her own immaturity but meeting him again had made it impossible for her to think of Marcus as anything but a poor substitute. She only needed the courage to live up to her beliefs.

It was surprising how easy it had finally been. She had said nothing to Marcus when he arrived. She had made herself attractive and had been entertaining and provocative, even making love with all the skill she had but her resolution had remained unchanged. Three days later, after turning down the job his friend in the City had offered her, she had taken most of her possessions by taxi to Jane's and had arranged to spend the last day of the holiday with her. Then, that evening she had told him.

The amazing thing was that he had accepted it calmly. "You've changed," he said. "I don't want to lose you but that's a foolish thing to say because I already have. It was always inevitable, I suppose. But why?"

"If I were to ask you to choose between me and Sarah. You would choose her, wouldn't you? And that's no longer enough for me."

He considered this. "You never asked me," he said finally. "Was that because you didn't want to know then?"

"It wasn't relevant because I thought I could be satisfied with that sort of relationship."

"And now you aren't?" They had talked for a time and then sadly but amicably had spent their last night together. Even the ending had been unreal, she thought, as she poured herself another coffee and probably neither of them had been completely honest, although they had come nearer to it than they ever had before.

Jane had welcomed her younger sister and had approved of the decision to leave Marcus. She had allowed Cleo to store her belongings in her spare room but, although nothing was said, it was quite clear to Cleo that there was no home for her here, especially as Jane was now expecting a baby. This was naturally far more important to her than Cleo's difficulties and worries.

This was a blow and for the first time Cleo was forced to realise how much she had relied on Jane being always there for her. In their rejection they had clung to each other but Jane, older and more stable, had now made her own life, from which Cleo was inevitably excluded. Robert had not made a great difference but the baby changed everything.

She did not resent what had happened but it forced upon her the necessity of planning her own life more successfully than she had done as yet. The only trouble was her old enemy - depression. Already the dark forces were massing. She felt that she was on the edge of a precipice and only by a tremendous effort of will could she keep her footing. It was imperative to keep her mask. No one must glimpse her real self, that frightened, rejected child, who felt herself unlovable and unable to trust anyone. It was impossible, however, to do this without an audience and it was a relief, therefore, when Cynthia unexpectedly came in search of her.

"I was hoping you'd be back," she said as Cleo opened her door in response to her knock. "No one else seems to be here. Apparently we are the keen ones."

"Unlikely as that seems," Cleo remarked with her brightest smile. "Come in," she continued, "I'll make some more coffee, if you have time, that is."

"That's just what I was hoping you'd say," Cynthia replied, coming and settling herself on the divan. "I expect you had an exciting half term with your lover in London," she remarked as Cleo began to prepare fresh coffee.

"We had lots of fun," Cleo said lightly. "Marcus had acquired tickets for the new play at the Barbican and also for the Opera. I was able to wear all my most fashionable clothes, eat delicious food and forget all about St. Elizabeth's. I was thoroughly spoilt, in fact." It was all true and yet so untrue.

"How could you bear to come back?"

"I enjoy the contrast."

"But surely Marcus doesn't like your being here? Doesn't it annoy him?"

"I expect it does." Cleo poured out the coffee into cups. "but he knows I like variety. If I do the same thing too long, I get bored." She handed Cynthia a cup of coffee. "Don't take it too seriously," she added lightly, "I don't."

"But you are going back, aren't you?" Cynthia persisted. "You don't want to stay here, surely? Although I'm sure Miss Stephens would grab you, if you did."

"I doubt if I'll want to stay here but I must admit I find teaching more interesting than I thought I would." That was probably the first honest remark she had made, Cleo thought, and then went on quickly, "but I'm not really sure what I want to do. The trouble is I'm not the settling down type. But what about you? Did you have a good half term?"

"Yes I did. Very good, in fact." Cleo looked at her in surprise. She did not sound her usual vague, irresolute self. "As a matter of fact," Cynthia continued, "I've made a few decisions at last. I'm not like you. I haven't your confidence. I just want to be settled and feel that I have a secure future."

"And what does that mean? Or don't you want to tell me?"

"Oh, I'm dying to tell you," Cynthia replied confidently. "In fact you'd better not try to stop me." She paused and then continued triumphantly, "I'm going to be married. Look!" She held out her left hand on the third finger of which a diamond and sapphire ring sparkled.

"That's marvellous!" Cleo exclaimed. "But how did it come about? You've never mentioned anyone. Is it a whirlwind romance?"

"On the contrary, it's sober and serious. I've known Francis for years. He lives nearby. Just over a year ago his wife died leaving him with three young children. I've helped out sometimes when I've been at home. This half term he asked me to marry him and I agreed."

"I see," Cleo said a little doubtfully. "I hope you'll be happy."

"I think we will because we both intend to work at it."

"But don't you think you might regret it? You might fall in love with someone."

"What is love?" Cynthia asked with a smile. "What we have seems to me to be a good basis for marriage. We know each other and we can help each other. I'm thirty. I'm not a particularly successful teacher like Bridget, and I'm not beautiful and confident like you. I'm rather scared and afraid of being alone. Francis needs help and companionship and I can give them. In return, I'll get the security of being needed by him and the children. It's not romantic, I know but I don't see why it shouldn't work."

"You certainly sound cheerful." Cleo was amazed at the change in Cynthia. Her somewhat melancholy vagueness had vanished. The colour in her cheeks and the sparkle in her eyes made her look prettier. Even her clothes were different. Instead of her usual floating neutral draperies, she was wearing a deep blue, tailored dress.

Cleo suddenly felt envious. How fortunate to know what you wanted when it was offered! "You're obviously doing the right thing for you. I'm sure you'll be happy."

"Thanks. At least I'm sure it's better," she continued with unusual candour, "than pretending I'd make a go with Nicholas, if he ever got round to divorcing his wife. That was moonshine."

"I hope it isn't moonshine for Stella," Cleo observed. "She seems to be getting very involved."

"Well, if anyone can push Nicholas into it, Stella will. She's pretty ruthless. But be careful with her, Cleo. She's seems to have got her knife into you."

"But why? I haven't done anything to her."

"You're simply too attractive to men. She's afraid Nicholas might stray your way."

"That's ridiculous! I'm not the slightest bit interested in him."

"Don't say that too loudly either," Cynthia warned. She doesn't want him undervalued, as it were!"

"I'm sorry for her."

"Perhaps. But don't forget she can be very unpleasant."

"I suppose you mean that she told you about my going out to supper with a parent?"

"She definitely did. Was it true?"

"Not exactly. It was Victoria's uncle and guardian, who was my tutor for a time at Oxford. His main aim was to discuss

Victoria with me, since I'm supposed to give her extra tuition. That's all."

"Stella managed to make it sound quite scandalous."

"Perhaps she should check her facts first. But it doesn't really matter. Let's talk about something more interesting. Have you decided when you're going to get married?"

Cynthia was only too pleased to talk about her plans and this discussion easily occupied the time until they were supposed to go to the foyer to dispense coffee and conversation to the parents who were returning with their offspring.

For an hour Cleo dressed formally in a jade green trouser suit did her duty conscientiously. She was bright and sparkling and mercifully there was no time to think. She was just turning to go when she was greeted by Merlin who came hurrying through the main entrance doors. "Good," he exclaimed, smiling at her, "I'm just in time. I thought I might have left it too late. I've been late for everything today."

"I wondered if I might see you," she replied, remembering that he had promised to look out for her.

"Victoria ordered me to see you but I intended to in any case. She has asked me to tell you that she's delighted to have you as her tutor and she's looking forward to your first lesson together."

"Thank you. What more can I desire?" Cleo smiled brilliantly. They were now standing at the front door and she was preparing to turn right to the corridor which would eventually bring her to the Staff House, when he stopped her.

"She would like to see you tomorrow, if it can be arranged," he added.

"Of course it can. I'll get a message to her."

He still did not move. "I was able to have a couple of talks with her and I am even more convinced that you are the best person to help her."

"I'll certainly do my best," she replied and meant it. This at least was something she could do well and would enjoy doing.

"Is there anywhere we can talk?" he asked suddenly. "I should like to tell you some more about Victoria." As she hesitated, he continued, "I can't stay long but perhaps we could have a drink somewhere?"

"I suppose so," she replied a little reluctantly, "but, if we're to avoid gossip, we'd better go to the pub at the end of the village. No one from school goes there."

"That sounds fine. Shall I get my car?"

"No, that's not necessary. The exercise will do us good. I'll get my coat." As she went to the cloakroom, she wondered if she wanted to do this but his manner was so detached that she thought she could have nothing to fear and she would be pleased to hear more about Victoria. At least, it would be preferable to sitting alone in her room, which she dreaded.

They set off at a brisk pace down the village street. Before they reached their destination he had told her of Victoria's great resentment against both her parents. "She never expected much from her mother but she thinks that Edward should have come home at least for a short visit and to be frank I agree with her. Edward, however, has always run away from emotional complications and prefers to take the easy way out. If that wasn't so, he'd have tackled Lucinda years ago and this might never have happened."

"I suppose Victoria feels very rejected?"

"Definitely, although I tried to persuade her it wasn't really so."

"But she must surely be grateful to you and your Mother?"

"To my Mother, yes. I don't see why she should be particularly grateful to me. I've only tried to persuade her that she has ability and should use it."

"As you did to me years ago," she remarked, then wondered quickly, if she had been wise to say that.

"Yes," he replied with a smile, "but that was more enjoyable for obvious reasons. Victoria is someone I feel obliged to help and I'm only too relieved to hand her over to you."

"Why do you say that" she asked crossly. "Why do you always pretend to be indifferent?"

"I'm not indifferent but I don't want Victoria to become too attached to me. I think she's looking for a hero and I don't intend to be forced into that role. I value my independence too much."

"I know that," Cleo commented involuntarily. Before he could comment, she continued quickly, "I'll accept the assignment as far as I can but you mustn't drop her that would be too hard."

"I won't," he promised. "If you're prepared to give me suggestions, I'll see they're carried out."

"We can agree on that then," she said.

"Good." He opened the door of the "Royal Oak". "We'll drink to that."

It's amazing, Cleo thought, as they chose a corner table in the almost empty lounge, how we can talk without embarrassment, after what has happened between us. They had, however, always got on remarkably well, considering the differences between them.

"I imagine beer is the best drink in a pub like this," he remarked as they sat down.

"It is, I believe but you shouldn't drink much since you have to drive."

"I don't intend to. I'll content myself with a half and the same for you, unless you have other ideas." On her agreement, he made his way to the bar, while she reflected that it was pleasant to be there talking, even if it was for only a short time.

"I hope you had a good half term?" he asked as he joined her again.

"Delightful," she said lightly. "Everything was arranged to please me. All my wants were attended to and every comfort provided."

"It must be difficult to come back to St. Elizabeth's?"

"Not really. I like variety, otherwise I get bored."

"But surely, the man you live with doesn't like your being away so much?"

"He doesn't but then he's in no position to object. I'm not his wife, he's married already and as an MP with a very useful wife, he has to be careful. I'm that reprehensible being the mistress - with all the delights and none of the responsibilities. It's been fun for two years." She smiled at him.

He did not smile back but said gravely. "I shouldn't have thought that would have satisfied you."

"Then it won't surprise you to know that I ran away. I'm rather good at that."

"I know," he said.

"But, unlike you, Marcus came after me. But it hasn't made much difference, so I have to admit that you were wiser than he."

"Wisdom didn't come into it," he replied but he still gave no further explanation. He took a sip of his drink, then asked, "am I to understand that you've now decided to abandon you lover as well taking up a new career?"

"Why not? Two years is a long time for me to be faithful. Perhaps I might try being virtuous now. It would have the merit of being different, at least." She stopped suddenly. In her attempt to hide her loneliness and depression, she was afraid that she had been led into saying far too much. It didn't matter, however, for he would soon be gone and any further communication need only be about Victoria, which was obviously all he wanted. She wished he wouldn't look so closely at her. It had always been difficult to hide things from him. She hated the thought of his possibly pitying her.

"Cleo," he began but, before he could continue, they were interrupted.

"Hi, there," it was Mike's voice. Cleo turned to see him coming towards them. "Where've you been? I was trying to get in touch with you."

"It was half term. I've been in London."

"Of course you did tell me. I should've remembered. I've just came in for a quick drink. Mind if I join you?"

"Of course not," Merlin said politely. "What will you have?"

"Thanks. I could sink a pint. I'm just on my way home from Scotland. I've got my wagon outside." He grinned cheerfully, as Merlin went to the bar. "Is that your bloke from London?" he asked.

"No," she said shortly. She wasn't happy about his joining them, nevertheless, she told him briefly about Merlin.

"In that case, I'll be in touch. I've just bought a new bike. You'll love it." She doubted that but did not argue for Merlin was returning. As he handed Mike his drink, she introduced them. As Merlin sat down, Mike thanked him and then said somewhat aggressively, "Cleo's just told me you're a professor at Wheaton. With lots of degrees, I suppose?"

"A few," Merlin seemed unruffled by Mike's tone.

"I'm a two GCSE man myself." Mike took a long pull at his drink, then putting his glass down firmly, he leaned across the table towards Merlin. It seemed obvious that he was deciding to be difficult, clearly resenting what he believed to be Merlin's claim to superiority. "And that's more than you need for a job like mine."

"I should imagine you need considerable skill and judgement," Merlin observed pleasantly.

"There aren't any degrees in that," Mike replied abruptly, "so no one thinks anything of it."

"Do you enjoy your work?" Merlin asked.

"Sure. It's tough at times, long hours and all that but I like going to different places and I like being independent. As long as I deliver the goods, nobody bothers me. That's what I like. He emptied his glass. "How about you? Do you enjoy your job?"

"Certainly, I do," Merlin replied firmly. "I'm pretty free too, as long as I produce results. You like going to different places, I like dealing with different people, so there's really not much difference between us."

"Except the pay," Mike said belligerently. "You get paid a lot more for a day's work than I do, so people think you matter more. You can't deny it but I don't suppose it bothers you." He looked challengingly at Merlin."

"I believe," Merlin replied coolly, "that everyone should be properly paid for his skill and hard work, whatever it is. You may be surprised to know," he continued, "that most university teachers think they're badly paid. Perhaps no one thinks he's paid enough. The truth probably is that no one ever can think he's paid enough, once he starts considering the time and effort he expends."

"I don't know about that," Mike persisted. "At least your lot can afford to get married, buy a house and support your wife and kids. My wife would have to work."

"Why not?" Cleo exclaimed, "perhaps your wife would prefer it. I see nothing wrong with that."

"I do," Mike declared. "I think a woman should look after the home and kids, while the man provides the cash."

"You're just an old-fashioned chauvinist," Cleo laughed, "a sort of dinosaur."

"Be careful, Mike," Merlin warned him. "Cleo's a very independent woman."

"Don't I know it!" Mike retorted. "She wouldn't even let me buy her a meal." He looked at his watch. "I'd better be going. We'll finish this argument some other time. My dinner's waiting."

"You have the advantage of me there," Merlin observed.

"You haven't arranged things properly, that's your trouble," Mike said affably, as he stood up. His hostility to Merlin had apparently vanished. "Thanks for the drink. My treat next time. See you."

"You seem to have overcome his prejudice," Cleo observed.

"I only spoke the truth and didn't attempt to deny he has a legitimate grievance. Do you know him well?"

"Not really. I've only met him about three times." She did not feel that it was necessary to explain further, especially as Merlin asked no more questions. He made no attempt to go, however, but sat apparently deep in thought. Having become accustomed to his silences in the past, Cleo did not worry, being happy to stay where she was a little longer.

"Do they serve food here?" he asked unexpectedly.

"I believe so. Someone told me their food was really home cooked, simple but delicious. Why do you ask?"

"I thought I might sample it. I'll make enquiries from the landlord." He soon came back with the menus. "The landlord recommends the mushroom pate and the steak and kidney pie. They're both home made and are available almost immediately."

"I thought you were in a hurry to get back?"

"I am but I have to eat and this seems preferable to cooking something for myself after a long and busy day."

"You've never liked cooking," she remembered suddenly. "You always used to persuade me to do it, whenever you could."

"And I still don't, although I'm getting quite good at it." He smiled at her. "I think I'll take the landlord's advice."

Cleo stood up. "I'd better hurry back before I miss supper."

"Need you? I was hoping I might persuade you to eat here with me." He looked unsmilingly at her. "But perhaps you'd rather not? There's much we can talk about."

"Surely, we've discussed all that needs to be discussed," she managed to say.

"I don't think so. There's a lot that still needs saying. But more importantly, I think you need a friend, just as I do - someone with whom you can talk freely."

"I think you're simply trying to be kind to me," she said quickly, "and I don't need that. I don't regret leaving Marcus."

"I'm sure you don't. But I'm not being kind to you, I'm being kind to myself. I would enjoy your company."

"We can't go back, Merlin," she protested. "I meant what I said when we parted, although I said it badly."

"I haven't the slightest desire to go back. But I don't see why we shouldn't be friendly, now we have the opportunity, especially as we're both exiles here in a way. Do you?"

"No," she said impulsively. "I'm pleased to join you." It would be preferable to being alone.

"Good. Then let's not waste any more time."

The dining room was small, comfortable and well heated with a log fire that was red and glowing. The only other occupants, two business men. were deeply involved in an earnest discussion. Choosing a table at the other end of the room but nearer to the fire ensured their privacy.

The mushroom pate arrived almost immediately and was delicious, so delicious in fact that Merlin seemed unwilling to talk. Cleo felt a little exasperated. "I thought you said you wanted to talk to me," she said, finally.

"I do," he replied, spreading the last bit of pate on the last finger of toast, "but I'm hungry. Why don't you eat your pate. You're far too pale and thin. Is that the fashionable model look?"

"How can you be so cruel," she retorted with mock pathos, "when you know it's my broken heart? I've been deserted for a constituency! But I suppose with an election looming, I can't blame him. As a good Conservative he must cultivate his wife and his majority, so I'm left lamenting."

"That's not what you said earlier," Merlin remarked. "You said then that the decision was yours."

"What do you want me to say?"

"Why not try the truth?" he asked abruptly. "Stop pretending you're frivolous and uncaring. I never liked your doing that."

She was angry. "What right have you of all people to say that to me?" Her voice was low but her tone was vehement. "I cared tremendously about you when I was twenty but it didn't do me any good. You left for the States because your career plans were so important. When you came back two years later you thought we could just go on where we'd left off. I ran away before I made an even bigger fool of myself. What I've done since and why is no concern of yours." She stopped as the waitress came to clear away their plates and they both remained silent until the second course had been served.

It seemed as he began to eat that he was not going to answer any of her observations. That made her angrier. She wanted to force him into answering. "I suppose you're not going to bother to answer me any more than you have done in the past. I expect that more important matters are awaiting your attention."

"Your happiness is important to me."

"Why on earth should I believe that?"

"Because it's true. I can tell you're unhappy and I care about it."

"There is no reason why you should," she retorted. "I was very unhappy when you returned from the States but it didn't worry you then. All you wanted was for us to become lovers again."

"You seemed to want it too," he answered, looking steadily at her.

"Yes, because I was weak and vulnerable. I fell into your arms and wrecked all my hopes of a sensible marriage with Simon. The only thing I could do was leave and try to start again. I didn't want you any more and I told you. I'm sorry for some of the things I said but the main points were true. As you accepted it then, your concern now seems somewhat hypocritical."

He put down his knife and fork. "I'm sorry," he said, "I seem to have managed this badly. You have every right to be angry I hoped I could make peace but…"

"Why don't you tell me how selfish and demanding I am, as you did before? Because that's still true." She looked at him curiously. "I think you've changed somehow."

"I hope I have. I needed to." He looked at his watch. "Damn," he exclaimed, "I really must go soon. But can't we agree to be friends? I think we still have much in common. I'll accept your decision." He finished off his meal while he waited for her to answer.

"I think perhaps we can," she said, finally. But that's all I want. I don't want any kind of sexual entanglement. I'm weary of all that."

"Fine. That suits me. Unlike you," he smiled at her, "I'm a practising celibate and have been for some time."

"You aren't!" she stared at him, amazed.

"You don't have to look so shocked. It's perfectly possible to be celibate and sane."

"Then you'd better instruct me how to do it successfully."

"I'll do my best to succeed at that somewhat unusual assignment, though you, I imagine, will attempt to divert me from the paths of virtue."

"I might," she confessed, "out of habit. But I don't want to."

They finished their meal quickly and set off back to St, Elizabeth's. As they walked quickly up the High Street she said impulsively, "You were right I do need a friend. But I'm afraid it's going to be rather one-sided."

"You have no need to worry about that," he replied firmly. "It seems, however, that the true irony of our situation has escaped you."

"Whatever do you mean?" She slipped her arm through his quite naturally.

"I'll leave you to discover that," he answered with a smile.

She considered this until they reached the Staff House. "You won't disappear now, will you?" she asked.

"I have no intention of doing so. But aren't you the one who disappears? Still we won't go into that, as time is limited. May I, instead, ask you if you'll meet me next Saturday after lunch? We might go to Birmingham. I can get some tickets for the theatre. What do you think?"

"I would love that."

"Then I'll phone you midweek." He kissed her lightly on the cheek, then walked quickly away to his car.

Chapter Eleven

Two weeks later Cleo was standing in the car park of the 'Red Lion' arguing with Mike whom she had agreed to meet there on the Saturday evening. "You can't deny she's beautiful," he was saying as Cleo looked crossly at the shining metal and smooth leather of his new and powerful motor bike. "She can do a hundred easily, even uphill."

"If you want to enjoy a love affair with your bike," she retorted, "that's fine by me but I don't intend to be the third party."

"Balls," he answered cheerfully with a wicked grin. "You're just chickening out. It'll be a great experience. You'll enjoy it."

"Experience yes but enjoyment never. You asked me to have a meal with you in Markhampton. I don't intend to go into Markhampton on that."

"You won't," he promised cheerfully, "we're not going to Markhampton."

"Then, where are we going?" That was a mistake, she realised, for it implied consent. "What I mean," she hastily corrected herself. "is where are you going?"

"To the gates of hell and back," he laughed.

"In that case I'm definitely not coming."

"I've brought a spare helmet and a leather jacket," he said, ignoring her. You'll be warm and safe. We'll go to this pub on the moors where bikers go. Good sound, good beer and good pub grub. I bet you've never been to a place like that."

"You're right. It sounds fascinating but not really me."

"How do you know, if you've never tried it? Anyway, you'll love the ride," he coaxed her. It's out of this world."

"That's just what I'm afraid of."

"Balls and again balls! You're just as mad as I am really. If you weren't, you wouldn't be here. You've nothing to lose and nobody to bother about, so why not take a chance?"

"OK," she agreed suddenly. It was all too true what Mike had said. She had nothing to lose.

"You won't regret it. It's the best way I know of setting rid of the devil on my back. It might scare yours away."

"I'd be glad if it did," she replied as she slipped into the jacket and gloves he offered her. Finally, with the helmet on, she felt a different person. Anonymous and ready for any risk.

"Just cling to me," he instructed her and lean over when I do. You'll soon get used to it. I won't go fast, not at first, anyway."

He kept his word at first but gradually as they travelled into the open, winding roads of the moors, his speed increased. She clung firmly to him as he went into the bends at a fearsome speed and miraculously came safely out of them. The air rushed past them, the hills were darker shadows all around. There was no moon and it was very dark, except for the piercing beam of his headlamp and occasionally the almost blinding light of cars coming towards them. There was no time to think or to be afraid. It was exhilarating.

Now, sitting in a pub which was rapidly filling up with young people, mostly bikers and their girl friends, she still felt exhilarated and detached from her entire past and future. Mike, after stopping to chat with various mates, was making his way to their table with a tray. He deposited a foaming glass of beer and a plate of beefburgers and chips in front of her. Then he sat down to his own meal. "It's not exactly up to your West End standard but it's the best they have, so you'd better make the most of it."

"It's fine," she replied. She felt so hungry after the drive in the cold air that any food was good food, even this. She couldn't remember if she'd ever felt like this, certainly not for years. Her hair was dishevelled, her cheeks were flushed and her eyes were sparkling. She felt beautiful and desirable and was aware of Mike's appreciation. On another occasion, she might have retreated from him but not now.

"You liked it," he stated, "you can't deny it."

"I did. It was marvellous. I understand now why you do it."

"There's nothing like a bike ride for raising the adrenalin," he remarked as he finished his glass of beer. "I needed that. I'll get another. Do you want one?"

"No, thanks. Do you really think you should, Mike?"

He laughed. "Don't worry. I always drive better after a few pints."

Protesting would be useless and anyway she didn't seem to care any more. It was more important to tackle the beefburger. As he came back to the table, she looked up and noticed a couple coming through the door. With a shock she recognised the fair, pale girl in her jeans and jacket. It was Stephanie St John. She was hanging on to the arm of a good looking fair haired young man who was similarly dressed.

Cleo looked away quickly, hoping that Stephanie would not see her. She was probably on a legitimate exeat just as Victoria was this weekend. It would be far less embarrassing, however, for them not to see each other. Then, to her horror, the young man waved to Mike who waved back. The couple then began to make their way towards them.

"Oh God," Cleo entreated Mike, "I don't know who he is but can't you head him off?"

"Why? He's Pete Mason, the younger brother of a good mate of mine."

The couple seemed to have been swallowed up in the crowd. There was still time. "I'm sorry about that. But the girl's in our Sixth Form. I simply can't meet her here."

"Too late," Mike replied, as the couple appeared again making their way towards them. Don't let it bother you. It's the same for both of you."

It was suddenly obvious that Stephanie had, for the first time, realised who it was with Mike, for she turned her back to them and said something urgently to Pete. "I'll sort it," Mike said casually. He made his way to the couple and spoke briefly to them. Cleo could not imagine what he said but, whatever it was, it was most effective, for the couple moved off quickly.

"Whatever did you say?" she asked Mike as he rejoined her.

"I didn't have to say much. Stephanie was already freaking out. I told her not to worry. No damage would be done, if they made themselves scarce. So, no sweat." When Cleo did not respond, he continued. "Forget it, woman. Drink up and enjoy yourself. That's what it's all about. There's a disco in the back room. Would you like to go? On second thoughts, better not. That's where Pete and Stephanie are making for. No need to stir it."

"I imagine she isn't out on an exeat or she wouldn't have been so worried," Cleo said dubiously.

Mike shrugged. "What you don't know, you don't need to worry about. You're a woman not a fucking teacher tonight. Let's have fun. I'll get us some more drinks."

During the course of the evening several of Mike's acquaintances and their girl friends joined them from time to time. It was easier Cleo found to listen rather than to talk much, since their language and their interests were so different from hers. Many of them, she discovered to her surprise, were married with children but they still insisted on their right to a night out with their mates when drinking, casual violence and sexual encounters seemed to be their main entertainment. But the real passion of their lives were their bikes and some of them had girl friends who shared this. Mike talked freely with them but it was obvious that they had a certain respect for him because of his wider experience and his greater recklessness which fascinated and almost frightened them. Several of his past exploits were mentioned with considerable admiration and Cleo learned that he had been both a soldier and a diver before he had become a driver. He was really as much an outsider and a wearer of masks, as she was. "You're fucking mad, you know that," one of his mates said and the others agreed. "You'd better be fucking, careful with him," another said to Cleo, "he's a devil."

As Cleo smiled, Mike put his arm casually around her and remarked cheerfully, "No need to worry. She's a bit of a devil herself, aren't you, Cleo?"

It was late when they left and Cleo was aware that Mike had drunk far too much, although there was little sign of it in his outward behaviour, except that he was more relaxed and confident. None of this worried her, however, as she seated herself behind him and clung on to him. With a roar they were off. Several other bikers left at the same time but they soon turned off and she and Mike were on their own. As they took the first bend at a frightening speed, she closed her eyes and prayed. They seemed to sway perilously but miraculously they made it. She felt a wild exultation. Nothing else mattered. Her blood seemed to throb with the bike. She laughed suddenly holding on to Mike's strong body, rejoicing in his skill and mastery of the powerful monster beneath them.

All too soon the lights of Barton Leas appeared. Mike slowed down at the last bend before the village and they came to rest quite sedately in the car park of the 'Red Lion'. The excitement, however, stayed with her. The ground no longer seemed firm and she swayed slightly as she dismounted. Mike caught her and held her close. Then, when he had taken off their helmets, he kissed her fiercely. It seemed quite natural to return his kiss. It was a fitting end to the whole reckless evening. She did not hold back or ask herself any questions.

She was almost disappointed when he said gruffly, "I'll walk back with you, then I must be off." She even wondered if he had another girl lined up for the rest of the night. As if sensing her thought, he explained as they walked towards the school. "I promised my Mum I'd be home in good time tonight. She's not well and I don't want her lying awake, worrying about me."

This surprised her but, before she could reply, he continued, "It doesn't always have to be like that." He did not speak again until they reached the gate, when he kissed her again several times. He released her reluctantly, "We'll make a weekend of it next time." he promised. Before she could answer, he was gone. "See you," he called, as he turned and waved to her.

The exhilaration and euphoria lasted until she entered her empty, bleak room. It was orderly but bare and unwelcoming. The piles of papers on the table were still waiting to be marked, an empty coffee mug was standing nearby. She walked across the room, drew the shabby curtains together and then sat on the divan. "I really must be mad," she thought. The room looked more repellently ugly than usual with only the single central light switched on. Normally, the subdued glow from the two reading lamps she had installed softened the edges.

As she sat there, she tried to understand herself and to answer the questions which came crowding in. It didn't seem wrong to have enjoyed the evening but it was both foolish and wrong to have encouraged Mike. Had they anything in common except depression and a reckless desire to escape from it? Had it been a similar recklessness that had ruined her mother's life?

She had told Merlin honestly, she had thought, that she didn't want any sexual entanglements. She had believed it to be true when she had said it. But how could it have been? Was she ever true to anything or to anybody?

Did it matter, however, when there was no one to care? She imagined Jane happily planning their baby's future with Robert. Marcus would be in Braxton planning future moves with Sarah to safeguard his majority in the election which could not long be delayed.

She had made many acquaintances but no real friends in London. She had deliberately cut herself off from the people she had known in Oxford. That thought brought her back again to Merlin. She had no idea what he was doing, as he had not attempted to get in touch with her since the pleasant day they had spent in Birmingham at the art gallery and the theatre. The conversation then had been friendly but impersonal and since then he had been silent. Perhaps he had regretted his offer of friendship. If so, she could not blame him. What friendship could she offer anyone?

She began to undress slowly. What do I really want, she wondered? The last five years had been a series of mistakes and fresh starts which had always failed. She had realised that evening that Mike's life had been somewhat similar. Perhaps they could help each other? At least he might need her, as Merlin never had and never would. His life had always proceeded smoothly and probably always would. What could they have in common, except a physical attraction, once strong but now no longer there? She must learn to stand alone.

The next morning after a disturbed night, she decided to go for the first time to Mass at the little Catholic chapel in the village, while the School attended the stately morning service in the Parish Church. It was a long time since she had been to Mass, for, while she had been living with Marcus, it had seemed hypocritical but now there was no impediment. She was not sure she believed anything but it was oddly reassuring to be there and to pray the familiar prayers with others.

The priest was a heavily built rather infirm, elderly man who performed the actions of the Mass slowly and with considerable difficulty, As he went to give his sermon, Cleo prepared herself for a boring and lengthy commentary on the day's readings. She was surprised, however.

"As you all know," he said slowly but clearly, "I have been very ill but, by God's Grace, I have been spared to be with you a little longer. And now at the end of my life, I find I have only one short, simple message to give you - Our Lord's own message given to his disciples just before his death - 'Love one another, as I have loved you.' I have given many sermons and tried to instruct many students and now, as I approach my own death, I know this is the only message worth giving. St John in his old age realised this too when he wrote, 'God is love and whoever remains in love remains in God and God in him.' And now I ask you, my dear people, to think about this and apply it to your own lives."

He paused for a few moments then began to recite the creed. Cleo, however, was scarcely aware of the rest of the Mass. It seemed almost as if God had spoken to her himself in her loneliness and perplexity. She was reminded why she had left her frivolous, loveless life in London because she had felt the need to identify with others and to care. If she was to be true to herself, she must not forget that nor allow herself to be tempted into yet another shallow relationship. But what was she to do?

She decided she would try to speak to the priest after Mass. At the end, she waited until her emerged from the sacristy and then went up to him. "May I speak to you, Father?" she asked. He smiled and waited. She went quickly on, "How can I love others when no one has ever loved me? I want to love but I don't think I know how."

He took her hand in his. "Let God show you how, he will if you let him."

"But I'm a sinner," she protested. "You don't understand. I've broken the commandments and turned my back on the Church. I'm not sure even that I believe anything now."

"We are all sinners," he replied gently, "and God longs to forgive each one of us. Since you are seeking him, although you are hardly aware of it, you will find him and the answer to your question." He placed his hand softly on her head and blessed her. "Go in peace, my child, and pray for me as I will pray for you."

She watched him make his slow and painful way out of the chapel, then she knelt down before the altar and fixed her eyes on the crucifix. She seemed to have no thoughts, no words, simply a feeling of peace. She remained there until she was disturbed by a mother and child coming in to light a candle, as she had done with her mother in those far off days when she still believed she was loved.

She left the chapel and walked slowly back hoping to avoid meeting anyone so that she might keep the feeling of peace that had come to her but it was already receding. She had scarcely reached her room when Pam called to her from the hall that she was wanted on the telephone. Mystified, she hurried downstairs. To her surprise it was Merlin.

"I hope I haven't left it too late to ask you," he said, as soon as she answered, "but I'm hoping you're free this afternoon."

"You've certainly left it late," she began but before she could continue, he interrupted her, "I need your friendly help", he continued, "but I shall understand if it isn't possible. I've had a difficult week which has been made more complicated by my mother deciding she felt too depressed to spend the weekend alone, in view of Victoria's unexpected announcement that she was spending her exeat with a friend. I've done my best but it's not a role that comes easily to me, as you probably realise, so I'm hoping you'll be willing to help me out." He paused.

"What exactly are you suggesting?" Cleo asked.

"I was hoping you would agree to have tea and supper with us, if I pick you up about half past three. Could you bear it? Perhaps you could consider it as your good deed for the week?"

Cleo laughed. "I'll be very pleased," she replied and realised that she meant it. "If you're sure that your Mother will not be annoyed at having me thrust upon her?"

"She'll be delighted," he assured her, "After two days alone with me, she's craving some female company. Will half past three suit you?" He rang off as soon as she agreed.

By half past three she was standing at the window of the staff sitting room, looking across to the village green where Merlin must park his car. As she saw him arriving, she moved out quickly, hoping to avoid Stella who was coming down the stairs behind her.

Unfortunately, however, as she neared the gate, Stephanie came quickly through it and spoke to her. "I was hoping to see you, Miss Lafay," she said. "I've been so worried since last night. Can I talk to you, please?"

Before Cleo could answer her, Stella interrupted them from behind. "Really, Stephanie," she said coldly, "you know you're not supposed to come bothering staff here. Miss Lafay may not know the rule but you most certainly do. I'm sorry to barge in," she continued, smiling sweetly at Cleo, "but I thought I ought to let you know." Stephanie apologised and stood aside as Stella went through the gate and paused, obviously expecting to meet someone.

Realising that Merlin was now walking across the village green towards her, Cleo said hastily, "I can't speak to you now, Stephanie. I'll see you at break tomorrow." There was no time for more, as Merlin had by now almost reached her. She was aware of Stella's keen interest in all that was happening and wondered briefly as she went to meet him what further comments there might be.

"I hope you're prepared to eat home made scones and cake?" he asked as they went towards the car.

"I shall devour them. But surely you haven't taken to baking? I can't believe it."

"You don't have to. Mother's daily help insisted on making them as soon as she heard I was coming for the weekend."

"And since you hate such indulgences, you thought you'd call on me to help." She smiled at him as he started the car.

"Naturally I haven't forgotten your healthy appetite. Your first thought whenever we met for a romantic weekend was usually about how soon we could eat."

"While yours was about how soon we could get to bed!" As soon as she had made it, she was a little apprehensive as to how that remark would be received but he only laughed and asked what else she would have expected.

It's a bit difficult for me to consider you as a family man," she remarked as they came out of the village. "You seemed to be totally detached from such commitments when we were in Oxford."

"I was pretty well but at the moment there is no one else and I'm conveniently close. Don't look so sympathetic. I'm unlikely to sacrifice myself, as you well know."

"I'm a bit nervous," she admitted suddenly. "I haven't much experience of mothers."

"There's no need to be. Although Mother is seventy seven, she's very young in outlook and easy to talk to."

"But you don't seem to think so or am I mistaken?"

"It's simply that I have been away from home for so long and am very different from Edward who did all the things expected of him. He became an engineer like my father and went into the business, then he married and settled down near the family home. I'm the odd one. Mother loves me, especially as I am her baby born ten years after Edward and, although she doesn't understand me, she wants to advise me and persuade me to change my life."

"I imagine that could be difficult, although I rather think it would be pleasant to have someone who bothered about me."

"I'm not as ungrateful, as you might think. I'm doing my best to please at the moment."

"I think you're doing remarkably well for you. But tell me what does your mother know about me?"

"Victoria has given you a glowing report and she knows that I was your tutor in Oxford for a time but nothing more. Does that reassure you?"

There was no time to say more as they were already moving into a wide tree-lined avenue with many Victorian detached villas on either side. They finally stopped in the wide drive of one of the largest. As the car drew to a halt before the wide steps leading to the front door, Mrs Evans appeared. She was using a stick but that was her only sign of frailty. There was little resemblance between her and her son, for where he was tall, lean and dark with clear cut features, she was small and plump with softly rounded features, rosy cheeks and bright blue eyes, which sparkled beneath her softly curling white hair. She was wearing a dress in fine amethyst wool with amethyst earrings and brooch.

She was obviously very pleased to see them both and greeted Cleo warmly when Merlin introduced her. "I was so pleased when Merlin said you could come!" she exclaimed, as the crossed the wide hall into a large comfortably furnished sitting room. An inviting looking tea was already laid in front of the fire.

"I see you have, as usual, disobeyed all my orders," Merlin remarked as he came in behind them. "You've prepared the tea, you've changed your dress and you obviously haven't rested." He smiled as he spoke and his mother smiling back was obviously unruffled.

"I've treated you as you would have treated me," she replied cheerfully. She turned to Cleo and invited her to sit on the settee next to her chair while Merlin was despatched to the kitchen to make the tea. As soon as he had gone, she said softly, "Merlin has been very good but it's not easy for him to make room for a neurotic, elderly woman in his well organised life, so I was very pleased when he suggested inviting you. I thought it would be good for us to have you here."

"It's very kind of you to say so," Cleo replied, a little surprised, "I thought I might be intruding."

"Certainly not. I particularly wanted to meet you because you're obviously so good for Victoria and for Merlin. He's had a difficult time in the last two years or so but he's been very pleased to meet you again, I think. You were obviously one of his favourite pupils."

Merlin's entry with the tea luckily saved Cleo from having to make any comment but she wondered about 'the difficult time' which he had never mentioned.

"Help yourself, Cleo," Mrs Evans requested as she poured out the tea.

"You don't need to worry about that," Merlin remarked, as Cleo took a scone. "Cleo has always had a very healthy appetite."

"I'm very glad to hear that," Mrs Evans answered, "it's so depressing when people say they're on a diet, as so many young people do today."

"I never need to diet," Cleo said cheerfully, smothering her scone with fresh butter. And I love home made scones and cake." It was very pleasant, she thought, to relax by the fire in a comfortable home with friendly people and she smiled happily at Merlin, as he offered her another scone. She was grateful to him for inviting her.

The next hour passed very quickly until Mrs Evans announced that she would rest until supper, leaving Merlin in charge. "I'm sure you'll have plenty to talk about and you can always make sure Cleo, that Merlin doesn't forget the supper. But beware or you will find yourself taking over."

"I know that very well," Cleo laughed as Merlin protested.

While Merlin disposed of the tea things, Cleo settled herself on the rug in front of the fire. "I'm so glad you invited me," she said as he returned and settled himself comfortably in an arm chair. "I thought you might have changed your mind."

"Changed my mind about what?"

"About our being friends."

"Of course not. I've had an unusually exacting week, that's all. University life is difficult at the moment. We're underfunded and the future's even more uncertain, particularly as politicians, thoughts seem to be entirely focused on the next election. Sweeping change seems likely but what we don't know. As a result both staff and students are under increased stress and feel threatened."

"But, that's been true for some time. Did something make last week worse?"

"I spent several hours with a third year student, who came to me with a half finished essay and a suicide threat. She refused to talk to any one else, so I tried to deal with her myself."

"Were you successful?"

"Temporarily at least but I'm not sure about the long term."

"Why is that?" She sat up and looked at him earnestly. "Surely, there is someone who would help her? I mean her family. Or perhaps they're not interested?"

"I received the impression that her family would be very helpful if she went to them. She's obsessed, however, with failure. Her boyfriend has left her and she thinks she's bound to fail in the Summer and won't get a job, so suicide apparently seems the best way out."

"How very cruel and selfish!" she exclaimed. "But then I think people who kill themselves are selfish. They simply don't think of what effect their action will have on those who love them. It's terrible to be rejected by someone in that way, given no chance to talk things over and to sort them out. It's so final!" She spoke with great passion and there were tears in her eyes.

"I didn't expect you to be so concerned, Cleo." Merlin was obviously puzzled. "Why are you?"

"It's because my mother committed suicide. I'd always hoped I would see her and she would explain things to me. But it seems she simply didn't care about me or about Jane or my father."

"You should have told me. When did it happen?"

"Shortly before you came back from the States. My father went to New York and arranged everything. She left no message for us. Apparently her lover had left her and she had no money. It didn't occur to her that Jane and I loved her and would have welcomed her back. Jane took it pretty calmly but I couldn't seem to cope with it."

"Oh God, I'm sorry," Merlin exclaimed. "If you had told me, I wouldn't have behaved as I did. No wonder you were angry with me."

"Oh, I was completely irrational. I committed a sort of suicide, rejecting everything and everyone and running away. It wasn't fair to blame you as I did but I didn't care. But I was right really, wasn't I?"

"How do you mean?"

"Not in the way I said it but in what I said. You let me go because in spite of everything you recognised the truth that we were finished. And now I don't understand. You suggest we can be friends. It seems to work but can it really?"

"I think so, as long as we are honest with each other."

"But are you being honest?" she asked. "Isn't it simply that you feel a bit guilty about me and want to feel better?"

"That is by no means the whole truth."

"But it has to be," she insisted, if you're honest. You could have found me at Jane's. I was there for several days, then we quarrelled bitterly and I did disappear for months."

"After I found you'd left your college the next day, I was going to ring Jane."

"But you didn't."

"No, because I had an accident. A lorry came rather fast out of a side turning and smashed me and my car. I was out of action for quite a long time, unconscious at first, then suffering from temporary amnesia. So I had difficulties."

"I wish I had known." She stood up and walked towards him. "You should have told me as soon as we met again. I'm so sorry. So that's what your mother meant when she said you'd had a difficult time?" She sat down next to him. "Did you have other injuries?"

"My spine was injured but after several rather painful months and a couple of operations, I'm more or less as good as before, although I do have occasional difficult days. I had one of those last week too."

"It's changed you hasn't it?"

"It gave me time to reflect and I realised that a lot of things needed improving in myself and in my life. But it's been a lonely business."

"So you really do want a friend, even me?"

"Especially you." He smiled at her.

"But you don't want to be my lover?"

"Not at present, perhaps never. Does that disappoint you?"

"No, it's a relief. But you must realise, Merlin, that I'm not a good person. I'm weak and unreliable, as always. But I am beginning to understand something about love and how important it is. That's why I left Marcus and my life in London. I want to care about people and learn to love them. But I'm afraid of myself sometimes and wonder who I really am. Not a satisfactory friend."

He took her hand. "There's one truth you haven't realised. One that makes all the difference. I love you. That became clear to me when I was in hospital. No one has ever come as close to me as you have and that's what I want to preserve. Does it sound very strange?"

"It seems a bit like a miracle to me," she said slowly, still leaving her hand in his.

"Hardly that, surely?"

"I don't know what else I can call it." She was silent, remembering herself talking to the old priest.

"Are you going to explain?" Merlin asked.

"Not now but I will, I promise. I need to think. But thank you for talking to me." She leaned over and kissed him on the cheek. "Now," she said, "I think we ought to do something about that supper. Don't you?"

"Unfortunately, yes." He too stood up.

"Shall we meet again soon?" Cleo asked as they walked towards the kitchen.

"I hope so. I think you should come to my home. I promise to cook the meal and we can talk as long as we like. No subjects barred. Will you risk that?"

"I'd love it."

"Shall we make it next Saturday?"

She agreed happily, remembering as she did so her implied promise to Mike. She would have to put an end to that, then she need not confess her folly to Merlin.

Chapter Twelve

The days, that immediately followed Cleo's talk with Merlin, seemed more tranquil. She felt as she had not done in years that there was something secure in her life and she looked forward to visiting him at his home. Her lessons too seemed to go well and Victoria, in particular, was an able and interesting pupil. She ate most of her meals with Cynthia and Bridget and found them to be friendlier than she had previously thought, perhaps, she admitted to herself because she too was more relaxed.

Her interview with Stephanie was brief. She felt herself to be in an ambivalent position, especially since she knew that Miss Wilson was particularly concerned about the girl. She deliberately did not ask Stephanie whether or not she had been out on an exeat but simply warned her about taking foolish risks. She was aware, however, that even by this she had compromised herself and that she might be viewed as an ally against authority.

Although this worried her briefly, she put it an one side when Miss Wilson asked her to help with House Dramatics for the end of term competition. This meant giving up some of her spare time but it was an activity she enjoyed, especially as she had been involved in drama both at school and college, moreover it brought her into closer contact with more of the pupils.

On the Thursday, however, her new found serenity was somewhat disturbed in several ways. It began when she lunched alone with Bridget. At first, they reminisced about Oxford until Bridget suddenly asked, "Have you thought any more about your future yet?"

"Not really," Cleo admitted, "to be honest not at all."

"You really ought to, you know," Bridget persevered pleasantly, "You must plan ahead if you intend to embark on a serious career. Have you ever thought you might take a postgraduate Teacher's Diploma? It's a useful extra qualification and, of course, it enables you to teach anywhere not just in an independent school like this. You could apply to any university - Wheaten has a good department. Why don't you ask Merlin Evans since you know him? That is, if you really want to be a teacher."

Faced with a direct question Cleo found herself in difficulties. She mostly enjoyed the teaching that she was doing but could not imagine herself settling down to such work regularly. "I'm enjoying teaching at the moment," she replied finally, "but I'm not sure that I want to commit myself to it. But then commitment has always been my problem," she added honestly, "both with people and jobs."

"That doesn't entirely surprise me," Bridget said with a slight smile.

"I suppose you always knew what you wanted to do?"

"Yes, but then both my parents were teachers. My father's just retired from a headship."

"Didn't you ever want to get married and have a family?"

"I was always career-minded but I did think I could have both once. Then ten years ago my fiancé was killed in a motorway accident and I've never wanted to replace him."

"That must have been terrible."

"It was but, looking back, I sometimes think that perhaps it made life easier for me, although that may seem a shocking thing to say."

"I don't understand." Cleo looked at her in surprise.

"Well, it solved the problem that most women have today. You see I really loved Stephen but he had a demanding job in banking. He would have been very successful. He didn't object to my having a job but it had to be in London, even if that wasn't the best place for me. He also very much wanted a settled home and children."

"And you didn't?"

"Frankly I don't think I could have managed it all successfully. I'm not sure any woman can, although lots try. I suppose I should admire them for trying but it's not my idea of a happy life - trying to juggle husband, home and children and probably feeling inadequate in all directions. I have a man friend whom I see occasionally in the holidays but he doesn't interfere with my life nor I with his. That suits me, although it wouldn't have done, if Stephen had lived. But you must have thought about these problems?"

"Not exactly," Cleo replied. "Perhaps because I've never seriously thought of getting married nor of having a permanent relationship. Oh dear," she exclaimed, "I don't seem to have thought seriously about anything, do I? I must be incurably frivolous. That's what my sister thinks, I know."

Bridget considered her for a moment. "I'm not at all sure that's true. You probably take things more seriously than most of us. I think you don't want a career, you want a vocation. Similarly, you are afraid of embarking on the average workaday relationship. You want something better. Am I right?"

Cleo thought about this. "I don't know," she replied finally. "You may be, although it sounds a little ridiculous. But in the meantime I still have to live somehow. Now I expect you've got your future planned. Do you intend to stay at St. Elizabeth's?"

"For a year or two, yes. Miss Stephens, has offered me Miss Wilson's House when she leaves in the Summer. After that, I plan to apply for a headship."

"I can just imagine your doing that. I do envy you your sense of purpose.

"Then, why don't you consider the year's training? It'll give you time to think and it could lead you to a higher degree and educational research. Why don't you ask Merlin Evans since he knows your capabilities?"

"Perhaps I will. In any case I'll certainly think about what you've said."

"Good." Bridget stood up. "I must go now but don't hesitate to ask me, if I can help in any way."

Left alone, Cleo continued with her lunch and tried to think seriously about what Bridget had said. It was clear that she simply could not drift on as she was doing for by the middle of July she would be both jobless and homeless. Even the coming Easter vacation presented a problem since there was now no Marcus with whom to take refuge. Jane and Robert she was sure would not want her for very long.

"May I join you?" A masculine voice interrupted her thoughts.

She looked up to see Nicholas Barnes smiling at her. "Of course," she replied as he sat down opposite her.

"It's just the opportunity I've been waiting for," he continued, "a chance to get to know you better. So far you've evaded me."

"Not consciously," she replied quickly. I assure you." She did not like him, she did not like the way he behaved but she had to admit as she had done before that he had a certain power of attraction. Certainly he was easy to talk to and she found herself readily agreeing to have coffee with him. His flattery was obvious but was made acceptable because he clearly did not intend to be taken seriously. She enjoyed the game even though she was tempted to wonder if Stella did not perhaps understand the rules.

"Presumably you have forgotten, Nicholas, that you promised to come to my room for coffee?" It was Stella who interrupted them. She managed to smile at Nicholas but her eyes flashed at Cleo, who immediately stood up.

"I'm sorry I've detained you," she said to Nicholas. "I must go anyway. I have some books to collect."

He stood up smiling at her. "We must find another occasion," he murmured as he turned towards Stella to apologise. Cleo thought it wiser to go without any further word. She was sorry that she had annoyed Stella again but she quickly dismissed the incident as unimportant.

A few minutes later as she was walking to the classrooms for the start of the afternoon lessons, she was surprised to be accosted once again by Stephanie who had obviously been waiting for her. For one who looked so pale and diffident, she was amazingly persistent. "May I ask you something, Miss Lafay?" were her first words.

"Of course," Cleo replied, wondering what she could possibly want now.

"Have you told Miss Harvey about seeing me with Pete on Saturday evening?" was the unexpected question.

Cleo stared at her. "Why do you ask me that?" she replied coldly. "If I spoke to anyone about you, it would be to Miss Wilson or Miss Stephens but I promised I would do nothing this time, so why are you asking me?"

"I'm sorry," Stephanie seemed nervous but was still persistent. It's just that Miss Harvey seems very suspicious. I was worried."

"How do you mean suspicious?"

"She spoke to me as I was coming away from Maths and said she hoped I was being more sensible now but from what she'd heard lately, she rather doubted it. Why do you think she said that?"

"I imagine she'd heard some silly gossip. You know how people talk in this place. I shouldn't let it worry you. Just don't break any more rules in future."

She was about to move on when Stephanie burst out spitefully, "She has no right to talk about anyone. All the Sixth

Form knows what she gets up to. I expect Miss Stephens would like to know about that too."

For a moment Cleo was at a loss how to reply. Finally, she said as calmly and as coolly as she could, "Please don't talk like that anymore, Stephanie. I don't want to know. We should all avoid this silly gossip. Just go away and get on with your work. If you do that, I'm sure you've no need to worry."

As she walked on, she was not pleased to be joined by Stella. "I see Stephanie's been bothering you again," she said, smiling with apparent friendliness. Take my advice. Don't let the Sixth formers get too close to you, especially not ones like Stephanie. She'll be lucky if she doesn't get sent away like Rosemary Jones last year but that was before your time."

"Yes, but I've heard there was some scandal."

"There certainly was. Two of us found her in the grounds after midnight with her boyfriend. It was obvious what she'd been up to. Miss Stephens wasted no time in setting rid of her. The school's reputation is very important."

They were standing outside Cleo's classroom by now. "I suppose that applies to the staff too?" Cleo asked. "In which case I should perhaps make it clear that I did not go to supper recently with a susceptible father but with Merlin Evans who was my tutor at Oxford and an old friend." Without waiting for a reply, she entered her classroom, reflecting that she might have been impulsive but that she did not regret it, even though she realised that Stella might easily think that she was obliquely criticising her behaviour with Nicholas.

There was no time to think about it, however, during the rest of a busy teaching day which only ended just before supper. It was only when she was sitting alone in her room, drinking a cup of coffee before settling down to prepare some lessons she allowed herself to confront some of the problems of the day. For three days she had felt confident chiefly because of the happy time she had spent with Merlin and his mother. It had been comforting to be appreciated and welcomed but now she was reminded that she had not solved any of her major problems. especially those which Bridget had discussed over lunch.

The Easter holidays presented the most immediate problem since they were only three weeks away. There was no obvious place for her to go, except perhaps to Italy where Helen, her only close friend from school now lived and worked. She had taken refuge there before and knew she would be welcome. Why was she so reluctant to do this? The answer was quite clear, although she did not want to admit it. She wanted to maintain her friendship with Merlin. Oh God, she thought, I must not let it happen again. That would be foolish. Nevertheless, she felt convinced that he had changed and that he wanted to build up a lasting relationship with her. Now perhaps it would be really good, if only she could trust him.

It was then she remembered that he had promised to ring her about the final arrangements for Sunday. It would be comforting to talk to him after the difficulties of the day and there was no reason why she should not ring him. His opinion would be impartial and helpful.

Merlin seemed pleased to receive her call. He had only just returned home and had been intending to telephone her as soon as he had eaten. In view of that she decided to postpone any discussion with him and merely asked him if he were able to confirm the arrangements for Sunday. "I suggest that I pick you up at midday," he said without hesitation. "We can then go for a pub lunch. After that I wondered if you might enjoy a walk on the Shropshire hills, since the weather, although cold, is supposed to be sunny. Or have you given up walking?"

"Certainly not," she replied indignantly, "I should love to get out on the hills". She remembered happy walks they had had in Oxfordshire and wondered if he did.

"Good. After that, we'll come back to my place and I'll supply that promised meal. Then we can relax and talk by the fire. Does that programme meet with you approval?"

She assured him that it did and went back to her room feeling surprisingly cheerful. The problems were still there but suddenly they seemed less pressing. As she was about to settle down to her work, she suddenly thought of Mike. Would he be expecting to see her at the weekend? Guiltily, she remembered that she had encouraged him recklessly. It was not the first time she had behaved in that way but she was experienced enough now to know that the end of such encounters was usually disappointing and depressing. She must not fall for that temptation again, she told herself firmly. She would make it clear to him, if she met him again that they could be no more than casual acquaintances.

On the following Saturday evening, however, her prudent decision was upset by Mike's totally unexpected appearance at the Staff House. It was an obviously disapproving Pam who brought him to her room. Cleo was indignant. She did not ask him in but standing in the doorway she challenged him belligerently. "Why on earth have you come here? You should have rung me."

He was wearing what looked like working shirt and jeans, he had obviously not shaved that day and he smelt of beer. Swaying a little, he supported himself by the door and appealed to her.

"Let me in, for Christ's sake. Cleo," he mumbled, "I must talk to someone."

From his imploring expression, she realised that he was in despairing earnest. It was impossible to turn him away. When she opened the door more widely he followed her unsteadily into the room and slumped down on the divan. Shutting the door, she stood and gazed wordlessly at him. He tried to give her a valiant grin but his eyes remained dark and sombre. "What the hell have you been doing?" she demanded finally, as he remained silent. "You look dreadful and you smell worse."

"I've been on the piss since last night," he answered her slowly. "Then I thought of you. You'll be kind to me, won't you, Cleo?" He stood up and lurched forward to embrace her. Firmly, she disengaged herself and pushed back on to the divan.

"Don't be stupid," she said. "You're in no fit state for such antics". She surveyed him once again. "When did you last eat?" He thought and with difficulty finally remembered. "I had some sandwiches for lunch yesterday. I didn't go home in the evening but just picked my bike up and joined some of my mates in the pub. I don't remember much after that until I came to just now and thought of you." Having made the effort to communicate, he subsided wearily again.

"Why ever?" she began and stopped. There was no point in that at present. He was not simply drunk. "I'll get you some coffee and sandwiches. Then, perhaps you'll be fit to talk."

By the time the food and coffee were ready, he was asleep an the divan but she roused him mercilessly. Suddenly, he seemed to become sober. Putting down his mug and plate, he stood up comparatively steadily. "Thanks. I needed that. I'd better go now. Sorry, but I'm not fit company for anyone."

It was a great temptation to agree and to forget about him. A good excuse to be rid of him. Instead, she found herself saying, Where are you going? What are you going to do?"

"God knows," he replied with an attempt to achieve his normal manner. "No need to worry. I've got over this sort of thing before."

"What sort of thing?"

"Depression," he said savagely. "Fucking, awful depression. It hit me on Thursday. Somehow I managed the journey back without killing myself or anybody else. But when I hit the depot on Friday, I'd had it. Couldn't hack it any longer, so I decided to go on the piss. Thought it might be better than topping myself. Now, I'm not so sure. Alcohol's no cure. I just go to sleep and when I wake up it's worse." He moved towards the door. "Thanks again for the coffee and food. See you maybe."

"Don't go," Cleo said quickly. "Sit down again. You said you wanted to talk, so why don't you?"

He considered her offer for a moment and then walked back and sat upright in the armchair. "It's no use," he responded bitterly. "I'm just a fucking failure, that's all. Talking won't put that right."

"That's not true," Cleo replied swiftly. "You've got a steady job now which you say you like and you've got a chance of becoming a transport manager one day, or so you said."

He shrugged. "So bloody what? I know I won't stick it. I've tried lots of things but I've never stuck anything yet. I work hard. I seem to be doing well. Then, suddenly, I can't stand it any more. I've let everyone down, especially my family. I'm the black sheep, the only one who hasn't done well at school and college. They're all nice about it but that doesn't make me feel any better. Why should it?"

"That's not really important," she tried to encourage him, aware at the same time of her own weaknesses. "We can't all be the same."

"That's easy for you to say," he retorted, "You've got both brains and beauty. Things have been easy for you." When she did not reply, he remained silent for a moment and then said grimly. "You're quite right of course, I could make good in my own way. The trouble is it won't happen."

"Why ever not?"

"Because," he replied with a strange calm, "I keep getting this terrible urge for self destruction. I've had it on and off for years but now it's worse than ever. You can't understand."

"I think I might," Cleo said slowly. She was reluctant to move towards the brink but it seemed necessary to try to help Mike. "Just a little anyway. Just over two years ago I was seriously thinking of killing myself. Everything seemed to have gone wrong. I seemed to have nothing left to believe in or to hang on to." She paused, shrinking from the memory.

"What happened?" She had caught his attention.

"I decided to change my life completely. I chucked up everything and went to London to seek my fortune as a model. It was quite as mad as some of things you've done."

"Did you succeed, unlike me?"

"Up to a point but then like you, I ran away again and came here."

"So that wasn't much good. Why didn't you top yourself?"

"Perhaps because I was lucky enough to find someone who liked me and enjoyed having me around. Also because I'm a survivor. I want to give in but I can't."

"Lucky for you," he said sardonically. Not all of us are lucky enough to find someone who'll put up with us. I never have."

"Never?"

He shrugged. "I thought I had. I met this girl and married her when I was diving. I thought it would work. It seemed to for a while but then we had a kid, chiefly because she wanted one, although I didn't feel we could afford it. It was the biggest shock of my life when she told me she was pregnant."

"Surely you thought it might happen?"

"You're joking! I thought she was on the pill but she'd decided to have her own way, like she always did."

"So what happened?"

"I tried to make a go of it but we rowed all the time. It seemed she didn't want me now she had the kid. I was foul to her at times but when I tried it didn't seem to make any difference. It was obvious she preferred to be a single mother. She was better off that way, she reckoned, so I buggered off."

"Don't you ever see them?"

"Sometimes. I'm fond of Ben, my kid, and he seems to like me but it never works long with Tracy. I was supposed to be going there today for his birthday." He laughed. "Fine father I'd be, pissed out of my mind. Tracy'd just shut the door in my face. Can't say I'd blame her."

Cleo stared at him. Her dominant feeling was one of amazement. "Why didn't you tell me about any of this?" she demanded. "You acted as if you were completely free. I thought we were supposed to be honest with each other."

He looked coolly back at her. "And how honest were you with me? Would you really have spent a weekend with me? And, if you had done, would it have meant anything? Come off it, Cleo. You're no better than I am. I might say you're worse. At least, I still care for my kid and support him."

So much so," she retorted angrily, "that you get pissed on his birthday and come round to me for comfort. What use is that to him. He'd be better without you." She was sorry immediately she had said it, especially when Mike readily agreed.

"Too fucking right," he replied savagely. "You've said it. I'm no bloody good at anything, so why shouldn't I top myself? Everyone would be better off without me. You might miss a bit of rough sex you fancied, but nothing else. Be honest!"

"I wish you'd stop being so sorry for yourself." she answered him furiously. "You make everything sound horrible."

"That's because it is, only you like to wrap it all up in fancy words. You should look at yourself before you start preaching at me. Is there anyone you care about more than yourself? I doubt it. We're two of a kind. That's what you don't like." For a moment they glared furiously at each other, then suddenly Mike laughed. "Admit it, Cleo. I don't suppose any bloke's ever spoken to you like that before."

"I should think not," she said. "but you aren't quite right. For some ridiculous reason, I care enough about you not to want you to commit suicide. It doesn't mean much, perhaps but for what it's worth its true."

"Then give me a good reason why I shouldn't."

"I've already given you one - I wouldn't like it. But more important your family would be devastated and so would Ben."

"They'd soon get over it," he said indifferently, "Ben wouldn't even remember me after a few months and a good thing too. My parents would be happier, if they didn't have me to worry about and Tracy'd be fine. She'd have my insurance money."

"How can you be so selfish!" Cleo exclaimed. "Don't you care about anything?"

"Not much. It all seems so bloody futile when you look at it. You can take risks, get pissed, have sex, even work hard but what does it all mean in the end? Don't tell me you haven't felt like this. You must have done when you thought of topping yourself."

Cleo strove to find an adequate answer. She was sure there was one but she didn't know how to express it. All she could think at this moment was that one should never approach this abyss, one should never ask these questions for only chaos lay ahead. But that was no answer for Mike.

"Be honest," he challenged. "You know I'm right."

"No," she said firmly, "I know you're not. There is one thing that really matters and that's love. And I don't just mean sex." She remembered vividly the homeless man who had aroused her compassion, the old priest with his simple, confident message. "We have to care about one another and not just ourselves, then things seem different." It was hard trying to tell him something that she hardly understood herself.

"And why the hell should I do that?" he demanded. "You'll start preaching about God next."

"And why not?" she retorted. "You were brought up like me as a Catholic to believe that God loves you. But I suppose you'll say you don't believe in him any more?"

"Oh, I believe in him all right. I just can't stand him. If he's so good, why does he let babies and little kids die of starvation all over the world? I don't mind him making me suffer I probably deserve it but they certainly don't. And, if he can't do anything about it, what's the use of him anyway? If I ever get to heaven, I'll tell him just what I think about him. God wouldn't stop me topping myself. He'd probably think it was a good idea, anyway." He stopped and looked challengingly at her. "No, you won't convince me with God."

"You're talking nonsense," Cleo replied. "It's time we stopped blaming God and took some responsibility ourselves. If we tried to make things better, instead of being so selfish, the world might begin to improve. You might be surprised."

"I hope you're thinking of applying this to yourself?" he asked with something like his old wicked grin."

"I'm not much good at it, I admit but I have listened to you, haven't I when I might have been enjoying my Saturday evening?"

"With some other bloke, I suppose?"

"Maybe, but that's no business of yours."

"OK, since you're mad enough to waste you time with a loser like me, what does Sister Cleo suggest I do then?"

"Go home," she responded promptly. "Have a shower and a shave and take Ben a present."

"You've got a nerve. I haven't even bought the poor little bugger one."

"Well, there's still time. You've got money and there's a shop in the village that sells sweets and toys. What's to stop you?"

"Nothing except that I don't feel like doing it. I'd rather stay with you."

"You haven't got the option," she replied ruthlessly. "Just concentrate on giving Ben a real treat. If you still feel like topping yourself afterwards, I shan't stop you."

"OK. I'll do it on one condition."

"I'm not so sure about that."

"It's not much. Just that you'll agree to meet me again."

"I'm not at all sure that's wise."

"Not for sex, just for talk. What do you say?"

"All right," she agreed reluctantly, "but you'd better keep your word."

"I promise and I always keep my promises. That's one thing my Mum taught me." He moved to the door. "I'm off now. See you."

Cleo sat down abruptly as soon as he had gone. She felt exhausted but she had somehow pulled him out of his suicidal mood. Then, slowly as she thought over the conversation, she realised what else she had done. She had tied herself more closely to Mike instead of extricating herself as she had intended. Yet, what else could she have done? He needed help and as a fellow human being she had been obliged to give it to him. She had left London, disgusted with the sudden realisation of her totally selfish life. She had only been trying to live according to that vision. Surely, it was right to help people?

She wondered what Merlin would say if she asked him. She had always regarded him as being both kind and rational and his second doctorate, when he had extended his studies in the States, had been in moral philosophy.

Suddenly she realised how much she was looking forward to spending the next day with him and how much his newly offered friendship comforted her. She must not do anything to risk spoiling it for it was necessary to have someone to rely on. It would be sufficient to ask his help with her more important problems. That resolved, she settled down to work.

Chapter Thirteen

It was late the following afternoon when Cleo realised that she had not mentioned any of her problems to Merlin. Over lunch he had been in a lively and entertaining mood and she had been happy to relax with him. Since then they had been driving and walking.

Now, at last, they were standing on the summit of the steep hill he had chosen for their walk. The path had been long and difficult at times and, although they had scarcely spoken she had been glad of his companionship and occasionally of his help. He seemed totally dependable as he stood beside her in his heavy jacket and jeans. They were looking towards the horizon where the sun, a bubble of fire was poised. The hills and the bare skeletons of trees were black and sombre but the winter sky was a delicate turquoise tinged with faintest gold. It was beautiful but, even as they looked, it was changing. The colour in the sky was fading, the air was colder and the wind was becoming stronger.

"We'd better not linger here much longer," he remarked, "It'll soon be dark and cold."

Cleo sighed. "You're right but I wish you weren't. Good moments begin to vanish as soon as one realises they are good." She looked sadly at him. "But, perhaps, the truth is that they never really are good anyway. It's just an illusion."

"It seems you are more depressed than I thought. Is there any particular reason?" He sat down on a large flat rock and made room for her to sit beside him.

"I had an extra lesson with Victoria this morning before church," was her surprising answer.

"I'm sorry that made you depressed. I hope that's not my niece's usual effect on you?"

"Of course not. It was just the discussion we had."

"Which was?"

"It was based on Trollope's novel, 'He Knew He Was Right'. Do you remember it?

"Vaguely. But remind me."

"Victoria is doing a project on the Victorian heroine and I suggested that she looked at Trollope's later novels for a slightly different point of view on the gender issue. They are relevant."

"I'm sure you're right but what has that to do with your present depression?"

"Well, there is a character in it called Priscilla Stanway and she is discussing the relationship between men and women with Nora Rowley who later marries her brother."

He looked puzzled.

"Priscilla says to Nora 'there are two things a man can't do; they can't suckle babies and they can't forget themselves."

She paused and when she didn't continue he remarked with a certain irony, "I would agree with the first proposition but I'm very doubtful about the second with its feminist undertones. I think it would be truer to say that it's a failing of human beings in general. Don't most of us find it difficult to forget ourselves? But perhaps you and Victoria were making a familiar case for the 'martyred' woman, sacrificing herself for her indifferent husband and family?"

"We did consider that," she admitted. "but we soon realised that our own mothers gave the lie to that illusion. Mine certainly did, as you know. No, it was the wider view which depressed me, the one you have suggested. How easy it is to deceive oneself that one is being altruistic when one isn't really being so at all."

"Well, as you know, many moral philosophers argue that pure altruism is impossible. I don't wholeheartedly agree but I admit that it is rare. But have you some particular situation in mind or is this just an abstract exercise? Or is it perhaps a devious attack on me? Are you still wondering whether you are wise to trust in an offer of friendship from me? Or are you worrying whether it's an attempt to get you to bed again after lulling your suspicions?"

She looked at him seriously and then smiled. "Why should you take so much trouble when you don't need to? No, I was really applying it to myself and feeling very doubtful of my own good intentions in almost everything I do." She paused, wanting to tell him about Mike and the complexity of her relationship with him but hesitating because of the effect such a confidence might have.

After waiting for a moment for her to continue, Merlin stood up. "I don't think you need to worry," he said pleasantly. "I expect your motives are mixed like mine and most peoples' but I'm equally sure they are predominantly loving, which is not so common." He reached out his hand to help her up and then continued before she could reply, "but I think we had better decide to get down the hill before we talk any more. Darkness is approaching."

"Do you mean that I should come down from my lofty heights and concentrate more on the practical details of life?" she asked with a smile as she began to follow him down. In her eagerness to keep up with him she hurried too much and began to slip.

"Exactly," he replied, as he caught her arm and steadied her "I'm afraid you'll just have to trust me at present. I know the path well."

"That's what worries me," she said and laughed. He did not reply but merely tightened his hold on her arm.

By the time they reached the road it had become quite dark and was very chilly. She shivered suddenly. "Everything's changed," she said mournfully.

"That's the illusion," he replied. "Nothing important has really changed. You'll be cheerful again once we reach the comfort of my home. There's a good fire and a casserole awaiting us."

"A casserole? You are domesticated these days!"

"Not really. My daily woman, Mrs Parry, advised me on that. I've always been good at getting advice."

"And help too."

"True. But nowadays, I do it myself. I'm the new independent male." He looked at his watch. "The meal will be cooked in about fifteen minutes. We should hurry. The car's not far away."

"Is your new home like the old one in Oxford?" she asked him as they drove back.

"Yes, but larger and more solid."

As soon as she saw it, she liked it. It was built of grey stone and had a slate roof and stood at the end of the village in a large garden with trees and hills behind. It was still clearly visible in the gathering dark, especially as Merlin had left several welcoming lights switched on.

"It's like a child's idea of a home!" she exclaimed. The sort you draw when you're about five - big and square and solid, a real home with three windows on the top floor and two and a porch below. I love it."

He smiled, obviously pleased with her enthusiasm. "Come inside and look round. But don't expect perfection. I only moved here last August from Oxford and there's still a lot of renovating and furnishing to do. He opened the front door and they entered a long, wide hall with a broad staircase and several doors opening off it. He pointed to the first doors on the left and right. "Those are the dining room and the lounge, as the estate agents say, but they are practically untouched, so we won't bother with them. Although I'll be glad to have your suggestions some time."

She followed him down the hall until he opened the last door on the right and switched on the light. "My study," he announced, "a mixture of ancient and modern with my antique walnut desk and my computer table and accessories and, of course, my books."

"I see you have a comfortable couch and two armchairs as well," she remarked as she walked across the room "and a door into the garden. Must be very pleasant in the summer. I'm envious."

He took her arm. "It's time I led you to the food," he suggested.

Leading her out of the study he opened the door opposite. As he did so a delicious aroma wafted out into the hall. "This is the living room," he explained, "once the kitchen, until the present, much larger one was added about forty years ago." He switched on the lights and drew the curtains.

It was a bright and cheerful room, dominated by the large Aga which threw out a comforting warmth and from which came the tempting smell of cooking food. The armchairs, the curtains and the cushions were basically a deep green with touches of gold and crimson. The table, chairs and dresser were solid country oak. There was a bowl of daffodils on the dresser, a welcome reminder of the approach of spring. Cleo delighted in it, for it seemed to embody her romantic ideas of the home which she had never enjoyed.

It also surprised her by its air of permanence and solidity. As she took off her jacket and sat down at the table, already laid for two, she watched Merlin as he took the dish out of the oven. He has changed, she thought. But why and in what ways? His Oxford home had always given her a disturbing feeling of transience, which his decision to move on to the States had justified, but this was different. It gave her the feeling that he had come to terms with life in a way which she did not yet understand. Not wanting to think about it at the moment, she turned her attention to the food.

"I'm ravenous!" she exclaimed.

“I’m pretty hungry myself,” he admitted, “so shall we postpone all serious discussion until after we’ve eaten?”

“It would be ungrateful not to,” she agreed.

It was over an hour later when they finally relaxed with cups of coffee in the two very commodious armchairs. Curled up comfortably, Cleo was not anxious to disturb the companionable silence. She simply wanted to relax and pretend that no contentious issues existed. After a few minutes, however, it became clear that this was not Merlin’s desire.

“I see you are comfortable,” he remarked with a familiar touch of irony. “Well exercised, well fed and warm. Your intention, I imagine, if you have anything as firm as that, is to chat with me about entertaining trifles for a time and then announce you must return to St. Elizabeth’s as you have some necessary preparation to do before tomorrow. Am I right?” He looked at her with the slightly mocking smile she remembered so well.

She was cross at having her complacency disturbed but being forced to think about it she could not really deny the truth of what he said. “Of course I have some work to do,” she replied defensively.

He laughed. “So have I, whenever I want to. It’s a very convenient excuse. But I don’t intend to let you get away with it.”

“What do you mean?” She straightened herself up and looked at him with the full power of her beautiful green eyes, curving her lips into a seductive smile. She was aware of the strength of her attraction.

He smiled back at her but did not waver. “May I remind you that we agreed to be friends? I’m quite capable still of appreciating your considerable charm but it’s irrelevant at the moment. You talked some amazing nonsense on the hill and I’m still wondering what is really troubling you.”

"It wasn't nonsense," she protested.

"No? Am I to believe then that you are really depressed about the somewhat outmoded feminist ideas you expressed which rapidly changed into a mistrustful view of human nature in general. Or was it all, as I suggested, just a devious way of expressing your mistrust of me and my motives?"

"Of course not," she replied quickly but before she could think how to continue, he interrupted her.

"I'm glad to hear it. Then perhaps you will tell me the real reason why you are so depressed and disturbed? Why your mood has changed so much from last Sunday?" He sat and waited.

"I don't see why it should surprise you," she replied finally. "I've always been moody and insecure. I often think my father's right. I'm destructive. Like my mother. I can talk about it quite rationally but it won't make any difference. You know that."

"I'm not sure that I do but I am certain that you're disturbed about something that you're reluctant to talk about."

Cleo leaned back and then, after a brief moment for decision, she began to tell him about her encounter with Mike. She had first of all to remind him of his meeting with Mike but, after that, he listened without interrupting her.

When she had finished he was unnervingly silent. "You think I've been very foolish?" she asked.

"More unkind than foolish. You should not have encouraged him to think that you could ever be seriously interested in him. You don't solve his problems by adding another one to them. You're far too intelligent not to be aware of that." His tone was cold and she realised that he was angry.

"But he needs help. How can I turn him away?"

"How many times have you made that your excuse? I thought you had decided to change your life?"

She was now angry. "You of all people have no right to say that. You deserted me remember?"

"That's never been entirely true. You were very young. I was eleven years older. I hoped you would be patient and trust me but you were unwilling because you thought it would be more romantic, if I wrecked my future for you. You were afraid perhaps of yourself as much as of me."

"But I loved you," she declared miserably. "I was so frightened of being without you. But I don't suppose you can ever understand."

"I think I can now," he said in a gentler tone. "But when I came back, you encouraged me and then deserted me and that might have been the end, if fate hadn't thrown us together again."

"I still loved you," she replied trying to speak calmly, "but I was ashamed of the way I'd behaved since you left and most of all of that stupid engagement which I'd sworn would make a fresh start but which I disregarded as soon as I met you again. I persuaded myself I was being manipulated by you once more. As I told you and at the same time I felt ashamed of myself and utterly worthless because I couldn't keep to any decision."

"I didn't think you were. I was angry but I would have found you and insisted on some truth, had it not been for my accident."

"Oh, how I wish you had; then I wouldn't have wasted two years in London, pretending I was helping Marcus in return for a certain security he offered me."

"But then you made a change and decided to start afresh?'

"I'm not sure that it's true to say I made a decision. It was more a gesture based on a sudden revulsion of feeling." She looked at him again but without any attempt to charm. "I want to be honest," she continued, "I might've gone back to him, if I hadn't met you again. In fact. I did go back and then I realised how meretricious it all was. I felt that I had been used or even abused by many men."

"Including me?"

She frowned, trying to find the truthful answer. "When you left me to go to the States, yes, but before then, no. But most definitely when you came back and tempted me to resume our relationship."

"Shouldn't you avoid me now?"

"You have changed. I wasn't sure at first but now I am. Everything confirms it - this house, your move from Oxford, your very different attitude towards me. I'm right, aren't I?"

"Yes," he agreed but seemed disinclined to say more.

"Tell me about it, please. I want to know. I want to understand. If you truly want us to be friends, you must tell me. I care very much, because you're the first person, perhaps the only person, I've ever felt really close to."

"You're right," he answered slowly, "I should try to explain more to you. but, perhaps, I should begin by admitting that you're the only person I've ever wanted to be close to, either before or since I met you. My relationships with other women have had little more than a physical basis. That seemed best to me. I preferred my independence. And you're absolutely right, I suppose, to suspect that it was for that reason that I left you in the way I did, not wanting to end it but not wanting to make any commitment. It was selfish. I didn't see it then but I do now. I was equally wrong when I came back two years later. I should have explained but I wasn't accustomed to that. I'm sorry." He stopped as if unsure how to proceed.

"But you *have* changed," she insisted.

"I think so. It would have been surprising if I hadn't. For several months, after I had recovered from the first shock of my accident, I faced the possibility that life might be completely changed that I might never walk again. For the first time I realised how alone I was and I saw my life in a completely different way and realised that in many important ways I had failed."

"But you have a most successful academic career," she protested. "And now you've added literary success with your novel. You can't possibly think of yourself as a failure."

He smiled warmly at her. "Thank you for wanting to console me. It's what I would expect. In spite of you own unhappiness, I believe you're always longing to put things right for everybody. I would have welcomed that when I was in hospital. During the long painful, unpleasant nights, I realised for the first time how alone I was and that you were the only person I would have welcomed."

"I wish I had been there," she said fervently.

"Perhaps, it was better that you weren't. I needed to learn a hard lesson and you might've protected me too much."

She stared at him in amazement. "I never imagined myself protecting you," she exclaimed. You always seemed so strong. I have always been the weak one."

"You're not really weak. You've survived too many disasters for that to be true. Whereas I, until my accident, had an incredibly easy life. I've never been short of money. I had loving, united parents who encouraged me when they realised I was gifted academically, even though that was not the career they would have chosen. I obtained a scholarship to one of the best Public Schools and from there to Oxford. And the rest you pretty well know."

"When I arrived in Oxford, I soon learned that you were considered a brilliant lecturer and that half the women were in love with you, although you were more or less indifferent. The most amazing thing to me was that you noticed me. Of course I was lucky to be introduced to you by a junior lecturer who was an old girl of my school."

"I was interested because you were not only unusually beautiful but also very gifted."

"And that was all," she said sadly.

"Don't be ridiculous, Cleo. You know it wasn't," he retorted swiftly. "I didn't intend it to be different but very soon it was. But I was still ambitious and selfish. I didn't want to lose you but neither did I want to commit myself nor change my plans. I'd not anticipated your reaction but that only shows how insensitive I was. That's why I say now I needed the hard lesson I had."

"I've been pretty insensitive too," she interrupted as he paused. "Since we've met again, I've not given much thought to you, I've been much too preoccupied with my problems. But tell me what you meant about failure."

"That's quite simple. I suddenly perceived that my life was an empty shell. I understood clearly for the first time that life without love is meaningless. I mean love in a very wide sense. Fortunately an old school and college friend unexpectedly turned up. We were far apart, you might think, because he had became a Jesuit. He didn't attempt to convert me but we talked seriously about the things that now worried me. He didn't give me the evasive consolations that most people went in for but instead encouraged me to face my problems and fears. As a result I had the courage to accept a second operation which succeeded where the first had failed and the will to struggle back to active life." He stood up and walked towards the table. "You've been a most patient listener but I think it's time I rewarded you with a second cup of coffee. That is, if you would like one?"

She accepted that, but as he sat down again, she said quickly, "But that wasn't the whole story, was it? You still felt that you had failed and that your life had to be changed. Am I right?"

"Absolutely. I still had to discover what was truly important, at least to me."

"I know what you mean," she said eagerly. "I suddenly had that feeling in London when I encountered the homeless man. At supper afterwards I saw my life as empty, frivolous and loveless. I had to leave. The only difference is you've achieved so much, while I'm still searching. You've written the novel you were always going to write, you seem to find your work much more satisfying though you haven't told me much about it. What are you trying to do?"

"I'm trying to persuade students, some of them from quite poor backgrounds that knowledge for its own sake is worthwhile and that the acquiring of it actually helps them to live more interesting and satisfactory lives."

"You're a rebel then against the accepted beliefs of today."

"So many people have told me."

"Wouldn't it have been easier to have tried your experiment in Oxford?"

"Possibly but not as exciting. In any case my encouragement came from the Vice Chancellor of Wheaten and a millionaire friend of his."

"And what about the students? Do they appreciate what you're trying to do."

"They are very enthusiastic. Some of them make me feel humble. Their lives have often been very poor and narrow but, given the chance, they're prepared to seek wisdom for wisdom's sake and forget commercial considerations for the time being at least. Many will go far, I think, as human beings."

"I envy you. I would love to be involved in something like that. You really care about what you're doing and the people you're doing it with. That's what I want."

"You can have it, Cleo, if you decide for it." He put down his cup. "Well I've given a brief summary of my life from my accident until I met you again."

"And since then?"

He smiled at her. "Since then my personal life has been richer, although more unpredictable. One other discovery I made, you see, during my illness was your importance to me. I very much wanted to put matters right but I didn't think I would have the opportunity."

"But aren't you disappointed to find how restless and unsettled I still am. I don't think I'm capable of being a good friend to you, although I want to be. I'm still too impulsive. My involvement with Mike shows that."

"It shows a lot of other things," he replied. Putting down his cup, he stood up and walked towards her, then stopped and sat down on one of the dining chairs which was close to her. "Do you trust me now?" he asked.

She looked up at him steadily. "Oh yes." She stopped and then continued quickly as if afraid she might not say it, if she considered further. "I need your help, Merlin. Nothing seems clear. In some ways it's worse than it's ever been. It's not just getting mixed up with Mike, it's everything. I'm nearly twenty five and I haven't a clue about my future. Jane would try to help, I'm sure but she's expecting a baby at last and Robert rather resents me anyway, so that leaves you with the unenviable position of Cleo's adviser." She tried to smile as she waited for his response. When it came, it was totally unexpected.

"What would you say," he asked calmly, "if I asked you to marry me?"

Completely amazed, she stared at him. "Whatever would you expect me to say?"

He laughed. "There are lots of things you could say, such as 'yes' or 'no' or 'maybe'"

"Since it's only a hypothetical question I don't have to answer it, do I?"

"I would like you to try. It wasn't meant to be hypothetical, just exploratory. If you hated the idea then we needn't pursue it and our friendship would be unaffected."

She frowned slightly as she considered his words. "I think I understand," she said finally. "But I don't know why you've asked me. You haven't shown any particular signs of being in love with me. Only last week you said you didn't want to be my lover."

"I don't. I want to be your husband."

"You don't have to ask me to marry you because you're sorry for me. That's carrying friendship a bit too far."

He leaned forward and took her hand. "You're a most exasperating person!" he exclaimed. "You seem to have no idea of how attractive you are. I could enjoy making love to you at any time. That's not the problem. I made that mistake when I came back from the States two and a half years ago and I realised when you left me, I should have told you instead that I loved you and wanted to spend my life with you. We've both come to understand, I think, that life without love is empty and that love can last, quite independently of sexual feelings. In the last few weeks I've realised that my love for you is stronger than ever. Will you answer me now?"

She allowed her hand to stay in his. "Oh, Merlin," she said quietly at last, "I do want to say. 'yes' but I'm frightened. I don't think that even you know exactly what I'm like. How I changed after you left. Since then, I haven't been faithful to anyone for long, not even Marcus at times. When I came to St. Elizabeth's I decided to change all that but I'm not being very successful am I?"

"Why do you say that?"

"Because of Mike," she admitted. "I don't just want to help him because I feel sorry for him. He attracts me physically and I've encouraged him. And what's worse I didn't intend you to know but it's got out of hand. I'm sorry."

He smiled cheerfully. "Don't look so tragic. I know about sex and I certainly know how susceptible you are. I'm just conceited enough to think that if we were together, all that would soon cease to matter to you."

"Perhaps you're right," she agreed, smiling affectionately at him. "I certainly don't want to lose you."

"You're in no danger of that." He leant over and kissed her very gently. "There's no need for you to make a final decision now. I think we should continue as we are and that you should have time to get used to the idea of permanence. But I warn you that I don't intend to cloud your judgement by making love to you. A serious matter should be decided with proper thought. I am prepared to trust you and you must trust me."

"That means no Mike or anyone else?"

"That must be your decision. I have made mine."

"I will try."

"Good." He stood up. "It really is time I took you back."

She looked at her watch. "I'm afraid it is. I really do have work to do before tomorrow. I wish I hadn't."

"Don't worry. I'll collect you on Wednesday at seven for supper in Markhampton."

"I shall look forward to it."

The journey back to St. Elizabeth's seemed all too short. Merlin was obviously pleased and Cleo felt happy and relaxed. She hadn't told him of her immediate problems but she knew now that he would be there to help. She no longer felt alone. As he stopped the car in the empty village green he kissed her warmly. "Don't work too hard," he warned her, "and don't get depressed."

She returned his kiss naturally. "I won't," she replied. "I'll look forward to Wednesday." He waited until she had reached the front door and then he drove swiftly away.

Chapter Fourteen

"You've been looking very pleased with yourself today," Cynthia accosted Cleo as they came out of supper on the Monday evening. "Have you won the lottery or something?"

"Hardly. Since I never enter it." She smiled back at Cynthia who was herself looking very cheerful after a pleasant weekend with her future husband and his family. "I had a good day yesterday, that's all."

"With the distinguished Professor Evans, if rumour is right."

"Oh, no," Cleo groaned. "I suppose that's Stella, since she saw me meet him? Nothing is private in this place."

"Right on both counts. It was Stella and nothing is private. A little gossip brightens up our dreary lives." Cynthia spoke mockingly and then added in a different tone, "Have you got time to have coffee with me? I brought one of mother's best cakes back with me."

"How can I resist that? I'm always hungry in this place. But I can't stay long. I've a set of marking I must do."

"Same here, so don't worry." Cynthia did not say any more as she led the way to her spacious and comfortable room, where she quickly busied herself preparing coffee in the cafetiére and putting out the cups. Cleo curled up in an armchair received her coffee gratefully, together with a large slice of home made chocolate cake. "Mothers are very helpful, aren't they?" Cynthia remarked.

"I wouldn't know," Cleo replied swiftly. "Mine left when I was twelve which wasn't exactly helpful. But from what you've told me, yours must be a great support."

"She is. That's why I'm glad that she approves of my marrying Francis, although my younger sister thinks I'm mad to take on a family and my father tends to question my capabilities. But then, fathers are like that, aren't they?"

"I suppose so," Cleo replied, "but again I haven't much experience. My father has as little as possible to do with my sister and me, especially since he's married again." She found it possible to talk quite easily about her situation, now that she felt happy and secure in Merlin's affection.

"You've had a rough time then," Cynthia said sympathetically. "I don't think I could have managed without my family at times. I suppose you find it difficult to believe in happy marriage."

"I very much want to," Cleo replied truthfully. "I think it's stupid to be cynical."

"Then you'd better not speak to Betty Anderson, Stuart's housemistress."

"Why what does she say? Is she married?"

"Divorced. When I told her I was getting married, she was quite sorry for me. She said I was better off as I was. Marriage, she said is ideal for men. They get some misguided woman to cook their meals, wash their clothes, etc. with sex laid on whenever they feel like it. She said she preferred to be on her own and to retire to bed with a good book and a bar of chocolate. She considers sex a grossly overrated pastime, especially after thirty. So there you are."

Cleo laughed. "What did you say?"

"I said she might be right but I preferred to make my own experiment, since it might depend on the people involved."

"I don't suppose that pleased her."

"It didn't bother her. She simply thought it showed my woeful ignorance of life. She might be right, of course. I haven't had much experience. Not like you, of course."

Cleo paused before taking another bit of chocolate cake. "And what is that supposed to mean?"

"I don't imagine that you've ever been short of men friends from what I can tell. You certainly don't seem to be at the moment. It's not surprising, of course. You're very attractive."

Cynthia looked admiringly at Cleo. "I don't blame you for having fun but it seems to make some people jealous."

"What are people saying? I'd rather know."

"We all thought, at first, that you had a steady relationship with someone in London who came down to Markhampton and whom you were spending half term with."

"I told you something about that," Cleo interposed swiftly. "It was pretty well finished when I came here and finally finished at half term. Do I have to make an announcement?" She was angry. "But I thought you, at least, were friendly."

"I am," Cynthia said firmly. "and I'm not involved in any of the gossip but things are discussed in my presence. Pam reports that she delivered a very disreputable but attractive young man to your room on Saturday evening and then Stella sees you going off with Merlin Evans on Sunday. She also hints that you've been doing your best to ensnare Nicholas as a side line."

"That's ridiculous! All I did was have coffee with Nicholas after lunch the other day. What's wrong with that? True. he was supposed to be meeting Stella but I didn't know that. Mike who's a friend of mine did turn up rather drunk but I sobered him up and sent him off to his wife and son. I didn't really think Pam would talk about it."

"She meant no great harm," Cynthia said quickly. "She thought it was strange. She likes a bit of excitement, that's all. Lots of people do. It's Stella who makes much of it. I think she must be scared she might lose her hold on Nicholas. And with good reason, perhaps."

"All the same I wish she would leave Merlin out of it. He's a very good friend and I wouldn't want Victoria to be upset by gossip. She's had enough to contend with. It seems to me that someone in Stella's position should keep quiet. I haven't talked about her but I'm sure some of the girls do. What do you think?"

"I'm sure they do." Cynthia agreed. "Many of the Sixth Form can hardly fail to see her bringing Nicholas back to her room or to see his car there in the small hours."

"Do you think Miss Stephens knows?"

Cynthia shrugged. "I wouldn't know but I have a suspicion that she is aware of most things that go on."

"Then why doesn't she say something? They're not exactly setting a good example."

"Nicholas," replied Cynthia with some cynicism, "is an excellent, though conceited Science teacher and Stella is that rare object a well qualified Maths teacher. If the parents were to complain, however, it would be quite different. That really affects the school. Oh dear," she exclaimed, "it's catching. I'm just as bad as everyone. And I only meant to wise you up." She looked very distressed.

"Don't worry," Cleo reassured her. "I won't repeat a word and I am grateful to you for helping me to find my way around. I seem to be amazingly innocent. Actually, I've decided to be a good girl from now on, so I should be all right."

"Would that have anything to do with Merlin?" Cynthia asked with a slightly mischievous smile.

"Perhaps." Cleo did not intend to confide any more even in Cynthia.

Apparently understanding and respecting this, Cynthia adroitly changed the subject and for the rest of the time they discussed less personal topics.

For the next two days Cleo worked hard and avoided everyone, except for Bridget and Miss Wilson who in different ways were both refreshingly detached. On the Wednesday evening, Merlin collected her at seven o'clock and they drove to Markhampton. Although he said very little Cleo felt happily that he was as pleased to see her as she was to see him. As they approached the town, he said, "I hope you won't object but I thought we would eat in the hotel. It's quieter and I thought it would be pleasant to sit and talk in the lounge afterwards." He smiled at her. "The food, however, probably won't be so good as in the Italian restaurant."

"I don't only care about food." Cleo retorted. "I enjoy conversation even more, although I am half starved at St. Elizabeth's, the gravity of which you don't seem to appreciate."

"I did my best for you on Sunday." he protested, as they walked into the hotel foyer.

"I certainly have no complaints. The food and the conversation were both excellent." He took her arm and she smiled, relieved to realise that nothing had changed since Sunday. As they walked into the restaurant to the table reserved for them, she had a fleeting memory of having come here with Marcus. But all that now seemed remote and unreal, almost as if it had happened to someone else.

When they had ordered after some discussion, she said almost without thinking, "Apparently our meetings have been observed. We are the subject of gossip, I'm afraid."

He only looked amused. "I am aware of that."

"How can you be?"

"You've forgotten Victoria. She rang me up last night, ostensibly to report on her progress but also to ask me if I would mind taking her shopping in Markhampton next Saturday. When I demurred on the grounds of unsuitability, she suggested that I should invite you to come with us, because you would be helpful to her and I wouldn't then be bored."

"She's outrageous. One simply can't have a private life at that place. Were you cross with her?"

He laughed. "Why should I be? It's quite flattering that I can still be seen as a romantic hero, worthy of the fascinating Miss

Lafay. No, I simply laughed and told her not to let her imagination run away with her."

"What did you say about Saturday?"

"I said I would, provided you agreed, otherwise she would have to wait until the holidays which are only a fortnight off."

"I'm surprised she hasn't put pressure on me."

"I'm sure she will. Now at least you are prepared."

"I surrender. I can't deprive her of such an innocent treat, nor can I condemn her to going alone with you. You'd probably be devastatingly critical."

"You must admit," he protested. "she dresses very badly."

"I won't deny that but all she needs is friendly help."

"And who better than you to give it? You can do a double good deed. Help Victoria and save me from a boring afternoon in dress shops. Surely you won't turn that opportunity down?"

"I feel very suspicious of you but I'll come."

The meal passed pleasantly and it was not until they were settled in the quiet, almost empty lounge with their coffee that Merlin spoke more seriously. He was lying back comfortably in his armchair with his long legs stretched out, apparently content not to speak. Looking at him closely, it seemed to Cleo that he looked rather weary and that he had mentioned in passing during the meal that his back had been painful recently, an unfortunate legacy of his accident. He had dismissed it lightly but she wondered now if it was not more troublesome than he wanted to admit. "You term ends in two weeks' time, doesn't it?" she asked, "just a few days before mine. I expect you'll be glad. I know I shall. It'll be lovely to have free time, won't it?" She thought happily that he would suggest some way in which they could meet.

To her surprise, he sat up and said calmly, "Unfortunately, I shan't have any free time."

She stared at him. "Why ever not? You have at least a month's vacation, haven't you? I suppose you'll have to do some work but not all the time surely? I hoped we might have more time to meet."

He put down his coffee cup carefully. "I was going to tell you tonight," he said. "I'm going to South America, San Salvador in fact, for about five weeks. It was arranged some months ago."

She was glad that he didn't look at her. She didn't want him to see the pain and disappointment she felt. With an effort, she managed to speak quite calmly. "I see. It seems a strange place to go for a holiday. Isn't it rather dangerous?"

"I believe it can be, if you move in the wrong circles. I'm not going just for a holiday. I'm going to help with an educational project out there." He turned at last to look at her.

"You haven't really changed, have you," she said bitterly. "Four and a half years ago you had to go to the States. Now it's South America. You know I must be stupid. I actually believed you on Sunday. I thought you'd changed."

"I meant every word I said, Cleo. I love you and I want you to marry me."

"Do you really think you'll find time for it between your various assignments?" she asked coldly. "I thought we might have time to get to know one another better but you don't seem to think that matters." She did not tell him how much she had already come to depend on him, for that was obviously something he hadn't considered and probably didn't want. She had been foolish once more, that was all.

"Cleo," he replied swiftly, "please don't say any more. I am very sorry that I have to go away at this time but it was arranged months ago when I had no idea that I would ever meet you again. I can't back out now. Surely, you can understand that?"

In spite of his appeal to her, Cleo was at first reluctant to yield. "Of course," she said finally, "since it must be important to your new career, you must obviously do it. It's childish of me to object, under the circumstances."

"It is connected with education and may have some influence on a book I plan to write but it's primarily a personal obligation. I made a promise to a friend. He has helped me considerably and in return I want to help him. Would you want me to break that promise?"

"No, I believe that promises should be kept, if possible. I'm disappointed. that's all. It seems as if there is always going to be something that comes between us. Honestly, Merlin, I'm not sure that you really have room for someone like me in your life. It would be better not to pretend, wouldn't it?" She tried to keep all bitterness out of her voice. She knew she needed a lot and it was hardly Merlin's fault, if he couldn't provide it. "Perhaps it was a mistake to make me feel differently, although I don't think you meant to be unkind. I want someone I can love a lot and who will love me in the same way. I want there to be a mutual support and dependence. I know now nothing else will satisfy me or keep me faithful."

"Are you saying then that you are rejecting me because I am going to keep my promise?"

Cleo hesitated. "That's not fair," she objected finally. "I wouldn't ask you to break your promise to a friend. It's just that it seems to leave me nowhere. Will you ever be free to be there, when I need you?"

"And you need me now?"

"Yes, in the holidays, that is. I hoped. Oh, what does it matter? I had no right to hope anyway."

"It matters to me," he said firmly. "It seems there are things you haven't told me either. We need to talk."

In spite of his firmness, he sounded unusually weary. For the first time she looked at him properly and saw that he looked pale and taut, as if he were making a great effort. She was surprised by the strange feeling that swept over her, it was a mixture of tenderness and compassion. She could not remember ever feeling like that about any man and certainly not about Merlin. Suddenly it occurred to her he might be vulnerable too, that he could suffer. "I agree we do need to talk but not now."

"Why not now?" he asked quickly. "Does that mean that you're still annoyed?"

"No, it means that I think you're more tired than you're prepared to admit and that your back is more painful than you have told me. Am I right?"

He hesitated for a moment, then admitted reluctantly, "I'm afraid you are. An unusually prolonged and severe bout of pain kept me awake most of last night."

"Does it often happen?"

"Not often but it's liable to on occasion. They warned me about that when I finally left hospital."

"And what are you supposed to do?"

"Take some strong painkillers and rest. But that's not always possible."

"It's possible now and you must do it, Merlin," she urged him. "It's already quite late."

"You haven't any need to feel sorry for me." he protested. "I'm very fit most of the time."

"It's not called feeling sorry," she said, "it's called caring. You cared for me once when I was ill, in Oxford so why shouldn't I care about you? We can have a much better talk on Saturday."

"With Victoria as umpire? I suppose?" She was pleased to see that he was smiling.

"Don't be awkward. We return Victoria at six thirty and then we talk. Everything will keep till then."

"And you won't disappear again before Saturday?"

"I promise. We'll go back to your house and I'll cook the meal this time. Then we talk and you can tell me more about your visit to San Salvador and I'll try to understand. Please forgive me for being unpleasant earlier. I'll try to be more patient."

"And I'll try to be more understanding, You should have told me more."

"I meant to but there has been so much to say." She stood up. "I want you to let me get in a taxi, so that you can drive straight home, without going to Barton Leas first." As he stood up obviously about to protest, she continued, "No objections allowed. I've decided." She took her purse out, "I'm afraid, however you'll have to pay for the taxi, as I haven't any money. That rather ruins my independent gesture, doesn't it?"

He laughed and took her arm. "I surrender and I love you very very much." She felt very close to him as they walked towards the exit and pleased that for once she had acted unselfishly.

He kissed her tenderly as he put her into the taxi. "I'll collect you and Victoria at twelve thirty on Saturday," he promised.

On her solitary journey back to St. Elizabeth's, Cleo felt confused. She was still very upset at the thought of Merlin's prolonged absence and still, she had to admit, resentful. It was unreasonable of her because he had obviously arranged it before they had met again and she could not reasonably expect him to alter such plans. It was not simply that he was ambitious but simply that she doubted whether there could be enough space for her. Some women might be happy with that kind of relationship but she knew that she never could be. She needed much more. Yet she had yielded suddenly not because she was being rational but because she had felt this unexpected tenderness for him. Having found him again, she was, she realised, unwilling to contemplate a life without him. All of which seemed confusing and irrational. As the taxi arrived at St. Elizabeth's she decided to think no more until they had talked again on the Saturday.

As she entered the badly lit hall of the Staff House, she was aware of people chatting in the sitting room but she did not feel tempted to join them. Instead, she walked over to her pigeon hole with the hope, unlikely though it was, that there might be a letter for her. To her surprise there was a letter which had been delivered by hand.

Opening it up she looked quickly to the end to discover to her further surprise that the writer was Mike. She went quickly up to her own room before she read it, not wanting to be interrupted.

'Dear Cleo,' he wrote. 'This is my attempt to say sorry for last Saturday. I can't remember much that happened at the beginning but I'm sure I was way beyond the mark. So, sorry. I did see Ben and take him a present. The silly little bugger was pleased, though I don't think Tracey was. Can't say that bothered me much. Thanks anyway for listening to me and sending me off less pissed than when I came.'

'I wouldn't blame you if you didn't want to see me again but I hope you do. You have a good effect on me. I've never said that to anyone before because it's never been true. I usually have a bad effect on them, instead. You're different.'

'If you are willing to risk seeing me again, ring me, if possible tonight. I'm sober and not depressed, I promise you. See you, I hope. Mike.'

She hesitated, read it through again but still could not decide what to do. Merlin had told her that it was foolish and unkind of her to encourage Mike. She had thought he was probably right. But was he? Perhaps, he felt threatened by Mike. And perhaps he was. She remembered her confession to him of Mike's attraction for her. Was she unwise to trust herself? Yet, there was a plea in Mike's letter which she found hard to ignore. Different though they were, they had much in common.

She didn't stop to think further. She had an obligation to Mike, just as Merlin had to his unknown friend, she told herself. She resented her dependence which Merlin seemed to be unable to understand. Running down the stairs to the telephone, she hastily dialled the number given at the end of the letter.

To her relief, Mike answered the phone, sounding pleased and sober. Their conversation was brief. He made no more apologies but suggested quickly, if she was willing, that they should meet that weekend. "I promise to behave myself," he said. "I just want to talk. You're the first girl I've ever been able to talk to. The sort I meet usually think that's a waste of time. But you're different. What do you say?"

She told him it would have to be Sunday. To her surprise he sounded a little reluctant but, when she pressed him, he admitted the reason. He planned to see his elder sister. "She's got husband trouble and needs a bit of support, so I promised to see her on Sunday afternoon. Christ knows why she should think I can help but she does. Still I can put her off and go over one evening. I don't suppose it'll make much difference."

"You certainly mustn't!" Cleo exclaimed, rather shocked at his indifference.

"Tell you what," he replied, "why don't you come with me? It might do you good to see a bit of real life, to see how the poor live. Claire's a single parent with four kids living on benefit. I bet your rich London friends have all the answers. Would you care to see what it's really like?"

Cleo remembered the revulsion she had felt just before she left London. She had excused herself for her flight by saying she wanted to widen her horizons by meeting those who were marginalised, whose lives were so different to her own. She hadn't achieved much of that by coming to St. Elizabeth's. Perhaps this was her opportunity. "All right, I'll come," she said quickly, refusing to allow herself time for further thought. This should also be a safer way of being with Mike.

He did not waste any more time but arranged to collect her on Sunday afternoon with his car and not his bike, as he had a box of provisions to take from the rest of the family.

Back in her room she wondered at what she had done. She had committed herself to seeing Mike again, in spite of her misgivings. She had rejected Merlin's advice and had made it impossible to meet him again on the Sunday. Why had she done this? Was it simply resentment against Merlin, in which case it was rather stupid. Was it perhaps a genuine desire for new experiences or was it really that she did not want to commit herself, even though Merlin was willing to do so. "But only as long as it doesn't interfere with career plans," she thought. She did not intend to be foolish again. But then what was foolish? She decided not to think about it until Saturday. She had plenty of work to occupy herself with until then. She had promised Merlin that she would talk to him and she would do so.

Going to the kitchen to collect water for her coffee, she encountered Pam. Looking a little embarrassed, Pam said quickly. "Cynthia tells me I've upset you. I'm sorry. I just didn't think. I was intrigued, that's all."

"I've got over it," Cleo smiled at her. "Mike is a bit disreputable and I certainly wasn't expecting him. He's one of those people who just can't help making difficulties for themselves. I tried to help, that's all. Nothing more."

"I never thought there was. I mean he's attractive but he's just not your sort, is he? I'd better say goodnight," she added quickly, before I put my foot in it again. "No more hard feelings, I hope?"

"Certainly not," Cleo replied, as Pam walked off, leaving her to fill her kettle. And that she thought is the common-sense verdict, 'he's just not your sort.'

Chapter Fifteen

"Well. I think the afternoon went pretty well, don't you?" Cleo asked Merlin as she entered the hall of his house. "I think there's no doubt that Victoria enjoyed herself."

"When I consider the amount of money she managed to spend, I sincerely hope she did. Fortunately, that is ultimately my brother's worry," he remarked as he led the way to the living room where they were to eat.

"Don't be curmudgeonly," Cleo protested. "You must admit she looked much better dressed at the end. And much happier. Which I think is even more important."

"I agree with both your statements," he said, as he conducted her to the kitchen. "She looked prettier and happier. You seemed to have enjoyed yourself too, I was glad to notice. Perhaps it wasn't too great a self sacrifice, after all?"

"You know it wasn't. I enjoyed it. It reminded me of shopping expeditions with Jane years ago." She looked with approval at his large and beautifully equipped kitchen. "Did you say that your Mrs Parry actually disapproves of this? She must be mad. I think it's perfect." She wandered round investigating various cupboards.

"If you still insist on cooking the meal, I suggest we have omelettes, salads and fresh bread. That will be easy and give us more time to relax and talk, which is our main object. What do you say?"

"Agreed but you'll have to show me where everything is kept."

"Good. You busy yourself with the omelettes and I'll see to the salads." He handed her a voluminous apron. "Mrs Parry's favourite," he explained, as he tied it firmly round her waist.

While the meal was being prepared, he returned to the subject of Victoria. "What is your impression of Victoria? Do you think she is happier?"

"I think she is. She is much more relaxed in lessons. She isn't afraid any more to express her opinions in front of others. She's very grateful to you, you know."

"I think she owes more gratitude to my mother for giving her a temporary home."

"She is very grateful to your mother but it's you she admires. She is aware that it must be boring for you to take on a seventeen year old niece but she says you've never shown it and you've been very kind." As Merlin did not answer but seemed absorbed in preparing the salads, she continued. "I think she's happier because her father has just told her that he hopes to be back for Easter and that, although he has to go off again, he promises to be home for the summer holidays and take her somewhere exciting. Did you know?"

Merlin paused. "Naturally," he replied, "since it was my suggestion to him. I told him that he could not leave mother alone to cope during the Easter holidays and that he must do something, since I had other commitments. I also told him clearly that I was tired of having the position of a father without the joys and that it was time he took on his own responsibilities."

"I think you were right. I don't suppose he liked it much, especially as you are ten years younger."

"He took it seriously, particularly when he realised that I was not available at all during the vacation."

"I see." Cleo slid the second omelette on to its plate. "If the salads are ready, we can start eating." For the next few minutes they were fully occupied with the final preparations for the meal. As they began to eat, Cleo said, "I see I'm not the only person affected by your South American plans. It could have been very difficult for Victoria and your mother if your brother had been unable to come back."

He looked straight at her with penetrating gaze of his dark eyes. "Are you suggesting," he asked, "that I should feel guilty? That I'm sacrificing everyone to my own selfish ends?" His tone was slightly mocking, as was the smile he gave her. "Remember in my defence the arrangements were made months ago when the situation was very different. I am willing to help but not willing to take on responsibilities that are not mine."

"But surely you have some responsibility for your mother?" she looked at him reproachfully. "Isn't that right?"

He met her gaze without flinching. "We've never been close, whereas she and Edward have always been so. She has helped him through several domestic crises and she'll be much happier if he's around. Will you now absolve me on these grounds?"

"What can I say? You have explained it all very clearly. I wish I could always be so rational. But then you always have been, haven't you?"

"You're still annoyed with me?"

"I'm not annoyed. I would rather say I'm disappointed, which is quite natural, don't you think?"

"I wish I was not going away now. But it's only for a few weeks, Cleo, and it might give you the space you need to sort things out. So much has changed for you in the past two months. And this time I've committed myself before I've gone away. You are the one who has still to decide. I would like you to do that without being over-persuaded by me. Don't you agree?"

"Perhaps." She applied herself to the food. There was so much she wanted to say that she was afraid to begin. How much right did his 'commitment' give her? Would she be right to make any claims on him? "Let's finish the meal first," she suggested, "then you can tell me what you're doing and why and perhaps I'll understand."

"I'll be happy to do that. There's a lot we both still need to explain, I imagine." He poured out another glass of wine for them both. "Who was that pallid looking Sixth Former who was speaking to you when I arrived?" he asked unexpectedly. "I was intrigued because Victoria was indignant that she should be bothering you on a Saturday afternoon. She said she was a frightful creep."

Cleo laughed, "That was Stephanie St. John. She is a bit of a nuisance at times. She thinks I should solve all her problems apparently. She wanted to speak to me urgently but I told her to wait until Monday break."

"You'll have to learn to be harder hearted," he advised. "She is not your responsibility."

"You mean I should learn from you?"

"Why not? I've had considerable experience." He began to clear the table. "I think it's time now for coffee, biscuits and cheese and fruit. What do you think?"

"I can't think of anything better, although I don't seem to have had much of a role as cook."

"Don't worry, there'll be many other opportunities, I hope. Still to console you I'll let you make the coffee."

After the meal they went into the study. Merlin drew the long, heavy curtains over the patio doors and switched on several lamps while Cleo comfortably settled herself on the wide couch. Having finally taken the armchair nearest to her. Merlin seemed content to wait for her to begin.

It was difficult but she plunged straight in. "I'm not suggesting that you have a moral obligation to do it," she said with a slightly mischievous smile, "but I would like to know why your visit to El Salvador is so important and how it came about."

"To answer you properly I have to go back two years to the time when I was still in hospital. The first operation, I'd had, hadn't been much of a success and the doctors were strongly advising a second one with far greater chances of success or so they assured me. I was very doubtful."

"But it was a success, wasn't it?"

"Yes, and with hindsight I can see it would have been utterly foolish to have turned it down. But I didn't know that then and quite frankly, Cleo, I was afraid and very confused. It's difficult perhaps for you to understand that, seeing me as I am now." He paused and looked at her.

"I'm afraid," she said remorsefully, "I've never really tried to appreciate what it must have been like. Seeing you so fit, I've minimised it all. I'm sorry."

"Don't worry. We all do it. I might not have wanted to talk about it once but I can confess to you now that I was pretty scared and felt quite unable to make a decision. It didn't help that I was also resentful of what had happened."

"I can understand that," Cleo answered him fervently, "there have been several times when I have felt very resentful about my life."

"I was fortunate, for it was at that moment that Lawrence came back into my life. He had been my only close friend at school and Oxford but, after we had taken our degrees, our lives had separated. To my amazement, he'd decided to join the Jesuits. I thought it was a terrible waste of his life and so we lost touch with one another. Now, home on leave, he heard of my accident and came to visit me. I had other visitors, of course, but he was the only one who tried to understand and to talk honestly with me. Most visitors pretended, without much thought, that all would be well and told me how brave I was etc. I realised they were naturally anxious to get back to the real world outside hospital, so I encouraged them. It was easier."

"I know what you mean. I discovered that, particularly when my mother committed suicide. People simply didn't want to talk about it. They were embarrassed or something, whereas I desperately needed to talk. The only way was to pretend. But you were lucky you actually found someone who was willing to talk."

"Yes, at first we simply talked, sometimes very seriously about life and sometimes quite light-heartedly. He didn't treat me any differently and after a while I was able to confide in him. He didn't try to convert me but in discussions with him I was able to sort out my beliefs and discover what was important to me. He gave me the courage to accept the operation because in talking to him I realised that the outcome didn't really matter. What mattered was to face the challenge and then make the best of whatever life was available to me afterwards. The operation, as you know, was successful and I then set out to rebuild my life, discarding much which had before seemed important. When I was fit I went to visit him in his large and poverty stricken parish in El Salvador, where he is trying to establish a school and in time a college. I learned a lot more there. Lawrence is not wasting his life because he really loves these people and cares more for their happiness than he does for his own and yet he seemed to be one of the happiest people I had ever met. I was pleased to have a share in this. It was something I needed and so last Summer I promised to go back this Spring for as long as possible to help him with his project. And that is why I'm going." He stopped and waited for her response.

"And you certainly must go," she said slowly, "I can see that now. I'm very glad you've told me. Does anyone else know why you're going? The real reason I mean?"

"No. Why should they?"

She frowned. "Because they must misunderstand you like me. It isn't right."

"The only person who matters is you. I don't want you to misunderstand me. When we first met you came closer to me than anyone had ever done but I still didn't value our relationship enough and so I failed you. Since then as a result of my accident and of meeting Lawrence I came to realise just how empty and useless my life was in spite of all my supposed success. I changed many aspects as you know but meeting you again seemed to offer the best chance of all to put things right and to make something good personally. I felt perhaps you had the same idea but now I seem to be failing you again. It seems I'm leaving you when you need help."

She made a big effort to smile and to speak lightly. "You're being unfair to yourself. I'm the sort of person who can never have enough help. I'm always doing foolish things and then trying to run away from the consequences, I seem to have made quite an art of it."

"I'm not at all sure I agree with that. But tell me first, what are your immediate problems. Why were you so upset when I told you I wouldn't be here for a few weeks?"

She hesitated. "So you really want me to tell you?"

"Of course. Why else would I ask?"

"It's simple really but probably not something that would naturally occur to you. I panicked because I suddenly realised I had nowhere to go for the Easter holidays. For two years I'd had a temporary home with Marcus. That had given me a feeling of security for a time but it was false. Jane's expecting a baby and so I can't land myself on her for four weeks. I've never had to anyway. I took this job chiefly because it offered me a home and I just hadn't thought about the end of term. Being virtuous is more difficult than I thought. But that's not your fault. I just thought I might stay in this area and see you and your family. And then like a spoilt child I was annoyed because you had different ideas." She stopped, unwilling to explain any more. None of it seemed very creditable or mature.

"You're perfectly right," he replied quickly. "I've never had enough imagination to understand the realities of your life."

"It shouldn't matter," she said. "The truth is I ought to be able to deal with it by now. I'm sure other people do. But there's no need for you to worry. I've solved that. I shall spend the first few days in St. Elizabeth's, go to Jane and possibly meet my school friend, Helen, who hopes to be making a quick visit to London from Italy. Then I'll spend the last week at St. Elizabeth's when the school opens up again. I may even find some time for serious thinking, which is long overdue."

"And so your immediate problem is solved and then I shall be back and we can plan our future, I hope. If you agree to marry me, you need never have these worries any more. Surely that is comforting?"

"It's tempting and if you'd been able to say that when I was twenty, I wouldn't have hesitated, though it might have disastrous but a lot has happened since then to both of us." She looked at him sadly.

"Are you really saying it's too late?" he challenged her. "I thought you enjoyed our times together as much as I did. Was I mistaken?"

"No, of course you weren't," she declared vehemently. "Your friendship is precious to me and very comforting. But it's not all I want."

"I love you. Isn't that enough?"

"What does it mean? I don't think I understand it. I'm sure you love the people you are going to help in El Salvador. I'm sure you have a more caring relationship with your students now than you had in Oxford. You are in many ways a much more admirable person. I admire your courage and your convictions, it would be better if I were more like you but I'm not. It's so horrible. It should be right but it isn't. It's all a bit hypothetical, isn't it?"

"It seems right to me. I loved you when we last parted, although I never managed to say it as I should have done. You said I over-persuaded you, used you by making love to you and you left me. When I was in hospital I wanted you more than anyone but you weren't there."

"Oh, how I wish I had been but I wasn't because we were out of phase and now we've moved on and we can't go back. You did without me then eventually and now you know you can."

"You're being very unfair, Cleo," he protested. "cruelly unfair. Knowing I can doesn't mean I want to. On the contrary. But isn't this perhaps just your excuse for once more evading a lasting commitment? Isn't that the real truth? You want to have me and yet be free."

"I don't know; you may be right." She stood up suddenly. "Oh Merlin, I can't help remembering the past. How wonderfully happy we were in Oxford! But that's stupid I know."

He too stood up, putting his hands gently on her shoulders looking deeply into her dark green eyes, now bright with tears. "I believe we can be happy again, even happier. That's why I want us to talk."

"But we can't just talk, necessary though that is. I need other things. Words seem so cold. I need.." she hesitated.

"Perhaps you need this," he suggested, putting his arms round her, he drew her close to him and kissed her with increasing passion.

For a moment she clung to him, returning his kisses, then she drew back a little. "If you want to make love to me," she said softly, "I would enjoy it very much."

For a moment, he still held her in his arms, then abruptly he released her. "I don't want to," he replied, "not now, not in this way. It wouldn't satisfy me and it wouldn't make you happy either."

She pulled herself away sadly. "It would for a short while. I doubt if I'll have ever more happiness than that."

"You could have," he insisted, "if you had the courage."

She laughed. "And that's just what I haven't got but I do have sufficient feeling for you not to want to deceive you. I think you're right to resist my advances. It makes me cross. I'm not used to that treatment. I hope it isn't too easy."

"You have no need to worry. It isn't."

She moved close to him again and looked up at him appealingly. "Then at least kiss me again," she begged, "I need some comfort and reassurance. Don't just talk to me. I'm so lonely."

He hesitated for a moment then taking her into his arms he led her to the sofa and crushed her close to him. She returned his kisses passionately and clung to him. "We've been so silly," she said, "it'd be wonderful, just like it used to be. Nothing matters, except that we want each other. Don't talk any more."

He released her abruptly and sat up. "Cleo," he demanded, "do you know what you're doing? Do you even care? This won't solve any problems. It never has." Shocked, she looked at him as he stood up quickly and moved away. It was obvious that he was having to make a tremendous effort to retain his self control. I'm a bitch she thought. Why did I do it? The answer was too unpleasant to be put into words. She could only think to say aloud, "I'm sorry, Merlin"

He turned and looked at her but didn't say anything. "I've been trying to tell you, now you know what I'm like." She stood up. "I think I'd better go back."

She waited but before he could reply, the telephone rang. He picked it up and announced himself. He listened carefully for a few moments, then said, "I think you're quite right, Miss Stephens. I'm very glad, however, that you didn't disturb my mother." There was another pause, while he listened, then he said calmly, "Of course I can." He looked at his watch, "It's only just gone nine. I'll drive to the hospital as quickly as I can and be in touch with you later."

"What is the matter?" Cleo asked. "Has something happened to Victoria?" It seemed unbelievable.

"She's had an accident," he replied, "just after supper. My brother rang. She talked to him about fifteen minutes, started to run downstairs, slipped and fell and broke her leg rather badly. The school nurse took her straight to hospital where she was fortunate to have immediate attention. She came back from the theatre about half an hour ago, since when she has been in a very distressed state so much so that the Sister rang Miss Stephens and suggested that her parents should be informed. Miss Stephens very sensibly spoke to me. I shall have to go, I'm afraid." He hesitated briefly. "I could take you back first, I suppose, or better still I'll phone for a taxi."

"Neither is necessary," Cleo spoke without hesitation. "I'll come with you, if you'll have me. You might need some feminine support. Please take me, Merlin." She looked at him anxiously, afraid that he might now reject her.

To her relief he smiled at her affectionately. "I'll be glad of your help."

"You will forgive me, won't you?" she asked as he offered her coat to her. "I was horrid and you were right. That's not the way for us."

"We don't need to talk of forgiveness." He laughed ruefully. "You might say I was over-confident." He picked up his keys, put them in the pocket of his coat and made for the door. "Come on, we'd better not waste any time."

They reached the hospital in Markhampton in record time and entered Victoria's small side ward barely half an hour after they had left Wheaten. She was sitting up, still wearing her hospital gown. Her hair was dishevelled, she was extremely pale and her eyes were red from crying. "Oh Merlin!" she exclaimed. "Thank you for coming. I told them not to bother you but sister said you must be informed."

"I've brought Cleo with me too," he said, walking towards the bed, so that Cleo who had entered behind him could now be seen. "We thought you might find it easier to talk to her, perhaps."

Victoria burst into tears. "It's marvellous to see you both," she sobbed. "I'm so sorry, though. I've spoilt your evening. And you were so good to me this afternoon." She sobbed even more. Merlin produced a handkerchief doubtfully and tried to console her saying, "Don't worry about that. It's unimportant. We want to help you, if we can." He looked helplessly at Cleo as Victoria clutched the handkerchief but still continued to sob bitterly.

Cleo came forward quickly and, sitting on the bed, she put her arms round the sobbing girl and stroked her hair gently. Then as the sobs began to subside, she offered her the handkerchief again. "Are you in a lot of pain?" she asked Victoria gently.

"It's a bit bad," Victoria whispered, "but it isn't really that. It's everything." She clutched Cleo's hand and then looked sadly at Merlin who had sat down on the chair beside her bed.

"You've had a very unpleasant shock," he suggested. "It's bound to upset you."

"I only had the accident because I was so upset. It was Dad's call that upset me, you see." She stopped, struggling once more with her tears.

Merlin frowned slightly. "I don't understand. Cleo and I thought you were pleased that he was coming back at last."

"I was but then he told me a lot more tonight." She was still battling with her tears but she managed to speak quite clearly. "He told me it was difficult for him to come back at Easter but he was making the effort since you had told him that it was his responsibility as you were going away." She looked at Merlin. "Is that true?"

Cleo too looked at him. She guessed that he was angry but he spoke calmly. "I did say something like that but I didn't expect him to repeat it to you."

Victoria even managed a watery smile. "I don't imagine you did. But Dad's like that sometimes, isn't he? But it wasn't that which really upset me. I asked about Mum. Said I wanted to see her and talk to her. I thought that we might all get together and sort things out a bit. We've done it before." She began to cry again.

"That seems to be a good idea," Merlin agreed, while Cleo hugged the girl more tightly.

"But not to Mum and Dad. It has never occurred to them. Dad said that there would be no point in that as he and Mum had already met a couple of times and sorted most things out. They had decided on a divorce and I could visit Mum when she had settled down with her new husband. There was no more to be said. I was so angry and so upset. They had settled my life without referring to me at all, as if I were a baby or a piece of furniture. Dad would try to live in England as much as possible and I would live with him. Mum would send for me if and when she felt like it. Neither of them even troubled to ask me what I thought. They didn't care what they were doing to me. I'd thought until then that they might sort things out again." She was sobbing bitterly again. "Neither of them cares about me at all." She clung to Cleo and buried her face in her shoulder.

"I'm sure your father does," Merlin said comfortingly, "in fact I know he does. He's simply very upset."

Victoria raised her face. "It doesn't look like that to me, Merlin. You've shown more interest in my future than he ever has and I'm very grateful to you and Grannie. And to you, Cleo," she finished, burying her face once more.

Cleo stroked her hair gently. "What happened then?" she asked.

"I told him I hated them both, banged the phone down and rushed out of the phone booth. I was crying. I didn't really see where I was going. I didn't bother. I lost my balance I think and just fell headlong down the stairs. I realised I couldn't move my leg and I just lay there and cried and cried until someone came. I remember saying, 'It's too much. I can't bear it. I want to die.' That's all." She was quiet suddenly. She rested her head once more against Cleo's shoulder and Cleo held her more closely.

Merlin was the first to speak. "I know your Father's first instinct is to try to run away from things but he usually overcomes it in the end. You must realise that he's been suffering from a shock too but he does love you. I'm sure of that."

Victoria did not respond but continued to cry, although more quietly while Cleo soothed her. As she sat there Cleo was for a moment in another room, a comfortable bedroom, where a girl of twelve lay stretched on her bed crying and crying until she had no tears left. Only no one came to comfort her. What was there to say? Could such wounds ever be healed? They might be but not yet and not easily. In the meantime, courage was necessary.

She lifted Victoria's face up, gently wiped away the tears with the now sodden handkerchief and then gave her a comforting kiss. "There's a time for crying," she said. "It's necessary but there's also a time for it to stop. I know. So let's make you look better first, that always helps. After that, Merlin will see how soon you can go home to Grannie and be petted. That's what you need."

"I'll go now and have a word with the authorities," Merlin said quickly, glad of something to do, "and leave you in Cleo's capable hands." He smiled at them both and left quickly. "Do you think it'll be possible?" Victoria asked, wiping her face with the damp flannel which Cleo handed to her.

"Of course," Cleo replied cheerfully, taking away the flannel and handing Victoria her brush and comb. "Merlin will arrange it. You must know he's very good at arranging things."

"I wish he wasn't going away for so long," Victoria sighed. "I'm sure he'd keep Dad up to the mark. You're not pleased he's going are you?"

Cleo did not answer immediately but offered Victoria her lipstick and powder instead. Victoria, however, was not to be put off. "You don't have to answer me but I'm sure you can't be pleased and I rather thought.." she hesitated, obviously wondering if she should proceed.

"Of course I'm not pleased," Cleo replied quickly. Suddenly it all seemed so clear. "But there are times when we have to be true to ourselves, even if we don't please other people. Merlin's keeping a promise he made to a friend. But I think you should ask him about it yourself. If he wants to tell you, he will."

She stood back and looked at Victoria critically. "You look heaps better now. That's right. Smile. I'll give you that. It suits you." She turned to smile at Merlin, as he came into the room.

"You should be able to go home on Monday, after you've seen the doctor. It'll have to be late afternoon because I'm not free until then."

Victoria's face lit up. "It's marvellous. You've fixed it. Cleo said you would. And I don't have to go back to school?"

"Not yet. I spoke to Miss Stephens too. Now, I'm told we must go so that you can get some sleep." He came over towards her bed and she clutched his hand. He smiled and released himself gently. "I'll bring your grandmother in tomorrow to see you. She'll insist on that. Just be careful what you say to her."

"I promise." She turned to Cleo who hugged and kissed her. "I will see you again, won't I?"

"Of course but not tomorrow, I'm afraid." She wished she had not so rashly agreed to Mike's suggestion. Seeing Victoria's disappointment, she added, "I could manage Monday after four but perhaps that's not a good idea."

Victoria turned to look pleadingly at Merlin. "I think it's an excellent idea." he said. "A womanly hand is definitely desirable. I don't exactly see myself in the role of mother." He turned to Cleo. "I'll collect you just after four and you'd better bring some useful books to keep your pupil occupied. We can make it easier for my mother by getting the supper." He took Cleo's arm and led her to the door.

"You'd better be careful," Victoria called to Cleo. "He's organising you now."

Cleo laughed. "I'm not worried. I know he just wants someone to cook the meal. Isn't that right?"

"Of course," he agreed. "Women enjoy being made use of. Men always think of themselves. I thought you two had agreed on that. We'll discuss that some other time, however. Now we must go." With a final wave they left, leaving a cheerful although argumentative Victoria.

A few moments later they found themselves in the large, practically empty foyer. Cleo looked with some distaste at the orange plastic tables and chairs which were scattered around presumably for the comfort of visitors, who were few at this hour. A young couple sat at one table and an elderly woman with crutches sat at another, apparently stranded. Two weary looking women were chatting idly to each other at the reception desk. The lights were harshly bright and the air was chilly. Cleo too felt chilly. In this crude light everything seemed raw, nothing could be concealed. She had comforted Victoria but she had not comforted herself.

To her amazement, Merlin said quietly, "Sit down. I'll get some coffee. There's a machine over there."

"Coffee?" she enquired incredulously. "Are you referring to that dark, evil tasting liquid in a polystyrene container? Surely you can't call that coffee?"

"Don't be so middle class and conventional," he replied cheerfully, "It's a hot liquid which stimulates, which is basically all that the finest coffee is. We need it." He felt in his pockets, "but we're not going to get it, unless you can supplement my small change."

She could and she did but she still protested. "But why here?" she asked, looking round with a shudder.

"Why not? Since we're here. We can sit and talk and no one will bother us." Taking the coins she offered, he walked off to the machine, while she sat down at the nearest table. Casually she studied the old woman, sitting almost opposite her. She was heavily built, wearing a shabby, tight-fitting tweed overcoat. From beneath a woollen knitted cap, her grey hair escaped in untidy strands, framing an almost colourless face lined with weariness and suffering. Her left leg was heavily bandaged. She waited patiently. Cleo felt a great pity for her.

Suddenly the old woman caught her eye and smiled. The lines changed. Her face was suddenly lit up. She looked kind and friendly, "Been visiting someone, have you love?" she asked. Cleo smiled back and agreed. "They're depressing places, hospitals." the old woman continued. "I've seen too much of them in my time. Still we have to grin and bear it. Be grateful for what the good Lord gives, that's what I say. Feeling a bit sad yourself, aren't you? Don't let it get you down." She looked past Cleo. "Here's your husband bringing you a cup of coffee. That'll do you good. It makes all the difference to have someone caring about you. I know."

"Can we get you a coffee?" Cleo asked as she took the despised cup from Merlin.

"It's nice of you to ask but no thanks, love. I'm waiting for my grandson. He's gone to get a taxi. He won't be long." She smiled again and then added proudly, "He's very good to me, my grandson. It makes all the difference."

Smiling back, Cleo agreed and then turned to face Merlin as he sat down with his cup of coffee. She took a sip. "You're right. It's not as bad as I thought."

"So she isn't marooned. I'm relieved."

"Why?"

"Because I was afraid that you in your usual impulsive way were going to ask me to take charge of her."

"Which you would have done?"

"Only to please you," he said with a slight self mockery.

"Don't be absurd. You know you'd do it, anyway. Just as you decided to stay here and comfort me. You were right. I dreaded going back to St. Elizabeth's on my own."

"You comforted Victoria."

"I hope so, but I'm so selfish, Merlin, I can't escape from myself. When I was consoling her, I suddenly remembered a twelve year old girl, sobbing on her bed and I thought there was no one to comfort her."

"Nevertheless, you comforted Victoria and now there is someone trying to comfort you even if it's only with a cup of poisonous liquid in a polystyrene cup." He smiled lovingly at her.

"I was horrid about it. I often am horrid. I can't think why you forgive me."

He sipped his coffee and seemed to be considering this. "It must be because I love you. That's what I've decided."

"But what if I don't love you?"

"I think you do but you're afraid to think about it."

"I'm not sure that I know what love means. Women seem to mean one thing and men another, when they talk about it."

"That's because they're talking about sex. I'm talking about love. That means trying to put another person first, trying to understand someone, to share things with them. Sex is just the icing on the cake, except when it's a serious attempt to produce a child."

"I don't feel free to marry," she said. "I suppose I just can't get away from my past. I wouldn't want a child, in case I made it suffer as I have. People are doing it all the time. There are lots of young people like Victoria. It makes me angry. I won't risk doing it." She drank her coffee furiously and watched the old woman as she was cheerfully collected by her grandson.

"Her grandson's come." she told Merlin. That's good." For some reason she felt unexpectedly cheerful.

"Just as I'll come." he replied, "but I want to marry you and I do want children."

"You're making it difficult for yourself." she said, but at the same time she put her hand on his. "Aren't you afraid of leaving me for so long?"

"No," he answered her firmly. "You have to face it by yourself now. But you know I'm with you." He held her hand for a moment and then said in a matter of fact tone, "I think it's time we left."

She watched him as he collected the cups and disposed of them, His certainty was restful and comforting. As she stood up she wanted him to touch her and so confirm it. He took her arm as they walked across the foyer and through the sliding doors into the cold, clear night. As they sat down in the car, he put his arm round her and drew her close to him. Her tears came suddenly but they no longer hurt as she buried her face in his chest and clutched his free hand. What had the old woman said, 'Be grateful for what the Good Lord gives." She was grateful. Thank you," she said. "I'm not afraid to go back now."

Chapter Sixteen

Everything was so different from what she had expected. That seemed to be Cleo's only thought as she sat on the shabby, sagging settee in Clare's living room that Sunday afternoon. She was alone for a while with the baby, eighteen months old Esther, while the three older boys played a noisy game of football in the garden. She could hear Mike talking to Clare in the kitchen, while she made the coffee she had eagerly offered and he unpacked the boxes of gifts he had brought with him from the family.

Absentmindedly, she watched Esther playing with her toys in the middle of the much worn carpet and tried to analyse her surprise and her other emotions. She hadn't wanted to come. She had been annoyed that because of her foolish promise to Mike, she could not visit Victoria with Merlin and stay in the warm world of his love which he had revealed to her at the hospital.

Throughout their hour's journey to this council estate on the fringes of the county town, Mike had tried to prepare her for this visit to his sister. She was, he told her, a trained nurse, twenty nine years old, the same age as Cleo's sister Jane, and trained in a similar London hospital only their lives from then on had been entirely different. Seven years before when Jane had married Robert, a solicitor with a future, Clare had married Dave. "We all thought she was totally mad," Mike said angrily, "and we were right. He'd been married before, divorced, thrown out by his wife who said he couldn't or wouldn't maintain her and their two kids. The Church didn't want to know, of course, Mum and Dad were very upset, so were we all but Clare insisted that she loved him and could change his life by giving him a fresh start a new home, a new family and a wife who loved him."

"But she didn't succeed?" Cleo was intrigued, hearing so much from Mike.

He shrugged, "What do you expect? This isn't a fairy tale. She's had four kids in six years, he's never had a regular job. Hasn't worked at all really for the last two. Now he's gone off for the second time on a bender. He's a drunk now only Clare won't admit it. He'll come back, worse luck, and she'll forgive him."

"But Mike is wrong," Cleo told herself, "it is a fairy tale, because Clare is like an enchanted princess." Until they had arrived at Clare's council house, everything had been much as Mike had led her to expect. Even in the March afternoon sunlight, the housing estate had a depressed and demoralised air. Repairs were needed, paint was generally lacking. Children swarmed over the once green patch in the centre, others were playing desultory football in the road, much to Mike's annoyance. Most of the people they saw looked defeated, especially the mostly overweight women, oppressed with children and poverty.

Then Clare had appeared at the door of her house in response to Mike's vigorous ring. As Mike greeted her and introduced her, Cleo studied this unexpected being in amazement. Clare was small and slim wearing a cheap but attractive bright blue dress. Her shining, naturally red gold hair, falling from a centre parting framed her heart shaped face and then cascaded over her shoulders and down her back. She gave Mike and Cleo a joyous, welcoming smile and her eyes an unusual deep blue sparkled. Her children clustered round her, delighted to see the visitors, Clare was shy and nervous, as her rather jerky speech showed but there was no hiding the pleasure she had in bringing them into her shabby but surprisingly clean and tidy home, She kissed Mike and then turned to Cleo, "Do come in," she exclaimed, "the children love having visitors and so do I!" After the introductions, Mike had gone to fetch the gifts from the car, Clare had pushed the small boys into the garden and had gone to prepare coffee, As she was going through the door, she had turned suddenly to Cleo with a happy smile and said, "I'm so pleased you can come, Mike has told me a lot about you." What had he said, Cleo wondered with some alarm.

Now, she leaned back and looked around the room. It was certainly shabby and furnished only with necessities, Apart from the settee on which she was sitting, which had obviously been enjoyed by many children, there were two armchairs in a similar state, a cheap dining room table and chairs, a small table with television and boxes of toys some of which Esther was exploring. One article of furniture was, however, unexpected. To Cleo's right, opposite the garden door there was a large well filled bookcase. She had just walked across the room to examine the books when Clare re-entered carrying a tray with coffee and biscuits. "You have a lot of books," she said examining the top shelf as she spoke. She was surprised to find not the children's books and romantic novels which she had half expected but several volumes of poetry and serious novels both old and new.

As she put the tray down the table, Clare said quickly and nervously. "I suppose you're interested in books. Mike told me you're an English teacher at the college."

"You've a pretty good collection," Cleo replied, walking towards Clare to accept the mug of coffee which was being held out to her.

"I don't have much time to read them now." Clare laughed nervously, "but I used to love reading. I did 'A' Level English and History and I particularly enjoyed English. I didn't pass." she added quickly before Cleo could comment. "I enjoyed the books but I never seemed to be able to write the sort of essays they wanted. I just wasn't clever enough."

"Not clever enough for what?" Mike asked as he came into the room and seized a mug of coffee.

"Not clever enough to pass exams," Clare answered cheerfully.

"Who the hell cares about that when you can make biscuits like these?" Mike asked, picking one up off the tray. He passed the plate to Cleo. "Try one. She's a brilliant cook." The boys who had just come into the room seemed to confirm this the eagerness with which they helped themselves. "The kids agree with me."

Clare laughed. "They're not all that good. You just like food." She turned to Cleo. "I've begun to think that men really just want someone to cook for them. I like cooking, so it doesn't bother me."

"I think perhaps you're right," Cleo agreed. Even Merlin could often be fitted into that category.

"My Mum's made a lovely cake for tea," Harry the middle boy confided to Cleo. He was a short, dark angular boy of about four with brown hair, bright eyes and a wide mouth which readily widened into an engaging grin, as it did now. "It's a birthday cake."

"Don't be silly," Joe, the eldest boy, interrupted him with the authority of his five and a half years. "It can't be a birthday cake. It isn't a birthday. It's a special cake, isn't it, Mum?" Joe was a rounder, fairer, more solid version of Harry.

Clare spoke quickly before the obviously wounded Harry could retort. "It's a family cake. We're having a party for Uncle Mike and his friend, Auntie Cleo." She looked apologetically at Cleo. "I hope you don't mind being brought into the family?"

Cleo laughed. "I think it's fun. I've never really had a proper family." She wasn't really sure that she meant what she said but it seemed important to support Clare who so obviously wanted to make everyone happy.

Somewhat to her surprise, Mike too was prepared to play his part. As soon as he had finished his coffee, he gathered the boys together and took them into the garden for a ball game, even including three and a half year old Mark, who desperately wanted to be involved. "Mike's very good with the boys," Clare remarked. "He likes children. It seems such a shame that he doesn't see more of Ben. I can't understand it. Perhaps I shouldn't have mentioned that," she added nervously, "but I suppose he's told you about Tracey and Ben. If he hasn't, I'm sorry, but he should've done."

"He has told me," Cleo replied unconcernedly. As Clare looked sharply at her, she added, "We're not lovers. Just friends. I'd prefer it to remain that way." As Clare still looked doubtful, she continued, "I'm still a sort of Catholic, I suppose and I think marriage should be for life."

"So do I," Clare agreed, as she lifted Esther on to her knee and cuddled her.

"Yet you married a divorced man," Cleo could not help saying. "Why?"

Clare hesitated for a moment and then replied with unexpected firmness. "I suppose you think it's wrong? Well I don't. It isn't always. Dave married first when he was far too young. It was a terrible mistake and it was completely finished when I first met him. He'd lost his family, his home and he was terribly lonely and depressed. Do you think it's right that he should stay like that, because the Church says so?" She hugged Esther even more closely and looked challengingly at Cleo with those amazing blue eyes.

"Of course, I don't think so," Cleo said quickly. "I just think one should avoid divorce if one possibly can and do everything to keep the marriage going, especially when children are involved."

"That's what I think." Clare said. "I love Dave and I want to keep my marriage going, although my family seem to think I ought to leave him. It's strange isn't it? They don't like divorce but they think I should leave Dave. I expect Mike's told you what he thinks. Well, there's my side too."

"I'm sure there is," Cleo replied swiftly. She hadn't expected to get involved in a discussion of this sort but, strange though it might be, it seemed better now to continue. "But Dave isn't with you now, is he I expect that's what worries them."

"No, he isn't but he'll come back." Clare put Esther down again and nervously began to sort through her toys.

Cleo hesitated then asked bluntly. "How can you be sure of that?"

"Because he's already been to see me," Clare replied almost fiercely. "He came in yesterday to say how sorry he was and to ask me to take him back."

"And you agreed?" Cleo was unable to hide the surprise and indignation she felt.

"Oh, I know what you think," Clare replied wearily. "Everyone thinks I'm stupid. Perhaps I am but I love him and I know he loves me and can't do without me really. The children love him too and they want him back."

"I don't know much about love," Cleo looked straight into Clare's defiant blue eyes, "but I think it must be wonderful to be needed and to love someone like that." She could not keep the sadness out of her voice.

Clare picked herself up from the floor and sat next to Cleo on the settee touching her hand gently with instinctive sympathy. "Don't be sad," she said, "You're so beautiful and intelligent, you're bound to find someone who loves you."

Cleo was tempted to be evasive as she would have been with most people but in the face of Clare's honesty, she could not be. "I think someone does love me," she admitted. "I'm the one who's wrong. I don't seem to know how to love properly. In any case, I'm terrified of marriage and children. I wouldn't want to fail like my mother did."

"There's no reason why you should fail," Clare protested. "You don't want to think too much sometimes. Do what your instinct tells you."

"Is that how you came to marry Dave?"

"I suppose so. Mike will tell you that I was stupid, that I had a silly romantic dream that I could change him and make up for everything."

"But you didn't really?"

"The truth's more complicated," Clare paused.

"It nearly always is, isn't it?"

"Part of me did hope that," Clare said rapidly. Although nervous, she seemed anxious to confide. "But part of me knew it wouldn't be like that. I had this feeling. Do you know what I mean? You have this instinct, though you don't put it into words. It's there in your mind. So when Dave chucks up his job and drinks, I'm disappointed but I'm not surprised, really. Deep inside me I knew what the risk was but I wanted to take it. Had to somehow. But I was angry when other people put it into words." Her rush of words came suddenly to an end. Embarrassed, she add, "I expect you think I'm silly too?"

"Not silly, just determined. Do you still think it's right?"

"Oh yes?" Clare's blue eyes were shining again and her smile was radiant. "We love each other, just as we are and we both love the children. I think that's more important in life than money and success, that's what I most wanted."

"But you must be terribly unhappy when he goes off?"

"I am and I feel very angry at times but I know he can't really help it. That's his weakness. I'm very weak too and he helps me. That's what marriage is all about, I think. Helping one another, having time for one another." She would have said more but at this moment Esther tired of her toys began to cry fretfully and clutch at her skirt.

Wanting to be helpful, Cleo awkwardly picked her up and tried to soothe her. Fortunately the child was attracted by the jade pendant she was wearing and began to play with it. Clare stood up hastily. “It’s time Esther had a rest,” she exclaimed “and I began to cook the tea. Would you mind giving her a bottle, while I start the cooking? She should go off to sleep, then I can put her in her cot for an hour.”

Inexperienced though she was, Cleo felt that she had no alternative but to agree and hope that somehow she would manage to achieve the desired end. To her relief, Esther snuggled up to her comfortably and in a short time she was asleep. Cleo looked down at her as she lay peacefully, still clutching the now unnecessary bottle. She was very pretty like her mother. Soft red-gold curls framed her delicately flushed heart shaped face.

She was about to get up to take the baby to Clare when she suddenly realised that she didn’t want to do that. She wanted to go on sitting on the settee holding Esther close to her. She could not remember ever having held a child in her arms before. There had been no babies in her life and she had never missed them. Now, however, it seemed to her that she had missed something very important. Esther stirred and sighed and she held her more closely, soothing her gently.

She remembered that she had briefly had a similar feeling of tenderness for Merlin when she had realised that he was tired and in pain. Was this love, she wondered. What was it that Merlin had said the night before. ‘Love means trying to put another person first, trying to understand them, to share things with them.’ And surely Clare had said the same thing when she said ‘it means having time for someone.’ It was strange she thought that two such very different people should have such similar ideas. Perhaps it was because they were right and understood more than she had ever done. At this moment it seemed possible to believe them and hope that she might feel like that. It might be possible that it would make her happy but could it ever really happen?

For the moment, however she was content to sit there until Clare came back into the room and whisked her daughter away with many thanks and there was no more time for peaceful reflection for Mike and the boys erupted into the room demanding to know if tea was ready. Clare's cooking was as good as Mike had said and tea was a cheerful meal ending with huge slices of the special family cake. In spite of all her difficulties, including the obvious shortage of money, Clare was clearly happy. Even Mike's disapproval of Dave's imminent return did not greatly disturb her. She simply laughed and said she thought it was best for them all.

"She absolutely crazy, isn't she?" Mike enquired of Cleo as they drove away.

"I think she's happy. It's a long time since I met anyone so happy. I was surprised."

"I suppose your lot would say she's one of the undeserving poor who ought to be struck off benefits and made to work?"

"I suppose my ex-lover's friends would have said that but they don't know her or anyone like her. It's easy to judge then." She turned to look at him. "You probably work harder than they do. Do you disapprove?"

Mike shrugged. "Why should I? I like work, anyway. Clare likes kids. She's good at bringing them up and making a home. Why shouldn't she do it? It's just Dave that worries me."

"I don't see why he should," Cleo surprised herself by saying. "Clare loves him and the kids need a father. She looks after him and gives him something to do. That saves society the bother."

"Are you being very soft or very cynical?" he demanded.

"I don't know. I've just been jolted out of my prejudices, I suppose."

"Well, that can't be bad. Shall we stop halfway and have a drink? We might even have a chance to talk. Kids certainly get in the way, as I know."

"You don't see much of yours. Why's that?"

"Clare's been getting at you, I see."

"I can think for myself."

"Well, the short answer is I don't want to." He seemed disinclined to say any more so they travelled in silence until he stopped and parked outside a large country inn. "The beer's supposed to be good here," he said abruptly, "and I definitely need a pint." Without waiting for her answer he went in leaving her to follow.

Although she was annoyed, she followed him quietly and asked for an orange juice. As it was a Sunday evening the lounge was almost empty except for two or three older couples. The upholstery, the walls and the carpet seemed to be predominantly dark and, although the usual garish lights were switched on, the general effect was sombre and somewhat depressing. Cleo found herself wondering why people came to these places when they had homes of their own. She was still considering this when Mike returned with their glasses and sat down. He too had a sombre look, she decided. Perhaps he was thinking of his own home.

"You're angry with me, aren't you?" she asked him, determined to get some response from him. "You didn't like my asking you about Ben?"

"Why the hell did you have to remind me? I've had enough family life this afternoon. You shouldn't listen to Clare. She sees everything in a rosy glow. Just look at her life. Even you are telling me how happy she is. What's the matter with you?"

"But she is happy," Cleo objected.

"And how long do you think that'll last? Supposing she has three or four more kids. She's mad enough to. How do you think she'll cope? And what's more important how do you think Dave'll cope. He's already had to take to drink and probably drugs." He took a long drink then put his glass firmly down. "I'm not criticising him. I know how he feels. I could be like that myself." He finished his drink morosely but to her surprise he did not suggest getting another one. "Tracey wants me back," he added, "but I don't want to go, she irritates me. I have to get away."

"But what about Ben?" she ventured.

"What about Ben? I didn't want Ben. That was Tracey's idea and she made sure it happened. Let her look after him. I give her money. I visit them occasionally. That's all intend to do. And I don't want to waste our time talking about it. For fuck's sake, don't you go all soft on me. And don't try to make me feel guilty."

"I had no such idea," she protested mildly. "I suppose I was just curious."

"Well forget it. Marriage isn't for people like you and me. Be honest. You'd be bored after a few years like me. The same place, the same person, day after day with sex twice a week because it's part of the bloody routine. And then having to find the money for it all, Would you really want that?"

"Probably not but my trouble is that I've no idea what I really want."

"Why should you have? Why not enjoy yourself? Try lots of different things. You might even try me?" He grinned at her suddenly, a cheerful, wicked grin. She smiled back at him. "That's better!" he exclaimed. "I'll get us another drink. You need something stronger."

"When does your term end?" he asked her as he came back. When she told him that it was in a little less than a fortnight, he asked what she planned to do.

"I shall be staying in St. Elizabeth's for a week, then I go to visit my sister in London."

"Couldn't be better," he replied cheerfully. "I've got the week off before Easter. We can meet up and get to know one another better. What do you say? Or have you got some posh bloke lined up?"

"No one for that week," she admitted. "I was planning on a quiet time."

"So was I. We'll have one together. I've got some long distance jobs next week and part of the following week but I'll be in touch."

"You seem to take my agreement for granted. I'm not sure I want to commit myself to anything."

He shrugged casually. "That's up to you. There's no need to decide now. I'm not offering anything permanent. How could I? Just a few good times, we'd both enjoy." He stood up. "We can drink to it." He moved off to the bar, leaving her to marvel at the complexities of his character and her own unexpected reaction. She should have turned him down but she hadn't - at least not yet.

As soon as they had finished their drinks. Mike decided it was time to go back as he had a very early start in the morning. Cleo was relieved because that enabled her to put off any further discussion of the future plans. On their journey back Mike said no more about his suggestions for their future meetings but talked casually about his job and several amusing encounters he had had in recent months.

Cleo decided that he probably had no serious intentions at all but had simply wanted to see how she would react. When they arrived in Barton Leas, he parked his car some distance from the school, remarking that he didn't want to be the subject of the sort of gossip that went on there.

"How do you know about it?"

He grinned. "From practical experience. Ten years ago I knew several of the Sixth Formers."

"Knew in the biblical sense, I suppose?"

He laughed. "I didn't tell tales then, so I won't now."

Cleo prepared to get out, feeling somewhat irritated. "I've enjoyed the day," she said coolly. "Thanks."

"It isn't quite finished yet," he replied. Putting his arm round her, he drew her close to him. For a moment, he studied her face. "Lots of blokes must have told you that you're beautiful and fucking sexy," he said, "so I won't waste time." He began to kiss her hungrily. At first, she remained passive but, as his other hand slipped inside her jacket and began to fondle her breasts through her thin blouse, her body suddenly sprung into life and she responded to him with kisses as demanding as his own.

For several minutes they clung together and then it was Mike who abruptly drew away not she. "What's the matter," she demanded, as she zipped up her jacket. "Have you changed your mind about me?"

He laughed. "I'm just not a kid any more. I want more than a quick fuck in the dark. Spend that week with me and I'll show you what I mean. You can't pretend now you don't want it. We'll have fun. Christ. I can't wait to see you without your clothes! What do you say?"

"And where would that get us?"

"He laughed again. "In bed, I hope. You want it. I want it. So why not? We don't have to stay together but we might for a time. Who knows? Be honest you don't want any ties, do you? You're like me."

"And how are you going to arrange this idyll?" she asked mockingly. "In your place or my place?"

He was completely unruffled. "That's easy. A mate of mine has a caravan in Wales. He'll let me have it for a week any time. No sweat."

"I suppose you've done it before. You're so sure about it," she felt he was too casual.

"No. This is special for you. What do you say?"

She got out, without answering and might have walked off, if he had not caught hold of her arm. "I don't know," she replied reluctantly.

"I'll be in touch next weekend," he promised. "You can tell me then." He released her and shut the door behind her. "See you?" he said, as she walked off.

As soon as he had driven off, she almost ran into the Staff House and did not stop until she found herself standing in the silent dimly lit hall. Shocked, she said to herself, "You wanted that. You encouraged him." Another part of her said defiantly, "Why not? Why shouldn't I? We are alike. Why shouldn't we enjoy one another and be happy for a time? It would be better than being alone." She walked quickly up the stairs and entered her own room, shutting the door firmly behind her.

She switched on the main light, revealing the room in all its drab ugliness. It was empty and unwelcoming. "I was a fool to leave Marcus," she thought. "What did I hope to achieve?" All the fleeting visions she had had of achieving a fuller, more meaningful life suddenly seemed absurd. The agreement she had had with Marcus had worked well enough. Why had she thrown it away for some romantic illusion?

She looked in the mirror as she brushed her ruffled hair. She had been born beautiful and desirable. Men wanted her and she had early discovered that she wanted them. "Who do you think you are?" she asked herself angrily, "Joan of Are or Mother Teresa?" It's time to stop pretending. All she had to do was get a job. Marcus had made it clear there were many available for her. Then she would be free.

"Free for what?" That thought came unbidden and unwanted. Suddenly, she remembered Clare and her children. Cynically, she tried to see her as the world saw her, as she ought to see her. Instead she remembered Clare's glowing smile, and the soft feel of Esther as she held her tenderly in her arms. She remembered once again that she had felt tenderly towards Merlin.

It seemed so long ago now but then only the evening before she had been happy, as he had gently put his arm round her in the car. It had been so different. She had still been happy when she arrived in this same room. "He shouldn't have rejected me when I asked him to make love to me," she told herself. "Perhaps he has forgotten how much that means to me. But, if he loves me, as he says he does, surely he should understand that? He seemed to once."

She turned away feeling very weary and began to undress. As she lay down she comforted herself. "I'm sure he will understand if I tell him properly. He can't just go away for five weeks without giving me that. He can't leave me to Mike." She would see him tomorrow and they could talk. She closed her eyes and determined to banish all conflicting thoughts, hard though it might be.

Chapter Seventeen

Monday morning began badly. After a restless night, Cleo managed to oversleep with the result that she was late for breakfast and only scrambled into the school assembly at the last moment. After which she had to dash back to her room to collect her books which she had forgotten and so arrived late for her first lesson, which was with a rather difficult fourth form.

The sounding of the break bell was a welcome relief. At last she had time to relax and enjoy coffee and a biscuit. Almost simultaneously she remembered that she had promised to speak to Stephanie St John at break. What could the wretched girl want? She hoped that it would be something easily dealt with so that she would not miss her coffee entirely.

She turned off the corridor to the dining hall and took a short cut through the gardens to the chapel cloisters where she had promised to meet Stephanie. Although cold it was an exhilarating blue and golden day and she noticed with pleasure that many of the daffodils were already in bud. Shakespeare's lovely lines suddenly came to her mind and she repeated them softly:-

'Daffodils that come before the swallow dares
and take the winds of March with beauty'

The world suddenly seemed a good place and she went to meet Stephanie more cheerfully, greeting her with a smile.

Stephanie who had been seated on one of the polished oak benches in the cloisters stood up but did not return her smile. Wearing the regulation straight navy skirt and cardigan over the white blouse and striped prefect's tie she looked very young and forlorn. Her fair hair which usually fell loosely was scraped back into a pony tail her pale face was devoid of make up and her eyes looked red as if she had been crying. Cleo had an intimation of disaster.

"I'm sorry to bother you, Miss Lafay, Stephanie began, "but I simply must speak to you. I don't know anyone else I can talk to."

"Shall we sit down," Cleo suggested. Stephanie sat down next to her but instead of saying anything began to cry.

"Whatever is the matter?" Cleo asked a little impatiently.

"I think I'm pregnant and I don't know what to do." The tears rolled down Stephanie's cheeks. She struggled to take a tissue from her skirt pocket and tried ineffectually to wipe her face.

"You think you're pregnant?" Cleo had certainly not expected this. She hoped fervently that this was just one more of Stephanie's attempts at drama. "You must be mistaken surely?"

"No, that is, I don't think so." Sobs choked Stephanie again. "I wasn't sure, so I bought a test on Saturday at the chemist in town." She stopped.

"And?"

"It was positive. It's early days, perhaps it could be wrong." She looked to Cleo for some reassurance.

"I'm afraid it's never wrong if it's positive," Cleo said gently. She put her arm round Stephanie. "I'm very sorry. Have you told anyone?"

"Only May Lewis. We've been friends since the third form. She helped me do the test. She won't tell anyone."

"No, I don't suppose she will. But what about," Cleo hesitated. "Who is the father?"

Stephanie stared at her amazed. "It's Pete of course," she replied quickly. "I thought you'd guess that."

With dismay Cleo realised swiftly that there was more to that relationship than she had suspected. How foolish she had been to have thought that the discipline of the school would have protected Stephanie. "Have you told him?"

"No, of course not. What's it got to do with him?"

"Well, he is the father and I thought you were fond of him and he of you. He should be willing to help. In any case it's his child also. Don't you think he has a right to know about it?"

Stephanie drew herself away. "I don't see what business it is of his. What can he do? I don't suppose he's got enough money!" She began to cry again.

"You don't think he would want to marry you and keep the child?" Cleo asked.

"He might do. I suppose. He's talked about it. But I don't want to marry him." She looked at Cleo with horror. "He's not the sort of boy I would ever want to marry. I just thought we could have some fun. Lots of people do. I don't see why this should happen to me. I never intended to have a baby and I don't want one. It would ruin my life."

"In that case you must tell your parents. They will help. I'm sure."

"I can't possibly tell them. They'd be furious. They've no idea of anything like this. Oh God, what shall I do? Please help me. Miss Lafay."

"What do you mean?" Cleo did not look at her. She was almost afraid to hear the answer.

"Well. I'll have to have an abortion. won't I? That's the obvious thing. I can't just wreck my life. I don't want a baby. I plan to get a good job and enjoy myself. You must understand. I thought you might be able to tell me how to set about it."

"Me!" Cleo stared at her astounded. "I've really no idea, Stephanie. But I'm quite sure such a serious thing shouldn't be decided without proper thought." She stood up as the bell sounded for the last five minutes of break. "We can't talk any more now. You must go and get yourself ready for your next lesson and so must I.

"But you can't just leave me." Stephanie protested. "You must tell me what to do."

"You must speak to your parents and then see a doctor as soon as possible," Cleo suggested. "Your parents are the people to help you and fortunately they will be able to do so. I'm not a suitable person to advise you. I don't think it's necessarily right to have abortion, under these circumstances. It's a very serious decision. You must think about it more."

"I've been thinking about it all weekend and it's the only thing I can do. Won't you help me? I thought you would." She stood despairingly without moving.

"I'm very, very sorry," Cleo replied gently. "I'm willing to discuss it with you but honestly I'm not really the right person."

"Can I at least see you after school and talk about it?"

"I'm going out straight after school but I'll see you here tomorrow after dinner. In the meantime, do try to think things out a bit more clearly. There's so much involved. You must realise that whatever you decide you will have to take responsibility for it for the rest of your life." As the second bell was now ringing they parted hastily. Cleo's thoughts were in a turmoil the rest of the day. It seemed now that she should perhaps have reported Stephanie earlier instead of trusting to the girl's good sense after she had been warned. She had meant to help Stephanie and prevent her from ruining her school career but it now seemed that she had been badly wrong in her judgement.

She would have liked to confide in Merlin when he met her but there was no chance. In any case she was also oppressed by the memory of her behaviour with Mike the previous evening. She must talk to Merlin about that. But when?

When he stopped the car in the hospital car park, Merlin did not immediately get out. Instead he put his arm around her shoulders and kissed her. Although he did not speak, his genuine affection and care for her were obvious. She held his hand tightly for a moment, glad of the comfort. After a few moments, he released her. "We'd better go and rescue our distressed maiden," he remarked with a smile. "She seemed more cheerful yesterday but she told us she was desperate to get home."

"I've brought her some books," Cleo said as she got out of the car. "I don't know whether she'll be pleased with them."

"It'll be good for her to have something to do. She's looking forward very much to seeing you."

For the rest of that evening, Cleo dismissed all thoughts of Stephanie, except when in the midst of a cheerful family supper. Victoria suddenly asked about her. " I suppose she's having trouble with her boyfriend," she suggested.

"You could say that," Cleo replied cautiously

"I don't expect you to tell me anything about it but we all know she's got a boy friend out of school. Most of us think she's being silly."

"I don't think you should embarrass Cleo by talking to her about it," Mrs Evans said before Cleo could reply. "You are forgetting that, although Cleo is our friend, she's still your teacher." She smiled consolingly at Cleo.

"You're right, Grannie." Victoria replied swiftly. "I'm sorry," she said to Cleo. "Please forgive me. Can we talk about the work you've brought me? Merlin can clear away the supper, can't you Merlin?"

Cleo was about to protest but Merlin intervened. "I'll do that, willingly but only on condition that when I've finished, Cleo and I have some time to ourselves."

"That's quite easily arranged," Mrs Evans said firmly before Victoria could object. "Victoria is going to bed to rest and she and I will watch television in her room."

"I'll be good," Victoria promised, "I'm much too afraid of my stern uncle to try to rebel." She smiled at Merlin to take away any sting there might seem to be in her words, as she settled down to talk to Cleo about serious matters of work.

It was almost an hour later however before Cleo and Merlin found themselves alone with a chance to talk. As he settled down in an armchair with a brandy, Cleo curled up on the settee looked at her watch, "It's later than I thought," she said sadly.

"I'm sorry." he replied, "my family commitments do seem to intrude at the moment. Something I had never imagined. I used to think of myself as a pretty self centred bachelor."

Cleo smiled. "And you were right in some ways, perhaps. But you've changed. At least your circumstances have changed."

He looked at her appreciatively and stretched his long legs more comfortably. "The one change I enjoy most is having you in my life again, as you're well aware, I'm sure. I was sorry you weren't free yesterday. It wasn't only Victoria who missed you. I felt, but perhaps I was wrong, that we came closer on Saturday evening. At least I felt that I understood you better." He took a sip of his brandy and seemed content to wait for her reply.

"You weren't wrong," she said swiftly. "I was so much happier."

"Of course," he continued, "I realise that I can't expect to monopolise your time, although I'd rather like to, especially in these last few days before I have to go away."

"There's no reason why you shouldn't, except for Wednesday evening when I'm involved in the House Drama Competition. Parents and guardians are welcome, so you could come to that and we could have a drink afterwards. It's not much of an invitation, I'm afraid."

"I'll accept it, at least I'll agree to the drink afterwards but in return you'll have to come to the Vice Chancellor's reception and concert on Saturday. The music is good and the food should be tolerable."

"I'd love to," she agreed. "Do I dress up?"

"You most certainly do. I expect you to be the most beautiful woman there. Fortunately that won't be very difficult for you."

He laughed. “And it should put an end to all the rumours about me.”

“Rumours?” She looked startled. “What rumours?”

“That I’m gay, of course.” He looked amused at her. “Simply because I’ve shown no interest in women lecturers or students. That’s the reward I get for my celibate life.”

“Oh no.” she laughed. “Not you Merlin. Everyone in Oxford would be astounded. But I’ll willingly come, if only to reveal you in your true colours.”

“I’m not sure I entirely like that. Couldn’t you say you are coming because you want to be with me?” He looked a little oddly at her.

“Of course I am! You know that!”

“Do I?” he asked her. “Sometimes I wonder, Cleo, just how much. I’m sorry,” he added quickly before she could answer, “there was no point in my saying that. I know the situation.”

She felt very sad and guilty, longing to confide in him but afraid to do so when the time was so short. She was again aware of a serious dissatisfaction with herself, At least, she decided she would ask his advice about Stephanie. “Merlin,” she said, “there is something I would like to discuss with you. “It’s nothing to do directly with you and me,” she added quickly. It’s connected with my work. I’m rather worried as to the right course of action and I think I may have been rash in the past.”

“I’ll help if I can but give me the facts first,” She quickly told him the story of her encounters with Stephanie, even though it did entail mentioning her evening with Mike.

As she had hoped he did not ask about Mike but went straight to the problem. “What is worrying you, Cleo? Is it that you’re not really sure of your response? I always thought that your attitude to abortion was quite definite, Am I wrong?”

“Not really, although now I think that there are perhaps very serious circumstances when it could be the better of two evils.”

"But you don't see this as such a case?"

"Not really, although I feel terribly sorry for Stephanie."

"But you won't help by saying something you don't believe. It is important to be kind but it's equally important to be honest. She has to decide and there'll be many people ready to put the opposite point of view."

"I feel so responsible and guilty, I suppose. If I had spoken to her Housemistress or to Miss Stephens could I have prevented this? I didn't want her to be expelled or something which would spoil her exam chances. But this is worse." She spoke tensely and twisted her hands in her agitation.

He stood up and came and sat next to her, taking her agitated hands in his. "You must not take on responsibilities which are not rightly yours," he told her gently. "You did what you thought would be best for Stephanie and it's possible that this pregnancy could have been started before you knew her."

"I expect you could be right," she admitted. "I suppose I just think that there, but for the grace of God, go I." She stopped, realising that this could involve him too.

He released her hands but did not move away. "If you and I had started a child," he replied quietly, "which was extremely unlikely, I would have insisted on providing and caring for it, even if you hadn't wanted to marry me. That child would have been conceived in love."

"I know," she said softly. "But I'm afraid Stephanie's child hasn't been. She just wants to be rid of it. She doesn't really think Pete needs to know unless he's willing to help to pay for the abortion. I find it so sad."

"It is sad," Merlin continued, "but the problem didn't start with the pregnancy. It started when they entered into the relationship without thinking of the possible consequences. Many people are unhappily involved: Stephanie, Pete, her parents, and not least the unfortunate child. But you are not involved nor responsible, so don't blame yourself. If you want to blame anything, blame the society in which we live, which encourages this sort of thing,"

"I was pretty irresponsible, I think, but I was fortunate that I met you. I trusted you." She stopped speaking and for a moment he did not reply. They were not touching but they were very close and she was content to remain like this.

"I hope you will soon be able to trust me again," he said finally.

"It's not you," she replied. "It's me. You know that." She paused and then went on quickly. "I saw Mike yesterday but we spent much of the time at his sister's. She's a beautiful girl with four children and an alcoholic husband whom she loves. Mike seemed to think it would do me good to see how the 'undeserving poor' live. He disapproves. I think, but I couldn't because I thought they were such a loving family. It was strange. You would like her, She is very honest."

When he did not reply, she turned to look at him. He seemed to be gazing into the flames of the fire. It was difficult, as so often, to guess his feelings. "Are you angry with me for spending time with Mike?" she asked him at last.

"Are you asking me if I'm jealous?" He turned to look at her at last but the expression of his dark eyes was hard to understand. "Do you want me to be jealous?"

She moved away from him. "No. That's not the reason why I see him. There is a bond between us. We've both failed. I suppose. At least, we haven't conformed to the pattern expected of us. We're both afraid of what we might do. I feel I can help him and I suppose that attracts me or flatters me." She waited for Merlin to say something but, as he remained silent, she added defiantly. "I find him physically attractive too but then I am susceptible as you know."

Merlin stood up and moved back to his chair. He picked up his brandy, looked at it and then put it down again. She waited, feeling a little afraid, almost. "What do you expect me to say," he said at last. "I suppose I should be pleased that you have been honest with me. But you know I love you and want to marry you, so what you have said doesn't just make me jealous but it hurts. I'm not sure that you understand how much that is. I can only hope that whatever you decide will be right for you."

"You can stop me from doing something foolish, if you want to."

"No," he said firmly, "I told you that on Saturday. I will not persuade you in that way. You must make a proper decision. Without that, any relationship we have, will be a failure." He was pale but obviously decided.

"You're prepared to risk that?" she asked almost incredulously.

"Yes, because I must." He finished his brandy and stood up. "It's time for me to take you home, I'm afraid. You must give me the details about Wednesday evening before we part."

Cleo did not demur for it was late and there seemed little more to say. She felt frustrated and annoyed with herself and with Merlin. She wanted to disturb his calm but could not think how to do it. Instead she returned to the subject of Stephanie. "I think you're right about Stephanie," she said. "I must persuade her to speak to her parents and to do nothing rash before then. I don't think it would help to tell Miss Stephens or Miss Wilson."

"Definitely not. She needs her parents' help and their protection against authority, particularly if she wants to keep it a secret."

"You mean, if she decides to have an abortion, no one need know at school?"

"Exactly. Now I think we've said more than enough about that, don't you?"

"I hate the thought," Cleo said passionately. "There are too many unwanted children, unwanted babies. People copulating and not caring, Stephanie doesn't care about Pete apparently. It's just fun that goes wrong and so then we get rid of the consequences. God, what a world. There must be a better way."

"You know there is," Merlin said calmly as he turned into the main village street. "But it's hard and when we're very young, we don't want to stop and think. Did you?"

"Oh, I'm no better. I wish I were but I'm not. That's what's so upsetting." She knew that she wasn't just thinking of Stephanie and Pete but was angry and disgusted with herself. "I can't advise her. It would be hypocritical. How do I know what I would've done if I'd been in her position? God knows I've done plenty of stupid and selfish things."

They had arrived at the Staff House. Merlin stopped the car but did not move or speak. As she waited he said at last. "I love you Cleo but I can't help you. We all have to make our own decisions whatever they may be and accept the consequences." She understood that he knew she had not simply been referring to Stephanie or to the past.

"In the meantime," he continued. "perhaps we can plan our next meeting and hope to enjoy ourselves away from your school and my family. Would a theatre trip appeal to you? There's a pre- London production at the Playhouse. A new play, very witty and entertaining or so I've been told. What do you say?"

"I'd love it," she replied, her mood changing instantly. "But do you think you can get tickets?"

"Easily, I believe. I'll make it for Friday. Then we can have a late meal afterwards and you can spend the night at my place. That's much the easiest thing to do since we're going to the University concert on the Saturday. Just bring all you'll need. I'll ring you to confirm the arrangements."

She was delighted. She had never imagined his suggesting anything like that. So he really did understand her! Impulsively she gave him a quick kiss and a hug. "But what about Wednesday?"

"That stands. We'll have supper in the village after the House plays. The rest of my free time, I need for sorting out my work and packing." He returned her kiss. "Now go away and don't do anything rash."

She waved happily to him, as he drove away and then went in the Staff House. There was a note in her pigeon hole. Surprised. she read it. 'Dear Cleo,' it said, 'will you have a word with me when you come in? I shall be in my room. Yours Stella.' Cleo was intrigued. What could Stella possibly want to say to her? She walked along the corridor to Stella's room which was on the ground floor at the back and knocked on the door.

Wearing her dark red lounge suit Stella was sitting at the table working with her lap top computer, which she closed down immediately Cleo entered. "Have a seat," she said, moving towards one of her armchairs and waving Cleo to the one that stood opposite.

As she sat down, Cleo looked quickly round the room. It was large and comfortable and most of the furniture had obviously been supplied by Stella. The background was dark but there were several touches of vivid colours, especially in the pile of cushions on the divan. It was lit by several small but brilliant lights. Stella looked rather sombre as always but she did not seem to be at all hostile.

"I wanted to talk to you about Stephanie," she began straightaway.

"About Stephanie?" Cleo stared at her.

"Yes. I'm her tutor. Perhaps you'd forgotten. I think you might've consulted me but that doesn't matter now. I spoke to her myself at four o'clock. She told me she had spoken to you."

“Do you mean..” Cleo hesitated wondering how much Stephanie had said.

“About the baby. Yes. I was curious and concerned. Her work has been unusually poor in the last couple of weeks and she behaved very oddly in her lesson with me after break. She looked wretched and did nothing and, when I reprimanded her, she burst into tears and left the room. Her friend, Maggy Lewis, said Stephanie was worried about something, so I sent a message for her to see me at four in my tutorial room. She’s a promising mathematician, I didn’t want her work suffering.”

“I see,” Cleo said. “and she confided in you?”

“She didn’t want to at first but I already had my suspicions, so it wasn’t difficult. She told me that you seemed to be against the idea of an abortion, which I would have expected since I know your opinions.”

“And you advised her to have one. I suppose. Do you think that is morally right? Or doesn’t it worry you at all?”

“I’m not concerned with morals but with practicalities.” Stella replied in cool, hard voice. She turned her sombre gaze on Cleo. “I don’t like seeing anyone in that situation any more than you do but since Stephanie is in it surely you can see it has to be dealt with promptly. It’s much easier while the pregnancy is still in its early stage.”

“But surely Stephanie needs time to think? There’s another life involved and the ending of it may have a much bigger effect on her than she realises.”

“Have you any personal experience?” Stella asked her.

“Not in my own life,” Cleo replied, “but one of my college friends had an abortion and she regretted it bitterly, so much so that she had another baby as soon as she could in circumstances almost as bad.”

"It doesn't have to be like that." Stella turned away. "I know from my own experience," she added. "as I expect you've already been told."

"No. I've not been told anything, although I did wonder that evening in Cynthia's room when I first met you."

"That amazes me," Stella replied mockingly. "I was pretty sure that Cynthia would have told you my guilty secret which I once revealed to her in a weak moment."

"You are wrong. She has never said anything. But how does your own experience affect your advice to Stephanie? That is what interests me."

"I told her that an abortion in my opinion was the only solution. And it is better done as soon as possible. When she seemed disinclined to listen to me, I suggested that she should speak to Miss Stephens or to Miss Wilson, her Housemistress. They are entitled to know since she is in their care and they would know what to do."

Cleo felt angry but restrained herself. "Surely her parents are the best people?" she asked.

"Miss Stephens will inform them. In fact. she has already done so. They will fetch Stephanie tomorrow. I thought you ought to know. It didn't seem necessary to mention your involvement, by the way."

"I suppose I should thank you for that," Cleo said coldly. "But I'm much more concerned about Stephanie. She must have been very upset at having to see Miss Stephens. Couldn't you just have got in touch with her parents?"

"That's not my job," Stella replied unemotionally.

"But surely it would have been kinder?"

"She has been very foolish and she has to take the consequences, as we all do. The best thing for her future is to get everything settled quickly and quietly. She must learn to behave more circumspectly, which is what I told her."

"Poor Stephanie! She must be very upset."

"Upset, perhaps, but certainly angry. I think perhaps that you have a rosier view of Stephanie than she deserves. I suppose you meant well but I can't quite see what you were aiming to do?"

"I wanted to persuade her to speak to her parents herself so that there could be a loving and helpful discussion of what is right. These decisions shouldn't be made in this cold blooded way. Surely you don't think that is wrong? There is a child to be thought of."

"In your view yes, in mine, no, There is Stephanie's future to be thought of."

"It needn't necessarily have been ruined, even if the child was saved," Cleo replied stubbornly.

"The parents may still see it in your way but I doubt it, after they have talked to Miss Stephens and to me. I pointed out that a mathematician's career is short anyway."

Cleo stood up. "Thank you for telling me," she said. "I don't agree with what you have said or done but I imagine you thought you were doing right. I only hope Stephanie is grateful for your understanding of her situation." She walked towards the door.

"I don't think so," Stella replied as she too rose to her feet. "In fact she is angry with me for interfering as she called it. She was pretty rude, in fact. If it's any comfort to you, she would have preferred to have dealt with you but I'm afraid that you might've been kind only to be cruel. I'm sorry but that's how I see it."

"I see it quite differently. I only hope you won't regret it. But then as you haven't regretted your own decision, you probably won't regret having forced Stephanie into this." Cleo went out quickly, closing the door behind her. She was outraged rather than angry with Stella's behaviour and amazed that Stella whose relationship with Nicholas Barnes was so widely known could accuse Stephanie of being lacking in circumspection.

She sat down on her divan and considered the situation. There was nothing she could do now. Stephanie's future seemed to be in the hands of her parents who would probably be influenced by the advice they had been given by Miss Stephens and Stella. Cleo felt a great pity for the girl who might so easily be persuaded into doing something she might later greatly regret.

She remembered Merlin's advice that she should not take on responsibilities which were not rightly hers and decided sadly that it might have been better to have reported Stephanie when she had first met her. Many times in her life she had tried to help others and failed miserably. It was time she learned her lesson, she decided as she began to undress.

As she turned out the bedside lamp and prepared to sleep, Mike came into her mind. Was he another person who was tempting her to think, perhaps disastrously, that she could help him?

Chapter Eighteen

The rest of the week passed uneventfully. It was accepted, openly at least, that Stephanie had been taken home because she was ill and that she would not be back until the following term. Cleo assumed that most of the Sixth Form knew the truth or had some inkling of it but nothing was said. They had closed ranks. As for the Staff, they were either ignorant or preferred to appear to be so. A notice finally came round from Miss Stephens confirming that Stephanie would be absent until the end of term but no one commented, at least not in Cleo's hearing.

Although Cleo found this strange and unexpected, she nevertheless preferred it to the usual gossip which would have been very upsetting to her.

On the Wednesday evening after an unexpected success in the House Plays' Competition which brought her a commendation from Miss Wilson, she was in a cheerful mood to meet Merlin but not in a mood to confide. He did not ask about Stephanie and so she did not tell him. He had been able to book seats for the theatre on the Friday he told her and had booked a table for a late supper afterwards. All of which seemed very pleasant.

He renewed his invitation for her to spend the weekend at his house. She agreed that it would be convenient and certainly save him from many extra miles of travelling but she no longer felt so confident about the nature of his invitation. If he wanted her to sleep with him, surely he would have said so? She decided it might be wiser not to investigate at this moment. They parted cheerfully. He kissed her goodbye and arranged to pick her up early on the Friday evening.

Friday afternoon brought her an unexpected letter from Stephanie, written late on the Thursday. 'Dear Miss Lafay.' she wrote. 'I am writing to tell you that it is all over. With my father's medical connections it was easy to arrange and my parents did not see any reason to waste time. They could think of no good arguments against an abortion and neither could I.

'I am grateful to you for talking to me, even though we didn't agree, I could see you cared about me, which is more than I can say for Miss Harvey. I shall never forgive her for the way she treated me. It is disgusting when we all know how she behaves.

'This morning, I was glad it was over and that I could forget about it. But now I feel empty and lonely. I didn't expect that. I keep crying. I expect I shall get over it. I know now that what you said about responsibility is right. I'll remember it in future.

'Please don't say anything to anyone at school. Stephanie.

'PS I enclose a letter for Pete which you might give to Mike to pass on. I have told him what has happened and that I don't want to see him ever again. My parents don't want me to tell him but I think he has a right to know as you said. S.'

Cleo read it through twice, then folded it carefully and put it into her handbag. She felt very sad and couldn't help wondering whether, if she had had a further talk with Stephanie, she might have persuaded her to act differently. Was that the hidden meaning of the letter or was it simply a way of ensuring her silence and of getting a farewell message to Pete?

There was no time now for her to think further about it, as she had to get ready for the evening and pack for the weekend. In any case, it would be useless, for there was nothing further she could do, except to pass on the letter to Pete as soon as she had the opportunity. She thought as she walked up the stairs to her room that it might be a good idea to remind herself about being responsible.

Merlin, as always, arrived on time. The theatre and the supper were as delightful as she had expected. It was very late when they arrived back to his home. He took her straight to his study and proposed a night-cap. Declining brandy, she decided on hot sweet milk, much to his amusement. "I always had that," she reminded him as they sat together in front of the fire. "and you were always amused at my childish taste."

She wondered how he would react to that reminder but he only smiled and agreed. As soon as they had finished their drinks, he took her with her case up to his spare room. "I think you'll be comfortable," he said. "If you want anything I'm across the landing." He put her suitcase on a chair and moved towards the door and seemed about to depart.

Suddenly he came back, put his arm around her and kissed her tenderly but not passionately. "Good night," he said. "I'm very tired and I expect you are too. I'll get breakfast about nine, if that suits you." With a smile he had gone and the door closed firmly behind him. His intentions were clearly obvious.

Left to herself, Cleo unpacked quickly and prepared for bed. It was almost amusing she thought to be so definitely yet pleasantly rejected. Only Merlin could have done that. As she lay down she realised, however, that she too was extremely tired after a busy and disturbing week followed by a late though enjoyable evening. It would be better to challenge him on the Saturday, if that was necessary. She hoped that it might not be.

Saturday morning brought fresh thoughts of Stephanie. Looking in the handbag for her lipstick, she came across the letter neatly folded away and re-read it slowly. Was there anything further she could have done. she wondered? How would Stephanie finally react to this? She was sure from what she had heard that no girl ever had an abortion without it affecting her, sometimes much more than she had expected. Perhaps that was the explanation of Stella Harvey? In spite of her bravado was she perhaps still suffering. Then how could she have advised Stephanie as brutally as she had?

That thought reminded her of Stephanie's bitter words about Stella. 'I shall never forgive her'. The words seemed chilling and almost menacing. Cleo was in a very thoughtful mood when she met Merlin for breakfast. He did not seem to notice as he greeted her and offered her a freshly prepared grapefruit. "Toast or cereal to follow?" he asked her.

"Both," she answered him quickly. "I should have remembered your hearty appetite." He smiled at her. "Perhaps you would prefer bacon and eggs" She declined shuddering but accepted a hot cup of black coffee gratefully.

He was looking very relaxed and attractive this morning in his casual trousers and deep maroon sweater over a carefully toning pink shirt. It was a cold but sunny morning and the sunshine came through the living room window and highlighted the daffodils on the dresser. A pleasant warmth came from the Aga as she sat down in a chair with her back to it. She was glad that she too had dressed carefully - electric blue check trousers and a soft matching electric blue cashmere sweater with a black gilet for added warmth. She was pleased to catch his appreciative glance.

He put some bread in the toaster on the table, poured out his coffee and sat down opposite her. "It must be nearly five years since we last had breakfast together," he remarked, as he helped himself to milk "You're probably even more beautiful now than you were then but your appetite hasn't changed. I'm glad to see."

"That may be true," she replied," but other things have, I'm afraid. I don't see life so simply now."

"Perhaps that's a good thing," he suggested.

"Perhaps but I'm not so sure." She hesitated wondering whether to say more.

"Something is worrying you, I think. Would it help to share it?"

"It's about Stephanie," she said slowly.

"Stephanie? Oh, I remember, the unhappy Sixth Former. Did your further conversation with her have any effect?"

"Unfortunately, it never happened." She told him about Stella's intervention and then produced Stephanie's letter. "I need to tell someone and there isn't anyone else."

He read it carefully. "It's a sad. little letter." he remarked sympathetically, "but that was to be expected. Obviously, her parents took the same line as Stella and Miss Stephens. There was not much she could do."

"She could at least have told Pete and found out what he wanted to do. It was his child too. Now, he's only going to find out about the baby, when it's dead." Cleo had not clearly realised until that moment how strongly she felt about that.

"So you think after all that Stephanie was wrong?"

"And you don't?" she challenged him.

He looked thoughtfully at her. "It's hardly right for a man to pass that kind of Judgement. You know how I would have felt about any child of mine. But Pete may not feel the same. Furthermore, would he be able to support a wife and child?"

Cleo took another sip of her coffee. "I don't know," she replied finally. "But probably not in the way she would have wanted to be supported."

"So in three or four years' time they would quite likely have been divorced? Stephanie would have her baby but would be without a career or a husband. Is that what you would have preferred?"

She stared at him in amazement. "I never thought that you would talk like that! Surely you have to risk something sometimes in order to do what is right?"

"But supposing you don't think it is right? What then?"

"Then I suppose that you have to try to do what does seem right to you."

"Isn't that what Stephanie and her parents might say they are trying to do?"

Cleo was upset. "Merlin," she asked vehemently, "why are you saying things like that? Is that all your study of moral philosophy has brought you to? A belief that all morals are simply relative?"

"Of course not. I'm simply trying to make an obvious point that the more one knows and understands about a person or a situation, the less likely one is able to pass judgement. One has to accept that some people are trying to do what they think is right, even though their ideals seem very limited. Incidentally, it makes one realise how necessary a sound moral education is. And that is why, I suppose, I have become involved in that myself."

"I understand that. I appreciate what you're trying to do but it doesn't make me think that abortion in Stephanie's circumstances could ever be truly justified. To me it is wrong and mistaken."

"I'm not disputing that. But sometimes, perhaps, you are too impulsive and emotional and tend to see matters as either black or white and not as they may be."

"You have every right to say that to me," she admitted suddenly "I judged you unfairly twice."

"I wasn't thinking about myself. I think I'm trying to caution you. You must not be too dogmatic in your judgements. Surely the Christian command to love should always prevent that, since it asks us to try to understand and to forgive."

"You think I'm not good at loving and forgiving. You're probably right. I doubt if I've ever forgiven my mother for deserting me. I might've done, if I'd had the opportunity but that was denied me. My father never forgave her and most people seemed to think he was right. My early life and my years in a Catholic school with its strict dogmatic teaching make it difficult for me to accept your undoubtedly wiser counselling."

"I had no wish to revive such memories or to upset you, Cleo." he replied gently. "I suppose I just wanted to encourage you to feel more kindly towards Stephanie and even towards Stella."

"That's not really difficult. I'm such a sinner myself. I would find it impossible not to do so, without being a complete hypocrite." She spoke more lightly and smiled. then suddenly she added more seriously. "It's love and loving I find more difficult. I'm not sure that I know what it's all about, even now." Putting down her cup. she stood up suddenly. "If you've finished." she asked. "shall we clear the dishes away?"

"We'll just stack them in the dish washer," he agreed. following her change of mood and leading the way to the kitchen. "Have you any ideas as to how you'd like to spend the day?"

"It's very bright. Why don't we walk somewhere and have lunch and then walk back. That'll give us time to rest and change. What do you think?"

"That sounds an excellent plan to me," he agreed.

It was nearly four o' clock when they arrived back after an invigorating day on the hills. They had been good companions but they had not carried on their earlier conversation. Cleo had, in fact, been very eager to learn more about where Merlin was going in El Salvador and what he had learned about it from his earlier, though much shorter visit. She had declared that it sounded likely to be a very hard five weeks for him and marvelled at his determination to do it.

They had tea and crumpets in the living room after they got back relaxing in the warmth of the Aga and the comfort of the armchairs, which was very welcome after their long and somewhat arduous walk. "It's amazing to me," she remarked, "how well you still walk, after your accident and operations."

“There are some things I no longer find easy but walking and swimming, I’m glad to say, don’t come into that list, or only on a bad day which I occasionally have.”

“But surely,” she persisted, “the sort of life you’ve planned out for yourself during the next five weeks won’t be exactly easy for you? You’ll work long hours and your comfort will be minimal? Are you wise to do this? Aren’t you, perhaps, overestimating your debt to Lawrence?”

“You think I’m being masochistic?” He smiled at her, “I hope not, although I can see why you might think so, but I am interested to gain a greater understanding of the education of people with special difficulties, I might even write a book.”

“Oh. I see,” she replied meaningfully.

“I’m not quite sure that I know what you mean by that.”

“Then you’ll just have to remain in ignorance because I’m now going to have a bath and start on my leisurely preparations for this evening. This is a matter of some importance since you have told me I must be the most beautiful woman there. It’s going to require all my somewhat considerable skill.”

“I very much doubt that,” he said. “I’ll come up with you and make sure you have everything you want. After that, I’ll rest and then have a bath too.”

“It’s most unfair,” she protested, “You don’t have to make elaborate preparations.”

“Neither do you. In any case. I’m determined not to be unworthy of you.”

He came into her room to make sure that everything was ready for her and then turned to go. At the doorway. he suddenly came back and walked up to her. Putting his hands on her shoulders he bent and kissed her on the mouth, lingeringly for a moment. Abruptly he moved away. “You look very lovely as you are,” he remarked. “I don’t quite know how you’re going to improve on it.”

"I most certainly intend to," she promised. With a smile he was gone, leaving her disappointed. She admitted to herself, she had hoped for more. "But I'm sure he cares about me." she told herself, "and tonight, he simply won't be able to resist me, if he really feels as I think he does." She contemplated with pleasure her simple black dress with its flattering tight fitting bodice and waist and the swirling skirt with the gleams of silver in it. She decided on the sparkling diamond earrings Marcus had once given her and the matching brooch. The black and silver shawl and shoes completed the outfit.

Merlin surveyed her with a certain ironical pleasure. "I admire your art." he remarked, "you have created a magical illusion. How could any man resist it? I shall certainly achieve my ambition. No woman at the University can possibly rival you."

"Your reputation will be secure," she said lightly but his irony disturbed her. Did he suspect her motives? If so, did it really matter? There was no time for further speculation. however, as he led her to the car and began to talk about the plans for the evening. The Vice Chancellor's reception and buffet came first, followed by the concert in Wheaton's very splendid hall.

As Merlin had promised, the food was tolerable and the music was extremely good. Cleo enjoyed herself, rather more than she had actually expected. She was introduced to several of his colleagues and their wives, the latter gazed at her warily but their husbands were obviously admiring. Merlin, she decided, was clearly the most attractive and intelligent looking man there but there was a difference from the Oxford days for here he was also respected as a senior and distinguished member of the academic community. She wondered why he had wanted to bring her. Was it that he wanted her to see him as he now was or was it simply that he wanted to have her company? His manner, charming, ironical, and slightly detached gave her no clue. She realised that she was still puzzled as to his real feelings.

On the drive home he said little except to comment favourably on the music and dismiss the food. As soon as he had parked the car, he took her into his study, switched on the lights and surveyed her with considerable appreciation. "You were very successful he remarked, "the belle of the ball, if there had been a ball."

"You were an excellent and entertaining partner," she told him as she took off her shawl. "I've been very good, aren't you at least going to reward me with a kiss?" She smiled up at him, her green eyes widely open and her soft red lips slightly parted. She was well aware of the power of her attraction. She had experienced that with many other men. Now. however. it was different. He was going away soon and she desperately wanted to feel sure that he loved her.

For a moment he hesitated. Then he smiled ironically. "Perfect!" he said. "How could any man resist you? How can I possibly?" He put his arms round her and bent and kissed her on her lips. For a moment he stayed very close to her and did not seem anxious to move away, then he released her slowly and walked across the room to draw the long, heavy curtains.

"Would you like coffee or something stronger?" he asked.

"Neither, at the moment. Can't we just talk?"

"Of course. I would like that." As she sat down on the couch, he came and sat next to her and put his arm around her shoulders. "I suppose it was wicked of me to ask you to dress up and play this part?" he said.

"Why did you?" she asked. resting her head for a moment on his shoulder. "Was it for your amusement or to satisfy your ego?"

"I suppose both of those reasons came into it, even though they don't reflect much credit on me, but more important, I wanted to see the other Cleo."

"The other Cleo?" She moved away and frowned at him. "What do you mean?"

"The Cleo who was a model and Marcus Fielding's mistress for two years."

She was surprised. "Does that matter to you?"

"Of course it does. I could not imagine the Cleo I knew so well in Oxford wanting to live like that or even being able to live like that."

"But you have known me for two months since I left Marcus and you've never said anything about it before. You didn't seem to think that I seemed so much different. So why now?"

"It has become more important."

"Because you're going away and because you've asked me to marry you?"

"Partly but also because you haven't agreed to marry me. It occurred to me that perhaps the other Cleo mattered more than I had realised and that I should perhaps meet her and get to know her."

"And now you're not sure that you like her very much, am I right?" she demanded. "You think she sets out to tempt and to make use of men, including you?"

"Didn't you do that and aren't you doing it now? Can you deny that?"

"Has it ever occurred to you that I only want to be sure that you love me? That you're going away again and I'm frightened. Is that so strange?"

"I've told you I love you and I've asked you to marry me. You're the first woman I've ever asked or ever wanted to ask. Doesn't that mean something? Can't you see that this is not the same as when I went to the States?" He remained irritatingly calm, as was his custom.

"I'm not the same either," she retorted passionately. "If you had asked me to marry you then, I would have done so without hesitation. I know I was naive and foolish but we were so close that I would never have believed it could be wrong?"

"But it would have been," he replied firmly. "I was not ready and neither were you. Nor were the circumstances right. But now it could be right and you aren't sure. You seem strangely dissatisfied with me. Why?"

"I can't believe in your cold blooded love. You talk of love but does it mean anything? When I even show that I want more, you politely and quietly decline. So, I think this is just some rational decision you have made for you own reasons. Perhaps you have decided that now is a good time for you to marry and I am available. That's not what I want."

"I see," he said. "You would prefer what has come to be the more usual scenario. Having been tempted by your beauty and charm so cleverly displayed, I should take you in my arms, caress your enticing body, smother you with my violent kisses. Then we should rush upstairs. tearing off our clothes and fall naked into bed. The details which should follow are familiar to you from your contemporary reading, so I won't bore you by reciting them. Finally, overcome with passion, hardly able to contain ourselves we have sex. In the modern jargon I enter you, you respond. The result - satisfactory orgasms for both of us."

"Why are you being so horrible? We have made love many times in the past and it was wonderful. Why do you mock it now? I need passion, you know. I couldn't be happy with some calm, frigid relationship. I wouldn't be faithful, I'm quite sure." She stood up suddenly. "This is ridiculous. I'll go to bed - alone if that's how you want it. I don't understand you? Why is it so different now?"

He too stood up. "If it's my body you want, you can have it, tonight if that is what you really wish. It would be easy for you to rouse me. It would be enjoyable while it lasted. We both know that." He took her in his arms and pulled her close to him. "Is this all you want, even now?" His voice was sad.

She pulled herself away. "Why do you speak like this? You didn't when we made love before. We were both happy then, why can't you be happy now?"

"The difference is that five and a half years ago we both loved each other. We weren't sure that it would last but we loved each other at that moment. Unfortunately perhaps for me, I discovered that my love for you was lasting but you don't feel the same. You aren't sure. You still want to experiment. That's not good enough for me."

"You have changed," she said, sitting down again. "Surely. you realise that?"

Before he answered, he moved across to his desk and sat on the chair in front of it. The light illuminated his clearly defined features and his dark sombre eyes. "You're thinking that my accident changed me, I imagine. The possibility of death and disablement does tend to make one see with greater clarity what is really important in life. I realised more than ever that a lifelong, loving relationship was very necessary to me. But before then I knew that I loved you, that was why I came to look for you after I returned from The States. The irony is that then I expressed my love passionately and you reviled me for it. Isn't that right?"

She could not deny it. "My life was chaotic. I wasn't ready for anything. My mother had just killed herself. Can't you see?"

"And so you ran away to a somewhat empty life without passion really and certainly without love. But when we met again two months ago you had left it. It appeared that you wanted to live differently."

"I did. I still do."

"You want to love and be loved but not yet as St Augustine might have said. In the meantime sexual excitement is still welcome. Is that it?"

"It doesn't sound very pleasant but there's probably some truth in it. But it's not the whole truth."

"Oh, I know. You like me as a friend, sometimes. And you also want to try me out again as a lover, without committing yourself, of course."

"Don't you see it might help me to be sure? I'm so afraid."

"I think you're afraid of loving but even more you can't believe that anyone could love you."

"No one ever has. So why should I believe you do? Especially when I'm not sure I even want you to do so, because I'd probably betray you and I'd hate that."

"So you offer me your body and want mine for the temporary consolation it might give? I don't want your body, I want you, the whole of you. I am ready to be committed but you're not. I can't accept that. It would degrade us both."

"Oh Merlin, don't be so hard!" she cried as he sat there regarding her. Nothing is as clear as that? If only you weren't going away! I can't bear that."

"I don't think I could bear to stay," he surprised her by saying. "I find it too painful. I want so much more than you are able to give. It will also give you time to think without me. Perhaps even to experiment more if that is what you want, as I sometimes think you do."

"You're thinking of Mike, I suppose," she accused him angrily.

"Maybe. That is for you to decide. If you want to decide, that is. I have to leave that to you."

She stood up. "And you're not prepared to help. I need help."

"Not mine any longer," he replied quietly. "That would be useless."

"You seem to have made up your mind."

"It is you who have to do that. I shall be away about five weeks. I will let you know the date of my return, when it's decided. If you want to see me again, it will be for you to tell me."

"How can you be so hard, if you love me?"

"It's because I love you, it's the only way. You must make your decision." He sounded very unhappy but quite resolute.

They gazed silently at one another for a while. "Did you expect this to happen?" she asked finally.

"I hoped it wouldn't." He said no more.

"I think it would be better, if you took me home now," she replied finally, "instead of in the morning. If you don't mind travelling so late."

"It will probably be best," he agreed. "Do you need to pack?"

"It will only take a few minutes." When she came down, he was already in the hall with her shawl which he placed softly round her shoulders.

She clung to him suddenly. "Oh, Merlin. I hate parting from you. I hope everything goes well for you." Her eyes were suddenly full of tears.

"I hope it goes well for both of us." He kissed her gently and led her out to the car.

Chapter Nineteen

The days that followed Merlin's departure were difficult for Cleo. She felt lonely and depressed but worse than that was the feeling that she had once again run away but this time without any justification. She could not attempt to plan for her future, everything seemed meaningless. What hope could there be for such a worthless person as she felt herself to be?

Even the weather reflected her mood. The blue skies and bright sunshine which seemed to have heralded the beginning of Spring vanished during Sunday morning and every morning she woke up to heavy grey clouds and a chill wind. Even the valiantly bright daffodils seemed to shiver as it passed over them.

Sunday was particularly depressing for most of the girls and the staff seemed to be unavailable. Many of the staff were away and the girls were obviously entertaining themselves in their Houses. The wind rustled down the corridors and the empty classrooms had an abandoned air. Cleo took refuge from her bleak room in the Library which was at least brightly lit and warm when the heavy curtains were drawn. It seemed a very welcome haven after a solitary damp walk. At least it was possible here to see other people without being obliged to talk to them.

Monday was better for then there was work to do. School was bustling with end of term activities and girls and staff were talking eagerly about the coming holidays. Bridget was going to France and Spain; Cynthia and Pam were both preparing to go house hunting, in readiness for their weddings in the summer. Cleo felt very isolated and on the pretext of last minute marking avoided them as much as possible. It reminded her far too much of the end of term at her own school when she had had no happy holiday to look forward to. It seemed as if her life had really changed very little.

Monday, Tuesday and Wednesday seemed to be endless and on Wednesday evening a phone call from Mike was a welcome relief. He sounded cheerful and relaxed and invited her to meet him in the 'Red Lion' for a meal and a chat. For a brief moment, she wondered if she would be wiser to refuse but that seemed ridiculous under the circumstances and furthermore she still had to deliver Stephanie's letter for Pete to him.

Thursday morning brought another totally unexpected event - a letter from Marcus. He was not to her surprise and to some extent chagrin, begging her to go back to him but on the contrary was offering her the use of the flat for most of the Easter vacation. 'I shall be spending much of the recess in Braxton and the South of France at Sarah's parents' villa and it occurred to me that you might perhaps be glad of a London base, for at least part of the time. Oddly enough, you still have your key, I believe so that presents no difficulty. So just let me know.'

He was obviously very much preoccupied with worries about the election which might be only a few months away. He did not appear to think that the Conservatives had much chance of winning and seemed to think that even his comparatively safe seat might be in danger. He was obviously, therefore, intending to spend as much time as possible at Braxton and would certainly not want to risk a disagreement with Sarah or her family.

Even so, he could not resist suggesting a meeting between them since he would be spending two or three days in London. 'If you remain adamant,' he wrote, 'we could at least have an enjoyable meal and conversation. Ever Yours Marcus.'

Cleo spent most of the day considering her response to Marcus' offer. It would be delightful to have the flat but would Marcus remain as undemanding as he now seemed to be, once they met? Was she, indeed, in a sufficiently resolute mood to resist him? She finally decided that the offer was too good to refuse and that there was no need for her to be nervous. Helen, her school friend, who was coming on a visit from Italy could stay with her there. It would be ideal. Thinking it would be much easier to write rather than to telephone, she wrote her letter on Thursday evening and posted it before she could have time to change her mind.

Friday evening found her sitting opposite Mike in a cosy corner table, More carefully dressed and groomed than usual, he was smiling engagingly at her and looked extremely handsome. He had been waiting when she arrived and said he had already ordered steaks and real ale for them, since those, though simple, were always good. He did not appear to consider that she might have preferred to order for herself and seeing his obvious pleasure in the arrangements, she made no objection.

As soon as they sat down, she handed him Stephanie's letter for Pete. He asked if it was important and when she replied in the affirmative, he suggested he might as well take it straight to Pete who was in the bar. "In that case," she replied, "it might be better for you to know what it's about. It'll probably upset Pete, at least I think it might," She told him quickly all she knew of Stephanie's story.

"The silly bugger'll be really cut up," he remarked, putting the letter down on the table. "He talked to me about marrying, and I'm sure he would've been willing, if she'd told him about the baby."

"Stephanie had no wish to marry him. She just wanted fun. Marriage is for later and for someone with her own sort of background. She made that quite clear to me."

"The bitch! We all warned him not to mess with her but he wouldn't listen." He stared at the letter for a moment then raised his troubled, brown eyes to hers. "I suppose I might as well tell him now. He's been wondering why he didn't see her last weekend." He stood up. "I won't be long."

Cleo sipped the real ale which surprised her with its pleasant taste and pondered once again over the sordid sadness of Pete and Stephanie's affair. She was interrupted by Mike's return. "He's really cut up about it," he said. "He actually thought she cared about him. Said she'd talked about them getting married one day. But, do you know what upset him most? The baby. He thought she should have spoken to him about it. I told him not to be a fucking idiot. Girls don't bother about that sort of thing these days." He took a long pull at his drink.

"I thought she should tell him," Cleo said. "but she didn't think it was any concern of his, since he wouldn't have enough money to get an abortion. I suppose you're right. A lot of girls think like that."

"But you wouldn't?' He finished his drink.

"No, I wouldn't, at least I hope I wouldn't."

"Fuck!" Mike said violently. "Why should we bother? Our steaks are just coming. I'll get myself another drink. Do you want one?"

"No thanks. What will Pete do?" she asked.

"Get pissed, I expect. That's what I suggested. Or get another woman, if he can be more careful this time." He sounded uncaring but she knew him well enough to realise that he was upset.

As soon as he came back to the table. Mike attacked his steak with vigour. "I'm bloody hungry," he announced. "I haven't had anything since breakfast and I've driven about three hundred miles since then. The motorway was hellish. There'd been an accident. It's no joke driving for your living." He grinned broadly at her. "You look good, he said. "and the meal's good so let's enjoy ourselves."

"Why not?" She realised that he did not intend to say any more about Pete and his troubles and she certainly had no desire to do so.

"How about these Easter holidays?" he asked suddenly half way through the meal. "Have you thought about my suggestion?"

"You mean that we should spend a week together?"

"Yes. But I'm afraid it'll have to be at the end and not the beginning. They've changed my dates because of a job on the continent. Still, the weather should be better then. What do you think? Wales should be quite pleasant. We could have a good time. What do you say?"

She finished the last morsel of steak before answering, wondering how to reply. "A friend of mine, my ex-lover, has offered me the use of his flat in London. Without him." she added quickly.

"And you'd rather go there?"

"Yes, it would be better than having to stay with my sister. My friend, Helen, is coming from Italy for two weeks, so she can stay there with me too. So I've accepted." She paused, waiting for his reaction.

"I see," he said with a grin leaning back and looking coolly at her, "that's my brush-off, is it? Why don't you just say so?"

"I hadn't made up my mind," she admitted. "But there's no reason why you shouldn't come there for the last week, if you want to. There's a spare room." She smiled at him, half expecting him to turn her down.

He finished his beer, appeared to consider the matter and said finally. "I get the message. It's a bit different from the one I had a couple of weeks ago." He shrugged. "But what the hell? My youngest sister lives in London but now she's got a kid, she hasn't got a spare room. It'll give me a chance to visit her and see the kid. I'll take up your offer." Seeing her surprise, he laughed. "You didn't expect that, did you?"

"I'm not sure what I expected," she admitted.

"You're not very sure about anything. are you?" he commented.

"I suppose you're right." She was amazed at his understanding.

"How do you know?"

"We've a lot in common," he replied but gave no further explanation. He looked at the menu. "I fancy home made apple pie and fresh cream. How about you?"

"Just coffee for me, black and strong." She hesitated. "We'd better fix our dates, before the end of the evening, if you're sure."

"I'm sure, as long as you realise that I'm still the same Mike. I'm not a rapist but I can be very persuasive, if I feel like it. And I expect I shall."

She laughed. "And I can be very indifferent, if I feel like it."

He turned away for a moment to order the coffee and apple pie, then came back to her. "But you're not sure. OK. I accept the challenge. Either way, it'll be a change from this part of the world and from driving every day."

"Your mention of driving," she said, as the coffee and pie arrived, "has reminded me that I wanted to ask you if you could help me to buy a car. It'd be much easier to get to London and I need one in Barton Leas. Something small but fairly good."

"How much?"

"What it needs. My grandparents left me quite a large sum."

"No sweat." he said cheerfully. "I'll take you to see a mate of mine this Saturday afternoon, if you've got a couple of hours to spare."

"Is he trustworthy?"

He laughed as he stuck his fork into his apple pie. "Not normally but for a mate of mine, he won't dare be otherwise. I guarantee you a good, little car at a fair price. Does that satisfy you?"

It did and they arranged to meet for a couple of hours on the following Saturday afternoon. As he left her, he said cheerfully. "I'll give Zak a ring. He'll have something ready for you. See you." He did not even attempt to kiss her before she got out of his car. Which was a surprise but a good omen, she told herself.

As she prepared for bed, her mind went over the conversation with Mike. She had agreed to spend some time with him at Easter but on a very different basis. They were still friends but she had put it on a different footing and, apart from Mike's usual banter there was no hint of a more intimate relationship. Why had she done this? She didn't have to for Merlin had left her completely free. Perhaps because he trusted her to be mature, she was determined to show him that she could be so. Or was it simply that neither she nor Mike had been in a romantic mood that evening? She left the question unresolved.

It was on the following Monday afternoon that Victoria warned her that trouble was brewing in the Sixth Form. They were sitting in the English tutorial room, a dismal, little, book lined cell away from the main classrooms, where they met three times a week for Victoria's extra classes. The lesson finished at tea time and they were having their usual chat afterwards. "I shall miss Merlin at Easter," was Victoria's opening remark.

"But your father's coming back," Cleo objected. "I thought you'd be pleased."

"Oh, I am, but he's not such fun to talk to. Merlin's very challenging, isn't he? He's good for me."

"He is," Cleo agreed. "I shall miss him." It seemed safe to admit that.

"But you're going to London. You'll meet lots of people I expect."

"Perhaps. At least I'm going to meet a school friend I haven't seen for sometime." She began to collect up her papers, preparatory to going for tea and then became aware that Victoria hadn't moved.

"Is there something else you want to say?" she asked.

Victoria was hesitant. "I don't know whether I should or not but you're a friend and not just a teacher, aren't you?" She stopped. Cleo waited and smiled encouragingly. "It's just that several parents intend to complain to Miss Stephens at the end of term, quite strongly."

Cleo frowned. "What about?" she asked. wondering how she could be involved.

"About Miss Harvey and Mr Barnes," Victoria replied nervously. "Their relationship. I mean."

"But that's not new surely," was all Cleo could think to say. "So why now?"

"Stephanie told her parents. She was furious about the way Miss Harvey treated her. So was Maggy Lewis and her other friends. Stephanie really was in a terrible state when she came back from seeing Miss Stephens. It wasn't that Stephie was so unpleasant but Stephanie didn't want people to know."

"Well, someone had to know, surely you realise that?"

"Of course, but it should have been her parents. They'd have hushed it up. You suggested that, Stephanie told me. But, because Stephanie was reluctant to tell them, Miss Harvey went to Miss Stephens and Miss Wilson. Stephanie and Maggie decided to punish her."

Cleo felt sick. "What do you mean?"

"Well, they've told their parents what most of the Sixth Form knows about Miss Harvey taking him to the Staff House late at night, and his car being there till about three or four o'clock. It wouldn't be so bad, I suppose, if he wasn't already married. But the parents aren't likely to think it's setting a good example, are they?"

"And what do you think?"

"I haven't had anything to do with it. Nor have any of my friends. We think that Stephanie and Miss Harvey are both rather horrid."

"Why are you telling me?" Cleo asked. "I hate the whole business. Miss Harvey disregarded what I thought."

"I know. Stephanie knew that. But there's going to be trouble and Miss Harvey might think you've said something. I just thought it might be better if you knew what was happening. People can be very vicious in this place especially when people are cleverer and more attractive than they are. It's the atmosphere. I suppose."

"I know," Cleo said. "I've been in a boarding school before." She tried to smile at Victoria. "Thank you for warning me. I'll try to avoid her. The term will soon be over, after all."

"You see I think of you as my friend, particularly after you talked to me in hospital. And Merlin is very fond of you. I don't want you to be unhappy." Victoria began to put her papers in her folder.

"Thank you." Cleo leaned over and kissed her impulsively on the cheek. "I'll see you tomorrow. Now I must go to tea." She hurried out, anxious not for tea but to be alone. She was grateful to Victoria but, even that, could not stop that dreadful feeling of isolation and depression that swept over her.

It was not until Thursday, the last day of term that the storm broke. The girls were due to leave by eleven o'clock and by the midday they were all gone. The house rooms and corridors were empty at last of all the trunks which had been piled up there. The multitude of cars which had clogged the narrow High Street had all departed and the village had sunk back to its normal holiday peace. Cleo who had never seen it in the holidays was surprised at the quiet. She wondered if the villagers preferred it this way or did they perhaps miss the bustle of the school.

It was just after midday when at Miss Stephens' request Cleo went to see her in her study. The study was immaculate as ever but Miss Stephens without her customary gown and with grey hair slightly dishevelled seemed more relaxed and friendlier. The summons had worried Cleo for she had wondered it could possibly have anything to do with Stella Harvey and Stephanie.

But to judge from the friendly smile with which Miss Stephens greeted her, it was obviously not that. Cleo arrived simultaneously with the housekeeper who was bringing in a coffee tray. "Good," Miss Stephens exclaimed cheerfully, removing a pile of folders from a chair. "Please sit down, Miss Lafay. And join me in a cup of coffee." Sitting herself behind the desk she thanked the housekeeper who placed the tray in front of her. Cleo found herself being offered strong fresh coffee in a delicate china cup while being scrutinised by Miss Stephens' penetrating but friendly blue eyes. "It seems you have survived your first end of term remarkably well," she remarked as she passed a plate of chocolate biscuits. "But then you're not unaccustomed to boarding schools."

Smiling back, Cleo agreed at the same time very mystified as to the purpose of this meeting and still a little apprehensive, It soon became clear, however, that Miss Stephens' first intention was to congratulate her on her first term's work, especially with the Sixth form and to encourage her. Soon, however, Miss Stephens came to the main point of the interview. "I was wondering," she asked, "if you would be willing to consider a more permanent post in the Autumn. As Miss Wilson is leaving, we shall be reorganising the English department and there could be a place for you, certainly with the Fifth and Sixth Forms. You might like to combine a part time post with further study as I seem to remember you have a doctorate to complete." She leaned back, sipping her coffee with a definitely encouraging twinkle.

Cleo could not have been more amazed. She had not expected this and had no ideas as to what her reply should or would be. She wished that Merlin were there to consult but in the meantime she must say something. She thanked Miss Stephens and asked if she could think about it as she had not yet made any clear plans for the future.

Miss Stephens remained most gracious and suggested that she should consider it during the holidays. "There is no need for you to make a decision before May," she said. For the next few minutes she talked graciously about Victoria's progress and then wondered if Cleo might be able to persuade Professor Evans to lecture to the Sixth Form.

Cleo was very relieved to be able to say that he was away for some time in South America but would surely consider it on his return. Thankfully, soon after this, she made her escape. As she came out of the corridor leading to the Headmistress's study, she bumped into Stella Harvey who was just coming out of the Staff Room opposite. They greeted one another briefly but neither stopped much to Cleo's relief. Since Victoria's revelations, she had avoided Stella.

In the evening, Cynthia and Pam had organised an end of term party in the Staff House. It was to be a casual buffet, which people could attend when and for as long as they liked. Casual though it was, it was necessary for her to attend, Cleo realised, if she were not to seem unfriendly. All the unattached men on the staff had been invited and boy friends were welcome. Cleo decided to go soon after eight and leave as soon as she reasonably could for she still did not feel in a party mood and was worried about the gossip Victoria had passed on to her.

Even though she arrived punctually there were several people already there. She was immediately hailed by Pam who introduced her to her future husband and soon found herself penned in a corner with them. This was pleasant until she was joined by Nicholas Barnes, who insisted on fetching her more wine and more food and who seemed determined to make himself her partner for the evening. As Tony and Pam remained with them and Bridget joined them she felt safe from his advances and could not deny that Nicholas could be an entertaining companion. As a result, she stayed longer than she had intended.

It was not until nine thirty that Stella arrived, looking very dramatic in a royal blue velvet trouser suit with snowy lace ruffles at the neck. For a moment, she stood in the doorway looking round the rather full room until her eyes lighted on Nicholas. Ignoring everyone else, she made her way towards him. If it had been possible, Cleo would have slipped away but instead she managed to turn towards Pam and Tony with her back towards Nicholas.

Stella stopped in front of Nicholas. "I expected you would come and fetch me," she said loudly. "I had a bottle of sherry for us to celebrate but, since you weren't there. I celebrated by myself." It was then that Cleo realised that Stella had indeed been celebrating. Her face was unusually flushed and her eyes had an unnatural brightness. "But I see you had more important people to see," she continued turning to Cleo. "You can't wait, can you?" Nicholas tried to restrain her, giving her his seat and offering to fetch food and drink for her but she ignored him.

"Haven't you done enough harm?" she asked catching hold Cleo's arm. "Are you never satisfied?"

"I don't know what you mean," Cleo said as quietly as she could, realising that the room was by now practically silent and that everyone was staring at her and Stella. She tried to move away but Stella still held on to her.

Stella laughed sardonically. "Of course you don't. You never do, do you? You're so sweet and good. You make me sick. The others may not see through you but I do."

"For God's sake come away, Stella," Nicholas said urgently. "You don't know what you're saying." He tried to take hold of her arm but she pushed him away.

"You're a fool," she replied angrily to him. "You're just as bewitched with her beautiful green eyes as every man. Even an intelligent man like Merlin Evans can't see she's two timing him, so what hope have you got?"

"I don't know why you're saying these ridiculous things," Cleo said coldly. "I can only think you have drunk too much sherry in your celebration." She pulled her arm away and managed to move out of the corner.

Stella, however, followed her. "And why do you think I was celebrating?" she asked. "You ought to know, after all!"

"I can't imagine what you are talking about," Cleo began but even as she spoke, she remembered Victoria's warning.

"Oh, but you do know, don't you," Stella responded bitterly. "I can see it in your face. You know why Miss Stephens sent for me this afternoon. You know because it was all your doing. You can't deny it." When Cleo remained silent, Stella turned to face everyone and continued in spite of Nicholas' protests. "You might as well all know. It'll save a lot of the gossip you all enjoy. I'm sacked! Or to put it more politely, as Miss Stephens undoubtedly will, I've offered my resignation to take effect as from May 31st." Before anyone could say anything, she continued in the same hard, bitter voice. "Do you ask why or don't you care? I'll tell you in any case. It's because I've failed to set a proper example in my behaviour. Miss Stephens has been told that I've entertained Nicholas in my room on many occasions at night and this has upset our moral little Sixth formers."

As she paused for a moment and looked round, Nicholas came forward, "Be quiet, Stella," he exclaimed. "You're not doing yourself or me any good."

Stella shook him off. "Don't worry, Nicholas. my darling," she said cynically. "Your offence will be overlooked, provided you repent. I'm sure you'll find that easy. It's the same old story. Men can get away with it but women can't."

She turned once more towards Cleo who stood horrified. "But that doesn't excuse you, another woman, for telling tales about me. Were you so furious that I got between you and Stephanie. That I objected to your pious advice. Though what right you have to give it, I can't imagine. You're just a lucky whore, that's all. At least everyone knows you for what you are now, and won't make the mistake of trusting you. I know it was you because I saw you coming away from her room this morning."

Cleo felt utterly frozen. She didn't even feel angry. Stella's grief and suffering were too terrible. But, before she could say anything, Bridget spoke in her usual clear, cool tones. "We all sympathise with you, Stella," she said," because of the way things have turned out but you are wrong to blame Cleo. Miss Stephens' decision has nothing to do with her, we were told last night at the Housemistress's meeting that several Sixth Form parents had complained, chiefly Stephanie's and Maggy's parents. Miss Stephens had already spoken to them all and told us of her decision last night."

Before Bridget could say any more, Stella rushed out of the room and down the corridor to her own room. Cleo waited for a moment to see if Nicholas would go after her but, when he made no move, she hurried after Stella. She had no idea what she would say but simply felt that someone must speak to her.

Stella's door was slightly open, so she went quickly in and shut it behind her. Stella had collapsed on her divan, sobbing violently. As she heard the door close, she sat up, tears streaming down her cheeks. "Oh, it's you," she said hopelessly I thought it might be Nicholas. You're the last person I would have expected. I suppose you expect me to apologise. Well, I've no intention of doing so." She began to sob again.

"I don't want you to do," Cleo began hesitantly. "As you said, I'm no saint. I spend quite a lot of time hating myself, so why shouldn't you?" When Stella didn't answer, she picked up a box of tissues and sat down next to her on the divan. Without thinking she put her arms round Stella and held her close. It was all important to try to share the desolation and misery of another human being. She knew only too well how overwhelming such feelings could be.

Stella did not resist her but with her head on Cleo's shoulder continued to cry but more quietly. Finally, she stopped and began to mop her face with the tissues Cleo silently offered her. "I don't understand you," she said suddenly, "why are you of all people bothering about me?"

"I just know what it feels like," Cleo replied gently, "I've made so many mistakes. Surely that's obvious?"

Stella looked steadily at her for a moment. "Perhaps you have after all. Why else would someone like you be in this place?"

"I had nowhere else to go at that moment. I still haven't actually."

Stella sat up and they looked silently at each other for a few moments, "I can go back to my mother again, like I did last time after the abortion," Stella said finally, "I'm a good mathematician. It won't be difficult to find another job. Miss Stephens has promised me a decent reference. But. Christ, what a fool I've been!" The tears began to roll down her cheeks again.

"It's Nicholas, isn't it?" Cleo asked.

"Yes, it must make you laugh but I actually did think he cared about me and that I could make a real life with him, at last. His marriage was finished long ago or so he said. But now look at him! He didn't move a step. He let you come after me. Men are all the same! I ought to have learnt by now!"

"Give him a chance," Cleo found herself urging. "He was stunned. I think. He's not the stuff heroes are made of. But he might be better than you think. He'll come round."

"Would you give him a second chance?"

"Why not, if I loved him. You can't expect people to be perfect. People like you and me have no right to anyway."

"I expect you're right," Stella agreed reluctantly. "I don't know whether I love him but he's all I've got and I don't want to lose him. Though I expect I have now. I don't know what to do."

Cleo stood up. "Freshen yourself up," she said firmly. "and I'll see if I can find him. I can be very persuasive with men, as you know." She left the room instantly before Stella could reply.

It was much easier than she had expected. Nicholas had left the party not surprisingly and was standing indecisively in the corridor, looking out of the window. He turned as he heard Cleo's footsteps. "That was good of you," he said. "How is she?"

Cleo regarded him steadily. Even now, with a little encouragement, he would turn to her for comfort. He was that sort of person. She did not intend to encourage him. "She needs you, although I can't think why. She must love you. But what about you?"

He hesitated and then said slowly. "I suppose I love Stella as much as I'm capable of loving anyone, but…"

"Never mind the buts," Cleo exclaimed. "I know all about them. I'm a bit of a 'but' person myself. I don't think, we get a lot of chances, perhaps you should take this one and stick to it."

He looked straight back at her and smiled slightly. "At forty four," he said, "perhaps you're right. Perhaps I should count myself lucky. I'll go and suggest some plans to Stella. Thanks." With a slightly regretful look at her, he turned and moved off.

Cleo watched him until Stella's door shut behind him. Slowly, she turned to go upstairs. She had no desire to return to the party. Only Bridget had supported her. She could be thanked the next day. Now, she preferred to be alone.

Chapter Twenty

By Saturday morning everyone had left on their holidays. Cleo was alone in the Staff House. One or two of the Housemistresses remained. Miss Stephens was still in residence and several of the domestic staff but, otherwise the school with all its many buildings was silent and empty. It had the strangely melancholy air of a deserted institution, which was familiar to Cleo from her own schooldays when she had been left behind to spend part of the holidays with the nuns. She found it more depressing than she had expected.

Not for the first time she found her thoughts straying in the direction of Merlin. How much better it would have been if he had not gone away. It was silly to think like that she told herself. She couldn't agree to marry him, simply because she didn't like spending time at school in the holidays. On Tuesday she would leave for London where she would spend a few days with Jane, then go to the flat to await the arrival of Helen Bennetti, her half Italian friend who now lived in Verona.

Now, however, she must decide how to spend the weekend. She got up reluctantly, slipped into her robe and drew the curtains. The sun was at last shining again and the quiet village had an almost medieval charm with its two half timbered pubs and ancient alms houses clustered round the village green, framed with trees which were definitely showing signs of spring.

She turned back to her room. At least it was enjoyable to be able to linger over her coffee and toast without having to worry about bells. She decided over her breakfast that it would be pleasant to go for a proper drive in the new car which Mike had helped her to buy a week ago. It seemed stupid to make the drive to London her first real journey in it. It would be wiser to get some practice first.

As she sipped her second cup of coffee, she tried to think where she might go but soon realised that she knew little about the surrounding countryside except where Merlin had taken her near his home. A solitary journey without an objective suddenly seemed very unalluring. A sudden thought struck her. Perhaps Mike might be free? He had given her the telephone number of his parents' home where he spent most of his free time. Why should she not try it? It was nine o'clock, it might be a good idea to do it straight away before he went out.

It was surprisingly easy. Mike answered the phone himself and was quite willing to change his somewhat nebulous plans to accommodate her. Saturday would be good, he said, as he had promised to spend Sunday with Tracy and Ben. The only trouble was that he sounded a little too easy. Confronted with the worry that she might be giving him the wrong impression, Cleo had a sudden inspiration, "I'd like to visit your sister Clare again," she said. "if that's possible. I was fascinated by her and the children and I'd like to experience some family life." With surprise she realised that her reasons were actually genuine.

She wondered how Mike would take the suggestion but he sounded quite unruffled. "If it's kids you want," he replied, "I might bring Ben along. Tracy's been moaning about needing a day off. We could take them all out for beefburgers or something."

She wasn't sure about this wondering whether she would be able to cope. On the other hand, Ben would be good protection, so she agreed and it was quickly arranged that he and Ben would arrive about two o'clock after lunch. My God, what have I arranged to do, she wondered as she went back to her room to dress. She had never contemplated doing anything like this in her life. Barton Leas must be having a strange effect on her.

As she tidied her room and sorted out her clothes ready for packing, she pondered over the events of Thursday and Friday especially her emotional moments with Stella. As was to be expected Stella had avoided her the following day, except to give her a brief apology and thanks on the way back from supper on the Friday. Nicholas, however, to her surprise, had taken her out to coffee in the lunch hour.

She had wondered whether she was wise to agree but he had been insistent and Stella, seeing them go off together, had for once seemed unmoved. He wanted to thank her, he said, for helping him to behave better than he might have done. "My divorce is almost final," he explained, "and I've asked Stella to marry me, as I should have done sooner." She had protested that he had no need to tell her but he obviously wanted to talk.

He seemed depressed. "I don't know if we'll make a go of it," he said, "but it seems we ought to try. I've damaged Stella enough as it is. Though she's not an easy person." he added, wanting some sympathy it seemed.

"I know," she had agreed, then continued, "but you don't have to marry her Nicholas, if you don't think you'll be happy. I didn't mean that. After all, this isn't the Victorian age. She isn't a fallen woman, nor is she helpless."

"I know but there isn't always much difference. I've made myself responsible. In any case," he added with sudden candour, "I don't think I'd be much good on my own. Too easily tempted." He looked at her. "You could tempt me any time but I know my limitations. In any case, you've always made them quite clear."

"Stella didn't seem to think so."

"She'll be better now," he promised.

"I doubt if I want to stay long enough to find out," she had replied.

"That's a pity. You could do some good work. I'm sorry, if we've driven you away."

"It's not as simple as that," she had replied. Now looking back, she wondered if she had really made a decision at that moment and, if so, what exactly it was.

Mike arrived on time. Ben turned out to be a quiet, withdrawn little boy with appealing brown eyes like his father. The car seat was adroitly transferred to the back of her car and he was quickly settled in it. "He won't be any trouble," Mike assured her. "He usually sleeps when he's travelling, and when we get there, he'll have a good time with his cousins. It'll do him good; he's too much on his own most of the time. Scarcely sees any other kids."

It was certainly true, for most of the journey, for he only bothered them twice, once to ask for his sweets and once to ask how soon they would get there. Mike was quite short with him on both occasions but Ben seemed not to mind. He obviously trusted his Dad.

As they set off, Cleo asked whether Clare's husband, Dave, was likely to be there. "Why not," Mike replied tersely. "Don't worry, he isn't drinking at present. And when he isn't, he's a pretty good father. We'll probably take the boys to the park with a football. I'm not much good but Dave's very keen. He used to be in a football team."

For a while, Cleo concentrated on her driving and was glad to have Mike's expert advice with her new car. As they neared the end of their journey, he asked her suddenly whether she was still willing to have him visit her in London. "Of course, if you still want to come," she replied.

He looked closely at her for a moment before answering. "There are times when I don't think I understand you at all," he said.

"Such as?" She smiled provocatively at him.

"Such as now," he said. "Why invite me today and then suggest we go to Clare's. It's not exactly what a man expects."

"So you decided to bring Ben? Did you hope I might change my mind then?"

He grinned. "I should've known better. You're not as easy as that. Anyway, I'm not sorry, I've brought him. He's no bother and it puts me in Tracy's good books, which might come in useful."

"I shouldn't have thought that mattered to you, being in Tracy's good books." She was genuinely surprised. "You're a bit of a puzzle yourself."

He did not pursue that but returned to his attack on her. "Why bother about me in London?" he persisted. "When we first talked about spending time together, I thought you wanted to sleep with me but you seem to have changed the goal posts since then."

"I thought I might but I'm not so sure now that it's a good idea. I don't think we would help each other much that way."

"I wasn't thinking of that, I was just thinking we might have a good time."

Cleo shrugged. "What's a good time? I've had plenty of those and I'm sure you have. It might be better if you took Ben away for the week."

"Better for who? Fuck it, Cleo! What's the matter with you? Have you been Born Again or something?"

"I want a future," she said suddenly to her own surprise. "I'm tired of dead ends."

"What sort of future?"

"I'm not sure, that's the problem. I can't stay where I am and I don't know where to go next but I want to go."

He grinned. "I could have said that myself. Perhaps we've more in common than you think. We might have a useful discussion."

"Perhaps but not now. Now I need some directions of a more humdrum kind. Such as how do I get to Clare's."

"Right. We'll discuss the other in London."

Clare was as pleased to see them as she had been the first time. She still looked lovely, although she was only wearing a shabby pair of jeans and a loose cerise coloured sweater. Cleo was very conscious of her own impeccable and very expensive chocolate brown trouser suit with her turquoise cashmere sweater and matching earrings. Clare, however, exclaimed without any envy, "You look lovely, Cleo, brown suits you. I look terrible in it."

She led them into the living room and quickly explained that Dave had just taken the boys to the park and was expecting Mike and Ben to join them there. Mike, at first, seemed disinclined to go but Ben quickly said, "Let's go, Daddy." At which Mike resigned himself to his fate. "Come on then, kid," he said, "don't stand about." Seizing Ben's hand he made for the door. "See you later. Have a good gossip, girls."

"We'll have a cup of coffee," Clare said, "and enjoy a bit of peace, while they're all away."

Cleo smiled her agreement and sat down on the floor to build a tower of bricks for Esther, who watched with great interest, then immediately knocked it down with much satisfaction. This continued until Clare reappeared with the coffee, when Cleo joined her on the settee, while they both for a few moments watched Esther's attempts to build her own tower, until she turned her attention to the toy telephone.

"It's nice to have someone to talk to," Clare remarked.

"But isn't Dave back now?"

"Yes and I'm glad to have him but we don't seem to have much time to talk. Anyway, I really meant it's nice to talk to another woman. Though with your exciting life. you must find me boring. I don't really have much to talk about except babies and things like that."

"That's not true," Cleo replied. "You shouldn't undervalue yourself. Besides I might like to hear about babies. I don't know anything about them or about family life really."

"Have you ever thought you'd like to have a family of your own?" Clare asked. "Or are you a career woman who doesn't want children? There seem to be a lot of those about these days. I suppose it's more fun to be free."

"Do you really think so?"

"I don't but then I wouldn't, would I? I enjoy babies. I like cooking and looking after people and things like that. I don't mind what other people do but I object to them telling me I should leave my babies and go out to work." She was unexpectedly vehement and almost passionate.

"I haven't said that," Cleo said gently.

"No, but I expect you do think I should have gone out to work, instead of having another baby, particularly as Dave lost his job soon after. But I don't mind being poor as long as we can all be together. Anyway, Dave's starting a new job tomorrow, so perhaps we'll be better off, if he can earn enough to live on and if he can keep it." She smiled nervously but brightly.

"I think you should stay with your children. You're obviously a very good mother. I envy you. At least, you know what you want."

"And you don't?"

"Not really. I'm just searching, it seems."

"I suppose that's what you and Mike have in common. He never seems to settle. We thought he had when he married Tracy and had Ben. But it doesn't seem to have worked. He seems to get tired of everything. Except," Clare hesitated, "I think he loves Ben and Ben certainly thinks the world of him. I wish he'd remember that." She looked worriedly at Cleo.

"If you think I want to take him away from Ben. you're wrong. We're not lovers. I'm not tying him to anything. He's free to make his own decisions."

"He worries me," Clare continued, "because he's so destructive. He always chucks up jobs and leaves people. Perhaps, if he had someone very stable..?" She looked at Cleo with an obvious question in her eyes.

Cleo looked directly back. "By your definition." she replied. "I'm afraid that I'm destructive too. I've done all those things. It looks like we might help to destroy each other, if we're not careful, doesn't it? I'm not your stable person."

Clare was silent for a moment, then she said slowly, "I just hope he won't ever desert Ben."

"Having been deserted myself, I wouldn't encourage him to leave his child." Cleo spoke coldly, rather resenting what Clare had implied.

"Good," Clare replied, ignoring Cleo's tone, "because, if he did, Ben might get over it, but Mike never would. It would be just one more failure. And it might be one too many. But perhaps you don't know what I mean?"

"I've seen him drunk and almost suicidal, if that's what you mean? I wouldn't want to encourage that. I suppose I'd like to help him to get over it."

Clare sighed. "It isn't always possible to help people, even when you very much want to."

Cleo looked closely at her and saw the unexpected tears in her eyes, "You mean that you aren't able to help Dave, as much as you thought you could?"

"Yes. I'm not sure he'll ever stick to any job. He's even weaker and more vulnerable than I realised. I suppose people were right about him and I was silly."

"Why does it matter?" Cleo demanded. She didn't want Clare to speak like this. It would spoil the picture she had formed of her. "You still love him, don't you? And he loves you? He's still the same person you were talking about last time we met. You can't give up on him, whatever people say. You have a family, don't let it fall apart! Your children need both parents, even if one isn't perfect."

Clare stared at her, shocked by her vehemence. "You really care, don't you? Why?"

"Because I know how important it is to have a family. I might be quite different if I had one."

"But you must have! Everyone has a family."

"Well, I suppose I have if you count a wealthy father who'd give me money anytime as long as he didn't have to see me, a stepmother whom I've only met twice and a sister who, although kindly disposed, is nearly five years older than me and fully occupied with her job, husband, and expected baby. My mother left years ago and anyway she's dead. My father doesn't want to see me, because I not only look like her but am like her, or so he says which isn't much of a recommendation. Oh God," she ended suddenly. "I'm sorry! I've only ever told one other person about this and he wants to marry me."

"Then why don't you marry him? You must care about him or you wouldn't have told him. And he obviously loves you."

"It wouldn't work," Cleo replied sadly. "I'd let him down. I've done it twice. When it's vital I can't believe in him or in me."

"But you think I can stick to Dave."

"I think you should and I'm pretty sure you've got the guts to do it. Don't bother about me," she added quickly. "I didn't mean to talk about myself. I'm just a bit upset because I've let him go away again and I can't help regretting it."

"Then why do you do it?"

"Because it's the right thing to do." Cleo said defiantly.

Clare, nervous though she normally was, looked as if she were ready to dispute that but, before she could speak, they were interrupted by a loud knocking at the front door and the excited sound of children's voices. Clare hastily went to let them in and Cleo followed more slowly to find Mike coming in with four little boys, who to judge from their muddy appearance and rosy faces had obviously been having a good time. There was no sign, however, of Dave.

"Where's Dave?" Clare demanded as she divested the boys of their muddy boots and coats.

"In the pub." Mike replied tersely. "He met a mate who offered him a pint."

"And he left you to bring the kids back. You shouldn't have let him, Mike, you know you shouldn't."

Mike shrugged. "The only alternative was to join them and I didn't fancy Ben hanging around outside a pub with a packet of crisps, nor the others for that matter, so I brought them back. We'd better be getting back soon any way. Tracy'll throw a fit if I bring him back late." He turned to Ben, seized his arm somewhat roughly and let him towards the cloakroom. "You silly bugger," he exclaimed. "Why did you have to get yourself so mucky?" He turned towards Clare before he closed the door. "Dave said to tell you he won't be long."

Clare turned unhappily towards Cleo, "He's scared of starting the job tomorrow."

"That's it," Mike agreed as he disappeared with Ben. "He's afraid he won't hack it and he'll let you down."

There was no time for Clare to complain or to grieve with five hungry children needing food and attention but her anxiety was obvious to Cleo, who tried to help, although conscious of her lack of expertise. It was quite obvious when Mike reappeared with a somewhat chastened but very clean Ben, that he was determined to get away as soon as possible, He insisted on their leaving almost as soon as the evening meal was finished, Cleo was reluctant to go, as Dave had still not returned and Clare was obviously very anxious. She was determined to help with the clearing up first but found it impossible to hold up Mike for very long. As soon as they were in the car and had left the depressed housing estate he said, "Well now, you've seen the flip side, what do you think of it? Do you still think it's a great romance?"

His tone was mocking and Cleo responded to it quickly, "It doesn't change my view that Clare loves Dave and her family and that she's remarkably faithful and gives Dave a lot."

"Perhaps but what about Dave?"

"Of course. I haven't met him but from his behaviour he seems pretty weak and irresponsible. He's drinking, while she's terrified that he won't be fit for the job tomorrow."

"And why do you think he's doing that?"

Cleo shrugged. "Because he enjoys it. I suppose, and because he doesn't care. Why do you think he does it?"

"I know why he does it. He drinks to escape, like I do. He knows he won't be able to stick this job long - he's too intelligent for it but he's got no qualifications - so there's nothing else. He can't face the thought of failing again, so he buries his head in a few pints."

"He doesn't seem to love Clare much."

"Balls," Mike retorted vehemently. "He loves her all right but he finds it too difficult to live up to her ideas of what he should be. Is that too much for you to understand? It's not much fun always having to say 'sorry' I know that myself."

Cleo did not answer immediately. Several upsetting thoughts had occurred to her while he was speaking. First, she felt obliged to acknowledge the truth of what he said and to admit that the fairy tale romance of Clare was not so perfect. Secondly, she saw herself in the same relationship with Merlin. Was that the real reason why she was afraid to agree to marry him? She did not want to imagine herself perpetually having to confess her weaknesses? Perhaps that was what had really happened to her mother? "I suppose you're right." she said finally. "Marriage partners should be more equal."

"It's probably better if people like us don't marry." Mike replied sombrely and lapsed into as somewhat grim silence. Cleo gave her full attention to her driving and they spoke very little until they were a few miles from Barton Leas, when Mike suddenly broke the silence.

"Have you decided yet what you'll do after this job?" he asked quite amiably.

"Not really but I had a long letter from my friend Helen who lives in Verona. She's the one who's coming to stay with me in London before you come. She suggests I might join her in Italy and make a fresh start. She says there's plenty of work and life's much freer. It sounds quite tempting. She says it's time I made a fresh start."

"It sounds a bloody good idea," Mike replied with unexpected enthusiasm. I might decide to go with you. There's a lot of driving jobs in Italy, I've been told."

"What about Tracy and Ben?"

"What about them? She wouldn't come. She's lost all her spirit of adventure since we got married. It's up to her. I'd give her the house and everything." He had obviously thought on these lines before. "I don't see why I shouldn't try something a bit more exciting. What do you think? I'm not suggesting we start a relationship but that we just go together as mates and see how it works out. No recriminations, if it doesn't. It might be better than being on your own. Good fun while it lasts but no ties."

In spite of her reservations, she was affected by his enthusiasm. "There isn't time to discuss it now," she replied quickly. "It's getting late for Ben."

"You could get more input from Helen and we can plan it when I come to London," he replied quickly, as if detecting her implied agreement. "I'd do better with someone like you around and you might even be glad to have me for a time."

"I might. Who knows. Stranger things have happened." Suddenly she saw herself as helping Mike. She could matter for a time. Wasn't that what she really wanted? To be strong rather than weak and dependent?

"We don't need to be too solemn about it." Mike suggested. "It'd be no big deal, just giving each other a helping hand. Think about it."

"I will." she promised as she stopped the car and waited for him to transfer Ben and his seat to his car. "But what about Ben? Wouldn't you miss him?"

He shrugged. "Not much. I've told you. I'm not a family man. That was Tracy's idea. Anyway. let me have your phone number in London and I'll tell you when I'm arriving." He gave a quick hug and a kiss. "See you."

The euphoria lasted only a few minutes after she had reached her dark. chilly and unwelcoming room. As she switched on the lights and drew the curtains, questions rushed into her mind, chief of which was what sort of a person was she to make important decisions in such a careless way? Would she ever be faithful to anybody or to anything? She had decided to leave St Elizabeth's simply because she disliked some of the people and events she had encountered. She had abandoned all thoughts of training for a teaching career, simply to dash off on one more mad escapade, this time to Italy with Mike. Why? Why? Why?

Apparently unable to think clearly, she began restlessly to tidy up her room. Picking up a couple of books lying on the table she moved over to the bookshelves with them. Suddenly her eye alighted on a slim volume of Donne's Songs and Sonnets which Merlin had given her in Oxford. Why should she notice that volume now? It had been an anniversary present he had said to mark the fiftieth day of their relationship. As she opened it, a sheet of paper slipped out. It was the note he had written then:

'All other things to their destruction draw,
Only our love hath no decay;
This, no tomorrow hath, nor yesterday,
Running it never runs from us away,
But truly keepes his first, last, everlasting day.'

"This expresses most perfectly what I want to say. I will not attempt to add to it. All my love, now and always, Merlin."

She remembered clearly standing in the porter's lodge, reading this note which had been delivered to her with his gift that lovely late spring morning. She had believed him with all her heart and yet she had not trusted him. She had not remained faithful when he had to go away because she had chosen to think he was deserting her.

It seemed that she had learned nothing since then. What right had she ever to his love? It seemed she would always fail. Some temporary pleasure would distract her. "People like us shouldn't get married," Mike had said. Perhaps he was right. It would be kinder and better to make a final break. For one moment she thought of tearing up the paper but, instead she placed it carefully back in the book and replaced it on the shelf. It would seem unforgivable to destroy it, she decided, for he had not been untrue to his words. She would keep it to remind herself of her weakness.

Chapter Twenty One

It was immediately after Helen's return to Italy that Jane decided to visit Cleo and spend the night with her, as Robert was away for a couple of days. The holidays, so far, had passed unexpectedly pleasantly. The Easter with Jane and Robert had passed without any incident and the two weeks of Helen's visit had been filled with excited planning of Cleo's eventual removal to Italy. Helen had been a little dubious about Mike but she had come to accept the possibility of his coming too. It was just one more of Cleo's impulsive adventures or so she decided to think.

Jane's visit was sandwiched between Helen's departure and Mike's expected arrival. Ostensibly she had come to shop for herself and for the baby now expected in four and a half month's time but clearly also she had wished to see the flat where Cleo had once lived and which she had never visited.

After a day of successful but tiring shopping they decided to relax over a 'take away' in the sitting room. Although it was late April the evenings were chilly and so they had lit the gas fire and Cleo was now comfortably ensconced on the rug enjoying the mock flames, while Jane, with an expectant mother's hunger finished off the last of the meal.

Suddenly, Jane asked the familiar question, "What have you decided to do when you have finished your job at St Elizabeth's" Since there had been no such question during Easter, Cleo had hoped that she had escaped this inquisition. But it was not to be.

Reluctantly, Cleo divulged her plan of going to Italy. Jane had never interfered in her life but she did not want to discuss her future with her. For a few moments, Jane received the communication in silence then, "Why are you going?' she asked calmly but in a voice which demanded a reply.

"Because I want to make a fresh start," Cleo replied rather lamely.

"But I thought that was what you were doing when you went to Barton Leas. If it wasn't that, I don't know what it was. Why on earth do you want to go rushing off again? I thought at one time that you told me you wanted to train as a proper teacher, as you put it. So why this sudden change? Couldn't you, at least, have stayed there? I'm sure you said at Easter that the Headmistress had offered you a further position next September."

"She did but I have decided that I don't want it. I'm not sure that I want to settle down as a teacher."

Jane sighed. "Robert said you never would but I thought that you were perhaps growing up at last. But now you're running away again."

Cleo was cross. "I don't see your problem. You didn't object to my running off to St. Elizabeth's. As a matter of fact, you encouraged me or so I thought."

"Of course I did," Jane replied indignantly. "That was the first sensible thing you'd done for years. Getting away from Marcus and finding yourself a job and a home. I really thought you'd build on it or at least stick to it. You can't go swanning around forever, you know!"

"What do you mean?" Cleo sat up and looked crossly at her sister.

"I mean wasting your obvious talents and just relying on your good looks and your charm to see you through. That's what you're going to do again, isn't it?"

"Helen thinks it's a good idea. She's really keen."

"I like Helen," Jane said judiciously, "I think she's a very good person but sensible - no. And what's more you know she isn't. What's the real reason for Italy? Who's the man this time?"

"There isn't any man," Cleo said defiantly. "It was Helen's suggestion and I realised it was just what I wanted. I thought it would be good to have a friend near. It's not been easy at Barton Leas."

"I don't suppose it has. But it wasn't meant to be was it? Real fresh starts are never easy. That's what makes me suspicious of this one. You haven't told me the whole story yet. Have you? Can you honestly say that there is no man involved?"

The trouble was that Jane knew her younger sister's weakness. Cleo had never been able to tell a direct lie. She knew better than even to try with Jane. "All right," she capitulated, "there is a man but he's only incidental." Quickly, she told Jane about Mike and her belief that they might help one another. "You don't have to worry," she ended somewhat lamely, "I am not so foolish as to think I can start a permanent relationship with him."

"Nor with anyone, it seems," Jane replied tartly. "For heaven's sake Cleo, you'll be twenty five next month, don't you think it's time you had some clear ideas about something?"

"Oh, I know you're going to tell me that when you were my age you were well started on your career, you were married and had a home of your own. Probably lots of people are but I'm not. Some people are divorced at my age too. At least. I've avoided that."

"Simply by not getting married," Jane retorted. "Leaving Marcus was, after all, a kind of divorce, wasn't it? And now you seem to be planning something even more stupid, if planning is the word. Do you make a point of avoiding anyone who might make a suitable husband or partner? What about the man you met again after knowing him at Oxford? He sounded quite suitable a writer and a professor - I thought you liked him?"

"He's gone to South America for the Easter vacation."

Jane looked curiously at her sister. "So what does that mean? Do you mean you can't wait for him to come back? You must have your fun whatever? Or does that mean he's tired of you?"

Stunned by her sister's critical tone, Cleo replied quickly, "He's actually asked me to marry him. It's simply that I'm not sure I want to, anymore than I want to be a school teacher."

"It all seems a bit dull and everyday, I suppose. It's more fun to dash off to Italy with an irresponsible and unsuitable man to say nothing of no job. At least when Mother ran away, she chose someone with money."

"But it didn't end up like that, did it? If you can't be faithful, you can't. I'm like her, I know, but I would like to end up hurting fewer people, that's all." In spite of her attempts, her tone was depressed.

Jane looked sharply at her. "You really mean that, don't you?, she asked. "When you've said that before, I've thought you meant it as a joky excuse. But you don't." She suddenly looked and sounded very worried.

"Well I am like her." Cleo explained defensively. "I look remarkably like her and I have a similar character. Father said so often enough. You must have heard him."

"I have and I don't believe a word of it. Because you look like her, you've created this image of yourself, based on what you think was her character. It's a sort of virtual reality thing. You've come to prefer that to the truth. You've got to face up to it before it's too late."

"I don't understand you." Cleo stood up quickly and faced her sister. She was obviously angry. "You've never said this before." She began to clear up the remains of the meal as that was the only thing that mattered. "There's no point in your lying now. It's too late."

"I'm not lying," Jane said firmly. "Stop mucking about. Those things can wait. Sit down and listen to me." She stood up, took the plates out of Cleo's hand and pushed her down gently into a convenient armchair, then returned to the settee.

"I'm waiting," Cleo retorted as Jane did not immediately say anything. "You really haven't got anything to say, have you? You just want me to pretend I'm different, then you can forget about it. I'm not your responsibility after all. You never seem to have thought about it before. Why now?"

"I should have done," Jane replied slowly. "After all, you are nearly five years younger than I am. I suppose it's because I'm having a baby myself. I suddenly see things differently. You have always been so beautiful and so very clever that I didn't see how you could want any advice from me, but I was wrong. I have just been selfish. Mother's going upset me but I was settled at school; I knew what I wanted to do in life. It was easier not to bother too much about you. But now I think if it were my child who was only twelve, how different I would feel. I'm sorry, Cleo. I've been a poor elder sister. There are so many things I should have told you."

Cleo sat quietly for a moment. The light from the lamp by her chair surrounded her with its golden glow. The loose waves of her hair shone like black satin, her eyes were like dark green pools. Her high cheek bones and the clear lines of her face were clearly silhouetted against the dark blue brocade of the high backed chair. Her soft, red lips were slightly parted. She seemed to be reflecting but it was difficult to imagine what she was thinking. She was not even sure herself.

At last she said slowly, "I don't see that you have any responsibility. It was mother who wronged me and you and it was mother who has left me her inheritance."

"I should have realised how much you were hurt and how little you really knew," Jane replied almost angrily.

"I still don't see that there is much for you to say." Cleo stood up and moved restlessly across the room to draw the heavy green, blue and gold brocade curtains.

"Please sit down and listen. If I don't say it now, I may never say it."

Cleo sat down obediently and waited, her hands loosely clasped in her lap. Jane leaned forward, as if she would touch her but then stopped. "You must believe me when I say that you're not at all like Mother. She was always egotistical and calculating."

"I don't see why you say that," Cleo interrupted her. "She wasn't faithful, just as I'm not but that doesn't mean she was totally selfish as you seem to be saying. I don't suppose she could help loving and changing. It's the unhappy way one is made. Because of her example I realise it more clearly and I don't want to hurt people as she did. It's better not to marry and certainly better not to have children if you're like that."

"But she wasn't," Jane said vehemently. "That's just where you're wrong. She didn't bother about hurting people. She just snatched what she wanted. She married Dad when she was twenty because, as he was ten years older, he was already doing well and he offered her a comfortable home in the South and he thought she was adorable."

"Well, you can't entirely blame her for wanting to escape from her dull, narrow life with her strict Catholic parents in that dreary manufacturing town."

"Is that what she told you? You never visited them, did you? Well, I did. When she had you, she found me boring and a tie, so she used to send me off in the Summer holidays to stay for weeks with her 'dreary' parents. You may find this hard to believe but they were very loving and kind and I had some very happy times there. I also realised that they were bitterly disappointed by their daughter's lack of affection for them."

Cleo frowned. "I hardly knew them. Mother seemed to think I wouldn't get on with them. That they would disapprove of me as they disapproved of her. After she left, I never saw them, then

Grandfather died and Grannie went back to Ireland where she died."

"So many things went wrong then," Jane said. "Dad retreated from us both and especially from you and I became absorbed in my own life."

"And I was left to myself. It seemed quite clear to me that no one loved me and that was probably because I was not worth loving." Cleo said it softly and factually, without bitterness. "And then I became unable to love faithfully myself, like her."

"You're right about Mother. She was pretty incapable of loving. She married Dad as an escape and she deserted him when something better turned up."

"She said she loved Jerry, that he was her first true love. It didn't last apparently but I thought she meant it."

"There had been other men before. I noticed but you were too young to realise. Jerry was the first one who offered her an alternative. He was an American and he was rich. But I suppose she left him for someone richer or something or perhaps he discovered what she was really like. Anyway, we know the miserable way she ended."

"I sometimes see myself ending like that," Cleo stated.

"You mustn't think of such a possibility," Jane said quickly. "If you're really like anyone, you're like mother's mother. You look more like her, because you have a similar expression. She was affectionate, warm-hearted and ridiculously impulsive, just as you are and Grandfather loved her. He was more serious but very kind. He was a headmaster, very gifted I think, but he chose to work in a school in a poor area because he wanted to help those who most needed it. Grannie supported him. And that was the dreary home Mother wanted to escape from."

"I see. I suppose that's why you became a nurse and then a Health visitor. You take after him."

"Even more likely it's why you thought of leaving your frivolous profession and becoming a school teacher. Mother would never have thought of anything like that, I can tell you. She would have laughed at the idea, just as she ridiculed my idea of becoming a nurse, unless it was to get a husband! Have I said enough to convince you?"

Cleo leaned back and shut her eyes for a moment. "I'm very confused," she said finally. "Why didn't you speak to me before? Why didn't someone speak to me? I needed help so much. Surely you realised that? I wasn't very old. I just felt bereft, particularly when I went to school."

" I should have done," Jane said remorsefully." Dad was so shattered. He just seemed to freeze but he never stopped loving you, underneath it all."

"Oh, he was always generous with money, still is, but he just couldn't seem to bear the sight of me. I thought it's because I'm like her and there's nothing I can do about it. So, I suppose I froze too."

"I tried to help several times," Jane answered her. "But you didn't seem to want it and it was so difficult at school with nearly five years between us. Then you were so bright. I didn't feel I could understand you, so I left it to Helen when you became good friends."

"I never confided much in Helen. I was just grateful for her friendship, She gives a lot and asks for very little, because she has a happy family. That was all I could take, until I met Merlin in Oxford. That changed everything for several months."

"You scarcely mentioned him to me," Jane remarked. "Were you lovers?"

"Yes and I deliberately didn't mention it to you. I was afraid you'd disapprove. I didn't want my happiness spoilt. But it was anyway."

"Why did it happen. Was it because he was so much older than you? Did he change his mind?"

"Not really, though I thought he had. He had arranged to go to the States for two years to do further research and take a doctorate in Moral Philosophy. It was a splendid opportunity for him and he did brilliantly. He published a successful book based on his research. I should have been pleased."

"But you weren't?" Jane asked gently

"No. I wanted to keep him with me. I was afraid to be without him. He said I was too young to tie myself to him. He wanted me to get my degree first, then decide. We had a terrible row. It was mostly my fault, I think. I wasn't really sane about it. I suppose he didn't understand. He thought I was being silly and possessive. He blames himself now but I don't really think he should. I went to pieces when he left. Well, you know a bit about that. Lots of men and then that stupid engagement to Simon just to prove I could be sensible. And you know that didn't work."

"The miracle was you got your First and started your post graduate work. But, why did you then rush to London and to Marcus? That seemed crazy."

"I suppose it was. I couldn't stand it any longer. Mother's suicide didn't help. I needed a refuge. I was also running away from Merlin who'd come back. I thought I hated him. I think I was mad and just came to my senses that evening when I suddenly had to leave Marcus and that pointless life. I was glad you took me in then."

"So it was quite an accident that you met Merlin again?"

"Yes and we had a lot to sort out, particularly me. But he had changed too, because he'd had a terrible accident and been disabled for months. It gave him time to think seriously, he said."

"And now he wants to marry you?"

"Yes very definitely. He doesn't want any other kind of relationship."

"Then what's stopping you?"

"That false image you've told me about. At least I suppose it is that. Virtual reality you called it, didn't you? That seems a good way of describing it. I wanted to experiment more but he didn't."

"So you decided to go off again with this character Mike and run away to Italy?"

"Put like that it sounds stupid. I suppose it is." Cleo stood up suddenly. "Let's clear away." she suggested. "I can't talk any more. I need to consider all you've said. I'm confused. In any case Robert will be cross with me, if I don't insist on your getting a good night's rest."

Jane acquiesced, realising that it would not be profitable to talk any further that night. Cleo needed time for reflection. "This is a beautiful flat," she said, as they went to the kitchen. "it must have been quite a sacrifice to leave it."

"You'd certainly think that if you could see the room I have at Barton Leas but I would hate to come back permanently. I'll show you round properly tomorrow. I've put you in the spare room. I shall sleep in the study. It seems better to avoid the 'connubial' bed, if I may call it that." The clearing up did not take long and they parted quickly for the night, without any further serious talk. Jane had to admit that she was tired and Cleo was quite obviously determined to say no more.

Cleo looked pale and strained when the sisters met for breakfast.

"You don't look as if you had much of a night," Jane remarked. "I suppose that was my fault. I'm not really sorry though, if it's made you think."

"If it's any comfort to you it certainly has. I spent most of the night awake, seeing many things very differently. If you hadn't been pregnant, I'd have woken you up at five o'clock and insisted on talking to you. You were lucky!"

"Well talk to me now," Jane suggested. "I don't have to leave until after lunch."

"I'm going to scramble some eggs first. Thinking's hungry work and I can't do any more until I've stoked up. Put some toast in and boil the kettle."

Jane laughed. "You've always liked your food. I can't think how you've kept such a beautiful figure. It makes me really envious but I think I'll join you this morning."

It was not until they were sitting down to a hearty breakfast that Cleo began to talk. "One thing I don't resemble Mother in is my healthy appetite. She was always worrying about her figure, just like you."

"But with more success," Jane replied ruefully.

"It's very hard you know," Cleo said as she took an extra slice of toast, "to try to see you own life in quite a different way. It isn't easy to have to admit to yourself that you've been slightly mad for years. For example spending two years in this flat was crazy."

"From what I've seen, it's a very splendidly expensive flat", Jane observed.

"Oh it is. Everything modern and in the best of taste. But I wanted a home and this could never be a home. It's just a transit camp where you accumulate as few personal possessions as possible. It was all right for Marcus. He has a home with Sarah. He never left it. But it couldn't satisfy me for long. Coming back has made me realise how empty and impersonal it really is. One thing did become clear to me during the night," she paused and buttered her toast.

"And what was that?" Jane asked.

"I'm a lonely little girl who wants a home. But it has to be a real home with a man who loves me and whom I love. And I realised one more thing. And this is all your fault."

"Whatever do you mean?"

"Well, we spent a lot of yesterday talking about your baby and buying things for it. I sat all interested. I realised for the first time in my life how important having a baby really is. You can say what you like about careers and doing your own thing but I don't think you've ever done it as a woman if you haven't had a baby." She stopped and looked defiantly at her sister.

"I'm not going to argue with you," Jane said, "I don't think I'd dare but aren't some other things necessary first, such as a father for example? Or do you believe that women should do it on their own with the sperm bank as some women seem to do?"

"Of course not. It's a loathsome idea. A child needs two parents as we know only too well. Perhaps it can't be avoided sometimes but I intend to avoid it."

"It seems you've pretty well solved your problem, then."

"How do you mean?"

"Well, all you have to do is to wait until Merlin returns and then agree to marry him. You obviously love him and I can't see any reason why he should have changed his mind. He seems to be the constant type. So what do we have to discuss?"

"At four o' clock this morning I thought that, then I realised to put it into the modern idiom that it's sentimental crap. I'm looking for truth and reality and that looks a bit like more 'virtual reality' as you called it. I'm not just a womb looking for a cosy nest. I'm a person who happens to be a woman and both sides of the equation have to be considered."

Jane sighed. "Oh dear, it sounds a bit like the late twentieth century angst again."

"Perhaps but it's still something I've got to deal with. I didn't leave Marcus so outrageously just to fly into the arms of Merlin.

I wasn't simply deciding to look for a for a more respectable and permanent set up which involved husband, comfortable home and family. I had very different ideas." She paused to put herself out another cup of coffee.

"Tell me," Jane urged her. "I don't think I ever quite got the idea. You found me puzzled and you left me puzzled, although slightly more hopeful."

"That's not surprising," Cleo answered, "I wasn't very clear about it myself. It was a sort of vision, I suppose you might call it, of a completely different way of life, a way which involved loving and caring. I felt stifled where I was and I hated the complacent way everyone was talking. It all came to head with their laughing about my concern for a homeless man. It was quite sweet but typically naive, they said. I had to get away. It's very distressing to see things properly for the first time - cold and frightening but you can't ignore it. So I can't just exchange that for another comfortable existence. I don't feel free to, somehow. I feel more at home with Mike who considers himself a failure and Clare, his unbelievable sister who has created a loving home on a council estate with an unreliable husband and four children."

"But you love Merlin, don't you? At least it seems pretty obvious to me that you do."

"I suppose I do. Probably always have." She looked at Jane. "Have you finished? I'd like to stack up." She began to clear the table and stack the dishes in the washer. She was irritated at the untidiness which marred the perfection of the kitchen.

"Sure," Jane replied, beginning to help her. "But don't try to change the subject. You can't run away at this point."

"I'm not trying to," Cleo replied crossly. "I admit I love him but that doesn't mean I should marry him. I don't want to become a university wife with two or three children and a little job that's tolerated as long as it doesn't interfere with husband's career. There are things I must do. I don't want to be stifled again."

"But aren't you assuming rather a lot? Rushing too quickly to a conclusion, as you tend to do."

"What do you mean?" Cleo paused in her tidying up and turned to look at Jane.

"Well, you may love Merlin. You may know him very well but to the detached observer it seems that you may be overlooking certain important characteristics of his. Of course I don't know him. But you did say yourself that he had had a serious accident which had naturally affected him a great deal you felt. Have you made allowances for this? Perhaps he too has changed more than you have realised. What do you think?" As Jane sat down at the kitchen table obviously determined to continue the discussion further, Cleo reluctantly abandoned further attempts at clearing up. She closed the dish washer and came back to her chair.

"What are you suggesting?"

"Two things really. Why did he leave Oxford when he seemed destined to spend his life there? And more to the point perhaps why is he now spending what must be an uncomfortable and exhausting time in El Salvador with a Jesuit friend when he might easily have enjoyed himself in the sun making love to you? I don't suppose you would have turned him down and I imagine he knows that?"

"Right on both counts. I wouldn't and he knows it. We parted disagreeing on those very points." Cleo was silent gazing at her sister. "What do you suggest?"

"I suggest you're seeing him too simply. It seems to be that he's a bit of an enigma like his fascinating namesake. Why don't you risk being really honest and challenge him to be the same. You might have a somewhat stormy time but you might have an unexpected outcome. That's what I'd advise you to do, if you were one of my clients."

"Well, if this is your professional advice, I'll consider it carefully." Cleo stood up again and continued clearing the breakfast table, while Jane watched her. She waited patiently while Cleo persevered with her efforts and then began to make fresh coffee.

Cleo rinsed their mugs, put the cafetiere on the table, pushed in the plunger and finally poured out the coffee. At last, somewhat to Jane's relief, she was ready to speak. "I think you're perhaps right," she said slowly. "I've learnt a lot in the last twelve hours. I think I can do it now. I couldn't have done it before. If I don't, I think I'll lose him and I really don't want to. I can be honest now and I can let him be honest, without my running away. Thank you. You've helped me a lot." She walked round to Jane and gave her a quick hug and a kiss.

"Good. It's about time I did, I think. You've been left too much to fend for yourself." She stood up. "The sun's shining. Do you think, we could go for a walk in the park. We expectant mothers need fresh air and exercise."

"Of course. I'll get our coats." Cleo was immediately solicitous of her sister's comfort. As they went out of the flat, she said worriedly, "I'm just left with one more problem that's due to turn up on my doorstep tomorrow."

"And that is?"

"Mike. Who's expecting to spend a week here on undefined terms and who is also planning to escape with me to Italy."

Jane laughed. "I can't help you with that. You're on your own there but I think you'll manage. You have considerable skill in this area."

"Not exactly. Mike is different. I don't quite know what to say."

"I can only suggest that the truth might be the best option."

"That seems to be my only option. I expect he'll survive. He's like me. In any case he's more attached to Italy than to me. I think."

"You haven't any real problem then," Jane retorted as they set out vigorously for the park.

Chapter Twenty Two

Cleo's optimistic mood did not survive long after Jane's departure as she waited in some trepidation Mike's arrival on the following day. He had promised to come between 7 and 8pm in time for an evening meal. The time came and went but there was no news of him. Soon after 10pm she ate a solitary meal and, when she had disposed of it, decided to go to bed as there seemed to be little she could do that night. She lay awake a long time and then slept fitfully expecting either his belated arrival or at least a phone call.

After breakfast, exasperated and tired, she decided that she must ring him at his home, his parents' home, in fact, as that was the only number she had. The phone was answered by his mother, who sounded pleasant but confused. She seemed to have no idea that Mike had been proposing to travel to London but said that he had gone to see his wife in response to an agitated telephone call from her about their son. This was the day before he should have set out for London and she had heard nothing since. She willingly gave Cleo his home number and suggested that she might find him there.

Cleo was very angry. Surely he could have communicated with her? She tried the number his mother had given her and on her second attempt succeeded in contacting Mike. He was obviously embarrassed and at a loss as she demanded an explanation from him.

"Tracey rang me up two days ago," he said, "out of the blue. She was very upset. I had to do something."

"I don't see why you had to let me down. You've never been worried about Tracey being upset before. In fact, you've always pretended to be quite indifferent to her." She felt even angrier now and made not the slightest attempt to hide it.

"This was different," he persisted. "It wasn't really Tracey. It was Ben. He'd suddenly gone down with asthma and pneumonia and she'd just gone to the hospital with him in the ambulance. She thought he might die. She couldn't cope, she said. She needed me, especially as he was calling for me. So I went straight away. What would you have done?"

"Of course you were right to go," Cleo replied immediately but she was still furious. "But that was about forty eight hours ago. Surely you could have found five minutes to tell me you weren't coming?"

"I suppose so," he said sullenly, "but at first I didn't think about it and then I didn't know what to say." He paused and then as she waited for him to continue, he burst out. "What the hell that's how I am - a useless, unreliable sod. You must know it really. You just have to accept it. I'm the same with everyone."

"I don't see why I should," she said icily. "I wouldn't have been unreasonable if you'd just explained to me. So why not?" A sudden thought struck her. "How is Ben anyway? Is he any better?" If Ben were still very ill, then Mike's unhappy mood was more understandable.

"The little bugger's fine now. He's driving us all mad, including the nurses. I've come to fetch his things, so I can bring him home in the car. They say he should be all right, as long as he's kept warm and has his medicine."

"So Tracey's feeling better now, I suppose."

"She's got me doing everything she wants, so she's fine, She enjoys a crisis. It gives her something to talk about." He sounded very depressed.

"But you're not coming to London. Is that what you're telling me?" When he did not answer, she pressed him. "Is that right? You've given up your holiday?"

"I've promised Ben I'll stay around and, if he's well enough, I'll take him out for a trip, I am his Dad and he's only three."

"I understand that," Cleo replied quickly. "We'll forget London then. I don't mind as long as I know. But why didn't you tell me? I was worried. What did you expert me to do?"

"I don't know. I know I should have told you but I just couldn't. What the hell. You know what I'm like. Tracey didn't know I was going away. It was difficult."

"So you funked it?"

"If you like. I wasn't obliged to tell you. I'd have got round to it. We're not tied to each other, after all."

A sudden explanation hit her. "It isn't just London, is it?" she asked. "It's Italy too. You're not going to do that either, are you. Or would you just leave me to guess that?"

"I can't," he replied aggressively but miserably, "I just can't. I was a stupid sod to say I could. I would like to walk out on everything but I can't. I always let everyone down."

"It's not the first time, then"

"No, I promised to go with a mate to Canada two years ago. Even bought the tickets. But I didn't go, He had to go on his own, you've had a lucky escape. Tracey makes out she can't do without me and I can't seem to let Ben down when it comes to the push. I'm just a big mouth, you see. Tracey'd tell you that. And she's probably right. I just don't like admitting it."

"So you'd have left me to work it out for myself? That's not very pleasant."

"I'm not pleasant. I never pretended to be. You can't say you didn't have some idea about me."

"I'm not going to." She no longer felt angry, almost amused instead. "I think you should stay with Ben. As for me, I doubt if Italy is for me, anyway. But that's no concern of yours now. I'll say goodbye and wish you well."

"You're angry aren't you? I don't blame you. I'm sorry, Cleo. I do like you a lot and we've had some good times but..." he hesitated.

"But now they're ended," she suggested quickly. "That's what you're saying. isn't it? Don't worry. We don't have to quarrel about it. I talked it over with my sister and she convinced me that Italy was a mistake. It would be throwing away all I'd achieved by coming to St. Elizabeth's. She's right, I'm afraid. It did seem a lovely dream but that's all it was - just a daydream. We both have to grow up, I suppose, and that seems to mean that you have to stick to Tracey and Ben and I have to carry on ploughing a lonely course."

"That sounds bloody miserable all round, for both of us," he commented. "Can you stick it? I'm not sure I can."

"That's your problem. We don't help each other."

"You've helped me," he said. "but you'd be mad to throw yourself away on me. Even I can see that. I've got nothing to offer."

"But you have got something to keep - your marriage and your son. And you must try to keep them. It's important. I would have despised you in time for leaving your child and you would have felt guilty."

"They don't make me happy," he protested.

"And I wouldn't for long. You've already made that clear. You seem to be forgetting that you turned me down first. Anyway, I doubt if you'll ever be happy, so you might as well do what is right and try that for a change."

"I might not be able to hack it," he said sombrely.

"Perhaps not but you've got to try - just as I have. So, for God's sake stop whinging. You can't get away from your Catholic upbringing any more than I can." She was angry with him again. "I've only put into words what you were prepared to do without saying anything. I think my way's fairer."

"Can we meet again?"

"What do you think? Sometime perhaps but not for a while. Now, go and collect Ben's things and get back to the hospital.

By the way, give my love to Clare, She'll understand and approve."

"She's already given me her opinion. Not that I thanked her."

"Now go and do what you were going to do anyway. Did you think I wouldn't bother to get in touch? Did you actually hope to get off as lightly as that?"

"I didn't think. I'm just a miserable coward, I can't make a real break."

"Rubbish," she replied crisply. "You'd have been a coward. if you'd left. You just funked telling me. It spoilt your image. Now go and get Ben."

"But what about you?" he asked suddenly. "What will you do?"

"Live."

"How?"

"That's my problem. I think I might solve it if I'm bold enough. Goodbye now. I'll be in touch."

"OK. I'll see you sometime then."

At last he was gone. She looked round the empty flat and realised that she had never felt so isolated. There had always been someone or some plan but now there just seemed to be emptiness. Italy had been a foolish dream but a dream has its consolations, however delusive. Now the only thing that seemed sure was that she would go back to Barton Leas and finish her teaching assignment there. And after that she had no idea.

She tried to think about Merlin but he seemed frighteningly remote. She had told Jane that she thought she might love him. But had she really meant it? The thought of being a university wife repelled her. And that seemed to be what Merlin was offering her. Did she even know that with any certainty? He had never spoken of their life together.

He had said he loved her. But what did that mean? Not enough, it seemed, to sleep with her when she begged him for reassurance and comfort. If he loved her, would he have gone off and left her as he had done for five weeks without a word, merely saying that, if she wanted to see him again, she must tell him? What kind of lover was he? No other man had ever treated her like that.

She remembered that he had said he could not help her any more. Why had he said that? The answer flashed suddenly into her mind. Because the time has come for you to grow up and help yourself, an inner voice said. You have to decide who you are and what you are and what you want. And about time too, she replied. That lonely child wanting a refuge must be banished forever. A woman able and willing to take her own decisions must take her place. How it was to be done she wasn't sure but it had to be. That was what Merlin meant and he was right. Perhaps his was a better kind of love. after all? But still she felt dissatisfied. Was it possible, she wondered for them ever to have a relationship of equals. Until now, he had always been in charge and she did not want that.

It was easier once she returned to Barton Leas a few days later. There was work to do and certain decisions which must quickly be made. She had a long conversation with Bridget one evening about the possibility of teaching as a career. That had much to attract her but, if she were to do it, she must take a year's training at a University and it would be best to apply quickly for the coming autumn. Miss Wilson, on the other hand, counselled her to return to Oxford to complete her doctorate with a view to University teaching which she thought would be more suitable.

How did people make such decisions, Cleo wondered It seemed to her that she had never really made a logical decision in her life, and that she was not trying to make one now but to decide something more important. But first of all she must try to see clearly why she had run away from London and her comfortable life there. Wasn't it because she had suddenly realised that she cared about people and what happened to them, particularly those destined for failure and rejection? She had a fellow feeling with them and that was what had led her to Mike and to Clare and her family. As a teacher she could begin to do this but to do it properly, she would have to have the courage to leave the privileged world of such schools as St. Elizabeth's and to give up many of the comforts she had always taken for granted. To go for training would be a start but she would have to live more and become more mature before she was ready for her real work. But, whatever she did in the intervening years, it was important that her life should be a caring one. It was essential for her to love. Did that include marriage and children? She remembered her words to Jane about the importance of being a woman and having a child.

She was sitting alone in her room one evening a week after her return when she reached this point. She had just posted a letter to Wheaton University. inquiring about the possibility of a place in their education department. Had she decided on Wheaton because it would keep her close to Merlin? She had seemed to do it almost without thinking about him but she was quite sure now that she did not want to lose him. She had missed him very much. Suddenly she realised that she need not miss him any longer. It was Friday May 7th. the day he had told her he would be back in his home. He had left her to get in touch with him and she would do it, at once. Without deciding what she would say to him, she went straight to the telephone. It was 6pm. He should have been home since midday. It seemed important not to waste any more time.

It was only when he answered that she thought that this was not the best time to approach him when he was probably tired, disorganised and jet lagged. It was too late to retreat, however.

"It's Cleo." she said. "I thought I'd welcome you home. I've missed you. It's good to have you back."

"Thank you," he replied. "I appreciate that." It was good to hear his voice but it was disappointing too because he sounded strangely formal and detached.

Surely he was not still annoyed with her? She was only doing what he had suggested. She decided to persevere. "I thought we might meet." she said. "Perhaps tomorrow?" When he did not immediately reply, she rushed on, "You don't have to bother fetching me. I bought a car at the beginning of the holidays, so I can come to Markhampton, if that would suit you? What do you say?"

"I would very much like to meet you but I'm not sure I can manage Markhampton tomorrow." He sounded weary

"I suppose I'm being tactless." she replied. "I expect you're suffering from jet lag but a good night's sleep should put it right. And I do want to see you. I want to tell you how sorry I am about the way I behaved last time we met. You were quite right and I was foul to you. I understand things better now. You're not still angry with me, are you?"

"I never really was angry," he said quickly, "but if I had been, it would be impossible to resist such a generous apology. It's not that I'm reluctant to see you, Cleo. On the contrary, I very much want to."

"Then what is it?"

"It's simply that two days of very difficult travel after five somewhat gruelling weeks, have had a bad effect on my spine. Remember I warned you that this could happen. I find myself in considerable pain and difficulty and I'm not sure that it will all be over by tomorrow. That's the situation, I'm afraid."

"What have you done about it?" she asked quickly

"I've taken painkillers and rested for several hours since I arrived home. I was just thinking I'd better try to get some food when you rang. There's no need for you to worry. It may take a day or two but I'll be in touch."

She knew immediately what she wanted to do. "I'll come to you," she said. "It'll take me less than an hour. I can cook us both a meal. I'll enjoy it. Have you got food or do I need to buy some on the way. And don't argue."

"Mrs Parry has left me well stocked. And I wasn't going to argue. I was wondering, in fact, if you could possibly stay for the weekend. We might then have time to talk. That is, if you want to talk."

"I'd love to. As long as you're not afraid to invite me, after my past performance. I promise to behave properly."

"I need you," he said simply, "please come."

In spite of her anxiety about him, she felt pleased that he needed her for in the past it had always been she who had leaned on him. Even a physical need was better than no need. "I'll collect a few clothes and come straightaway," she promised.

It was slightly less than an hour later when she drove up to his familiar, friendly house. Spring had arrived since her last visit and the large Magnolia tree in the front garden was covered in delicate pale pink blossom, while brilliant red and yellow tulips were splashed around, reminding her of daubs from a child's paintbox. She loved it as she had done the first time she had seen it. It was a home.

Merlin opened the door to her before she could knock. In spite of his deep tan, his face looked drawn and weary but he still met her with his usual piercing gaze and the loving smile she knew now that he kept for her. He was wearing a dressing gown and his normally smooth black hair was untidy. "You've been very quick," he said, "I'm glad to see you."

Impulsively she went straight up to him and hugged him, lifting her face for him to kiss her, which he did most lovingly. For a moment, they stayed together, then she detached herself. "I must get my case," she said, "and get to work." As she entered the hall, she looked around approvingly. Nothing had changed. She followed him down the hall and into the study where he had obviously been resting on the big sofa.

"Sit down." she commanded him. She had noticed that, in spite of his efforts. he walked with difficulty. "I shall make us some coffee, then you can go and have a long, hot bath while I cook the meal. We can eat in here. You can recline and have a tray and I'll manage with the armchair and the coffee table. Will that suit you?"

"I wouldn't dare to oppose you," he replied, smiling. "I see you have everything worked out. I feel like a small boy again. I'll be obedient."

"Don't you know that there's a mother hidden in every woman, even in an unlikely one like me? I suppose we enjoy it." She noticed that he was glad to sit down, as she hurried off to get the coffee.

As soon as the coffee had been drunk, she banished him to his bath on the grounds that she was very hungry, even if he wasn't. She watched with some anxiety as he made his painful way upstairs but did not offer help. Whatever the outcome, she felt quite sure that she had made the right decision to come.

Her plans worked perfectly. The meal was ready as soon as he was. It was simple but appetising and obviously met with his approval. By the time he had eaten and was drinking more coffee, she was delighted to see that he looked much less weary and far more relaxed.

"I don't expect you to talk much tonight," she said. "But I would like to have a full account of your visit to El Salvador, sometime, especially as you didn't tell me much about it beforehand. Did you achieve what you set out to achieve?"

To her surprise he did not answer immediately but appeared to be considering her question thoughtfully. Finally, he answered. "To a large degree, I suppose, the answer is yes." He paused, then added. "I learned a lot, some of it unexpected."

She felt rebuffed and a little irritated. Physically, he might be glad of her help but he still did not want to share his life with her. He was still in control and she could not see that he really needed her.

As if guessing her thoughts, he said unexpectedly. "Perhaps we can talk more about this tomorrow, Cleo? I'm still very tired, I'm afraid. But I'm very pleased that you have come. It is far more than I deserved after so long."

She was immediately repentant. "Of course, I understand. Would you rather go to bed now?"

"Soon but I'd like to hear a bit about you first. You look happier. What have you been doing in my absence?"

"Learning a few useful lessons about myself. And missing you. There were lots of things I wanted to talk over with you but I stumbled through them myself in the end."

"That was probably much better. Now you must have more confidence, because you have done it successfully. Would you be willing to tell me about them?"

"That's just what I want to do but it's hardly fair when you're tired and in pain."

"Don't worry. I feel much better now than I did when you arrived. I'm also relieved because I've reproached myself a lot for parting with you as I did. I was afraid I'd been too brutal."

"You were brutal but I'm no weakling either. I needed to be made to grow up. Things were very difficult at school to begin with." She told him briefly more about Stephanie and about Stella's public disagreement with her. The outcome pleased him.

"You did well to sort that out," he remarked. "You didn't need my help."

"I just wanted your shoulder to cry on. I was really angry with you for not being there. I nearly ruined everything by deciding to run away again." She paused and looked at him. "Do you really want to know this? It concerns me and Mike?"

"I want to know," he said firmly. "If we are to be happily married, we must be able to talk freely about everything don't you agree?"

"Of course. I agree," she answered swiftly. "Marriage is no good, unless it's a real partnership, a real sharing, not just of bodies but of minds and souls". Did he really understand this. she wondered. Was he prepared to share? Nevertheless, she accepted his remark. "But are we going to be married? Isn't that still to be discussed?"

"I hoped your coming tonight might mean you had decided but perhaps there are still some things you want to discuss first?"

"I think we need to, if I'm to be sure. And I must be sure. I'm sorry, Merlin. There are things I want to tell you too. Five weeks is quite a long time."

He smiled. "I see. I promise to answer all your questions tomorrow but perhaps you'd like to tell me your guilty secrets first, while you have me captive. What have you been doing in my absence?"

"I've been very sensible in deed but not always in thought." She told him briefly about Mike and her plans for going to Italy. "It was all your fault for going away again," she ended, "It frightened me to be left again."

"I understand now," he said. "I promise I'll never go away again, at least not without you. Would that help you to decide about marrying me? I can't promise to stay put. There are too many things I want to do but I can promise to keep you with me, if that's what you want."

"I do with all my heart," she said fervently, "I want to do lots of things too but I would prefer to do them with you." She laughed suddenly and light-heartedly. "At last I think I know what loving means, I know now I really love you. I've never said that before," She looked surprised.

He laughed too. "It's wonderful to hear you say that, without being worried or afraid. I think perhaps you know now how much I love you."

She stood up, walked across the room and sat beside him on the sofa, He put his arms round her and they kissed, a long tender kiss. He stroked her hair. After a few moments, she moved away a little. "I'm still not sure about marriage," she warned him, "because that has to be for life."

"I agree. Tomorrow I'll be ready to talk but may we enjoy our reunion a little while tonight? Just two old friends happy to be together."

"Why not?" She smiled and kissed him, "But I'm sending you to bed early so that you will be fit to talk tomorrow."

"I'm too tired to object to that," he assured her.

It was after a late breakfast that Merlin suggested they should talk. He seemed much restored and assured her that the pain was practically gone. "It's time," he said. "for you to put your worries into words." They were in the study with the patio doors slightly open as it was a very sunny late spring morning.

"And time for you to be honest with me," she responded.

He frowned slightly. "So you think I'm dishonest then?"

"No, not exactly. It's just that I feel there's still too much I don't know, too much you haven't shared with me yet. I've probably told you everything about me at different times. You've helped me and advised me and that's fine but it won't do for a marriage. It's too one sided. I need you but do you need me?"

He met her challenging gaze calmly, as always. "I think my asking you to come this weekend proves that?"

"Up to a point yes, but it's not enough. And it is important because of the way we started."

"What do you mean?"

"Well, when we first met you were one of the gods and I was just an ordinary mortal. In other words you were a very successful, charismatic lecturer and I was just a humble second year student. And even now, nearly six years later our positions are still much the same. It makes it hard to have a satisfactory relationship."

"Do you mean that I am too old, that eleven years is too big a gap?"

"Not really. I mean that you are very sure and self - sufficient and I most certainly am not." They were sitting side by side on the sofa, as she said this, he stood up and walked over to the door. For a few moments, he stood apparently looking down the garden, while she waited. She became aware in the silence of the birds singing and wondered if he were listening to them, then he turned slowly and came back, seating himself at the desk instead of returning to the sofa, as if he suddenly wished to put a distance between them.

"You're wrong," he replied at last. "I thought you had understood that what happened to me two and a half years ago, the loss of you, followed by my accident changed me considerably. I no longer felt sure of anything."

"I can understand that," she said quickly, "but you've sorted yourself out again, haven't you? Your novel has been very successful, you've established yourself at Wheaton with a new and interesting department."

"I suppose it could seem like that." He looked at her. "But you are underestimating the affects of a close encounter with death and disablement. It left me questioning all my earlier values and assumptions and feeling very unsure about most things. It seemed to me that most of my previous values had been meretricious, that through my own folly I had lost you whom I loved and that I was left with a somewhat empty existence. Hence my complete change of life."

"And you still feel like that?" She looked at him. "Why did you agree to go to South America? Had that something to do with feeling unsure or was it just an educational experiment? That has puzzled me."

He replied slowly. "My motives for agreeing to go in the first place were mixed. I was very grateful to Lawrence for the support he had given me and I also envied him the confidence he had in God's love and in his mission. I wanted to go and lose myself there, I suppose you might say, perhaps to share his security."

"You thought you might go and work permanently. Perhaps even join the Jesuits?"

"Perhaps even that. Then, of course, I couldn't go straightaway and I had to make other decisions, even if they were to prove only temporary. I had re-established a certain stability and pattern to my life when I met you again. Less, however, than you assumed, I think." He stopped as if waiting for her to comment.

"You certainly seemed settled to me. I suppose that attracted me, although at the same time it frightened me because I felt so inferior, on occasions. I didn't simply want to feel dependent again. I wanted to feel that I was necessary to you. That I was loved and wanted."

"Surely, you know that you are? You know now, or so I thought from what you said, why I would not make love to you when you tried to persuade me earlier?"

"I think so," she replied quickly. "Because it would've made it easier for us to avoid making a proper decision."

"Right. So what is worrying you now?"

"Your going away as you did and your reluctance even now to tell me about your experience in El Salvador. Have you now decided that it is, after all, the better life for you?"

He looked puzzled. “I think you’re making difficulties. Would I speak as I have done, if that were so? You must have more trust both in me and in yourself.”

“I know you’re right but I find it very difficult.” She looked pleadingly at him.

“I’ll try and make it easier. My visit to Lawrence convinced me that his life could never be right for me, not even if I went as a lay worker. I’m not convinced it’s right for anyone. I came to feel that perhaps the people in the developing world should be allowed more freedom to sort out their own destinies, even if it means they have to suffer. Although I think I did some useful work helping Lawrence to set up his new college, I don’t want to act as God. I learned quite a lot about other people but more importantly I learned more about myself and what I want to do.”

“Which is?” she asked firmly

He smiled, stood up, walked across the room and sat beside her once again on the sofa. “Ask you to marry me as soon as possible, so that we may start the adventure of our life together, without wasting more time.” He took her hands in his. “What do you say?”

She did not answer him directly. “I’ve decided that I want to train for a year as a teacher. I could do it at Wheaten.” She waited for his comment.

“Good. I’m happy to spend another year here but, after that, I intend to relinquish full-time teaching, as I want freedom to write creatively and to lecture. I would also like time to be with my wife and the family I hope to have. Does that conflict with your ambitions?”

She smiled at him. “Not a bit. I need time to experience security with you in our home and with a family. Once I’ve trained, my career can wait for a few years, I think. I suppose it sounds very old fashioned but that’s how I feel. It seems a wonderful prospect to me, after the trauma of the past twelve years. I suspect many homeless people feel like me, only they aren't so fortunate."

"Will you marry me then, as soon as it can be arranged?" He held her close to him, waiting for her reply.

"Of course," she said quickly, "but," she added before he could kiss her, "we don't have to wait till then do we? Not now we've decided?"

He laughed. "You haven't changed a bit." As she put her arms round him and pulled him closer, he whispered. "The time is ripe now, my darling. It never could be more so." They were lost in each other as the birds sang unheeded in the garden.

THE END